Praise for ~~Jubilee~~

'Loved *Jubilee*. Absurdly fun, smart science fiction.'
Anthony W. Eichenlaub,
author of *The Man Who Walked in the Dark*

'Quirky, witty, and wild sci-fi fun.'
Zabé Ellor, author of *Silk Fire*

'Sharp with flawed-yet-relatable characters.'
Jennifer R. Povey, author of *The Lost Guardians* series

'A wild adventure across worlds.'
David Dvorkin, bestselling author
of *Time and the Soldier*

STEPHEN K. STANFORD

JUBILEE

This is a **FLAME TREE PRESS** book

Text copyright © 2023 Stephen K. Stanford

FLAME TREE PRESS
6 Melbray Mews, London, SW6 3NS, UK
flametreepress.com

US sales, distribution and warehouse:
Simon & Schuster
simonandschuster.biz

UK distribution and warehouse:
Hachette UK Distribution
hukdcustomerservice@hachette.co.uk

Publisher's Note: This is a work of fiction. Names, characters, places, and incidents are a product of the author's imagination. Locales and public names are sometimes used for atmospheric purposes. Any resemblance to actual people, living or dead, or to businesses, companies, events, institutions, or locales is completely coincidental.

Thanks to the Flame Tree Press team.

The cover is created by Flame Tree Studio with thanks to Shutterstock.com.
The font families used are Avenir and Bembo.

Flame Tree Press is an imprint of Flame Tree Publishing Ltd
flametreepublishing.com

A copy of the CIP data for this book is available from the British Library and the Library of Congress.

PB ISBN: 978-1-78758-884-4
ebook ISBN: 978-1-78758-886-8

Printed and bound in Great Britain by Clays Ltd, Elcograf S.p.A.

STEPHEN K. STANFORD

JUBILEE

FLAME TREE PRESS
London & New York

TRANSLATOR'S NOTE

Many have questioned the wisdom of translating Gr★n Br★thx's mid-period novel into Ancient English. However, the author of this project feels that providing fresh, relatable material may be more enticing for Primitive Languages students than the stale canon of ancient texts.

The present novel was largely dismissed as escapist nonsense in its time and fell out of currency soon after the author's death in MP: 50,712. However, being loosely based on the Sirrelian Insurrection, this work has seen a resurgence of interest in recent years.

Idioms and expressions have been translated using language believed to have been in use in the 'twenty-first century'. However, as the apposite use of proper names and the variations in the slang used between the various communities of Ancient English speakers are still hotly disputed, no assurances can be given as to the authenticity or correctness of these.

One of the major problems we have faced was in finding appropriate translation for words dealing with technologies and materials. To obviate this issue, neologisms have been coined that accord with the cadence and structure of Ancient English. For instance, our everyday material xr★mxzslv is translated as 'hardiplaz'.

Many thanks go to my colleagues at the Shmwx#wr Institute for Ancient History, to the author, who, despite being legally dead for eighty-four years, agreed to collaborate from stasis backup, and of course to my hive husbands, Grn Br*grx (1) & (2).

Brn Sh*grx
May, 50,796

CHAPTER ONE

There we were, Danee and I, sitting off the white dwarf star MGNA#12, alone in our little flyer, waiting to go to Jubilee.

A very ordinary star, the one before us. Just another point of light among the billions. Not especially bright or dim, large or small, and with no real planets to speak of – certainly none capable of supporting life. So ordinary no one had even thought to name it, so pilots used the designation number: HD223948-PC11-MGNA#12. Most called it MGNA#12 for short.

And yet to some people this star was far from insignificant. To some people this star was one of the most famous in the galaxy. Because from here, and *only* from here, you could jump to Jubilee. Something about the peculiar gravity waves, still not properly understood and, bizarrely, never investigated. But by entering the right code into your quantum drive you could be taken, not to another point in our galaxy as usual, but to a parallel universe instead. A universe containing only one human artefact – Jubilee.

We were waiting on the old pockmarked drone sitting five klicks away. After thirty minutes it finally came to life, sending an encrypted message containing the jump code, the strangest I'd ever seen.

"Really?" I asked Danee.

"Yup," she said, smirking.

Danee had already been to Jubilee three times before, which was highly unusual. Controversial even. I guess that's why they'd picked her as command on this mission even though I was technically her superior.

I keyed in the coordinates manually: 000000.000000.000000.008000 – the weirdest, emptiest set of numbers I'd ever seen. As we all know, to make a quantum jump you need the three spatial coordinates plus time, the fourth. This had everything set to zero – except time. You shouldn't

4 • STEPHEN K. STANFORD

be able to jump with these numbers. I flipped up the safety cover over the launch button.

Sometimes you look back on a particular moment and wonder, *What if I'd chosen differently?* Those moments where everything branches off. If I'd turned around there and then, not gone to Jubilee. Would that have spared us all what came next? I guess you can't really answer a question like that.

"Here goes nothing," I said and hit the jump button.

CHAPTER TWO

The screens didn't even flicker. The smoothest jump ever.

"Here we are," I said. "Eight-tenths of a second into the future."

Everything on the monitors looked the same as before. MGNA#12 was still there and so were the local stars – all in the right spots. But my comm's unit was another story. For the first time in my life nothing showed. No data, no faster-than-light streams, no traffic of any kind – just background static from nearby stars. This entire universe devoid of sentient communication. It was chilling.

"Bringing her round now," said Danee, "and there she is, pleasure garden of the galaxy."

The stars slid across our monitors as we rotated. Danee zoomed in on a point of light, which expanded into a giant object hanging in space a few hundred klicks away. My stomach lurched.

For some reason we build our ships and space hubs with a particular aesthetic. All sleek and smooth. No real reason for that – after all, if something doesn't have to pass through an atmosphere, why make it streamlined? But that's how we've done it for thousands of years, so that's how we do it still.

Not Jubilee.

Before us was the wildest collection of space junk you could imagine, assembled into a roughly flat shape twenty kilometers long and ten wide. Though calling the components *space junk* might almost be too kind. No piece of metal too crappy. Every object, large or small, shiny or dull, round or square, randomly bolted and welded together into a mad concatenation. Crisscrossed with wires and cables, festooned with antennae and electronic components. If something in the vacuum of space could rot, it would be Jubilee. Toward the port side I caught an occasional bright flash where it seemed construction bots were welding on a new section.

The comm's unit bleeped. "Docking code received," I said.

"OK, let's go."

I accepted the code. There was a soft ping as it took over our craft, then we moved off toward Jubilee. Danee leaned back and stretched with a sigh, piloting work over. I snuck a sideways glance. Beneath the androgynous flight suit there seemed the promise of a pleasing shape and, despite the no-nonsense short hair, an attractive face. Inappropriate thoughts bubbled up from the male lizard brain – surprising. For these past three years I'd been focused like a laser on only one thing: making it work with Sana. No other woman had existed for me.

The mad chaos of Jubilee grew large in our screens. To politicians of a certain stripe, this place was evil incarnate. Chairman Nees himself had recently called it 'a foul stain on the moral fabric of the galaxy' – though technically, of course, Jubilee was not part of our galaxy at all. Existing in its own parallel universe, free from any government jurisdiction or control, Jubilee was said to be a free-for-all. A seething cesspit of gambling, prostitution, drug-taking and indulgence of every kind imaginable *and* unimaginable. At our poker nights, hardened Services guys talked about it in hushed tones. Those who'd been there were mini celebrities – and now here I was.

"There's a sound package with the code," I said. "Do you want me to run it?"

Danee smiled. "Your first time, may as well."

I hit play and the cabin filled with a booming voice.

"Hello, kiddies! Welcome to Jubilee!"

A bizarre accent, one I'd never heard before. I shot Danee a quizzical look.

" – So right now, if ye're hearin' this ye're probably comin' to dock and ye're probably all nervous and excited, right? Well don't worry! Coz ye're going to have the time o' ye lives here on Jubilee. Ye get me?"

"That's Douglas," said Danee, "the AI that runs Jubilee."

"An *AI* runs Jubilee? Isn't that illegal?"

She raised an eyebrow. "Remember where you are."

The voice went on. " – *Now before ye get stuck into everything, I'm going to explain the rules here on Jubilee. And there's only three o' them, so nobody say it's too hard, all right? The three* golden *rules. Are you ready?*"

There was the sound of a drum roll.

"*Rule number one is this: ye have to be an adult.* Got that? *No children allowed on Jubilee.*"

We were coming up close to the structure now, flying under the long, flat side. Craft of every kind were coming and going, drones as well. A halo of activity.

"*And here comes the second, are you ready? Golden rule number two is this: you may not harm another being on Jubilee. You can do whatever ye want to yourself, but no one else. And finally rule number three: once you run out of money, ye have to go home.*"

The last was widely known. To get to Jubilee you needed an invitation – the means of securing which was mysterious (long books written on the subject). You also had to have a prepaid return ticket, which would automatically activate the moment your credit ran out. There were stories of people doing their dough at the tables and being bundled straight onto a ship home.

"*And that's it, folks, apart from these golden rules ye can be as* naughty *as ye like! Oh, and one last thing.* Complaints. *The complaints department closed – let me see – about* two hundred fucking years ago, *so if ye're not happy with anything ye can just* bugger off! *Got that? Thank you and do* have a nice day!"

The cabin fell silent. "Quite the character, eh?" said Danee.

"Indeed."

She shook her head. "You know, I gotta say, it's not like everybody thinks. It's possible to have a very tame weekend on Jubilee."

"Really?" I smiled. "Doesn't sound like Chairman Nees had a tame weekend."

Jubilee loomed above us. You could see where sections had been added onto, then added onto again. Many of the pieces had old, incomplete snatches of writing still on them. We passed under a large square shape stenciled with the words:...*DERSMYTH SPACEWORKS XIVVX*....

Our ship zoomed toward the open door of an industrial dock about a klick away, green flashing light above it.

"I guess that's us," said Danee. "We'll keep this short and sweet, right?"

"Roger that. Retrieve the body, then get the hell out of here."

We flew into the open dock and landed lightly on the pad. I felt the rumble of heavy doors closing behind us, then heard air flooding in. My console pinged to say it was safe to alight, and I was just about to open our hatch when Danee touched my arm.

"One more thing," she said. "Let's not mention that we're Investigators. They don't much care for them around here."

I opened the hatch and stepped out. The air smelled OK, gravity a little light. In all respects the dock looked standard and other than our ship the only thing it contained were some scanning devices. A door at the far end opened and a man stepped through smiling warmly, one hand raised in greeting.

"Investigators Hasum and Perolo, *welcome* to Jubilee!"

CHAPTER THREE

It was the voice we'd heard flying in. So this was Douglas, or more correctly one of his robot avatars. I looked at Danee with a half smile.

She kept her face neutral. "Thank you, it's a pleasure to be back on Jubilee, albeit under such tragic circumstances."

"Very tragic," said the robot, sounding not at all sad.

These days of course it's possible to build robots so they look indistinguishable from humans in every way. But for some reason, maybe galactic convention, we always make them look just a little artificial. Perhaps it makes us feel secure? 'Douglas' was medium height and impossibly thin. He had short, dark hair in an unfashionable bowl cut and a bland face with one highly distinguishing feature: dark, heavy eyebrows, now beetling with concentration. He looked at Danee with affection and a hint of amusement through mild blue eyes.

"Basically, this is a retrieval mission," said Danee. "Our orders say not to undertake an investigation, just collect the body and go home. So we won't be in your way for long."

"Oh, don't worry, you aren't in my way at all, Ms. Hasum."

"Please, call me Danee."

"Thank you, Danee – we're not exactly big on protocol here. Welcome to our humble home." He did an exaggerated bow and then turned to me. "First time for you, sir?"

"Yes, and it's Col."

"Pleased to meet you, Col," he said, vigorously shaking my hand, then turned and gave Danee a bear hug. "Fourth time's the charm, I'm sure."

Danee extricated herself. "Yes, well, as I was saying, we don't plan on being here for long."

The android looked solemn. "Now ye see, that's where we might be having a wee problem. Fella that runs the morgue here goes by the name Zanders. He's off on a bender right now. Got a problem with the old—" He mimed drinking from a bottle. "Gampa to be specific. Without him we can't sign anything out."

Danee's eyes widened. "How long are we talking?"

Douglas rubbed his chin. "Let's see…he's six hours into it, will probably go for another six. Then he'll have to clean up and sleep it off. Could be looking at thirty-six hours?"

"And there's nothing you can do? Surely you could sign the body out yourself?"

"Well, you see, *there's* the problem. People are always sayin' *delegate*. But then you have to leave 'em to it. Otherwise you end up doin' everything yourself. You get me?"

We all stood there awkwardly for a moment.

Douglas went on, "We have our own ways here on Jubilee. But let me make it up to you. We'll put you up nicely in one of our good hotels. It's evening period now anyway, so why not stay a couple o' nights? *On me!*"

Danee looked at me, stricken. "I might just confer with my colleague, in our flyer."

"Please, take your time," said the android, beaming. "I'll wait out here."

We stepped back into the ship, then I closed the door and switched on the cloaking device for privacy.

Danee slapped the console. "What's this fucker up to?"

"Surely he could release the body if he wanted?"

"Of course! This is bullshit. The mortician is *drunk?*"

"A gampa hangover *is* pretty bad," I said, trying to lighten the mood. I'd overindulged a couple of times myself and it wasn't pretty.

She glared at me. "We can't even talk to Command from here on Jubilee. What'll they make of it when we don't come back?"

I pondered for a moment. Douglas was watching from the dock and when he saw me look up, gave a big smile and waved. An idea came to me. "Let's do this: first we go back out there and *insist*. If he doesn't budge, then we can take up his offer but demand he sends a message back to base for us. He'll be obliged to do that much."

She thought about it for a moment and then sighed. "Not much else we can do, is there?"

"We *could* just go home and let Command deal with it."

She thought again. "I like the first idea better. Going back empty-handed would *not* be a good look."

And so it was that we made the fateful decision to stay on Jubilee.

Things went as I expected. Douglas politely refused to release the body, but did agree to send our message to Command. "Why don't we do it right now?" he asked.

"OK," said Danee, "give me a moment."

"Why don't ye stand over there in front of the ship, will look nice and professional like!"

Danee stepped back to the ship, head down, then looked up. "OK, ready."

"Recording," said Douglas.

She looked straight ahead. "Commander Huk, I am reporting there has been a delay on Jubilee. There is a...*technical* problem with the morgue here" – Douglas gave a thumbs-up as if to say 'good explanation' – "and we're being advised it will take thirty-six hours to sort out. With no orders to the contrary, I've decided to stay on Jubilee and wait until the body is released. If anything changes, I'll report back to you. Hasum out."

An intelligently calibrated message, I thought.

"Splendid," said Douglas. "Now let's get you sorted out. Do ye have clothes and all that?"

"Yes," I said, grabbing our packs out of the flyer, "we've got overnight bags, we'll be fine."

We walked out of the airlock down a short corridor to a bank of elevators. So far, everything inside Jubilee looked surprisingly normal.

As the lift rose I asked Douglas, "So how do you get messages back to the 'normal' galaxy?"

"Good question, Col, I can see you're a smart fella. I have a wee device that jumps over every sixty seconds and handshakes with my communications drone off MGNA#12. Then it jumps back and brings me all the news."

"Right, so you could, if you wanted, carry everyone's traffic back and forth from Jubilee, it would just be on a sixty-second delay?"

"Sure, but we've got an intranet on Jubilee and that's enough. I don't want them playing with their koms all day, I want them gambling and whoring and spending their money! Here we are…."

The elevator gave a gentle ping, the doors opened and I had my first view of Concourse, Jubilee's famous main drag. A large corridor really, but twenty-five meters wide with a high ceiling. It was humming with people and noise and activity. A well-dressed woman walked past with a large cat (or small lion) on a leash. The cat had its head and tail in the air and seemed very satisfied with itself.

"Who's she?" I asked Douglas.

"Oh, just one o' the residents."

"There are *residents?*"

"Sure, we've got lots o' people living here – if you've got the money, you can stay as long as you like."

Shops and businesses of every kind lined the corridor. We passed a grocery store, a café and a tattoo parlor. Across from us a young man with a long, bushy beard was busking on the street.

"This is Concourse," said Douglas. "It runs the length of Jubilee right through the middle. Everything from here and up, that's for the guests, and everything below's for the staff and services."

"The people here to *spend* money are upstairs and everyone else is below," chipped in Danee.

"Spot on," said Douglas. "I'm taking you to Excelsior on Three, one of our swankier establishments. It's only a few minutes' walk if you don't mind hoofing it?"

There was a transit system running along the center of Concourse as well as air taxis painted bright yellow.

"I'm happy to walk," I said. There was plenty to see.

We passed a store selling a range of booze and drugs that would have been banned pretty much anywhere else in the civilized galaxy – its collection on proud display. Then a brothel, a lurid hologram promoting the various activities on offer. No one seemed to pay it any attention.

"This is a *residential* zone?" I said.

"Well, we do have the red-light district in Sectors Nine, Ten, Eleven and, come to think of it, a bit of Twelve as well. I guess zoning's never been one o' me strong suits. Here we are...."

We stopped in front of a gold shopfront above which was written *The Excelsior*. Inside was a bank of elevators and a uniformed concierge who pushed the lift button for us – possibly his only job. Despite everything, I couldn't help feeling a tingle of pleasure at the prospect of staying in a fancy hotel.

As we ascended Douglas said, "We're going straight to your suite, I've already checked you in."

Danee whistled. "Private lift, *on* Concourse."

"I told ye you'd be looked after," said Douglas, grinning.

Two uniformed figures waited upstairs – our robo-butlers.

"Investigator Hasum," said one of them, bowing, "my name is Susan. Welcome to the Excelsior on Concourse." The bot was designed to look female. She took Danee's bag and ushered her away.

"And I am Batum," said the other. "If you please, I'll show you to your room." His accent was aristocratic, following some ancient law of hospitality.

"First you gotta see this," interrupted Douglas excitedly.

He led me to a large living space. On the far side of the room was its breathtaking feature – giant floor-to-ceiling windows *with a view to the outside*.

Some large object had been repurposed to make this section of Jubilee. It must have been considerably larger than its immediate surroundings for it jutted up, creating an 'aspect', an exterior view of Jubilee in all its mad complexity, and beyond that a distant sun the size of a tennis ball. There was an endless churn of activity, with ships docking at every point, others moving in or out, and farther away many more waiting their turn. I watched as two ships winked out of existence, no doubt jumping back to our home universe, and saw at least one appear. Behind all this a backdrop of intensely bright, unblinking stars strung out over the velvet black of space.

"They call this the *Starview* Suite," said Douglas. "Magnificent, eh?"

He dimmed the lights for greater effect.

It is a cliché to say the one thing you never see in space is stars, but like all clichés there's an element of truth to it. Portholes are tricky and expensive, so we don't build many. You can spend months in space without seeing outside the ship. I put my palm up against the glass. The surface was cool, but no more than a window back home on a winter's morning. I marveled at the engineering that had gone into this, protecting me from the vacuum, the radiation and the minus-270-degree cold of deep space.

"Yeah, it's amazing," I said. "Tell me, is that nearby sun the same as MGNA#12 back in the normal universe?"

Douglas turned away from the window and looked at me. "You know, the thing I like about you, Col, is you're *curious*. People just ain't curious much these days."

"Well, I am an Investigator."

"They're usually the least of all."

True, unfortunately.

Douglas went on. "Can you name a single major scientific breakthrough from the last few hundred years? How come no one's studying MGNA#12? What makes it possible to jump over here to our little playground?" He gestured toward the window. "It's all about making baubles for rich people these days." And then he sighed. "Not that you can't do both, I guess."

I thought about the flyer I'd arrived in. Basic design unchanged in a thousand years. It was as if, after putting galactic civilization back together after the trauma of the Collapse, humanity had decided *well that's enough of that then* as far as science was concerned and collectively gone to sleep. Even worse, for systems that were part of the Movement, further progress was judged to be somehow unwholesome.

"Now to answer your question," continued Douglas, "the star you see is the same age and size as MGNA#12. If you measure the other stars around, there are slight variations between this universe and yours. The farther you move away from here, the more these variations add up."

"Fascinating," I said. "And while I have you, can I ask something else, a personal question?"

Douglas turned with a look of mock surprise, "Well *I'll* be! I'm gettin' all *fluttery* now, Col – and we only just met!"

I laughed nervously, and stammered, "Just – I just wanted to ask – what is the accent you speak with? I've never heard anything quite like it before."

We had been walking along the length of the window. Beyond the kitchen was a corridor and the other bedroom, Danee's. I'd been wondering if the 'star view' extended into her room.

"This accent I'm talkin' with now? That's called Scottish Ancient Lite."

"And why do you use it?"

"Because I was programmed this way, o' course. By the boss, back in the day."

"Who's the boss?"

Douglas looked up at the ceiling for a moment, perhaps in reverie. "Fella by the name of John Hudson. Been dead five hundred years now – though I do have a backup. Had a fascination with Old Earth. Said the only way you could understand the way o' things was by studying ancient history."

"Couldn't you override the programming?"

"Probably. Suppose I must like it this way."

This, I would learn, was a typical conversation with Douglas – answers leading inevitably to more questions.

Now he looked at me intently. "Col, can I ask *you* a question?"

"Sure."

"Why don't you come live here and work for me?"

I was thunderstruck. "Work for *you* here on Jubilee?"

"Why not? I need a new head of security and you'd be great. You could bring Sana along and, besides, things are turning to shite on Brouggh."

I tried not to react. Douglas had done background on me – enough to know the name of my wife. And what did he mean about Brouggh?

"But why me? We only just met – how could you possibly know I'm the right person for this job?"

"Because I'm a fuckin' quantum AI computer, mate, and you're exactly the right type: smart, security background – the kinda guy who *gives* a shit. I always follow my gut in these things. Think about it. You don't have to decide right away."

The offer was flattering but ridiculous of course. Why would I ditch everything to come work in a madhouse? And what about Sana and her political career? Up to that point, I'd built everything in my life so carefully, step by step. If Douglas really knew me, he would have known that I simply did not make impulsive decisions like that.

I countered with another question.

"Douglas, why do you have humans working for you anyway? Running the morgue, security – couldn't you just do it all yourself?"

"Sure," he said, "but where would be the fun in that?"

Batum, the robo-butler, appeared to announce my room was ready.

"OK, see you round, Col," said Douglas as he left. "Call if you need anything."

My room contained a vast bed turned down and made up with brilliant white sheets softer than air. The en-suite bathroom was lined with white stone, trimmed with gold and lit with a pearlescent glow that emanated from everywhere and nowhere. My reflection in the full-height mirror looked somehow taller and more handsome. I tried not to think of my own crappy bathroom back home.

Batum called from the bedroom, "Sir, would you like a *mint*?"

He spoke the word 'mint' as if it were highly significant.

I walked back into the bedroom. "Would I like a what?"

"A *mint*, sir. Many of our guests enjoy eating them."

He stood with robotic perfection, ramrod-straight, holding a tray with half a dozen small, white pills on it. Seemed like altogether too much fuss about a humble sweet and I was instinctively about to refuse, but then had a change of heart.

"What the hell, let's try one, shall we?"

Batum produced a pair of silver tongs, picked up a tablet and dropped it onto my open palm. I put it cautiously in my mouth – delicious! Surely the nicest mint I'd ever tasted, even given the bizarre buildup.

"Batum, I take it you're an android?"

"Yes, sir, they only have human butlers in *mid-tier* establishments."

Batum was starting to irritate me. He gave the impression that his usual guests were a notch *better* than me – though of course that was probably true. "So, are you part of Douglas or an independent entity?"

"Sir, I am a TR-six thousand domestic droid, beta. I have a separate consciousness to that of Douglas."

"And what do you do, usually?"

"Sir, my duties include catering, cleaning, assistance with grooming, security and providing companionship as required."

Some mischievous impulse had me ask, "Does that ever include sex with your guests?"

Batum looked at me coldly, and I swear with a tinge of disappointment. "Sir, you scan as hetero-standard, although I could of course, *if required*" – he paused – "offer manual relief."

I laughed aloud. "No, I'll be fine, I was just curious. Do you happen to know what Danee, I mean Ms. Hasum, is doing right now?"

He paused for a moment. "My colleague advises Ms. Hasum is presently located in a women's apparel store on Concourse. She has sent you a dinner invitation for nineteen hundred hours."

I checked my kom and sure enough there was a message from Danee.

"Do you require anything else, sir?"

"Nothing, thanks, Batum."

"Would you like me to prepare breakfast for you, sir?"

"Yes, why not, shall we say oh seven hundred?"

I lay on the bed and looked around, agog at the sumptuous room – was all this part of Douglas's plan? Obviously he was up to something. Had he delayed us just to try and get me to work for him? Madness, surely? As if I could just leave everything behind on Brouggh?

An idea popped into my mind. I asked my kom to interrogate the Jubilee intranet and a holographic list of services sprang up. I could just as easily have projected this to my optic nerve, but have always been old-fashioned about such things. I scrolled to *M* for Medical, found the subcategory I was looking for and then a doctor.

An appointment was available for 16:00 the next day.

CHAPTER FOUR

Danee took us to some place called the Hot Pot. On the corner of Concourse and Fourth Avenue, it was elevated a few steps and had a pleasing view over the endless parade.

Danee looked nice. She was wearing lipstick and makeup, and smelled fragrant. I know little about women's clothing, but let's just say she was wearing some kind of light blue jumpsuity thing that was figure-hugging, matched her eyes and had a subtle shimmer through it. The tables were small and we sat close. It felt uncomfortably like a date.

"Got a message back from Huk," she said.

"Saying?"

"Not much, *Continue as proposed.*"

That was a relief. "At least they're informed. Can't say we went off-mission."

"Doesn't seem like much of a mission right now." She laughed. "Fancy hotel, nice restaurant."

"Agreed – but what can we do about it?"

"Nothing! So we may as well enjoy it. That's what I decided, anyway."

I smiled, having come to the same conclusion. "Do you think we'll get reimbursed for expenses?" Judging by the menu, my salary wouldn't go far here.

Our dinner arrived, served, as you'd figure, in a big pot, with side dishes and dipping breads, the latest food trend: cucina marana. To me it looked like an ordinary stew – though the wine at least was good. The waiter, a bored young guy dressed in a traditional embroidered tunic, set everything up for us.

"Are you from Marana?" I asked.

He raised an eyebrow. "My mother was born there, but I've never been."

"Is anyone here Maranian?"

The waiter snickered and slouched off without replying.

"No tip for him then," said Danee, tucking in. "So, I assume you're curious about my previous trips to Jubilee? Everyone always is."

"Yeah, guess so."

"Not that exciting really." She dipped her bread and started eating with gusto. "The first two times were with an ex, Braden" – she said his name like a swear word – "a gambler. Had some crazy scheme to break the bank. Spent six months conniving to get the invitation to Jubilee and we slept on the couch of a buddy who worked here."

"Not exactly the Excelsior on Three."

"Opposite end of the spectrum."

"How did the gambling go?"

"Oh, you know – hey, this is good, isn't it?" She waved at the food enthusiastically. "Days on end playing cards, winning a bit, losing a bit, me bored out of my brain. Then eventually he lost everything and we went home."

I tried to imagine Danee hanging around doing nothing: she didn't seem the type. "And what happened to Braden?"

She made a face. "Charming and handsome, but not too bright was our Braden."

This was a different Danee to the one I knew from work. I'd spoken to her class during final year, seen her around Command a bit. She was prettier than average without being one of the "hot" girls. Seemed smart and ambitious. A bit uptight, maybe. But not tonight.

"And the third time you came?"

"That was a hen weekend, a whole bunch of girls came over."

I whistled. "Expensive weekend."

"Bride was from a rich family, paid for everything. Afterward had this huge wedding, and now of course" – she took a slug of wine – "I never see her. She's some kind of *society* person."

"And how was it, the weekend?"

"Exactly as you'd expect. Hours and hours and hours in all these bars. A stupid club with male strippers. Some of them hooked up, with guys or other girls or whatever – the bride-to-be didn't hold back, let me tell you. I ended up going to my room and reading a book."

"That's a bit boring."

"Not as boring as thirty drunk bridesmaids."

The food was surprisingly good and the wine was giving me a warm buzz. It was becoming harder by the minute to pretend I was not enjoying myself.

Then a booming voice from the door. "Look at you two *lovebirds!*"

Douglas.

He strode through the restaurant with a big smile. "Do ye mind if I join you?"

I didn't think it would matter much if we did.

"Please," I said, pulling over a chair.

"You folks doing OK? Can I tell you, there's no change with our friend Zanders. Still a ways off yet."

Douglas clearly meant to keep us on board for these two nights, whatever his motive.

He grabbed me around the shoulders affectionately. "So, Mr. Perolo, how are you finding Jubilee?"

At that moment a couple in a rear banquette started having sex, the woman mounting her seated mate.

Douglas swiveled to look, threw his head back and laughed. "Humans! Just like bloody rabbits – any chance they get!" He bellowed, "Someone throw a blanket over them!"

No one took any notice and the sounds of lovemaking eventually petered out.

"I kind of imagined Jubilee to be like *that*," I said, gesturing toward the back of the restaurant, "a nonstop orgy or something."

"Yeah, I know. That's what people think," said Douglas glumly.

"Not too far off the mark if you go to Sector Ten," said Danee.

"Indeed, but we're not really about all that. Not really."

I raised an eyebrow. What else was Jubilee about?

"All right, let me ask you something, Col," he said. "Ever heard the expression *What happens in Vegas stays in Vegas?*"

"Sure."

"What does it mean and where do you think it comes from?"

I'd never considered it before. Just one of those things people said that didn't make any sense but everyone knew what it meant. "From Old Earth? And I suppose it means *we're going to keep something a secret.*"

"Correct!" said Douglas. "Except Vegas, *Las* Vegas, actually, was a real place. A ramshackle, shit-poor town in the middle of a desert on Old Earth. Poor bastards didna have so much as a pot to piss in. Then one day someone had this brilliant idea: why don't we legalize sin? Mind if I have one?" He picked up a wineglass from a neighboring table and poured a drink from our bottle. "So they opened up the town. For all the usual stuff, you know, gambling, prostitution, money laundering." Douglas ticked them off in a bored monotone. "Business was boomin' but after a while, Col, let me tell you, somethin' *funny* happened." The android drank his glass in one long gulp, then banged it down on the table. "Now that's a good drop!"

I wondered what effect or even pleasure a glass of wine would have for him?

He went on. "The city fathers realized they were makin' more money from all the normal business – you know, food, entertainment, hotels and the like – and less from all the naughty stuff. Turned out, sin was just a lure. A way to get people thinking this shithole in the middle of the desert was someplace worth goin' to!"

"And you're saying Jubilee is like that town on Old Earth?" I asked.

"Except," said Danee, "it's located in its own parallel universe, point zero eight seconds from our own."

"True," said Douglas, looking me in the eye, "but like Vegas, the conventional economy is where the real money is."

Outside people thronged in the late 'evening' – overhead lights now dimmed. I spotted an Aurelian walking among the crowd, his Drax trotting behind. He was easy to make out, a foot taller than any human and, like all Aurelians, wearing a grim expression as if a tiny rain cloud was following him, and only him, around.

"Don't see many nonhumans about," I said.

"Nah, not many," said Douglas. "Jubilee don't seem to appeal to 'em. Only humans get hung up with all that sin and redemption crap. The other races just do whatever the hell they want."

Instinctively we all glanced toward the back of the restaurant, where the amorous couple were now enjoying a postcoital feast, cooing and tenderly feeding each other titbits.

A moment later Danee gave a big yawn, setting me off as well. "Time to put that fancy bed to use," she said. "We'll need plenty of energy for what I've got planned tomorrow."

CHAPTER FIVE

Dozing, half awake, half asleep …empty bed.

Did she not come home again?

Instantly wide awake.

Where am I?

On Jubilee. Of course, in a hotel room.

Parched and surprisingly hungry – must have had more wine than was good for me. Checked my kom: 06:00. There were faint sounds from the kitchen. Perhaps Batum could make breakfast early?

I got up and put on a white hotel gown – fluffy, gorgeous and heavy as lead. Probably worth a week's wages. Walked out into the living area. Pitch-black with stars splashed across the viewing window like frozen fireworks.

Batum was in the kitchen, working in the dark. "Good morning, sir, would you like the lights up? I do not require the human visible spectrum to operate."

"Don't worry, Batum, the view's majestic."

"To be honest, sir, it's the best thing about this job, working by starlight."

For the first time I found myself warming to the android. "Do you think I could have breakfast now? Woke up early."

"Certainly, sir. And may I point out, sir, there's no need to come out of your room to ask for anything, just call my name anytime, day or night."

"Thanks, Batum, I'll remember that."

After a kingly breakfast and a high-tech shower to restore a dead man, I sat in the lounge waiting for Danee, gazing at the stars.

"Amazing, eh?" she said perfunctorily when she arrived. "Ready?"

"Yes," I said, trying not to sound resigned. It's true we had a whole day to kill, but even so her plan seemed frivolous, if not lethal. We took the lift down to Concourse and boarded one of the transit cars.

"Buckle up," she said, grinning. "We're going all the way across Jubilee, so that means passing through Sector Ten."

The red-light district, famous galaxy wide. It was hard not to feel a tingle of excitement. From our carriage I took in the view of life on Concourse. Heaving with humanity from every system in the galaxy clad in every conceivable mode of dress. Each kilometer we crossed into a new sector, delineated by one of the major avenues. Sector Four seemed to be full of banks and jewelers. Sector Five, fashion. As the numbers grew higher, the atmosphere changed. There were more casinos and nightclubs, and more people out of it on booze or drugs.

"You know, Douglas offered me a job yesterday," I said. "Head of security."

Danee turned from the window, astonished. She had been unpacking while I was having that conversation. "My god, that's incredible!"

"Came out of the blue, I'm still trying to digest it."

"Would you consider it?"

"Nah." I laughed ruefully. "Of course not." Then I remembered something that had been nagging at me. "But in that same conversation he made a comment about Brouggh."

"Brouggh?"

"Just in passing, but it was strange. He said: *Things are turning to shite there*. Did you hear anything?"

Danee looked nonplussed. "Just the one message from Huk."

"Guess we'll find out soon enough," I said, trying to shrug off a tight feeling in my navel.

The lights dimmed as we entered Sector Nine, a perpetual nightscape for the red-light district. Sounds of muffled debauchery permeated the train, exploding when the passenger doors opened. Every shopfront here was a nightclub, brothel or gambling den. Neon lights and gaudy holos splashed across the street promoting every kind of illicit activity – not that anything actually *was* illicit here of course. As we crossed into

Sector Ten I spied a couple handing out holo-balls, a very buff man and a curvaceous woman, stark-naked except for cowboy hats. Others too: a topless woman with three breasts, a person divided down the middle, half male, half female.

Rowdy young men walked near our carriage, one of them slapping our window. They were wearing 'beer hats' – cans stuck in them with straws running to their mouths. No one batted an eyelid. At one of the stops a couple were kissing enthusiastically right in front of us. The woman suddenly pushed the man away, palms in the air, bent over and puked violently on the street. When she stood back up her partner had moved on and, seemingly unaware, she resumed with another man.

"Imagine kissing *that* mouth!" said Danee.

Music pulsed from endless venues lining side streets thronged with impenetrable crowds. Couples and groups copulated wherever there were shadows – indeed, even where there were none.

Concourse would be OK. It's the side streets where you'd get the real problems. Some part of me that processes these things was taking careful note. Of the cameras, the guards (uniformed and undercover, human and robotic) and the enormous security infrastructure clearly in place. It took a huge amount of organization to allow for all this chaos.

We passed through Sector Eleven. Drunken revelers got on and off, and then as we reached Sector Twelve the overhead lights went back to daytime.

"What do you think?" asked Danee sweetly. "Nice little trip up the country?"

I tried to form words. "Overwhelming. It's the Jubilee I imagined, but with stuff I couldn't even imagine."

Foot traffic thinned out. We passed through a commercial area – offices and store fronts for lawyers and accountants, travel agents and Realtors. I noticed a number of signs reading *R&D Broker*. Could it be, with all the pushback from the Movement, people were actually getting original research done here on Jubilee?

A kilometer ahead, Concourse ran into a flat wall and stopped. End of the line.

"Nearly there!" said Danee.

I scanned my kom to get off (fifteen credits, ouch). In front of us was a glowing arrow and sign reading *Lo-G World!* A holo was embedded in it with the image of a man and woman holding hands, bouncing high into the air.

We walked down Avenue Nineteen for half an hour following the signs – *THIS WAY to Lo-G World!* It seemed like it was quite the attraction.

"Still don't get it," I said, a little grumpily. "Why the big fuss?"

"Because," said Danee, "it's unique! With gravity dialed down to ten per cent, you can do all sorts of cool things, like fly. Just try and have an open mind!"

I grunted assent. Maybe she was right. Most people experience zero G only a few times in their lives – if at all. Maybe on an interstellar trip if the captain turns off the gravity to give everyone a thrill. This was something else again and I could think of nowhere else like it. No planet could support life with gravity at only one tenth of a G – the air would bleed off into space. It was an artificial mini habitat that existed only on Jubilee.

We queued at the entrance window, above which was a list of prices:

One hour	*20 credits*
Two hours	*35 credits*
Full day	*50 credits*

A bored-looking guy with long, greasy hair sat inside, a guitar leaning against the corner. He scanned our koms for two hours and handed us helmets and kneepads. We stepped around the corner to a staging area and put them on. Naturally they were old and dinged-up, and Danee's helmet was way too large, falling down over her ears.

"Do we really need all this stuff?" I asked, knowing the answer already.

"Of course! This place is five hundred meters high. If you fell from up there, even at the low G, it would be like fifty meters back home."

"Well in that case, kneepads won't help much, will they?"

Danee raised an eyebrow. "I thought you were going to be open-minded?"

We readied ourselves, then stopped for a moment in front of the entrance. Danee looked comic in the too-large helmet. Cute too – I couldn't help thinking. Our eyes met and we both laughed: one minute here to collect a dead body, the next making whoopee in a theme park. Oh well.

We passed through the door and, feeling the change in gravity, I made a rookie mistake instantly: stepping down too hard and bouncing high into the air. I performed a clumsy somersault before floating gently back down to floor level. Danee did far better, copying passers-by and adopting a sliding shuffle to move along.

Lo-G World turned out to be a huge cylinder half a kilometer high and roughly 250 meters wide. Must have been an old reservoir or gas tank from a colony somewhere and now repurposed and welded onto the side of Jubilee. The giant space was alive with activity. Excited shouts and shrieks bounced off the round walls creating strange, distorted sounds. There were trampolines with people jumping to astonishing heights, a swimming pool with clear hardiplaz walls to retain the water that sloshed in high, slow-moving waves. In the center with paths radiating outward were shops and food stalls, and some kind of games area, and above us the air was filled with flying machines. Not just machines – I watched as a young woman glided to an elegant landing using nothing but a slinky batsuit with webbed arms. All possible and *only* possible in the ultralight gravity.

Danee pointed to the trampolines and slid off in that direction. Next to us a group of older guys were playing a low-G ball game. One of them kicked the ball too hard and spun helplessly forward in a somersault from the opposing force: Newton's Third Law in action. His mates laughed and jeered – proving human nature constant even if gravity wasn't.

I faced more humiliation at the trampolines. First bounce sent me way too high and despite a frenzy of midair twisting and writhing, I returned to earth headfirst. Danee on the trampoline next door was – of course – doing far better.

She called to me. "Come over, it's better with two!"

I settled to the ground and joined her. We held hands facing each other and started bouncing. Slowly at first, then ever higher till the trampoline was a tiny square below us. Danee was right, with two people it made everything more stable and we could go higher. She shrieked with joy, face flushed, hair sticking out from under her helmet flopping up and down with each jump. Afterward we lay on the ground recovering, watching a couple of gyrocopters swoop around and over us.

"That's next!" Danee said.

A bored-looking young woman with purple hair and piercings was working at the copter station, popping gum and playing with her kom. "Two?" she asked, barely looking up. Then without a word turned to fetch them from a nearby rack.

I have to say, they were beautiful pieces of work. The bodies were made from a single piece of hardiplaz, featherlight in the low gravity. With a large rotor on top and a smaller one on the tail for stability, they looked a bit like ancient helicopters from Old Earth but running off pedal power, a monofilament drive train running up through the cage to the top rotor.

The young woman strapped us in, adjusted the seat and pedals, and launched into a well-worn spiel. "Welcome to the Lo-G World gyrocoptering experience," she said in a nasal monotone. "To ascend, simply start pedaling. To return to the ground, stop pedaling and your craft will gently descend." She popped her gum loudly. "To control direction in flight, toggle the control stick like so." She fiddled with Danee's stick. "Seat belts must be worn at all times. Please observe all safety precautions and enjoy your Lo-G World gyrocoptering experience." Before the last sentence was finished, she was already slouching back to her station.

"Race you to the top!" I said and pushed down hard on the pedals.

Blades whirred and the craft lurched into the air. Seconds later the ground was far below, but something was wrong with Danee's machine. I saw a hand waving from the cockpit, the small figure of the attendant returning, bent over doing something, then moments later the blades turning. Good, that gave me a head start! I pedaled even harder, zooming into the higher reaches of the vast cylinder.

Then without warning I lurched violently to the right, so sharply my head whiplashed. At the same instant one of the winged flyers zoomed through the flight path I'd been taking. Interesting. The machine had performed that evasive maneuver on its own. No way could a pedal-powered rotor craft do that. Had to be a small gravity engine hidden away somewhere on board connected to sensors and some rudimentary anti-collision AI. Clearly these things were designed to be idiotproof. Which was good. In less than a minute I'd almost killed someone – and I was a trained pilot.

Down below everything was a toy town populated by ant people. A lift cable ran up the side of the cylinder, turning back around at a ledge near the roof. The cable had footrests and handholds at regular intervals. I watched as one of the winged flyers was hoisted to the top, then stepped out onto the ledge. An elderly man, thin with bronzed skin and a large beaked nose. He adjusted his wings and flexed his fingers, testing the control system that feathered them. Then he leaped off the ledge out into space, tucked into a dive to build speed, opened his arms and swung around into a graceful banking turn.

Opposite us on the far wall, climbers neared the roof. They'd obviously clambered all the way up using only handholds (and no ropes or safety gear). I wondered what they would do on reaching the top – climb back down? My question was answered immediately. A young woman got to the very last handhold, then sprang backward out from the wall, performed a midair twist to face the ground and opened her arms to reveal a batwing. She swooped off, effortlessly adjusting her bodyweight to control the glide, seconds later finding a thermal current and circling back up to the roof. Real flying. If I lived on Jubilee, I'd be here doing this every day.

Danee had nearly caught up to me, her craft whirring and rising in small circles. "There was something wrong, the girl had to fix it," she called out, pointing to the blades.

"Yeah, I saw."

We pedaled around the wall of the cylinder, taking everything in. The airspace was filled with small figures soaring and swooping, the distant sounds of people having fun percolating from the floor half a kilometer below. A moment of pure bliss. I stopped pedaling and floated in space, idiot grin on my face.

Eventually we tired. Danee pointed to the ground and I gave a thumbs-up. I stopped pedaling and the craft began to sink, auto-rotation by the blades naturally slowing my fall to a safe speed in this ultralight gravity. As we sank, I kept waiting for my ears to pop, but of course that was not going to happen in the artificial habitat of Lo-G World – same air pressure all the way down.

Close to floor level, a flight school was in progress, the instructor drilling her students. I watched as one of them botched a launch and sank ignominiously to the floor, wings flapping comically askew. We circled the park, watching people play in the pool and bounce on the trampolines, then set our copters back down at the station.

Danee took off the helmet and shook her hair out, eyes shining. "Had enough?"

My legs were burning and anyway, how could you top that? "Yep, for today anyway."

On our way out Danee dashed over to one of the souvenir stands and returned with a gift. A cheesy-looking, deliberately retro-styled badge she pinned to my shirt. Kinda thing they make in the millions for a fraction of a credit. Across the top it read:

I got high…

And along the bottom:

…at Lo-G World!

And in the middle was a 2D drawing of a grinning couple holding hands, bouncing in space. There were little lines running from the figures signifying great speed.

"See, that's us," said Danee, "on the trampoline!"

"Why, *thank you!*" I said with exaggerated gratitude. "I shall treasure it till my dying day."

CHAPTER SIX

My kom gave me the directions: only twenty-five minutes by foot, plenty of time before my appointment at 16:00. From the Excelsior I turned right onto Concourse, heading into the lower numbered sectors, which seemed a little more residential. I passed a gymnasium, health spa and, surprisingly, a church – albeit with a rowdy bar right next door, drinkers spilling outside. I took a side alley lined with stores selling homewares and stopped before an elevator that had been summoned electronically by my kom – manual buttons being of course only for places like the Excelsior.

The doors opened onto a swanky reception area with shiny white floors and a large holo reading *Beartreaux Medical Suites*. A receptionist sat behind the counter: human (I guess), female and entirely unnecessary. An elderly couple reclined on a plush leather couch. Soft music tinkled and a low table was set with objets d'art. Someone had been making good use of the designerware stores in the street below.

"I'm here for a sixteen hundred with Dr. Lam," I said to the woman, proffering my kom for scanning. "I'm a bit early."

She smiled sweetly. "It's OK, Dr. Lam is available – please go through to room four." She gestured to her right.

Down a short corridor was a sign reading *Dr. Priscilla Lam: consulting dermatologist* followed by a string of letters. I entered to find a plump lady of indeterminate age dressed entirely in black, examining a holo.

"Come in, sit," she said, pointing to a chair without looking up, then continued her work while I waited in silence. Eventually the holo disappeared and she fixed me with penetrating brown eyes. "How can I help? I thought this appointment was for a *Ms.* Perolo?"

"Yes, that's my wife," I said, "but she couldn't be here. I mean, I'm on Jubilee without her."

She pursed her lips. "Well, how can I examine her if she's not here?"

"I have a very good holo of her condition. Do you think you could look at it?"

The doctor made a face and then shrugged. "OK, but it's still four hundred and twelve credits consulting fee."

"That's fine," I lied, trying not to think about my vanishing bank balance. This fancy clinic was clearly not meant for the likes of me. I brought up a holo showing the angry red weal in the middle of Sana's back.

"Can you send that to me?" the doctor asked.

She reopened the holo on her own kom, zooming in on the red mark. Fine blisters and tiny pustules became visible on closer view. "High-quality holo," she muttered, concentrating.

"Military-grade kom," I said.

She looked up for a moment, surprised, then zoomed in tighter. We were now at the highest magnification. Individual skin cells could be made out, a faint silver sheen visible between them. The doctor nodded in understanding and then looked at me quizzically. "Mr. Perolo, is your wife politically active, would you say?"

The question blindsided me. I stuttered, "Y-yes, actually, I'd say she is."

"And your home system, has M4M reached there yet?"

I felt a burning in my chest. "We're half and half. The Movement has seats in Congress, but not control. It's a tense situation."

"And your wife, she's an opposition politician?"

"That would be accurate."

Dr. Lam pointed toward the silver sheen in the holo. "What you have here are nanides."

I think somehow I had already guessed this, but it was still a shock. "So it's artificial," I said flatly.

"My word, yes," she said. "Artificial and remotely controlled."

I closed my eyes. There was a roaring sound in my ears.

The rash had started six months after Sana was elected to Congress. She had sat up in bed in the middle of the night screaming and writhing in agony. I'd rushed her to the closest clinic, where ointment, painkillers and a sedative were prescribed. But with little effect. Over the next few weeks, a pattern emerged: maddening itchiness during the day, then throbbing and burning at night, destroying sleep, destroying sanity. I had taken Sana to every doctor and specialist I could find, but no one seemed to have a clue.

I took a breath, tried to regain composure. "Could you remove them?"

"Not hard, you just need the right gear."

"We visited many doctors on Brouggh, how come *they* couldn't?"

She laughed knowingly. "They could. Of course. But someone from M4M pays a visit. If they know what's good for them...."

That's right! One appointment I remembered clearly, Dr. Rallis. He had been all sweaty and nervous, wouldn't look me in the eye. Bundled us out within minutes, claiming he couldn't help. My Investigator radar had pinged that something was off but for the life of me I couldn't figure out what. In the end I'd decided he was probably just an oddball.

Had to hand it to the Movement, clever ploy. Strike your opponent down with a strange malady. *The Lord's wrath.*

That's what you might think, especially at three in the morning. Fairly simple to pull off too. There aren't many doctors left these days, with most diseases eliminated or easily treatable at robo-clinics. Hell, there were only a handful of dermatologists on all of Brouggh. Not hard to get to them. Just the one little problem of nano-weapons being outlawed by galactic treaty for the past seven thousand years.

"How did they get them onto her?"

Dr. Lam thought a moment. "Not difficult. Just a light touch with a dispenser. Maybe in summer if she wasn't wearing much?"

Summer, yes. That's when it began. Sana probably wearing something brief with a low back. A stranger brushes against her, just for a moment....

I'd always considered myself above politics. Of course I'd supported Sana in her run, but as a Services employee I was supposed to be neutral. To be honest I didn't really have a beef with M4M anyway – Services people are conservative by nature. But in that moment in Dr. Lam's office, something snapped. Sana had been right all along. The Movement had to be stopped.

"And those bastards are always talking about morals," I said. "What kind of people would do this?"

"Your wife is lucky. With that same technology they could strip the skin right off her back."

"Oh, I should be grateful then," I said bitterly. "These people are capable of anything."

The doctor smiled sadly. "Why do you think I have to practice here on Jubilee?"

CHAPTER SEVEN

Sana and I had just started dating. We were in that dreamy phase, couldn't keep our hands off each other. So when she'd suggested checking out the M4M rally, I was less than excited. Why do anything else when we could be getting horizontal?

We'd met a month before at some cop thing – a retirement, I think. She was there with the band and stood next to me at the bar as I loaded up with drinks for my buddies.

"Thirsty?" she asked, eyes twinkling.

I tried to think of something amusing and clever to say. "Thirsty friends," was the best I could do.

She was wearing a tiny black dress and was tiny herself, with dark skin, a mane of black hair and flashing black eyes. We got talking. She was graceful, outgoing and funny. Came from a large, artsy, inner-city family full of musicians, poets, dancers and the like. I was big and clunky. A country plodder. An only child and lifelong member of the Security Services.

It was love at first sight.

The rally was held on a crystalline summer's evening. We'd walked through Central Park holding hands and made out on the lawn near the ornamental lake. She sat on top of me, brushed her hair off my face and tenderly stroked my cheek.

"Who'da thought, eh?" she said.

"Thought what?"

"Me and you."

She looked deeply into my eyes, the rest of the world melting away. If there were a heaven, it could not be better than this.

"You make me feel safe," she said after a while, "and you're not aware of how attractive you are – which is a very good thing."

In those days Sana was always praising me, building me up.

"OK, time to move," she said. "I've heard so much, don't want to be late." And with great effort she got me onto my feet.

We headed toward Harrison City Hall, where a big crowd was building – though far from the stadium-filling masses that would soon follow.

Sana wrinkled her nose at the giant banner reading: *Movement 4 Morality*. "That's a bit corny, isn't it, using the number four that way? It's like they're trying to be cool."

Typical Sana, picking up on the discordant note. On that night, though, all I could think about was wanting to nibble that cute little nose. We walked into the reception area, where they scanned our koms. It was crowded and intense. A crew of young, hyper-enthusiastic volunteers, all with the same idealistic gleam in their eyes, were running everything.

Sana recoiled and looked back toward the door. "Maybe this was a bad idea? Why don't we go to your place like you wanted?"

But my curiosity was aroused. "Look, we're here now, why not see what all the fuss is about?"

We were given brochures to read and ushered to our seats by a young woman with the same gleaming eyes. A band played up-tempo religious tunes and the crowd swayed and clapped along.

"At least those musos know what they're doing," said Sana.

A warm-up guy came out on stage, young and charismatic with a Brouggh accent. Had clearly done this before. Tonight we would hear from Gilham himself, founder and spiritual head of the Movement. The excitement was palpable. It was said that Gilham had started M4M as a teenager on his home planet, Rethne. He lived monk-like in a small apartment, ate only one vegetarian meal a day and lived by a self-imposed vow of celibacy.

The warm-up guy finished, the music faded and the lights dimmed. We waited expectantly in the dark hall as long minutes passed, anticipation building. Finally the stage lights came up and a tall, thin man dressed entirely in white walked smoothly onstage to rapturous applause. He stood calmly at the lectern and looked out toward the audience with a benevolent smile, waiting for the noise to die down.

Eventually there was silence. Stretching out, becoming pin-drop in the large hall.

Gilham had longish, dark hair that he flicked away from his face. He cleared his throat, looked down at his notes and began speaking in a gentle, surprisingly reedy, almost feminine voice. "Thank you for coming tonight. I would like to welcome you with all my heart."

He spoke quietly, making us all sit forward and strain to hear. He seemed humble and modest. We were already on his side – this after just one sentence.

"With your permission," he said, "I would like to enquire into something here tonight, something I consider very important. Will you indulge me?"

Positive murmurs from the audience.

"Thank you. So the question I would like to pose is this...." There was a long pause. "What *is* it to be a human being?"

Surprising. I hadn't expected that.

"A simple question, isn't it?" said Gilham. "And yet the answer is *not* simple. Is being a human something to do with your position in life or your relationships or your qualities – good and bad?"

The crowd murmured again, perplexed.

"No," said Gilham. "If you think about it, it's not really to do with any of these things, is it?" Another long pause. "So what *is* it to be human? It's a question I've spent my whole life considering."

We were now paying rapt attention. We wanted Gilham to tell us the answer.

"And let me ask you another question, a related question – what is it that truly makes us happy? When we get money or fall in love, we feel happy for a little while, don't we, but then what happens?"

He spread his hands, palms open. He had large, liquid, black eyes that seemed bottomless. When he spoke, it felt like he was talking directly to me.

"What goes up must come down," he said sadly. "All these things we assume will make us happy, they're only fleeting, aren't they? Imagine this, imagine you were the richest person in the galaxy, married to the most beautiful and loving partner, famous and healthy – would that make you truly happy?"

"No," the crowd muttered.

Gilham's voice was starting to rise now. "That's right," he said, "you'd be happy for about five minutes – if that! All these things are fleeting and yet we pursue them as if they were the *answer*, and here's the crazy thing: we already know in advance they won't work! Isn't that crazy?"

I looked around. The gleaming-eyed volunteers were positively jumping out of their seats, the new people muttering in agreement.

"As a species," said Gilham, "we've conquered poverty and disease, nearly beaten old age. Once we came up with interstellar travel, we rampaged through the galaxy, obliterating any species or things that stood in our way. But has all this" – he was shouting now – "has all this made us even one *tiny little bit* happier?"

"No!" the crowd roared. I found it hard to disagree with anything Gilham said and his charisma was so powerful I didn't want to anyway.

"Why do we do it, then? Why keep expending so much energy on things we know in advance will not make us happy? Why?"

Someone yelled, "Tell us!"

Gilham laughed. "OK, I'll tell you." And now he spoke so quietly it was almost a whisper. "It's because we've been lied to."

There was a shocked silence.

"The people who run this planet, the so-called *elites*. They don't care about us." Gilham slapped the lectern, his voice rising again. "What *do* they care about? Power. Power for themselves, power for its own sake. They want us to run around, distracted. Chasing baubles, indulging in one *dreary* pleasure after another, so we won't notice what's really going on."

The mood in the hall grew darker. People were muttering angrily, calling out, *That's right!* As though Gilham had a wire running directly into their heads and was generating a negative current.

"These people," he snarled, "think they're so clever, with their fancy artworks and *open-minded* morality. They love to jet off to other systems to have their little symposiums on galactic harmony. But what good does any of that do for *us?*"

Sana grabbed my leg, her nails digging into me. "I have to get out of here, right now!" she spat.

I stood, taking her hand, and we squeezed our way along the row of seats and exited the hall.

Outside, she turned on me. "Why did you make me stay there!?" She was shaking like a leaf.

I was taken aback. "It was your idea to come!"

"Yes, but I wanted to go, you made me stay!" She turned – "I have to get away!" – and stormed off into the night.

And so it was we had our first real fight over the Movement.

Gilham went on to speak in all the major cities across Brouggh to ever-expanding crowds. He railed against the establishment, urged a return to simple living and old-fashioned morals, and by tour's end was packing out sport stadiums. A few weeks after he left, Movement candidates blitzed the global congress elections, picking up twenty-five per cent of the seats, shocking the established parties to their cores. As part of this wave, a small-town mayor by the name of Rubichek Nees was elected to Congress, where he joined the Ethics Committee and in a few years became its powerful chairman.

From that first night Sana had set herself against M4M, saying, "Gilham is dangerous, he's got everyone fooled."

She was performing comedy and added a venomous satire of what she called the *Bowel* Movement to her act. Privately I questioned the point. The crowd was always full of creative types like Sana. Wasn't this just preaching to the converted?

Occasionally I wonder to myself: had I not married Sana, would I too have been taken in by Gilham and the Movement? The uncomfortable answer is, quite possibly, yes. Many of the things he spoke about rang true for me and I had an instinctive resentment of the people he was attacking. It didn't seem so bad if they got taken down a peg.

But I was spared (and damned) by my relationship with Sana.

One night after a show some political person had sidled up, suggested she run for Harrison City Council on the Justice Party ticket. She'd built something of a profile, why not put it to good use?

CHAPTER EIGHT

And put it to good use she did, taking to politics like a natural.

Where had this person been during our first two years? She gave interviews – straight to camera like a pro – speaking off the cuff and skewering Movement politicians at every opportunity. She was insightful and clever and always funny, and during that election – that first rung up the political ladder – no one was able to lay a glove on her.

One night she dragged me to an event, the Harrison City Waste Department Annual Gala or some such thing (after a while they all blurred together). A tall man with a gleaming pink pate – a big cheese of some kind – strode over to where Sana and I were chatting with a group of her supporters. He towered over her in a manner some might consider intimidating, hand outheld.

"Hello, my dear, Sana, isn't it?"

She looked up at him, barely half his size, squinting in a way I knew spelled trouble. "I'm not your *dear*," she spat, hand clenched at her side as if to ensure it could not hold itself out to be shaken.

"Come now," he said, his voice booming and hearty, "we may be on opposite sides of the aisle, so to speak, but that doesn't mean we can't be civil, surely?"

"You and I have nothing to talk about, *Chairman*." She fixed him with a withering glare and held her ground in silence until the man shrugged, turned and strode away.

"What's that motherfucker doing *here*," she growled, "at a Harrison City municipal function?"

I was shocked – was it necessary to be so uncivil? – and wasn't it the whole point of democracy that everyone agreed to disagree with their political opponents? Unless of course those people were in fact enemies of democracy itself, a concept I could never have entertained at the time.

Looking back, I'm pretty sure Chairman Nees attended that obscure local event for one reason only: to take a close look at the new rising star everyone was talking about.

Of course, Harrison City Council turned out to be just a stepping stone. Before year's end Sana was handed a prime slot on the state ticket, shunting aside seasoned political operatives. She was recognized everywhere we went now, people often assuming I was her security rather than her husband. Something we both laughed about – though it got less and less funny as time went on.

Was I resentful or jealous? Not at all. I was proud if anything, starry-eyed and worshipful, even if a slight condescension crept into her voice at times and even when the nights she was away grew longer and ever more frequent. Besides, there was work. All-consuming, never-ending. Work buddies and work functions that I might have once skipped – back when the shoe was on the other foot and it was always her complaining about my long hours. I figured that somehow things would eventually change, go back to being better like they were before.

The state elections were a triumph and Sana's maiden speech to a packed gallery was met with rapturous applause and widely disseminated. The more scorn and venom (and threats, public and private) that Movement people poured upon her, the more her star seemed to rise in the eyes of everyone else.

Finally it was Brouggh Global Congress, inconceivable only a few years earlier. A slot was found and in that fateful cycle when M4M achieved near-control of Congress, Sana was the sole new candidate from a liberal background who bucked the trend. Almost half of her Justice Party colleagues were turfed out.

Making her even more of a hero to certain folk. She was away for months at a time now and when home, never off her kom, handling media and urgent politics. I became less current with whatever the crisis of the moment was and my own work stuff seemed inconsequential compared to hers, so there was little for us to talk about.

And as for sex – forget about it.

Still, my heart was hers only. There were the occasional flashes of our former life: a chat by kom late at night while lying in beds a continent apart, a meal snatched here or there. I pined for her, tried my best to not be 'clingy' or 'annoying', and when I noticed them at all, other women seemed like pale shadows compared to her blazing light.

A year after the Congressional win came the rash. For a short time it brought us closer together as we visited doctors and tried every treatment, conventional or otherwise. But at some point, she turned inward. Became stoic, uncommunicative. The very sight of me seemed to annoy her – and it was this finally that tipped me over the edge. I grew sullen and resentful. It was easy to forget she was living with chronic pain because she never spoke of it. I began to question our marriage. Had we ever been truly in love, or was it just a shallow attraction of opposites? Some days I'd blame myself – I had to be more patient, more kind. Surely her skin would clear up sooner or later and everything would go back to normal?

She often slept in the spare room and even when there were no scheduled events, went out anyway to distract herself. There was drinking and substances. There was the political crowd and the artsy friends. And there was the comfort of others.

★   ★   ★

I don't remember much about the last meal on Jubilee. Danee took us through a park at the top of Sector Five, the first open space I'd seen. The grass was artificial but with live trees growing in pots. The high roof above was part of the outer skin of Jubilee – and here you could see the random nature of the structure. A giant weld ran above us joining to another section on the far side, which jutted off at a strange angle.

This part of Jubilee was said to have a bohemian vibe and at dinner our waiters all sported strange facial hair – even the women. Some kind of androgynous trend, I guess. Opposite was an art gallery hosting what appeared to be a launch, a large holo sign reading:

O B F U S C A T I O N S: *Kat Blair.*

A milling, murmuring crowd with the same strange facial hair were being served cocktails and nibbles by what looked like human waiters. Must be a *mid-tier* gallery, I thought, remembering Batum. In the center of the crowd a tall, red-haired woman dressed in black was holding court – Kat Blair presumably. Sana would have been right at home.

Danee and I didn't talk much. I was mulling over the appointment with Dr. Lam and the prospect of returning home seemed to hang in the air between us.

Douglas buzzed in on Danee's kom. "How're you getting on, folks? Col, what's your story? I hear you've been tryin' to take out the gliders over at Lo-G World?"

I laughed. "Those copters wouldn't let you take out anything, there's so much tech hidden in them!"

Danee looked at me in surprise. I hadn't told her about my near miss.

"Not much gets past you, does it, mate? That's why I want you workin' for me here on Jubilee!"

"Sorry, Douglas, don't think I'm your man."

"Well, you never know," he said cheerfully. "Just givin' you a heads-up Zanders is back on track. He'll be ready for you at oh eight hundred. Does that suit?"

It did. We decided to meet at 07:30, finished up our meal and headed back for what was meant to be a quiet night in.

Dear reader, if you've been following closely, what occurred next may not be a surprise to you. But rest assured, it was a massive shock for me. There was a soft tap and a figure silhouetted briefly in the doorway – Danee, wearing next to nothing. Slipping into my bed, forming herself to me, soft lips finding mine in the dark.

I suppose a better person would have put up at least *some* resistance.

Who knows why I didn't – perhaps it was the free-for-all atmosphere of Jubilee? But in one instant, Danee unleashed something in me I thought had been lost forever and to no one's surprise more than mine, I fell into her arms without a moment's hesitation.

She was long and lean with small breasts, a toned body. So different to Sana. For modesty's sake I draw the curtain here – but you can assume the chemistry was good. Afterward we lay together and I tried to regroup – a crawling feeling growing in my belly. Guilt and shame.

"You know—"

She cut me off with a finger to my lips. "It's OK, I know about Sana. And I know *about* Sana. I know you're a good guy."

I didn't feel like a good guy – in fact I was appalled at myself.

There was pillow talk. Turned out, she'd always had a thing for me. "You spoke at my freshman class and I thought *that's the guy for me.*"

"Really? I never got that sense from you." In the few dealings we'd had, Danee had given nothing away, always been completely professional.

"Yes, I know," she sighed, "but then I was lying in my room this evening and I suddenly realized it was now or never."

"I don't under—"

"Because if I left it up to *you*, my dear, nothing would ever have happened, would it?" She stroked my face, relaxed and amused. "Don't worry, sometimes it's only another person who can see what's really going on."

We talked until late. Danee asked about my life, wanted to know why I'd become a cop – definitely not a subject for that night. I told her, growing up in the hinterland, I had been curious about the big, wide world – not a lie exactly. No way was I going into what had happened with Mother and Tim.

Eventually she drifted off in my arms, then I too fell into an uneasy half sleep.

CHAPTER NINE

Flowing in. Flowing out.

One of those dreams that's pure sensation, impossible to put into words. Morphing into a tropical scene. Beach shack at night with a wooden floor, open door to catch the sea breeze and a net over the bed for mosquitoes. But one has found its way inside the net. Whining noise, so annoying. I came half awake with a dreamy question: *How could there be mosquitoes here on Jubilee?*

Then understanding – *nanosassin.*

Everything that happened next took place within two seconds – no more. They say your life flashes before your eyes when you're facing death, but that's not how it went for me. Time slowed to a single moment of crystalline clarity as my mind worked through the options for survival.

Flight?

Impossible, could never outrun it.

Protection?

Lying naked in bed.

Defense?

It's dark and there's nothing to fight with.

By elimination, call for help.

But who – Douglas? Security?

Minutes away, too long.

A flash of memory. Batum, speaking yesterday "…my duties include… security…."

Half a second gone. One point five seconds remaining.

Call Batum then.

Unless he's part of this somehow?

Then we're dead anyway.

OK, must get the words out clearly. No time to stumble.

They formed in my mind.

"*Batum help nanosassin!*" I screamed.

At the same moment putting my hands over Danee's ears. One of us might survive, let it be her.

As the words were halfway out of my mouth, perhaps by the time I had cried '*Help,*' Batum, acting with inhuman speed, burst through the door, which blew off its hinges, leaped across the bed in a blur of motion and stopped dead, crouched over us with his hand next to my ear. There was something caught between his finger and thumb. Buzzing angrily.

"I've got it, sir," he said. "Please be still, I'm going to back away now."

His fingers were a millimeter from my left ear. An instant longer and my brain would have been turned to mush from the burrowing nano. The lights came on, Danee waking up dazedly while Batum stood near the door, eyes fixed. Concentrating on holding the nano, which was trying to chew through the artificial flesh of his finger and thumb, blue fluid falling to the carpeted floor.

"I could crush it," he said without looking up, "but Douglas has given orders not to. He will be here in zero point three-eight with containment."

The room was silent apart from the sound of the trapped nano. We counted down the seconds, each of which felt like an hour. I heard the elevator ping and next the room was full of security droids, one of which spoke with Douglas's voice.

"Everybody calm now. Batum, you'll be needin' work on the hand after this."

Douglas produced a small, clear container and slid it over the nano. The lid snapped shut with a loud click, slicing off Batum's finger and thumb. The nano broke free, zipping around furiously inside its tiny prison, dashing against the walls, trying to burrow out. Nasty piece of work. A droid took the box and raced off while Douglas handed Batum a cloth to wrap around his hand. The lift pinged continuously, more security arriving by the minute. Danee and I were still lying naked in bed.

"Could Susan bring me some clothes, please?" Danee asked.

A different type of droid entered, inflating a balloon that emerged from its out-thrust arm. The balloon puffed up ever larger, passing around us, rejoining itself, contacting the walls, roof and floor until a grayish-brown film lined the entire room. The droid Susan entered through the broken door, the film parting to let her through.

"This is an intelligent membrane," said Douglas. "It allows air through and any object with permission. But nothin' else. We're going to keep it up till the place is secure."

Douglas left and Danee jumped up to pull on her clothes. I did the same and we both sat on the bed in shock while the security detail did its thing.

Douglas returned a few minutes later, shaking his head gravely, and asked, "I take it you spent the night here together?"

I glanced at my kom; it was 05:22. "Close enough to all night."

"Well, that saved your life, Danee. Probably both of you."

I looked at him in disbelief. "How?"

"That thing cut its way through the air grille, which is not supposed to be possible since it's made of fuckin' Titex. This suite is supposed to be hardened for nanos, which is why I put you in here."

Surprising. Why would Douglas worry about our security when he had so clearly manipulated events to keep us here on Jubilee? And anyway, how the hell did that thing get through Titex? It's almost impossible to cut in a workshop with special gear, let alone by an insect-sized nano.

"That bug's got a tiny cutting wheel made of somethin' we've never seen. Found the same hole in Danee's room, so we think it went there first – no one home – so then it tried this room. Seems the cutting wheel got slightly damaged on the first grille and that's why you heard it."

I got up and looked at the air grille above the bathroom door. There was a hole, just three square millimeters in size, cut through the dark gray Titex.

Douglas spoke again. "Do ye want to say goodbye to Batum? He's off to the shop to get his hand fixed."

"Of course," said Danee. "He saved our lives."

"Something you should know," said Douglas, a little sheepishly. "Strictly speakin' Batum and Susan are not domestic droids. They're from security. I had 'em posted here to be on the safe side."

Batum entered, thumb and finger patched with hardiplaz where they'd been amputated by the containment box.

"Guess I'd better shake your hand," Danee said, "the left one anyway. Thanks for saving our lives."

"No problem," he said, shaking with Danee, then me. "Had a weird feeling the whole time something was going to happen." He leaned against the wall, his personality seeming quite different now to the Batum I knew over the last few days.

"You seem pretty relaxed despite getting your finger and thumb chopped off," I said.

"Yeah," he laughed, "especially now I don't have to pretend to be a bloody butler!"

CHAPTER TEN

An hour or so later the suite was pronounced clear and the membrane in my room deflated. Douglas left two anti-nanobots to stay with us till we met again.

I kept turning over the events of the night. Who was behind this? Was it some incomprehensible play from Douglas?

If he wants us dead there's a thousand ways he could do it.

Or what if he merely wanted us to think we'd been saved by him? My instincts said no. The whole thing was too close and Douglas appeared genuinely rattled by it.

So if not Douglas, who then? Something was very wrong.

At 07:30 we met in the lobby. Outside on Concourse, an official car waited to whisk us to the morgue. Finally we could collect the body of Chairman Nees and get the hell out of here. It felt like we'd been on Jubilee for an eternity.

"Have you worked out how the nano got on board?" asked Danee as we traveled along Concourse, relatively quiet in the early morning.

"We're scanning from one end of Jubilee to the other," said Douglas, "but so far nothin'."

"You must get so much freight here," she said, now back in uniform and businesslike. "Maybe it was smuggled in with food or inside something solid like a piece of equipment?"

"Impossible, you've no idea how sophisticated our scanning is. Couldn't get a grain of sand on board without us knowin'."

"Well, *something* got through, didn't it!"

Douglas muttered a stream of expletives under his breath.

"Anything on the nano?" I asked.

"Committed hara-kiri once it realized it was trapped. But we're working to see what we can retrieve. We have our ways."

An idea occurred to me. "You're doing building works on the far port side, aren't you?"

"Yeah, we're putting Sector Twenty-One on at the moment." Douglas paused. "I can see where you're goin' and if that were to be the case, it raises a whole bunch of curly fucking questions. But you see? This is exactly why I want you here on Jubilee, Col."

"Yeah, well, I mightn't last long if I took that job!"

Douglas muttered more expletives. "Everyone's a fuckin' critic – though not without cause, I suppose."

We arrived at a large goods lift, which took us down a few levels and opened onto a hangar door inscribed *Jubilee Morgue*. Finally.

A pale, chubby man with loose jowls and scraggly gray hair waited inside. His eyes were watery and bloodshot, and his hand trembled when I shook it. If you wanted to draw a portrait of someone who'd just been on a two-day gampa bender, this would be it. The room was brightly lit, a bank of lockers filling the far wall that presumably contained bodies. I knew from our briefing notes that Jubilee gave seven days for the next of kin to claim a body and after that it would be buried in space – a tiny parcel shot off toward MGNA#12.

"Better take a look at the *naughty* boy," I said cheerily. I wasn't planning on doing much grieving for Chairman Nees.

Zanders touched a button and a coffin-shaped stasis unit slid out from the wall. He hit another button and the hardiplaz window went from opaque to clear and *that* was when the bombshell dropped.

Lying in repose, arms crossed, was the smooth-cheeked figure of an adolescent male, around fifteen years old.

Danee swore. "What the fuck is this, Douglas?"

Zanders bent over the unit in consternation. "Says *R. Nees* in the file."

Douglas brought up a holo-video of the place we were standing in. We saw the body of a middle-aged man being loaded into a stasis unit, then time speeding up, nothing happening for days, the odd figure flashing by.

"No one's touched this unit since it was loaded, I've checked the log," said Douglas.

"Do you have vision from inside the coffin?" I asked.

Douglas fumed. "Now why would I have a camera *inside* a fucking coffin?"

"Yikes, I got a match," said Danee. She had scanned the face of the corpse and run it through the database on her kom. "Lachy Nees, the chairman's *son*."

There was stunned silence. The chairman had a son? That wasn't in the file and you wouldn't assume, given how few people have children these days. But of course, he was Movement; they were supposed to have kids.

"But how did he get here to Jubilee? Didn't you scan him on?" I asked Douglas.

"Of course!" he replied defensively, bringing up a holo of a middle-aged man entering a landing dock. "Scanned as *R. Nees, Brouggh*."

"Hang on," said Danee, "that is *not* the face of Chairman Nees."

I looked closely. She was right.

"So," I said, "let's get this straight. A middle-aged man scans onto Jubilee posing as our esteemed chairman, dies and then his body somehow transforms into that of his teenage son?"

No one spoke.

"How did he die, anyway?" I'd not asked the question before.

Douglas brought up a holo showing the last sad days of Lachy Nees in high speed. We saw him scanning on board, then running the gamut of earthly sins in comically fast motion: gambling, drinking, sex with multiple partners – little white bottom bouncing in the air – snorting and shooting drugs. The vision slowed toward the end. He looked at himself in the bathroom mirror, gravely swallowed a pill and lay down slowly on the bed. In a final tragic note, holding a stuffed toy to his chest for comfort. I glanced into the stasis chamber and saw a clear bag with personal effects, on top a mangy old toy monkey. He was still a boy, really. What had driven him to take his life? And in such a way, calculated to damage his father?

"Tell me how this corpse goes from being a middle-aged man to a boy?" Danee asked.

There was silence. We stood there gawping, as if the body were going to wake up and explain.

Zanders cleared his throat theatrically. We all turned and looked at him.

"DNAging," he said.

"DN what?" asked Danee.

"Illegal of course," Zanders said. "The young ones do it, to get into clubs or bars or whatever. Temporarily ages you a few years older, then wears off. Hard to detect coz it's your actual DNA. This boy turned it thirty years ahead—"

"And reprogrammed his kom to be his father—" cut in Danee.

"Which is not supposed to be possible," I said.

We stood there, still in disbelief.

"And then he *tops* himself," said Douglas.

I turned around and paced the room, mind whirling.

This was bad. On many levels.

It was one thing to be collecting the chairman's body – good riddance – but this kid? They had to have known at Command.

I had received a priority message on my kom: *Report to Commander Huk immediately.* She was waiting in her office, white-faced and agitated. Motioned for me to shut the door, then sit.

"Urgent mission, highly sensitive."

I nodded OK. It was already unusual to get briefed this way rather than a new file popping up on my kom.

"You've heard of Jubilee, I presume?" she said.

"*The* Jubilee?"

She smiled grimly. "The very one. We've received a message to collect a body. VIP."

Stranger and stranger.

"OK and our VIP is …?"

She leaned forward. "This is *top* secret. The subject is Chairman Nees."

I let out a breath. Rubichek Nees dead on Jubilee? Fuck me. No wonder this was hush-hush.

"On this mission you will be second and Danee Hasum will be first. You know her, right?"

I thought for a moment. "Yeah, I've seen her round."

"A flyer's waiting. You're to leave immediately, collect the body and bring it straight back. This is *retrieval* only. You are not to investigate the cause of death. You are not to tell anyone where you're going or even that you are going, and you cannot speak about this afterward. Status one top secret."

Sana wouldn't know where I was. That would be OK, I supposed, it wasn't unusual for me to disappear on a mission for days at a time sometimes – and anyway, it wasn't like we hung out much anymore.

"OK, that's it," Huk had said, pointing to the door.

I saluted – "Commander!" – grabbed a daypack from my locker and found Danee waiting in the flyer. Minutes later we were off to Jubilee.

That was only two days ago, I realized with a start.

My mind churned. Chairman Nees would have known – obviously – that this body was not himself dead on Jubilee. So let's assume they knew who the body really was – his son Lachy would be missing, they'd figure it out. So they'd cobbled together a scheme: they would have Danee and me bring home 'Chairman Nees' hoping we didn't notice.

The face might not look quite the same, but a man of the right age with family resemblance – and anyway, people look different in death. We wouldn't have questioned it. Chairman Nees would lie low for a few days till the body was back and then a cover story would be put out.

Then what?

Danee and I would know some inconvenient facts.

But we're Services, trained to keep secrets.

Yes, but why pick us instead of any number of department factotums?

They'd selected two controversial agents: Danee, who'd been to Jubilee multiple times – a black mark these days – and me – in a compromising marriage. Why choose us unless something was up? What was supposed to happen after we returned home?

Nothing good.

Then the delay. They knew we'd find out who was in the casket.

So then the nanosassin.

Was that Command? Or was it M4M?

Either way, how could anyone have a bug ready to go here on Jubilee?

And why kill us *before* we got home? I looked up and saw what I assumed were the same thoughts playing out on Danee's face.

Douglas too. He said, "Are you sure ye want to go home now, given everything? Job here on Jubilee could be just the ticket? You too, Danee."

I shook my head. What about Sana, what about everything? Staying on Jubilee would be dereliction, I could never return – and besides, there was the kid. "We can't forget," I said, "there's a young man here who deserves to be given his last respects, whatever the circumstances."

"Such a *boy scout* you are, Col, that's why I love ya!" said Douglas.

I looked at Danee and she nodded grimly.

We loaded the body into our flyer.

Before we closed the doors, Douglas said to me quietly, "You can always come back, y'know."

"Even if I wanted to, how would I get here?"

He leaned in and whispered, "There's a way. If it comes to it, you'll know what to do."

He walked off without looking back.

We sealed the doors and set off back to Brouggh, where things had utterly changed in the forty-eight hours we had been away.

CHAPTER ELEVEN

A large party was waiting for us in the airlock, weapons drawn. Way more uniforms than needed – it was standing-room only. As soon as I opened the flyer door, a team rushed inside our ship, then rushed straight out again with the casket, whisked off to who knows where.

Henderzon, an agent I knew well, pointed a blaster at me. "This way, Perolo," he said, gesturing toward the door.

I'd been expecting an awkward reception, but this was ridiculous. "What's going on, am I under arrest?"

He sniggered. "Buddy, a lot's happened while you've been away."

I'd never liked Henderzon much. He was lazy and incurious, and we'd clashed over the years. I got on with most people in the department, so it was significant he'd been chosen to greet me. I was bundled out of the airlock by an armed detail, Danee, looking pale, in a different direction.

"At least tell me what's going on?" I asked with no reply as we marched briskly down the long antiseptic corridors of Command.

Everything seemed crazy. Why was I being treated like a criminal? I was acutely aware of the blasters pointed impolitely at my back, itchy trigger fingers at the ready. If they wanted to take me out, this was where they could do it – *subject attempted to seize my weapon and was mortally wounded in the ensuing struggle* – but I didn't figure that likely. There'd be questions they wanted answering, my only leverage. I thought about the upcoming debrief. Reminded myself I'd done nothing wrong.

Command was buzzing, people rushing everywhere in high anxiety. Whatever had gone down was big. We came to Commander Huk's office and here was the next shock. The sign on the door had been changed to read *Controller Brimheed*. Controller? When was that ever a thing? What had happened to Huk and who the hell was Brimheed?

Henderzon opened the door and we all walked into the office – or tried to, anyway. There were so many overzealous officers, they bounced off each other trying to get inside.

Henderzon pointed to a chair – the one I'd used a few short days ago. "Sit there."

I complied while my detail stood around, tense and flushed from the rapid walk. There was barely enough room for them in the office, which struck me as perilous. They were on such a hair trigger, any sudden noise might set off Armageddon.

"Boys, you look hot and puffy," I said. "Surely there's no need for nine of you to guard little old me?"

Henderzon's eyes narrowed. "Shut the *fuck* up, Perolo. You and your bullshit are done around here."

Nevertheless, he sent all but two of the cops to wait in the corridor. Someone I didn't know, a small, skinny man with bad acne, came into the room, scanned my kom, then left immediately.

I recognized the two remaining guys, tried pushing a little more. "Addison, Roth – *remember me?*"

They both found something fascinating on the floor in front of their shoes.

"Henderzon, we didn't always see eye to eye, but hey, that was work. We're the good guys, right?"

He looked away.

"Listen, I don't know what they've told you but" – here I had to be cautious, Huk had declared the mission category one – "all I can say is, for the last three days I've been following orders, I have no idea—"

"We *know* you were on Jubilee, Perolo."

His voice cracked, a pulse beating in his neck. Henderzon was clearly stretched beyond his meager capacity – but he'd mentioned Jubilee! A voice of intuition told me to throw caution to the wind, put my version of the story out there.

"Listen, guys, I was sent to Jubilee by *Huk* to collect a body. Very hush-hush. Was supposed to be Chairman Nees but turned out to be his *son*, Lachy Nees. That's who was in the casket you unloaded! I'm being set up somehow."

All three were looking at me now – that had gotten through. These guys were professional Investigators like me. They knew when something sounded right, and when it stunk of bullshit from Command. Even Henderzon got it; I could see the conflict in his eyes.

Before anyone could speak, the door opened and a very young man in uniform, presumably Brimheed, walked quickly into the room and sat at what I still thought of as Huk's desk. "OK, guys, I can handle things from here," he said a little nervously.

The three cops walked out, looking back now with some concern. Brimheed pushed a button under his desk and my whole body became inert like a statue. An immobilizer, fuck. This was a highly aggressive move – and before asking a single question.

"Your mission to Jubilee was category one," Brimheed said in a prim, moralistic tone. "Why did you just discuss it with the men here?"

My anger rose. "Why are you using an immobilizer on one of your own men who's done nothing wrong?"

My mouth still worked, of course, and my eyes. But nothing else. I couldn't even swivel my head to look away from Brimheed. He seemed incredibly young, barely old enough to shave, with light blond hair and pale blue eyes gleaming with the same zeal I'd first seen at the M4M rally. How on earth could he be in charge here?

Then the penny dropped: *political appointee*. The Movement had to have taken charge somehow. They'd parachuted in one of their own to run things at Special Services Brouggh. No wonder everyone was so freaked out.

Brimheed looked up at the ceiling for a moment in silent communication. Could even be Nees on the other end somewhere; he'd certainly have an interest. "I'm going to have you take me through exactly what happened from the time you left Command until you returned today. OK?"

The voice trembled slightly. Had he interviewed even a single suspect before today? Must be some first-year graduate. Why pick him? Plenty of guys were fans of the Movement. If you wanted to take charge of SSB, why not install someone more senior?

Because Brimheed is a true believer.

And that was a scary thought. Because nothing's more dangerous than a true believer – especially one that's out of his depth.

I forced myself to adopt a reasonable tone. "Of course, I'm happy to debrief, but why don't we turn that immobilizer off? Makes it hard to concentrate."

I had an itch on my nose I was desperate to scratch. One of the terrible things about immobilizers – the complete loss of power. In training we'd learned how to use them and experienced what they felt like. In my whole career I'd only ever used the device twice, on highly dangerous suspects with serious mental conditions.

"No, um, sorry." Brimheed looked agitated. "You've already shown yourself to be...noncompliant. Let's start at the beginning."

There was no point in arguing, so I took him through the events of the last three days, all the while sitting there like a piece of stone. He was especially interested in the nano attack and how it was stopped. He paused at regular intervals for instructions.

After what seemed like hours, I finally asked, "Look, I'm very happy to keep going through all this, but wouldn't it be easier to just get everything off my kom?"

"Your kom is blank for the entire duration.... *Newtech*." He spat the last word as if mouthing an obscenity.

Good old Douglas. Couldn't help himself, I guess. It's supposed to be impossible to wipe a kom – but these days many impossible things seemed to be happening.

"Look, I understand the sensitivity," I said, trying to sound reasonable, "but none of what's happened is my fault—"

"Investigator Perolo" – Brimheed cut me off – "did you have sexual relations with Investigator Hasum while you were on Jubilee?"

Ah, there it was. That's how they were going to get me. Technically I had been on duty the whole time. Not supposed to be doing things like drinking wine or having sex with my number one. By custom this rule was never enforced for long layovers. But this time it would be – and now Danee had been brought into it. I had to be very careful, as anything I said could land her in trouble.

"I'm sorry, but that's a personal question and I'm not going to dignify it with a response."

"Investigator Perolo, there's been a lot of changes here on Brouggh. It is no longer an option to deny one's…*wrongdoing*."

"It's nobody's business what I do in my private life."

"Oh, it *is* our business and you were on company time. You must answer the question or there will be consequences."

"My answer is, *no comment*."

Brimheed paused for instructions from whoever was running him, then trembled visibly. "So be it, Perolo."

Dear reader, if you're one of those sensitive souls who fast-forward through the *violent bits*, then you might want to think about doing that now.

The small, skinny man with the bad acne scurried back into the room, this time bearing a large metal spike. He fixed little red eyes on me and smiled nastily, exposing a row of teeth filed down to points. Time slowed to a single moment of horror as he grabbed me by the hair with one hand. I felt his hot, excited breath on my face, smelled the foul odor from his unwashed armpit. With his other hand, he thrust the metal spike deeply into my right eye. Blood ran down my face and I screamed in agony and shock, unable to move. He worked the spike farther into the socket and my eye popped out.

"Did you have sex with Investigator Hasum?"

Blood was pouring, pooling in my lap and dripping onto the floor, my right eye hanging from its socket. I screamed wildly, uncomprehending. This couldn't be happening.

"I repeat, did you have sex with Investigator Hasum?"

The little man still had me by the hair. He raised his spike again and brought it to my left eye. That one next.

"Yes."

"Have you told us the truth about what happened on Jubilee?"

"Yes," I moaned.

Brimheed got up and walked out. My heart was pounding, the room spinning ever faster, everything fading to gray, then black. I lost consciousness – which was a good thing.

CHAPTER TWELVE

I came to lying on a bed in the medical center – memory and horror flooding back. *The man, the spike. My eye hanging out of its socket, blood pouring from the vacant hole.* I reached up to find a patch over my eye, a strange hollow flatness beneath it. Someone must have cleaned me up and cauterized the socket because I felt only a dull, throbbing pain.

But my right eye was gone.

Next to the bed was a box containing personal effects from my desk as well as my daypack from Jubilee and some boxes of medication – I was being cashiered. A guard walked in, Aballa, one of my friends and one of the few SSB guys who got on with Sana.

He drew a breath when he saw me. "I'm supposed to give you a ride home."

He flicked a look at my left wrist, my kom. Until recently an indispensable portal to the world, but now a surveillance tool – we had to speak carefully. We took a company ground car, black with red letters: *Security Services Brouggh.* My last ride in one of these, I supposed. I felt numb, in shock probably. Every so often an image from the torture session flickered before me, then a wave of terror. Try to think of something else.

"Is Sana OK?" A safe question for Aballa to answer.

"No one's heard from her in days."

I frantically checked my kom. Nothing. No messages and no updates. Tried calling but got a complete blank, not even a busy signal. Hot panic filled my heart. I prayed to god there was a message for me at home. Looked at the news feeds – noticing my kom had been detuned to civilian grade – and slowly pieced together what the fuck had just happened here on Brouggh.

The day we'd left for Jubilee, an elderly congresswoman from the Justice Party had retired due to ill health. On the same day, another government MP had met with a fatal ski accident, giving the Movement a temporary majority of one in the Brouggh Global Congress. Using their new majority, M4M politicians voted to remove the prime minister and install their own – who else but my boy, Rubichek Nees.

That same evening a plot to blow up Congress had been discovered and promptly blamed on the opposition, giving Prime Minister Nees the pretext to call a state of emergency, suspend *habeas corpus* and declare himself Potentate with dictatorial powers. These actions were supposedly constitutional, but of course a petition was now pending before the Supreme Court. In the past two days, opposition figures had been rounded up and sent to 're-education' facilities.

All this was surely straight from some M4M playbook. I would love to investigate the 'ski accident' and 'bomb plot'.

"How are you feeling?" asked Aballa sympathetically.

What to say? Could things be any more fucked up? "I'm OK. What story did they put out about Danee and me?"

Aballa smirked. "You and Hasum kidnapped Lachy Nees and took him to Jubilee, where he met with foul play."

Despite everything, I laughed aloud. This was surely the juvenile hand of Brimheed at work – could they not come up with anything better? Sometimes M4M was smart, and sometimes amazingly dumb.

Anyway, fine. No one was going to believe it. I had already put the real story into the system by talking to Henderzon and the other guys before the torture session. It would get around. There are two things I know about cops: they love to gossip and they look after their own. By day's end everyone in SSB all over Brouggh would know Perolo and Hasum had been stitched up. That was something. A start.

Giant posters of Nees had been installed around Harrison. Some had him shaking hands with Gilham, beaming for the camera. Must have been a busy few days for him, what with taking over a planet and all – not to mention his own kid disappearing.

Aballa helped carry my stuff up to the apartment. I opened the door and sang out, "Hello, *Sana?*" but knew already she wasn't there. The place felt shockingly empty.

I hugged Aballa goodbye. "Please have everyone look out for Sana, try and find out where she is?"

"Of course, we're on it. The moment we have something, I'll let you know."

The door closed behind him and I was on my own in the quiet flat. I did a walk around looking carefully at everything. Every so often images from the torture session swam before me unbidden, but I forced them out of my mind – focus on the present.

The spare bedroom had nothing in it anyway. The lounge room was exactly as I'd left it, but the kitchen seemed wrong. This was Sana's domain, she loved making exotic meals and it was never left completely pristine. But the coffeepot, for example, had been put away in the cupboard rather than left sitting in its usual spot out on the bench. Had a cleanup team been through here?

My stomach clenched: *Cleaning up what?*

M4M was capable of anything. They'd ripped my eye out for refusing to answer a question. What would they do to Sana, one of their highest-profile critics? Or was this just paranoia? Maybe I'd put the coffeepot away myself? I looked around the bedroom and the bathroom. Sana's clothes and toiletries were all still there. Looked for a note or sign, but nothing.

My eye started to throb, so I took some of the medication – a painkiller and sedative – thoughtfully supplied by my torturers. I lay on the bed fully clothed and gave in to a wave of self-pity. In the space of seventy-two hours I'd indulged in an extramarital affair, lost my job, lost my wife and my home world had been taken over by homicidal fanatics. Oh, and my eye had been gouged out.

And what about Danee? I tried reaching her on my kom – but as with Sana, no response. The medication was making me groggy, the shock settling in no doubt. It was evening and I drifted off to a fitful sleep.

CHAPTER THIRTEEN

I woke up early morning. Straight away checked my kom for Danee or Sana – nothing. Took more medication, just the painkiller this time, and unpacked my stuff. Something fell out of my daypack and rolled across the floor – the button Danee had given me:

I got high – at Lo-G World!

A joyous couple, bouncing eternally. I smiled sadly – it already felt like years ago. I put the button on the dresser and dumped the rest of my stuff in the spare room – a meager collection for two decades of service.

I stripped for a shower. Reluctantly peeled off the eyepatch and shuddered at the sight. A hollow where my right eye had been, covered with a layer of pink artificial skin.

The man, the spike, the eye lying against my cheek.

Enough – keep the mind off it. The skin over my eye socket looked delicate but was probably safe to get wet. Hauled myself into the shower – for what point, though? Stood there for what seemed like hours, barely moving.

Then from the depths of depression, something astonishing. Hope. I stepped out of the shower, looked across at the steamed-up mirror and nearly fell over. Writing. In Sana's childlike hand, reversed out of the foggy mirror:

gone 2 jubilee

I smacked my forehead in astonishment. This was a game we used to play, especially in the early days. The exhaust fan was useless and the bathroom always steamed up. She'd write something silly or cute on the mirror with her finger – *you're my country luvva* – and it would stay invisible till after I showered. Sana had found a way to leave me a message. One the Movement would never discover – clever girl!

I got dressed, my heart suddenly brimming with joy, mind spinning with plans. Had to get back to Jubilee – that was the obvious move, what was left for me here on Brouggh anyway? – but how to accomplish that? My kom would have a travel stop on it, the authorities would never let me off-planet.

But Douglas had hinted at something. "*If the time comes, you'll know what to do.*"

What did that mean?

Maybe I could just call him on my kom? He'd be listening for sure.

But no. If it weren't blocked, it would be monitored. Something else.

Then I got it.

CHAPTER FOURTEEN

I dressed and left the apartment. It was surely bugged so I couldn't put my plan into action there. Caught the elevator to the ground floor. When people saw the eyepatch, they looked away or found something interesting on their koms. I later learned that an eyepatch had rapidly become a potent weapon for the Movement. A symbol of shame, of 'wrongdoing', and a terrifying deterrent for dissenters.

Something else too, something primal. It seemed *biblical* to me, satisfying a deep sadistic urge in M4M's psyche.

Out on the street I walked slowly, like a depressed man with nowhere particular to go. In reality my heart was filled with bliss. I picked up snatches of conversation and was amazed at people going about business-as-usual. How quickly they'd fallen in line! Two women praised the new prime minister, what a relief all that partisan rancor was finally over. Way behind me, far enough for them to think I wouldn't notice, were some young men wearing gray t-shirts and dark glasses. Despite my very slow pace, they managed to always stay a few hundred meters away. These guys weren't SSB – had to be Movement – and not good at their jobs either.

I arrived at the local park, where Sana and I had spent blissful hours in the early days lying together on the grass. A large square with paths leading from each of the corners to a central fountain. I sat on a bench, looking aimlessly through my kom for a while – a man with too much time on his hands. Off in the distance, the gray t-shirts were now hanging around each of the four entrances. I pulled the button Danee had given me out of my pocket and had a close look.

I got high – at Lo-G World!

A crappy, mass-produced souvenir. The back made of tin, the cover clear hardiplaz, a cheaply printed image sandwiched between. This plan was either a stroke of genius or utter folly – but how to execute it? My kom would be listening to everything. How could I take it out of action for just a few moments?

Think outside the box, Col.

The fountain.

Perfect!

I sauntered over to the ornamental pool and sat on its edge. Gazed into the water and as if seeing something interesting, plunged my left hand in. With my other hand I whipped the souvenir button out of my pocket and spoke into it like a microphone:

"Douglas, it's Col, please come and get me!"

My left hand emerged holding a pebble, which I examined for a moment, then threw back in – skipping it across the water.

How long would it take for Douglas to come? Assuming, of course, this wasn't just idiocy. We were talking about technology I had never heard of before. *Newtech*, Brimheed had called it. So who knows, an hour, two hours?

Three hours. And if nothing happened, then plan B – whatever plan B was.

It was a warm, sunny morning, the park cool and pleasant. I took my position back on the bench and listened to the happy cries of children in the nearby playground. In the early years Sana and I had talked about having kids – very hypothetically – but decided there was plenty of time. Such were the advances in human longevity, making babies was something couples put off till later in life – unless they were Movement, of course. But now I thought, *why wait?* If the chance came, I would bring it up again, for life was tenuous and fleeting – so I'd discovered.

Time passed.

The gray t-shirts lounged around looking bored. A couple walked by holding hands and a woman entered the park from the south gate pushing one of those high-tech prams. She walked cheerfully, head high, and stopped at a bench opposite. Quite pretty with long, dark hair, wearing stretchy athletic clothes and large fashionable sunglasses. A *yummy mummy*,

Sana would have called her. She picked the baby up and sat it on her lap facing me. It was drooling, looked about six months old.

But it fixed its eyes on me and spoke aloud. "You took ye time. Thought you'd never call!" Douglas's voice.

I looked again at the mother – a familiar twinkle in the eyes – Danee!

Unbelievable! My heart soared; this was almost too good to be true. But dangerous. The gray t-shirts continued their lounging around, oblivious to my salvation that had just appeared by magic. I glanced pointedly at my kom.

"Don't worry about that," said the baby Douglas, "all they'll be hearin' is the birds."

My brain whirled with questions: how could Danee be here with Douglas, and so quickly? *Must have some kind of prior relationship. And a way of communicating.* And how come she wasn't being followed like me? *Guess I was the one married to a prominent anti-Movement leader.* Had they tortured her as well?

"Are you OK, Danee?" I whispered.

"Better than you, I'd say."

My hand went unconsciously to the eye. "So what happens now?"

"Right, well, listen up," said Douglas. He gave the name of a popular downtown ice-cream parlor where we would meet in an hour. "Best if them gray t-shirt guys didn't follow you. I don't want to give this joint up – makes a fucking *mint!*"

So Douglas owned businesses here on Brouggh – how did that work? How far did his operations extend beyond Jubilee?

"Douglas, they'll just track me there on my kom."

"Nah, they won't, I'll turn your tracking off."

Turn off a kom – who'd ever heard of that? How many impossible things could Douglas do?

"The moment you turn off my tracking, they'll know something's up and grab me."

"OK, true, let's think," he said. "What about this? Head into town and when you give 'em the slip say something aloud like *What a lovely day.* When I hear that, your kom'll go nighty night."

I thought for a moment. It seemed workable.

"Go through the staff door, out back in the warehouse – you'll find us with the flyer. But be careful not to scan anything. Your kom won't be transmitting but a scan will show up. Got that?"

Good point. This was going to take some fancy footwork – but the germ of a plan had formed in my mind. I encouraged it to sprout and grow.

"OK," said Douglas, "let's move it. *Mother*."

The 'baby' gave me a wink and started to cry. Danee cooed and rocked it, then put a pacifier in its mouth with a little smirk. She placed it back in the pram and walked off as if we'd never spoken.

I stayed slumped on the bench pretending to scroll through my kom, watching Danee exit calmly through the north gate out of the corner of my eye. One of the gray t-shirts said something to her. She would be catnip to those guys – pretty young mother with child, exactly the kind of thing Movement people adored. If they only knew. She continued across the road and disappeared around the corner.

I waited another twenty minutes, silently working through my plan. It was crazy – but wasn't everything? With luck I'd be off Brouggh within the hour.

Time for action. I walked over to a nearby rent-a-bike stand and pulled one off. The Harrison City Council had conveniently installed these all over town, along with a network of raised tracks. I casually mounted the cycle, did a few circles – they say you never forget, but it *had* been years – and took off through the park, straight out the north gate. Past the waiting gray t-shirts, who looked stunned at this sudden change in circumstances. One of them stared slack-jawed as I zoomed by – I almost felt like giving him a wave.

I turned down a side street running alongside the park, then moments later rode up a ramp and onto the raised track. Now I was riding along a bicycle freeway five meters up in the air. Navigating was harder than you'd think with only one eye, but what a glorious late-spring morning! Yesterday's horror was receding – how quickly we forget pain – and I had to stop myself from saying, *'What a lovely day!'* Riders coming the other way flashed past. To my right stretched the green inner suburbs and to my left downtown Harrison City. From here the track would curve around, cross the river and take me into the heart of town.

Back at the park there would be consternation and finger-pointing. Their ponderous, labor-intensive tail had fallen over in the blink of an eye. Following someone on a pushbike is actually quite tricky. You need air cover and a team ready with bikes of their own. Always a headache.

By building these raised paths, the city elders had provided Harrison City's small band of criminals with a perfect way to get around. The gray t-shirts would be scrambling – should they grab some bikes and send a team after me? The smartest among them would call for air support – and on cue, there it was – the silver glint of a drone appearing a few hundred meters above.

All going to plan.

I cycled along merrily, not too fast or too slow. Over the river and into town. Up ahead lay the off-ramp to CenterPoint Mall, our city's largest. I took this exit, knowing it would terminate at the fourth-floor parking lot – the whole place familiar from my days as a beat cop. I rode to the bike stand, conveniently located near the entrance, scanned mine off, then strolled in through the sliding doors. After a dozen steps I stopped and said aloud, "What a lovely day!"

I waited a moment, then ran back out the door and across the car park to the emergency exit. Tore down the stairs four at a time – hell on the ankles. The aim was to get out of CenterPoint, across the alleyway and into the mall next door before the team scrambled. They would head to the last place my kom pinged, so best to get far away.

Halfway down the stairs, some instinct had me stop and listen. I heard the unmistakable crunch of boots coming up the stairs, many pairs of them. I took a quick peek: a whole squadron of troops. How did they get here so fast? No time to ponder that. I turned and ran back inside the mall. This was bad. I was in the exact place they were going to look for me. How had my lovely plan derailed so quickly? I forced myself to stop and take a deep breath in, then out. Panic leads to fuckups.

Think, Col.

A corridor ran to my left with signs for the public bathrooms. From memory, a security door was down there. I could use it to make my way out through the bowels of the mall. That's better! I walked rapidly – but not conspicuously so – down the corridor. Put my wrist up to scan through the security door, but instead of a green light and satisfying click, a nasty beep and flashing red light. Of course! My clearance had been downgraded and worse, *fuck*, I'd just *scanned my kom*.

I'd just sent a signal telling them exactly where I was.

No time for deep breaths, act on instinct. I ran to the male toilets, into one of the sit-down stalls, which I locked from the inside, then slid back out under the door – this might buy me twenty seconds. Then back up the corridor and into the disability toilet, locking the door behind.

What now?

I jumped up onto the sink, leaped into the air and was able to push a ceiling tile out of position. OK, good. Jumped again, grabbed the edge of the hole and agonizingly pulled myself up into the ceiling, fingers burning from the sharp edge. Panting, I looked down and saw large dirty shoeprints on the wet sink unit. Shit. May as well leave a note with an arrow saying: *he went this-a-way*.

I pulled my shoes off, jumped back down onto the sink, slipping and falling hard, the left side of my chest collecting the edge of the basin. I lay on the bathroom floor, searing pain running up my side. Pretty sure I felt a *click* – was that a rib cracking? Probably. Fuck. No time to think. I splashed water over the vanity unit, then looked around, no paper towels, only an air dryer. Whipped off my top – hot pain up my side – wiped down the unit. Then I jumped back onto the sink and leaped for the ceiling.

A hot poker burned into the side of my chest. Unbearable. I hung in space for a moment, unable to move, everything starting to spin and go black.

Focus, remember the training.

I took the pain, put it inside a small box. Buried it somewhere deep down. Now the pain was still there but it didn't matter so much. I hauled myself farther up – ribs and arms and fingers screaming. Swung my body, swiveled my hips and somehow got a foot inside the hole. Dragged myself up into the ceiling. I lay next to the open hole for a moment, panting. Waves of pain washed over me, finally subsiding. I looked down into the bathroom – no footprints, good. I carefully slid the ceiling tile back into position. From below came the sound of troops charging down the corridor and then *kaboom* as blaster fire blew up the toilet stall where they thought I was hiding.

At least that answered one question: *What were they going to do if they caught me?*

Now what? I got to my feet and ran in a crouch along the ceiling cavity. In addition to everything else, I'd now be filthy wherever I touched anything. I dropped to my knees, slid a tile ajar and took a peek. I was over a main passageway of the mall. To the right was a store with suits in the window and a sign reading *Adriano: The Gentlemen's Outfitter.* A crazy idea came to me. But there were no sane ones, so this would have to do.

I crawled along, checking my position twice, then opened a tile over the area I was looking for. Bingo. Slid the tile aside and dropped down inside the changing room of the clothing store, putting a hand over my mouth to stop a shriek of pain. I peeked out to see a serving robot, low-grade. Perfect.

I cleared my throat and called out, "Hello there, Adriano?"

The robot – which was standing near the front door to welcome customers – turned and did a double take. It was dressed in a formal black suit and bow tie. "I'm sorry, sir, I didn't see you come in! My name is Roberto, how may I be of service?"

"Hi there, Roberto. Say, do you have a washbasin here? I took a bit of a tumble riding my bike."

The robot approached. "Sorry, sir, the restrooms are to our right, down there." It pointed to the corridor I'd just left, from which sounds of great commotion were emanating. "But could I offer you a pre-moistened towelette?"

A wet wipe slid out from a slot in its chest.

"Thanks, Roberto, I'll take a few of those. So look, crazy story, but turns out I have this important meeting in just a few minutes. Got called on me suddenly while I was bike riding." I improvised the thinnest tissue of lies. "So I need a complete outfit, put together immediately – do you think you could do something like that?"

The robot looked at me, the gleam of service in its eyes. "Certainly, sir, I'll put together an *ensemble* this very second!"

Roberto scurried off and I turned to the mirror. Staring back was surely the least plausible customer Adriano's had ever the pleasure to serve. My clothes were torn, my hair awry and a large scratch, still bleeding, ran the length of my arm. I was hunched over my painful right side, wearing a soiled eyepatch, face and hands comically blackened like a chimney sweep from a historical holo. Thank god this robot was only a sales model. I pasted down my hair, wiped my face and hands clean as best I could. Outside in the passageway a bunch of troops rushed past carrying a ladder, their hysterical sergeant barking orders. Fortunately no one had thought to look inside the stores yet – an oversight they would soon remedy.

Roberto came back holding a choice of three outfits. I picked one in off-white, the most casual.

"I'll also need shoes, a hat and sunglasses to match, please, Roberto."

"In a trice, sir!"

The robot would have scanned my size, so the clothes fit perfectly. I threw on the shirt, tie, pants and jacket, catching a glimpse of the price tags. Bloody hell, this was going to cost a fortune.

But hang on. No way could I scan this suit. I'd be pinpointing myself again for those trigger-happy troops. Damn, it was just so automatic to use your kom. I'd have to come up with plan B, or C, or whatever I was up to now.

I stepped out of the change room. The shoes were brand-new and stiff, but fit perfectly. The eyepatch went into my pocket – they'd be looking out for that – and on went the sunglasses and a white Panama hat. I looked like a dodgy real estate agent with tropical swampland for sale.

The robot purred. "You look magnificent, sir!"

I edged toward the front door. "Roberto, old chum, would you mind fetching the other tie from the change room?"

"Certainly, sir!"

The moment the robot turned, I was off. Out of the store, along the passageway and onto the escalator, feeling guilty. I didn't like shoplifting, but then again, I didn't like the thought of being blasted into my component atoms either.

Resisting the impulse to run, I stood straight with one hand on the moving rail, ignoring the pain in my ribs. Time crawled as we dropped down to the next level. Around the mall dozens of the gray t-shirts were darting in panic, looking into shops and generally making nuisances of themselves. The troops had obviously figured out I'd gone into the roof. They'd have found my shoes – *eureka!* – then started a vector search. Hot, dirty work. Nowhere near as much fun as blowing shit up.

I stepped off at level one, turned calmly and walked onto the next escalator. I could see daylight through the main entrance below. In a few moments I'd be clean away. The seconds ticked down.

From above there was a new commotion. "Stop, *thief!*"

I looked up. A haggard, skinny man in a ridiculous mall security uniform – all epaulets and gold buttons – was standing at the level-four rail pointing at me. Summoned by Roberto, I guess.

"That man's stolen a five-thousand-credit suit!" he shouted hysterically, running down the escalator two steps at a time. Probably the gravest crime he'd ever dealt with.

There were gasps and stares from the people around me. An alarm sounded and the doors to the front entrance began to close, but I'd finally reached the bottom of the escalator – freedom was in sight. I darted out the ground-floor entrance onto the street and through the crowd. Walking briskly, not daring to run. How long before my pursuers joined the dots? Adding to the rib pain and throbbing eye was a fresh misery: the brand-new dress shoes torturing my feet. Should I kick them off? No time.

Back at the mall entrance someone was shouting and pointing in my direction. I reached the first cross street on my left – a small lane – immediately turned down it and started running, ignoring protests from my feet. A garbage truck was coming. Salvation! I jumped in through the passenger-side door and crouched near the floor. A robot emblazoned with a sanitation services logo was sitting on the driver's side, looking down at me quizzically.

"I'm from City Council, inspecting routes, which unit are you?" I asked with as much command as I could muster.

"Twenty-first, Sanitary, sir," said a tinny mechanical voice. These machines had only the most basic interface. "Operating schedule fourteen."

"Very good, Number Twenty-One, continue on. I'm just – retying my shoelaces down here." The last comment was unnecessary, these units had barely any smarts beyond collecting rubbish.

I spoke into my kom. "Hey, Douglas, are you tracking me?"

"What the fuck are you doing, laddie? Stealing fancy suits?"

"You don't know half of it. Listen, I've got the whole planet on my tail. I'm hiding in garbage truck Twenty-One, can you log on and direct it to Banks Street?"

"Done in a jiffy."

The truck moved off, hopefully to the right place. I stayed low as we turned back onto the main street. Took off the shoes and massaged my aching feet. I heard panicked shouting and uproar coming from the mall entrance, fading as we drove away. It was two minutes to the gelataria, hopefully a short enough time that no one would think to check this truck.

I sat up and looked around at shoppers on the street going about their business. Only a few short days ago I'd been like them. Unthinking, caught up in normal life. The truck turned into our destination, Banks Street. It drove a few meters and then stopped. The robot got out, emptied a bunch of rubbish bins into the hopper, drove another few meters and stopped to do the same thing again. Just a few blocks away was my safe haven, Peaches, the famous gelataria, but at this rate it would take half a day to get there.

"What's going on, Douglas?" I hissed into my kom.

"This thing is dumb as a rock. It recognized the street and locked into some hard-wired program. I can't stop it."

I was hoping the truck would take me all the way to the shop, but forget it. Back to mad flight. I jumped out and ran, shoes in hand. The footpath was crowded with shoppers, making it hard work. A military

truck drove slowly past scanning the crowd, so I flicked off the hat and
turned to look in a store window. From behind came the sound of
blaster fire and explosions. Probably the garbage unit – sorry about that,
Sanitation Unit Twenty-One. More trucks were arriving every moment,
troops pouring out.

Now or never.

I took off, sprinting the last few hundred meters. I bolted past queueing
customers and into the ice-cream parlor, two soldiers hot on my tail. What
were they going to do, shoot this place up with wall-to-wall kiddies? I
heard a *pop, pop* – *s*tun balls. These release a fast-acting sedative along
with a thick black smokescreen. I took a deep breath, knowing it would
be my last for a while. All around was the sound of screaming, quickly
followed by the thuds of falling bodies as the store filled with impenetrable
black fog.

Good, this was helpful. Now where was the staff door? I put my
hands forward and felt something. Cold. The ice-cream counter. Quietly
I moved to the left, trying not to step on anyone. The soldiers were
blundering around behind me. They'd have nose filters for the gas but
be just as blind as me. I reached the end of the counter, lungs starting
to burn. What was the layout again? I tried to remember from the brief
glimpse I'd had.

The door was to the left of the display fridge and behind it.

Had to be fast, body screaming for air. I kept my hand on the end
of the counter and slowly moved around it. Stepped forward into space.
Took another step, then hurrah! A door and a handle.

Which turned. I stepped through into clear air and freedom.

"Get ready, Douglas!" I shouted, sprinting through the corridor. "I'm
coming in hot!"

"Go to the very end," said Danee through my kom.

I ran past a room full of machinery. Behind me, the door I'd just come
through was blasted apart, sending smoke and debris everywhere – such
drama queens! Why not turn the knob? I got to the end of the corridor,
everything hurting. I dived through the door – blaster fire passing over
my head – and landed in a large storeroom. Sitting in the center of the

room was a flyer in the process of closing its side door. I brought my feet under me, got into a crouch and dived into the machine, the door closing instantly behind me.

Danee was at the controls with 'baby' Douglas strapped next to her. Through the monitors I saw the room fill with troops, blasters aimed. I hoped for their sakes they had enough impulse control to resist shooting at a powered-up flyer.

"Shields up," said Danee. "We're ready to move."

"But how do we do that?" I screeched, thinking of the roof above us and the air space beyond, no doubt filled with hostiles.

"Like this," said Danee.

She hit the jump button.

CHAPTER FIFTEEN

The image in the monitor flicked from the storeroom filling with armed troops to a gray-brown rocky wall.

That was it.

"Where the hell are we?" I croaked.

"Inside a hollow asteroid off MGNA#12," said Douglas. "Jumped here coz the Movement's got eyes on the space around this star. Don't want them seeing our comings and goings, so we'll pop over to Jubilee shortly."

Of all the 'impossible' things recently occurring, this jump was without question the most mindboggling. According to the physics we're taught from childhood, space/time is too distorted inside the gravity well of a planet to make a quantum jump. That's why our ships must travel at snail's pace far enough into space to do it safely. But we had just jumped straight off the *surface* of Brouggh to the inside of an asteroid. Impossible. Or a breakthrough in technology not seen in millennia.

"I can't believe you just did that!" I spluttered.

"Just coz everyone else's gone to sleep doesn't mean I have to," said Douglas.

Danee pointed and snapped her fingers at the shoes, still in my hand. I must have been clutching them the whole time. "They look nice."

I passed them over and, feeling self-conscious, put my eyepatch back on. Didn't want anyone getting grossed out.

Danee examined the shoes with the laser focus of an expert shopper. "Off-world!" she said, flipping them over. "Hand made in Marana, very fancy."

I groaned, remembering the price tags at the men's store. "Douglas, when I've saved up some money working on Jubilee, can you please transfer five thousand credits to that clothing shop?"

"So you're working for me now?"

"Guess so."

Danee passed the shoes back and looked at the controls, "OK, we're reset – back to Jubilee, folks."

"Jeez," said Douglas. "Fella's just had his eye ripped out and he's worried about the fucking *tailor!*"

★　　★　　★

Jubilee appeared in the monitors, growing large as we zoomed in. An adult-sized Douglas was waiting for us in the dock. He reached into the flyer to help me out, then retrieved a large insuplex carton from the back.

"Won't be getting any more of these," he said, handing around ice creams from Peaches, "so we may as well enjoy."

'Baby' Douglas waddled off and the rest of us sat on the edge of the loading dock. I felt numb. One minute running for my life and the next here on Jubilee – eating ice cream? The cone in my hand was labeled *choco-vanilla swirl* and it looked pretty good. In a daze I took a bite – delicious.

Douglas ate with relish. What pleasure could an android possibly get from ice cream? "So," he asked between bites, "how did you figure out to use that souvenir button? Danee and I had bets on it."

"Just came to me. It was the only object I brought back with me from Jubilee, so however unlikely, that was it."

"And what happened to the idea of losing your tail?" asked Douglas. "That ice-cream business is gone now."

"I *tried*. It should've worked, but they were on to me so fast. I don't understand it." I had many questions about the last twenty-four hours on Brouggh. Something – actually, a lot of things – didn't add up. "What did they do to *you*, Danee?"

"Oh, they questioned me about everything, then they asked if we'd had sex, so I just told them *yes* and then they fired me." She didn't sound fazed.

"I tried to protect you, lost an eye over it!"

"Well," she said with very little evidence of concern, "you do look dashing with that patch!"

"Don't worry, Col," said Douglas, "we'll get you a new one in no time. Just need to decide – do ye want organic or mechanical? Mechanical ones 'sposed to be better."

Now we were back on Jubilee I wasn't feeling concerned about the eye. Besides, there was a far more pressing matter.

"So, how is Sana getting on?"

"Sana?" asked Danee.

"Yeah, she's here on Jubilee, right?"

They both looked at me in surprise.

"You're sayin' Sana's here on Jubilee?" Douglas asked.

I told them about the message in the mirror, anxiety rising.

Douglas shook his head. "I just scanned the past seven days. Nothing. Apart from you two, no arrivals from Brouggh at all."

A sick feeling grew in my stomach.

And a horrible thought. What if they knew about the mirror trick?

But of course they would. Movement people must have had our flat under surveillance for years.

But the writing was in Sana's hand.

That just means they made her write it, not difficult. I saw the scene playing out: Sana in the bathroom with a blaster at her back, told to write on the mirror, just like she always did. So clever of them.

Except.

Except something. What?

Something about that message wasn't right. It had been troubling me since I'd first read it, just below the surface of my awareness. Something about the wording.

I let my mind go blank, allowed whatever was in there to bubble up.

gone 2 jubilee

Then I saw it. The number '2' instead of the word 'to'. A small thing, but one of Sana's pet hates – using a number for a word. She'd even made a comment about it the night we saw Gilham speak. She'd never write a message using that construction.

Therefore, it was code.

For what?

That she was being forced.

The more I thought about it, the more certain I was. Clever of Sana, at least I didn't have to waste time looking for her on Jubilee. And M4M would not expect me to know this. A small victory, but something, and it told me two things: Sana had definitely been abducted and they wanted me off Brouggh.

But why? To get me out of the picture? They could have rubbed me out in so many other ways. Didn't seem strong enough. Then it hit me.

They must have wanted to flush Douglas out.

Find out where his base was on Brouggh, see his newtech in action. Someone was playing a very subtle game here – in stark contrast to those moronic troops. Or were they all part of the same ruse? Now I thought about it, those guys had anticipated every move but allowed me to slip the net each time. Maybe in some ways it had been too easy?

I let out a big sigh and the other two looked around. Something about all of this was off, but how exactly was beyond my understanding. I shared my thoughts and there was silence for a moment.

Douglas took the last bite of his ice cream. "Well, you know, I've been thinkin'. About the Movement. I have a question for you both: how would you describe the way they get things done?"

Danee spoke first. "They're hard to read, sometimes they seem very clever and sometimes surprisingly dumb."

"Precisely," said Douglas. "Those guys in the gray t-shirts, they couldn't organize a fuck in a brothel, right?"

"Err, yes," I said. "They were amateurs. And the troops – your standard half-trained morons. Except always a step ahead of me. That's what I don't understand."

"So," said Douglas, "could you summarize it as: *good strategy/ bad execution?*"

I rubbed my chin for a moment, then nodded.

"So that's why I believe there's an LAI behind it all somewhere."

Danee and I looked at Douglas, thunderstruck. Large AIs were virtually banned across the galaxy these days, most particularly in space controlled by M4M. Gilham constantly railed against artificial intelligences, saying they were against God's will or God's plan or whatever.

"I can feel it in me bones," said Douglas. "Don't take this the wrong way, but the Movement's strategy has always been way too clever for humans to come up with. Somethin's out there. Playin' 3D chess. Thinking two hundred moves ahead. Then when the humans execute, they're the same village idiots as usual – no offense."

"None taken…I guess," said Danee.

"And then there's the energy signature. Me and my AI pals, we recognize it. It's in the encrypted FTL streams. It's very clever, it's tryin' to disguise itself, but we know it's there."

"You can decode faster-than-light messages?" I asked, incredulous.

Douglas grinned. "O' course!" Then his face darkened. "But this thing's outsmarted me every which way and I tell ya, it's starting to piss me off!" His mood lightened again. "Oh, and ye should also know, we figured out what happened with your nanosassin attack."

Turned out there had been a plant: Danee's robo-butler, Susan. Not that it was her fault. The nano had penetrated Jubilee from where I'd suspected – the building works at Sector Twenty-One. A surveillance gap had opened for a fraction of a second as a wall broke through and the nano got in, infecting eight security droids with malware (one good reason to have both human *and* nonhuman security). They found a deleted comms link to Susan and were able to recover it and restore the data. It all made sense now. Once M4M knew Danee and I were delayed on Jubilee, they must have decided to take us out. They could pin whatever story they wanted on us to explain Lachy Nees' death. I marveled at the planning – having nano capability ready like that?

"Perhaps you're right, Douglas," I said, "maybe there *is* an LAI out there running things for the Movement."

"Or maybe the Movement is being *run by* an AI?" said Danee.

"Whatever," said Douglas. "I've decided to give myself an upgrade.

Once upon a time I was likely the fastest quantum computer in the galaxy. Nowadays, with that fuckin' thing out there...."

I realized the conversation had gone offtrack – at least as far as I was concerned. "Listen, Douglas, I've *also* decided something. I *will* come and work for you here on Jubilee. But first I need your help with a couple of things."

"And what might they be?"

"First, we have to rescue Sana, and second...we have to destroy M4M."

Douglas laughed. "Nothin' else? Wouldn't like me to solve the meaning o' life while we're at it?"

"Think about it, how long before the Movement comes after you?"

"Oh, they don't like Jubilee all right, but don't worry, I've got my ways of lookin' after meself."

"How long would you last without customers or supplies from our home universe?"

"The galaxy is a big place, Col. My projections show M4M falling apart from its own contradictions within four hundred years."

"But you just said it's being run by an AI – what other tricks might they have up their sleeve?" I stood up, passion rising. "And even if you're right about them falling apart, think of all the suffering before that happens! Don't you have a duty to intervene if you can?"

The conversation was getting heated.

"It's not my problem, matey! I'm not programmed for a humanitarian mission, I'm here to sell the dream: sex and drugs and rock 'n' roll!"

"That's not true, Douglas, you came to rescue me on Brouggh. You do care."

"Yeah, I care. I care about havin' a good security guy – that's why I came to get you." Douglas was getting defensive and his Scottish accent stronger. "Ye can't be puttin' all this on me. I can't help the way I been programmed."

"Well, maybe it's time to change your programming, and anyway—"

"*Boys!*" interrupted Danee. "Instead of arguing, why don't we take the matter up with John Hudson?"

CHAPTER SIXTEEN

We passed through the final sliding door, labeled *Control Room,* to find a dusty old space full of equipment and racks of hardware.

"That's me over there," said Douglas, pointing to a large bank of machinery.

This place had clearly not operated as a control room for a long time, probably not since Douglas came online and took over running Jubilee. There were unlit video monitors, desks heaped with papers and junk, and a pile of new equipment stacked up on the floor – materials for Douglas's upgrade, I assumed.

We had traveled here from the landing dock by gravity sled. It took us through the underbelly of Jubilee – a maze of interconnecting corridors. We passed row after row of giant receiving docks humming with activity as human and nonhuman staff processed pallets of goods and material, putting them on conveyor belts to be whisked off to god knows where. Giant pipes thrummed with water and air moving to and from the recycling plants, and various workers and droids passed constantly, going on and off shift. We traveled for half an hour till we reached Sector Nine, then took a goods lift to Floor-1. The construction here seemed cruder and the paintwork flaky – making me think this was an old part of Jubilee, possibly the first constructed. Everything else must have been added on from here.

In the control room, we walked through a door at the far end to find a theaterette with half a dozen chairs facing a large glass cylinder floating in the air. The room lights dimmed and the cylinder turned a cloudy white color. The clouds coalesced into the shape of an old man seated on a chair wearing a hospital gown, then resolved into a full-color holographic.

The man in the tube opened his eyes and smiled. "Hello, Douglas," he said haltingly, looking around the room. "So where am I?" Then realization seemed to dawn. "Oh, this is a stasis projector, right?"

"That's right, John." Douglas's voice was surprisingly tender.

"OK...so that means I'm...dead and therefore talking to you from backup?"

"Yes, John, you're in stasis backup," said Douglas. He nudged me and whispered, "We go through this every time."

"So how long ago did I die?"

"About five hundred years ago."

"Really? I remember being ill, but not the end."

"I edited out the last three months because they weren't...pleasant. I can restore them to the file if you wish?"

"No," he sighed, "probably for the best.... So, five hundred years? That means Jubilee must be doing OK then?"

"Yes, John, it's goin' real well. We're workin' on Sector Twenty-One right now, got nearly five million residents."

"Sector *Twenty-One*. Wow! Douglas, that's amazing. *Amazing!*"

He was a small, lightly framed man with an elfin face, large eyes and longish gray hair. Despite his advanced age, he had an air of boyish enthusiasm.

"So, John, we wanted to ask your opinion on a few things if that's all right?" asked Douglas.

"Of course, but you know I left you in charge for a reason. Don't know how much use I can be."

"Well, it's a moral question really, about our purpose with Jubilee. But first, let me introduce you to my friends, Col and Danee."

I waved hi.

Danee said, "I've met you before, John, but in a different session, so I guess you don't remember me."

"Pleased to meet you, or re-meet you as the case may be."

Douglas took him through recent events: the rise of M4M and takeover of Brouggh, the death of Lachy Nees and the nanosassin attack, and now the presumed abduction of Sana.

"OK…" said John cautiously, "that all sounds terrible, but I don't understand what any of it has to do with Jubilee?"

"Well, that's my fuckin' point exactly!" said Douglas.

"John, I know it might seem off-mission to you," I said, scrambling to gather my argument, "but Jubilee has a lot of resources these days and there's not many things standing in M4M's way. The Galactic League is moribund and the planetary governments are asleep. The Movement is—"

"That anti-technology trend we were startin' to see while you were alive," interrupted Douglas, "has gotten heaps worse. They've been switchin' AIs off all over the place. Even in places not run by the Movement."

John tut-tutted and shook his head. "Ridiculous. Criminal."

"What I'm saying, John," I continued, "is that Jubilee could be a great help. Even if M4M *is* destined to fall over, we could cut short the suffering by hundreds of years. If we *can* make a difference, why shouldn't we?"

John shook his head again. "You know I never started Jubilee to help people, I started it to get *away* from them! I was always a bit of a loner, you know, a mad scientist if you like. When I found this star, MGNA#12, and learned what it could do to a jump drive, I thought: *Great, now I can get away from everybody in my own private universe!* I found some old space junk. Jumped it here and fitted it out. But then of course I needed money to keep going, so I started a card game for high rollers and to my absolute amazement it just took off."

Douglas was following John's words intently, like a child hearing a story told many times by its parents. "Yeah, and all those rich fuckers, they just *loved* comin' over here with no law or government or taxes."

"And then it got too big, too many headaches," said John. "I was running around day and night. I escaped from everyone – to my own private universe – only to find they'd followed me here!"

"So he built me. Set things up so I could handle everything," said Douglas, beaming.

"That's right. And after you came online, everything was much easier. In fact, things were great. But then I got sick."

"That was a bad time." Douglas looked sad.

"Anyway, my point is, we never set Jubilee up to be the galactic police. Quite the opposite. I saw it as a place outside society, a place free from all rules or boundaries."

"Where everyone can do whatever the hell they like!" said Douglas.

"As long as they're not hurting anyone else while they're doing it."

Douglas smiled triumphantly. "So that settles it, Col. Sorry, but M4M is none of our business."

"But hang on," said John, "let me think for a moment." He closed his eyes, rubbed them wearily and then sighed. "Look it's true, it's none of our business. And it's true we never set out to be do-gooders. But I do feel bad for Col and all the people affected. What if we compromised? What if we offered some *assistance?*"

"How?" asked Douglas.

"Information and support. That's a middle path, no?"

Douglas was wrestling with John's words, but I sensed he was coming around. "OK, OK. If that's what you think, John," he said eventually, "we can help 'em out. Least we can do."

They talked some more, figuring it out, then got onto the topic of Jubilee itself. John was astonished to learn it now had an economy worth many trillion credits per annum. News to me. I couldn't help wondering what Douglas did with all that money. Buy ice-cream shops, I guess.

Finally, it was time to end the session.

Douglas looked sad. He said softly, "Bye, John, and thanks for your help."

John looked at the android with affection. "Bye, Douglas, and I just want to say something else to you. I think you're doing a terrific job, I'm very proud of you."

"Thanks, John."

The image in the cylinder disappeared and the room lights came back up. Douglas brushed a tear from his eyes and Danee put an arm around his shoulder.

"It's OK," she cooed.

Douglas made a small sob, then looked around in embarrassment.

"What?" he said defensively as if I'd been mocking him. "How many times do *you* get to meet your creator?"

We sat in silence for a few moments, then a thought came to me. "Why don't you add some memory to the file and leave it running? It would be like having John around as a living entity?"

"Tried it. Biologicals don't get on well in the digital environment. They miss having arms and legs and all that. Then you put 'em in an android and they don't like that either. Nothin' feels right."

"They go weird eventually," said Danee. "He tried with John, but nothing worked."

Douglas shrugged and stood up. "Time to get busy. I've got some upgradin' to do. Then I'm gonna put the word out and see if we can find Sana. Meanwhile, the two of you should get settled."

CHAPTER SEVENTEEN

We were taken to Sector Fourteen, where an apartment was assigned to each of us. Mine was a one-bedroom with living area and kitchenette. Not exactly the Starview Suite, but comfortable enough. A pile of fresh clothes lay folded neatly on my bed and the bathroom was stocked with basic toiletries – enough stuff to get me through my first few days. Nice of Douglas.

I stripped off and showered, then stood at the basin and examined myself in the mirror. The eye had almost completely healed over – the nano compounds doing their work. A huge purple bruise covered the right side of my chest and there were cuts and scratches on my face and arms from the wild flight across Harrison. Sore, but nothing that was going to kill me.

What next?

Get a new eye, save Sana and destroy M4M. In that order. All in a day's work.

And what about Danee?

Now that was a tricky question. Obviously I had to stop being intimate with her – sexually *and* emotionally. How could I work to save Sana while carrying on with another woman? I stared hard at the person in the mirror, spoke to him sternly. "Col, that's *it*. Under no circumstances will there be anything more with Danee. Got that? The night with her, that was a one-off, an aberration never to be repeated – *even if just the thought of her lying in the room down the corridor makes you hard?* – OK, stop it, stop that line of thinking immediately, Col, just snap out of it!"

As if on cue, there was a knock at the apartment door. I opened it a crack, only a towel wrapped around me, to find Danee, smiling and fragrant from the bathroom.

Thirty seconds later we were in bed.

Turns out that being tortured, chased and nearly killed multiple times is quite the aphrodisiac. We spent the afternoon and night together and after that, her things started turning up in my apartment, a subliminal migration that I only became conscious of weeks later.

So I shut it down again. "Sorry, but we just can't *do* this."

Danee was understanding, kept her distance for a day or two, and then somehow or other (I'm not sure how) we always ended up in bed again. The whole thing was very perplexing.

Douglas took me to an ophthalmologist, who installed a new mechanical eye that looked identical to the original but worked even better. On macro it was like a magnifying glass, on telescope I could see for miles and when I wanted it to, it could also step down to match my left eye, giving me normal stereovision. A marvel of engineering.

Danee told me about her life. She'd grown up wealthy. Mother was a career woman, focused and serious, worked as legal counsel in a big corporation. Father was a socialite, flamboyant and charismatic, a dandy and a serial philanderer. They must have had some arrangement because they were both still together and still in love after all these years. "Without him," said Danee drily, "Mother would have *died* of boredom."

She was loved and cherished, had been sent to good schools and with little application had scored top marks. She had been a party girl, friends with everyone, but by young adulthood was jaded and world-weary. One day out of the blue she'd decided to join the Services. "It was the only career choice that would shock my parents. I could've been a lawyer, a hausfrau or an artist and they wouldn't have cared less. But a *cop?* That blew their minds."

A few days later, she asked about my life.

"Not much to tell," I said. "Country boy made good, that's about it."

We were lying in bed together. Danee had 'dropped in' with a bottle of wine before the inevitable happened again.

She sat up, frowning. "Come on, you have to do better than that."

"Honestly, there's not much to tell."

"Well, how come you have a sealed psych section in your file?"

I leaped out of bed, angry and upset. "What have you been doing? Snooping in my file?"

"What do you reckon? Checking up on you, of course."

I didn't know what to say.

"Look, you know I like you. *Of course* I'm going to look up your file and if you've got a psych record, I want to know what it's about."

I threw on my clothes and stormed out.

To be honest, I've never been one for big dramatic scenes. This had been a problem between Sana and me. She *liked* having window-rattling fights, then passionate make-up sex. I could understand Danee pulling my file. Given time, I would probably have done the same with hers. It was technically illegal of course, but every cop did it. The real problem was having to explain what was in there. It was a locked vault and until now, I'd only opened it – barely opened it – for one other person in my life.

I walked the corridors aimlessly and cooled down. Went back to the apartment, but of course Danee was gone. I sat for a while, then called her kom. She answered, audio only.

"Danee?"

"Yes – gotten over your little hissy fit?"

"I'm sorry, but…it's painful. Hard for me to talk about."

Her tone changed. "It's OK, you can take your time. But you have to give me something."

Two days later, I called her again.

"OK, tonight. Let's talk."

CHAPTER EIGHTEEN

Jerbet was a town of ten thousand souls nestled in the forests of the northern hinterland. Compared to many other settled planets, Brouggh has a highly tilted axis, so the summers and winters are extreme up that way.

When I was five, Mum and Dad had decided to have a second child. This was highly unusual of course, even for country people. Mother's belly grew large and a nursery was set up for the new baby – a boy they were going to call Tim. Then the doctors found a problem. They called it a *genetic defect*. They said in the past, on Old Earth, the baby would have died before it was even born, but these days they could fix him while he was still inside. Everything was going to be fine, but everyone seemed worried. Mother had to rest a lot. I played outside in the cold spring sunshine, riding my new red bike, and imagined taking my brother along with me.

Mum went to hospital and a week later I came home from school to find the new baby. He was incredibly small, but beautiful, born earlier than normal because the doctors were worried. I held him and his tiny hand grabbed my finger. His eyes were the same color as the spring sky outside – a light frosty blue – and I loved him from that moment.

The doctors were right. Tim *was* healthy and normal – or seemed to be, anyway – but he took a long time learning to speak and occasionally did weird things. For instance, every once in a while, maybe a couple of times a year, he would stop dead and gaze unfocused into space for minutes at a time, a strange glow in his eyes. I would shout and try to snap him out of it, but he never answered. When I was older, I thought a lot about those trances. I couldn't shake the idea that Tim was somehow staring into the void. That it was calling him.

Tim spoke in his own special baby language that only I could understand and that I translated for Mum and Dad. He was sweet and happy. He had an infectious burble of a laugh that made everyone else laugh too and I thought it was the happiest sound in the world. He would throw his head back and it was like his face split in half. I worried about him. I took him everywhere. We played outside in the forest during the summer afternoons and in the long winter months we made up games inside. I felt lucky compared to my schoolmates because I had my own little friend, someone I could play with all the time.

One late summer afternoon, when Tim was five and I was ten, Mother had taken us to town for shopping and a treat. She was at the counter paying with her kom when she looked around and noticed Tim was nowhere to be seen.

"Where's your brother?" she asked. "Go find him."

I ran around the food aisles, calling out. "Not here, Mum!"

She went to the shop entrance and looked out at the street. I followed. No one there. She went back into the store and with mounting panic looked around the aisles and under the displays. Tim was nowhere.

"I've lost my child!" she said to Ms. Lodder, the shopkeeper.

I still remember the fear in her voice.

She told me to wait and ran off. Ms. Lodder called Father and he arrived a few minutes later along with the police. In half an hour the streets were full of people and the sky buzzing with drones.

In the days that followed, the town of Jerbet was seized by hysteria. Parents kept their children indoors and a news crew arrived, followed by another one and then several more. The other kids at school started looking at me strangely and police from neighboring towns turned up to 'help'. Our two hotels filled with amateur sleuths, conspiracy theorists and interested onlookers.

The effect on Mother was terrifying. It was like a new person had occupied her body. Her hair and clothes became unkempt and her eyes red from weeping. At night from my bedroom I heard her pacing and muttering. Beating herself up for losing Tim.

Looking back, I think it was apparent even to my ten-year-old self that the local constabulary were out of their depth. Littering was the most serious crime they ever dealt with. One afternoon two police ground cars collided in the middle of town, such was the state of pandemonium.

Into this circuslike atmosphere a team from SSB landed to take over the search, led by a large, very dark-skinned woman, Investigator Sunter. She had striking features I'd not seen before, implying off-world origin, but spoke in a Brouggh accent. All of the SSB officers were calm and competent, and for the first time it felt like there were people in charge who knew what they were doing. On the second day after SSB arrived, Sunter came to our house and interviewed Mother for a long time while I waited upstairs in my room. Then I was called. We sat together in the kitchen with milk and biscuits. She told me I wasn't in trouble, she just wanted to see if there was anything I could remember that would help.

"It must be very upsetting to lose your little brother that way?"

I nodded.

"Well, we won't stop looking till we find him. I've been doing this for many years, Colin, and I can tell you we *always* solve these things."

I was impressed. She seemed strong and clever, and nice too – even if she spoke with that posh city accent.

"Now, Col, I want you to think back to the moment when Tim disappeared. Tell me exactly where you were and what you did."

I *really* wanted to help. I closed my eyes and thought back to the moment in the shop. "I went to the freezer to get ice creams. Chocolate for me and vanilla for Tim, that's his favorite."

"OK and then what happened?"

"I took the ice creams to the counter so Mum could scan them."

"Was Tim with you?"

I tried to remember. Where was Tim? He had been with me when I went to the freezer, then he'd walked away. Which direction? To my right and behind. Toward the door? I concentrated hard – yes, there had been a tinkling sound. "At first Tim was with me, then he walked off. He often does that. I'm pretty sure he walked out the door of the shop."

"Why do you think that?"

"Because I heard that little tinkling sound the door makes."

Investigator Sunter was recording our conversation with her kom, but had a notebook as well. She wrote *front door* with the word *front* underlined. "So Tim went out the door, you went to the counter. Is that the order of events?"

"Yes, then Mum realized Tim was gone and we started running around looking for him."

"OK, think now. Did anything happen in between the time you came to the counter and the time your mum noticed Tim was gone? Think, Col, this could be important."

I closed my eyes and tried to go back in time. I'd been standing next to Mother. I'd smelled the stale onions in the shop, felt the coldness of the ice cream in my hand, heard the purring of the air conditioner. Then another sound. What? Whirring, familiar. "I think a drone came and delivered something."

Sunter was very interested in this. "How do you know?"

"Drones come to Jerbet all the time with stuff because we're so far away from the city. I heard one drop something off at the door of the shop and when I went outside with Mum, there were boxes on the pavement."

"And those boxes weren't there when you first went into the shop?"

I thought back again and shook my head. "No, I remember Tim was holding Mum's hand when we walked in and he couldn't have done that if the boxes were there."

Investigator Sunter seemed excited. "Colin, *thank you*. This is critical information. Not many people would remember all those details. Well done."

She got up from the kitchen table. I followed as she strode outside to the flyer, already talking on her kom.

"– the older brother remembers a delivery drone arriving at hour zero. I want it found and the camera footage downloaded *immediately*."

Years later, as an Investigator myself, I reviewed the files and felt the drone lead was indeed critical and should have broken the case. However, the unit in question hit a powerline two days after Tim disappeared, fritzing its memory, which had not been backed up. Was this suspicious? Possibly. But the larger issue was timing. SSB hadn't arrived until four days after Tim vanished and by then every man and his dog had been through town dirtying up the scene – and of course, if they'd come earlier, they might have found the drone before it crashed.

Three days later the searchers caught a break. An old blue teddy bear turned up in the woods not far from the back of our house – Tim had been carrying it the day he disappeared. Mother and I both remembered and it was verified by CCTV. How did it get there, three kilometers from town? Could he have run home, then got lost in the woods? The security camera directly in front of the grocery store was not working (of course), but others in town on any route Tim might have traveled showed nothing.

The operation moved to the area behind our house, with drones, sniffer dogs and search droids combing the thick woodland. The case now changed from missing person to suspected abduction. All the men in town were summoned to city hall and willingly agreed to have their koms scanned, and all traffic through Jerbet during the period in question was hunted down and investigated. All of this turned up nothing.

Mother took to wandering the woods at all hours of the day and night, calling for Tim or talking to him as if he were there. Looking back, she should have been hospitalized or put on medication, but at that time everyone was so preoccupied with Tim.

When Father poked his head into my classroom, gray with grief, I knew it could only be one of two things. Had they found Tim's body it would have been a relief, but instead it was Mother. Missing. I was taken out of school and questioned, but knew nothing. Her behavior had been so disturbing I'd been staying away from her. Another thing for my ten-year-old self to feel guilty about.

The search redoubled. Father joined them in the woods while a

nice lady from up the street, Ms. Veitch, looked after me. She made hot
chocolate and scones, and tried to comfort me with the same lie I was
being told by all the adults: *Everything is going to be all right.* The search
continued, but after a few days an autumn storm blew in with howling
winds and a massive snow dump. The search had been planned to restart
the moment the weather cleared, but instead winter set in and nothing
could be done.

In spring, Mother was found by hikers in a gully twenty kilometers
from home. The snow was melting and her body had been gnawed by
animals. The area was surrounded by steep granite hills, explaining why
her kom signal hadn't pinged. The whole town of Jerbet turned out for
the funeral and mourned intensely – even more perhaps than what might
be considered normal, because of course there was someone else not
there, someone who could not be grieved for.

A few months later (a period of time considered way too short by the
good folk of Jerbet) Ms. Veitch, the nice lady from up the street, moved
in with Dad and me.

★   ★   ★

Danee lay silent for a full minute. "So, they never found Tim?"

"The search ground on for a year, then fizzled out."

"And you went through the files when you became an Investigator?"

"Totally. It was my dream to reopen the case and solve it. But Sunter
was a pro, she did a perfect job. Though now I can't help wondering what
a quantum AI – let's say Douglas, for example – might turn up if we fed
in all the data."

"That would be interesting."

"Yeah. Something to do after…all this is over." I waved my hand in
the air.

We were silent again.

"Poor booby." She stroked my arm gently. "That's a tragic story. I feel
guilty for taking you back there."

"It's OK, I've spent a lot of time…working on it. When I applied to the Services, the shrinks were all over me. Wanted to make sure I didn't have a 'negative motivation' for joining. They supposedly took the trauma away."

"Those events made you the person you are."

"True. I made decisions. Didn't want to stand out anymore, so I learned to be easygoing – *one of the guys*. Got serious at school so I could join SSB, which eventually I did." I paused, remembering recent events. "And now I'm fired."

"Me too!" said Danee, amused. "I guess that's the difference between us: I always feel like somehow things will work out OK."

"Whereas I know that sometimes they don't."

"Well, yes," she said, "but maybe both points of view are true."

CHAPTER NINETEEN

The next day Douglas summoned us for a 'wee chat'.

"On our way!" I replied, anxious to finally get things moving.

The control room seemed tidier now, the piles of new equipment gone – probably installed as part of the upgrade.

"I won't beat around the bush," said Douglas. "She's on Rethne."

Danee and I gasped. Home planet of Gilham and the Movement 4 Morality. How had Douglas gotten this intel?

"She's working as one of Gilham's personal staff. From what I can tell she's not been harmed, at least for now."

It made horrible sense. Sana had been such a prominent critic, a thorn in Gilham's side for years. What better revenge than to make her into your personal servant? – if you happened to be a sadist of course (and also if you had no regard for the potential fallout).

"There's more," said Douglas. "That LAI I've been talking about, I reckon it's based on Rethne as well."

Where else would it be? I stood up and started pacing. "Douglas, you have to get me there."

"Yeah, I figured you'd say that – and look, *maybe* I've got a plan. I've been talkin' to a fella I know, a royal prince from the Grendeva system. He's run up a rather large, frankly unpayable tab here on Jubilee and consequently become highly agreeable to certain requests. I think we can get you onto Rethne as part of a royal delegation from his planet."

"Wow," I said, "that would be perfect." As VIPs we'd be taken directly into Gilham's orbit, then find a way – god knows how – to get Sana out.

"But don't kid yourself – my projections show ninety-eight per cent chance of failure for this little jaunt."

I turned to Danee. "I want you to come as well."

She looked amused. "So let me get this straight. You want *me* to join you on this mission – the one with a two per cent success rate – impersonate royalty from a far planet, travel to the headquarters of M4M and save your *wife* – who you've been *cheating on* with me?"

"Yes, that's right."

Danee shrugged. "I'm in."

"*Thatta* girl!" said Douglas.

"And I want Batum too," I said.

"Fine. Though we'll have to modify his energy signature so he can't be identified. In fact, we'll have to do that for all of you. And that eye, Col, sorry, but you'll have to change it back. They'll be lookin' out for a bloke with a new right eye."

"Damn, and I was just getting used to it."

Douglas laid out his plan. We would travel to Grendeva, taking a circuitous route to throw off M4M's supercomputer. From there we'd board a royal spacer for Rethne. A delegation was being sent supposedly to study the Movement and decide whether to invite it into the Grendevan system. Of course, the real leaders of Grendeva were well briefed on M4M and wanted nothing to do with it. They'd somehow been persuaded to go along with this whole charade by Douglas's contact.

Before leaving Jubilee, we would undergo a process called DNAltering to make us look like real Grendevans – right down to the cellular level. Social media and official documents would be set up for our new fake personae and we would be downloaded with artificial memories and authentic accents. In other words, we'd become indistinguishable in every respect from natural-born Grendevans.

"Also," said Douglas, "there's some quirky things about these people. For starters, no koms. They use a portable device called a *mobile* with only some of the functionality. So your koms will have to come out."

After the Collapse, some systems like Grendeva had never fully reintegrated back into galactic civilization, so elements of their culture were evidently quite different from Galactic Standard. The thought of having my kom taken out was horrifying, it had been part of me since I was fourteen years old and was as familiar as my right arm – how could I live without this indispensable tool?

"And another thing," said Douglas, "Grendeva is a matriarchal society. True, there's a king, but he's elected by the Council of Wise Women, which organizes and runs everything."

Matriarchal? If I was hearing right, it meant that only one sex, the females, was in charge. It was hard to imagine a place where that was possible. "What do the men do?"

"Bugger all! Laze around gambling, boozing, humping sex droids – and contributing a little DNA now and then when required."

"And this," asked Danee innocently, "is different to everywhere else, how?"

"Ha, ha," I said, the best retort I could come up with.

"So, the women rule," said Douglas, "and if you want to head this rescue, Col, you'll have to transition to female."

I considered for a moment. Despite opposition from the Movement, it was relatively common for people on Brouggh to change sex. A person could be male, female or nonbinary, and change back and forth as many times and in whatever combination they liked, and with today's long life spans, why not experiment? But the thought had never appealed much to me. Perhaps I *am* just an unreconstructed country boy at heart? "Hmm, don't think I'd make a good woman. And anyway, it's going to be hard enough pretending to be Grendevan, let alone female. Danee, can you be lead?"

She shrugged. "Just one more thing."

*   *   *

With all the preparations it would take a month before we would be ready to leave for Grendeva. Later that day we started the medical procedures, the DNAltering – which would take weeks to integrate – followed by a small operation to remove our koms. I begged Douglas to delay this, but he pointed out we needed time to familiarize ourselves with these strange devices they called 'mobiles'.

Also (and sadly) my amazing new eye was swapped back for a biological one.

Next came the language and backstory downloads in the form of a large and terrifying injection into the neck – leaving me with a headache and a strange sense of living in two worlds.

My character's name was Prince Humphrey. He came from an obscure rural backwater called Cantabriach – a clever touch explaining why polite society would never have heard of him. I had new memories of growing up in the family's crumbling manor. Doing princely things like riding white horses and hunting rabbitlike critters with a trained hawk called Trin, which I'd brought up from a chick and loved more than anything else in the world. Mother was often away on 'business', but Father was a kindly chap, if overfond of brandy and the dispensing of unpleasant advice.

"Humphrey, you are fair of visage and maidens will come calling," he would say in an archaic dialect through a mouthful of rotting teeth, "but never forget marriage is a business. It matters naught she be lovely, learned or pleasant of demeanor. 'Tis important only she be generously favored with rank and prosperity."

Father's plan had been to send me to an expensive finishing school in the capital, Strakencz. There I was to learn the fine arts of courtship and grooming, and hopefully catch the eye of someone important. The plan paid off handsomely when I met an obscure heiress, Lady Darmley (Danee), at a royal ball. I had become Second Concubine and as her latest *enthusiasm* was selected to travel on the 'mission' to Rethne.

Where did all this crap come from? Were these real memories from a real person, or completely made up? Either way, it was a shock to be immersed in a world where the accident of birth-sex could matter so much. As a student I had learned that in primitive societies like Old Earth, gender and even skin pigmentation had been causes of great social discrimination – but had always found that hard to believe.

Danee took great delight in practicing the dialect and pretending to boss me around. "Prince Humphrey of Cantabriach," she commanded, "come hither at once and service your good lady."

An order I found extremely easy to obey, especially given the startling changes occurring in her physiognomy. Danee's hair was growing out jet black, her breasts swelling and her skin turning a deep olive brown – reminding me (uncomfortably) of Sana more than a little.

I was changing too. Looking younger and taller, becoming physically stronger. In the mornings I stared in the mirror, fascinated as my face gradually morphed into one I didn't recognize. Of course I was a fairly big guy to start with, but now my clothes grew tight and I started bumping my head into things – unused to being *this* tall. Apparently Prince Humphrey had little to do all day other than work out and groom, so I spent a lot of time in the gym, where I developed washboard abs and rippling biceps. I also grew a cleft chin, my eyes became almond-shaped and my skin darkened to a betel-nut brown.

Dear reader, a confession. Somewhere along the line during adult life, I came to understand that I was a reasonably attractive guy. Certainly not *model* good-looking, but a seven, say – or maybe an eight on a good day. I didn't think about it much or care, really, and once I met Sana, stopped paying attention to other women anyway.

But *Prince Humphrey?* There must be some threshold of physical attractiveness beyond which everything changes, for I started getting stares and come-ons from women wherever I went. And men, too, of course – gay and who knows, probably even straight (and, being Jubilee, and especially in the red-light areas, from persons of every type of sexual orientation, identification, predilection or concatenation).

One night, a plump, middle-aged, conservative-looking lady playing a gambling machine in one of Jubilee's vast casinos reached around and without looking up, grabbed me so hard with viselike fingers it left a massive red bruise on my ass.

Prince Humphrey was a stud muffin, a *piece of fluff* – Douglas must have made him this way on purpose. Maybe for a laugh, but more likely to make sense of the relationship – he was Lady Darmley's toy boy.

After a few weeks the changes to Danee and me were almost done, but we had to wait for her hair to grow long so she could wear it in the plaited braids of a Grendevan noblewoman. Burning with impatience, I wanted to try attaching artificial hair, but Douglas reminded us everything had to scan as authentic. The waiting was interminable. My skin crawled whenever I thought about Sana and what might be happening on Rethne.

Batum needed a makeover too. His CPU was swapped and his body shape altered to resemble a royal serving droid. "How come I always have to be the fucking *butler?*" he complained when I broke the news.

We had to assume that M4M – or its AI – would scan everything. We could take nothing with us that wouldn't be part of a normal diplomatic mission. So, none of Douglas's newtech or concealed weapons of any kind. All of which made me wonder – given he was a security model – what might the robot be capable of hiding?

"Batum," I asked, "do you happen to have any secret weapons or hidden compartments built into your person? If so, could you please show them to me now?"

For a moment I thought the robot had exploded.

Jutting from every part of his body were weapons of all shapes and sizes: knives, small arms, Taser-like equipment and cavities containing bombs and grenades.

"They all have to go," I said.

Batum shrugged sadly. Everything fell to the floor with a clang, making a pile of weaponry fit for a small army.

"Nothing else?"

"No, that's it," he said, looking at his feet.

"Are you sure?" I asked skeptically.

There was a long pause. Then a tiny cavity opened in his neck, a drawer popped out, turned itself upside-down and a small bomb joined the pile.

"Nothing, Batum, nothing at all. We have to go in completely clean."

"I get it," he said, sounding depressed.

"You'll be rebuilt to look like a royal droid, but don't worry, there's a vital role for you to play on this mission."

During this time, we took jobs on Jubilee – Danee in the Intelligence section. I learned she had been recruited years before when she'd first joined SSB and had spied for Douglas ever since. Following protocol, I never asked what she did each day and she never told me. I started over at Security, throwing myself into the vast apparatus.

Turns out, running a society with no rules takes a huge amount of organization.

I caught a glimpse of it firsthand with Danee one night. We had taken to exploring Jubilee. Touring the myriad bars, theaters, galleries, restaurants and cultural hot spots. Sometimes we hit the red-light district and sometimes Douglas tagged along as well. One night he told us that Jubilee was probably the most densely populated place in human history.

We visited a bar deep in the red-light district called the Reef. The theme – as you'd expect – was tropical, with sand on the floor and fluorescent coral glowing on the roof and walls. A two-piece played on the small stage, though you could say it was really a three-piece because one of the musicians was Theridian. I stared in wonder as it used its four tentacle-like arms to skillfully strum and pluck the famous sixty-eight-string vina, accompanied on congas by a dark-skinned man clearly enjoying himself. The place was packed.

As we entered, my cop brain pinged a couple sitting at the bar, swaying drunk. The man, dressed in trendy red overalls, was vibrating at about a seven, muttering to himself angrily. We took a table in the power corner on the far right-hand side facing the bar, a position known to all law enforcement because it gives such commanding views of everything.

We sat and for a moment I stared in wonder at Danee. The face was no longer hers – a stranger looked back at me – but her eyes shone with the same light, possessed the same consciousness. She was still undeniably Danee in a way I couldn't define. Outside the window behind us was the eternal night of Sector Nine, the endless pulse of music and thrum of activity. A waitress dressed in skimpy tropical-themed clothing brought us coconut bowls of *quavaa*, said to be mildly narcotic.

But one taste of the bitter liquid was enough to know it wasn't for me. Besides, narcotics, even mild ones, have never been my thing. I went to the bar for a real drink, found myself next to the out-of-it couple. The man glared at me, muttering something incomprehensible but clearly aggressive. He was at an eight or nine now – building up. In my beat days, I would have judged it time for this chap to be escorted elsewhere. Perhaps with a tap on the scone to induce good behavior. But how would that work on Jubilee? Was anyone going to sort him out?

The band picked up momentum. The music had a hypnotic, trancelike quality. People stood and swayed along, probably a bit stoned from the quavaa. Danee too, cheeks flushed and pupils dilated. It was all quite enjoyable – except for Mr. Overalls at the bar. Not mellowed out, not having fun. Probably lost money somewhere, bitter and upset. He stood up lurching, pointing a finger, shouting at the girlfriend. Here we go. Should I step in?

He smashed the head of his glass on the bar, and I watched in horror, in slow motion – too far away to get there now – as he lunged at the woman's face with it.

Then action. Blindingly fast.

One of the 'stoned' dancers swaying next to the bar snapped both arms around the man with astonishing speed – was that a glint of robotic silver above its collar? – pinning him, the weaponized glass falling to the floor. Another 'patron' swiftly cuffed and whisked him outside. All over in a few seconds and no one seemed to have noticed – not even the girlfriend, who looked even more out of it than the man. Slick work.

Douglas later showed me how all of Jubilee was wired for sound and video with a phalanx of personnel – human and robotic – constantly on hand to deal with trouble, particularly in the red-light district.

"What would happen to someone like Red Overalls?" I asked the next day.

"Off to dry out, then on the first ship home."

"What if he'd attacked her back in their room?"

"We're always watching. We've got algorithms. He would never be left alone with her."

At the bar, Danee and I sat for a while more till I got bored.

"Wanna split?" I finally asked.

She giggled. "Col, I've got a problem."

"What?"

"I can't stand up, I think it's the quavaa. I've been busting to go to the toilet for ages!"

"Try," I said.

She pushed her hands down on the table and leaned forward, then fell back into her chair laughing. "I really can't!"

"Looks like I'm carrying you!"

I pulled the table out, then picked her up. I left with Danee in my arms, her face buried in my chest with embarrassment. A stoned guy danced around us on the way out, laughing with glee.

In my new job at Security, I decided to investigate the building works at Sector Twenty-One. Instinct told me something wasn't right there. During the torture session, Brimheed had been supremely confident in accusing me of sleeping with Danee. Information had gotten back to him. But how? There had to be a piece of equipment planted somewhere that was capable of receiving a signal and jumping back to the normal universe to pass it on. Call this thing a *jumpcom*. The obvious place for it to be hiding was Sector Twenty-One where full security was not in place yet.

Douglas was skeptical. "I dunno, we've been vigilant over there, I'm tellin' ya."

I was unmoved. I had him rustle up a spacesuit (extra-large for my new body) and we took a flyer over to Sector Twenty-One with work halted for the day. Gravity had not been activated yet, so I wore magnetized boots. We landed on the roof, beneath which would soon be a vast expanse of condos and luxury accommodation. I fitted my helmet, gassed the suit and, after getting a thumbs-up from Douglas, depressurized the cabin and opened the flyer door. Douglas had sent a mechanical robot as his avatar rather than the usual semi-organic droid, which would have been macerated by the radiation and vacuum of space.

I pushed myself up from the seat with only the tiniest effort now we were in zero G, grabbed the top of the door and swung out of the craft. There was a slight pulling sensation as my magnetized boots were sucked onto the metal structure.

What now? The flat roof stretched away in every direction. This new sector was huge with clean square lines because, unlike the rest of Jubilee, it was being constructed with new materials rather than old space junk, Douglas finally making use of his ill-gotten billions. It was an eerie sight. Harshly lit by arc lights mounted on poles, the eternal blackness of space bearing down, pierced by the unblinking stars burning in their billions.

Was this crazy? What could I possibly see that robot eyes might have missed? This thing could be anywhere on or in this structure and searching for it properly could take weeks. I set off across the featureless expanse feeling like a fool.

In the end, though, it was almost comically easy. In one of the far corners I spied a jumble of metal and clomped my way toward it with Douglas following nimbly behind. We had to communicate via suit radio rather than kom, because of course I no longer had one of those.

"Over there, can we check that out?"

"You're the boss," said Douglas.

In the corner was a large pile of gear, tools and equipment held to the surface with magnetized stays and netting. One box stood out immediately. A square meter in size and a different color to everything else – burnished silver – with the word *Tools* stenciled across the top. There might as well have been a sign pointing to it: *suspicious object*.

"What does that scan as, Douglas?"

"Ahem...just a box with welding equipment inside."

"Really? Doesn't look right to me."

I moved closer. There was no lock or lid, no apparent way of opening it. Surely that wasn't right? I reached out to touch it, but Douglas grabbed my arm.

"Best let me, might be booby-trapped."

Of course. Should have thought of that. I walked about twenty steps away from the pile. "OK, let's see what we've got."

Douglas reached for the box and then everything went white.

★   ★   ★

There was the sound of static and a loud hiss. I felt sick – nauseous.

My body was stuck straight, arms pinned above my head. Where was I? An image formed of Douglas reaching for the box. Then what?

I opened my eyes to see stars streaking across my visor in a twisting blur. I was spinning crazily, backward, end over end at great speed. That's why my arms were above my head. Held in place by centrifugal force. I tried to bring them to my sides, but couldn't. Must be rotating very fast, hence the nausea. And the hiss? A leak somewhere. The suit was humming and whirring, trying to compensate. How long could it keep that up?

The box must have exploded. Cracks in my visor – something had hit me full in the face with enough force to damage the safetiplaz and knock me out into space. Where was Douglas? Surely he'd send something to find me. Jubilee swooped past with every second or third rotation, getting smaller each time. My tumbling motion must include some spin – like a high diver – because the view kept changing with each rotation. I tried calling. No kom, of course! And the suit was giving me only static.

"Douglas? Douglas, can you hear me? Come in!"

Had to get my arms down, try to play around with the suit radio. I locked my hands together and slid them slowly down to my chin. But this only made things worse. Like an ice-skater bringing her arms in to twirl, I'd reduced the moment of inertia and sped up the rate of spin. I frantically tapped and pressed the suit radio on the left side of my helmet and tried paging.

No response.

I let the arms go and the spinning slowed back down a bit. But I was still tumbling madly through space. Not a damned thing to do about it.

I must have blacked out again. Came to when the suit spoke to me:

"Warning: air remaining five minutes."

A bunch of red holo messages flashed inside my helmet: body functions critical, suit integrity critical. I was venting air. Bleeding out. The suit would be trying its best, had probably shot me up with adrenaline and drugs and whatever, but it wasn't a hospital – which was what I needed.

I ran through the options once more, talking aloud. Surely *something* could be done? What would they have said in training? Hard to know, because no one trains to be blown off into space from an artificial habitat existing inside its own parallel universe with only an eccentric AI computer to potentially save you. The manual was sketchy on that. My mind churned and churned, eventually running down to nothing.

And then it hit me.

This was it, *really* it.

I was going to die here, spinning in space off Jubilee.

And what had it all been for? This life?

Losing Mother, losing Tim. The big career, the difficult marriage with Sana – she'd be stuck on Rethne now, I'd never get to save her, save us.

Then something remarkable happened.

I heard a sound. Laughter.

It was me.

Everything felt suddenly absurd. Why had I taken it all so seriously, worried so much? When you least expect it, all your fleeting dramas could be snuffed out just like that. A cosmic joke.

A feeling of peace came over me. And understanding. A *knowing* that everything was perfect and exactly how it should be. I felt connected to the space and the stars around me. A feeling of oneness, of no separation between myself and the universe.

It was ecstatic.

My last thought was, *If this is death, bring it on.*

CHAPTER TWENTY

I slammed into something solid with huge force – like being hit by a truck. The suit took much of the blow, but was sounding two or three new alarms now. At least the collision stopped the tumbling motion, but what had I hit? All I could see in front of me were stars, Jubilee so far away now. Whatever it was, I must have crashed into it backward, then rebounded. I tried to look behind – but you can only turn your head so far in a spacesuit. The stars were moving slowly left to right so therefore I was rotating. In a minute or so I'd be facing the opposite way. I hung there in space, panting, gradually spinning around, waiting for whatever I hit to come around into view.

A ship!

A sleek medium-sized spacer. Must be moored off Jubilee, waiting to dock – what were the odds of hitting that? Growing larger by the moment. Shouldn't it be the other way around? Getting smaller as I rebounded away? They must have heard or felt the collision. They were moving in to investigate.

"Warning: air remaining two minutes."

The ship loomed closer, but the suit was having a tantrum. A new message told me it was going into *saver mode*, whatever that was. It was dying. Its energies running down, just like me. I didn't care. I felt relaxed and amused, still high. If I died here within sight of salvation, so be it!

The ship was meters away, then within touching distance. I grabbed a handhold and pulled myself up from the underside. Light streamed from a porthole above. *Porthole!* My visor was fogging at the edges, the cracks growing larger. Sooner or later those cracks would join up and my faceplate would blow out. Ah well.

Above me a woman gazed out of the porthole, framed in the oval light like a portrait. She was dressed in a black evening gown for a glamorous night out on Jubilee. Makeup and red lipstick, hair pinned up. Sparkly necklace probably worth more than my apartment. Must be an upmarket cruiser, this – anything with a porthole had to be.

I pulled myself level, smiled and waved at her. She stared blankly for a second, then her eyes widened and she screamed – silently on the other side of the window. Her face disappeared. I tried tapping the glass, then two men and a different woman appeared, bunched together.

"Warning: air remaining one minute."

I mouthed, *"Help me!"* and started laughing at how crazy everything was. The people inside were all talking at once. Debating something, maybe.

I bashed the window. "Let me in, *let me in*, little pigs!" I was laughing hysterically. Caught my reflection in the porthole glass. Cracked visor misted red, blood running down my face. No wonder the woman had screamed. Anyway, how could they help me? Ships like this didn't have grappling arms, they carried rich people from one pleasure world to the next. The emergency airlock would take twenty minutes to open – if anyone knew how to do it – and as per regulations there *would* be a suit somewhere on board, but probably still in its box, never used.

"Warning: air remaining thirty seconds."

The woman in the porthole – probably the ship's captain since she was wearing a uniform – waved at me and pointed to my left. I looked across to see a sliver of light pouring into space. Growing larger. The departure gate airlock. Opening! How could they do that without docking? These things are specifically designed *never* to open into space. Question for another day. If there was another day.

I pulled myself across to it. But how to get inside? There was nothing to grab hold of, only a clean wall and fully retracted door. I was floating just outside the lock with no way to pull myself inside.

Then the air ran out.

Only the remnant of air trapped in my spacesuit was keeping me alive. One minute or so before unconsciousness and death.

I reached across to the handhold nearest the door. I grabbed it firmly, using my wrist muscle to rotate my body around into the open cavity. I was captured by the ship's gravity and fell heavily to the airlock floor, but my legs were dangling outside, strangely unresponsive. In fact, my whole lower body was inert.

I rolled over a couple of times deeper into the airlock. Right leg inside now, but the left still dangling over the edge. Had to get it in or the door wouldn't close. Why was it stuck? Why wouldn't it move? Everything was spinning, starting to go gray. Hypoxia.

I rolled onto my back. Painfully, using every last erg of energy, I willed my body to sit up. Leaned forward, grabbed my leg as though it were a piece of wood and pulled it. The knee came up, the leg was sliding in, but then my heel seemed to catch on something – the lip of the airlock door. I shook it side to side, pulled hard, felt something rend and tear. A loud hiss, turning into a roar. The suit was pierced, blowing out. Somehow I dragged the mangled mess of my left leg into the lock. The last thing I remember was banging the airlock wall to let them know I was inside.

CHAPTER TWENTY-ONE

"He's conscious now." Douglas's voice.

"Col, can you hear me?" Danee.

With great effort I opened my eyes to see them peering over me, worried expressions on each of their faces. Above was a plain white ceiling. Probably some kind of mediclinic. "Hi, guys," I mumbled. "Hey, can't move my body."

"It's OK, Col, you were banged up," said Danee.

"*Very* banged up," said Douglas. "We need to do a couple of tests with you conscious, OK? Then you'll be going back to sleep. Do you remember what happened?"

Memory trickled back, the grogginess falling away somewhat – I was probably being pumped full of amazing drugs. "Yeah," I said, "we were playing golf at Harrison Central and I got hit by a ball."

They looked at each other, concerned.

"Just kidding. Explosion. Hurtling through space."

"Jokin' around! Can't be too bad," said Douglas, smiling.

"You know, something happened to me out there."

"Yeah, you got blown up and nearly died," said Danee.

"No, something else, something amazing. I had an experience."

"OK, we're good." A voice from the other side of the room.

Douglas looked over, then turned to me. "You can tell us all about it real soon."

Everything went black again.

Turned out I'd been hit by blast shrapnel traveling at 1,600 meters per second, fracturing my skull and pelvis, and blowing me off Jubilee and out into space. I also had liver and spleen damage, and a perforated bowel.

The spinning motion had sent blood to my head, which filled my brain and poured out of my skull, and the collision with the ship had broken my back in three places. Without nano-surgery I would never have walked again and if the injury had occurred even a centimeter higher, my upper body would have been paralyzed too.

I survived only because of the incredible redundancy built into the suit and the fast work of those passengers aboard the *Tropicana* – the ship I'd hit. Luckily for me it was owned by a prominent surgeon who had administered first aid on the airlock floor in the critical minutes it took to land on Jubilee. With no time to release my helmet, they'd used an ice-bucket hammer to crack my faceplate open – who said these luxury items have no use?

I spent a week unconscious in the mediclinic. Doctors were especially worried about brain damage and were amazed I survived. There was a further two weeks in a nano-bath with tubes hanging off me everywhere, followed by rehab. All this pushed out our departure to Grendeva.

In the moment it exploded, the box had sent an EMP pulse that knocked out Douglas's comms and sensors. That's why there was only static in my suit radio and why Douglas couldn't send a ship.

"Had to do a partial reboot," he said. "First time in two hundred years."

By the time I'd collided with the *Tropicana* Douglas was already back online, talking to ship computers in the area and sending out drones. He immediately took control of the ship, overrode the airlock code and brought it in to Jubilee. He reckoned the odds of hitting something like that at five million to one – and if I'd missed, he never would have found me in time. I had literally cheated death.

Bring on Rethne, bring on Gilham!

Drones were dispatched to collect everything from the expanding debris sphere made by the jumpcom. All pieces, no matter how small or damaged, were brought to a secure room, reassembled and reverse engineered. The box worked largely as I'd imagined: programmed to receive messages from Jubilee, then jump back to the normal universe and send them on via an FTL stream. It also contained sensors and AI. It had been carefully observing activity on Sector Twenty-One, kept itself mingled with construction equipment and been blithely ignored by the construction droids, who even moved it occasionally with all the other gear. When Douglas and I had arrived, it was smart enough to know the game was up and intentionally sent its suicidal blast in our direction. Fortunately I was standing behind Douglas's avatar robot and had been partially shielded.

"*Nasty* piece of work," said Douglas, "and technology like nothin' we've seen before. Doesn't even look human to me."

"What do you mean by that?" I asked, astonished.

"Just the way it's made, programmed. Not the way you lot do things."

"So you're saying it was made by an AI? Or by another race altogether?"

"Not sure."

All work stopped on Sector Twenty-One. They found other devices and booby traps, large and small. The worker droids were infected with malware and the whole site so badly compromised I considered it a write-off. Thank god Douglas had kept a *cordon sanitaire* between it and the rest of Jubilee.

"If I were you," I said one afternoon from my nano-bath, "I'd cut the whole dammed thing off from Jubilee and send it into the nearest sun."

"No way," said Douglas. "You've got *no* idea how much money I've spent."

False economy. I'd been researching the ancient Scots in all my spare time and learned they had had a reputation for being tight with money. Maybe Douglas had inherited more than just the dialect?

"You'll never be able to clean it up. There could be nanos hidden anywhere, even inside solid walls. Cut your losses!"

But Douglas was adamant. The worker droids were deactivated and scrapped, and a fresh team began scanning the sector from one side to the other – a job scheduled to take a standard year.

"You know this is a complete balls-up?" I said in exasperation.

"I was never meant to be doin' this," said Douglas defensively. "I was programmed to run a flophouse!"

He was right. Until now the main security threats to Jubilee had always been internal – bad behavior from guests.

Douglas would need to lift his game.

"Actually," I said, "till now you've had it easy."

The aftereffects of my strange experience lingered. I felt euphoric but also calm. It was like I'd caught a glimpse of a truth that had always been there but I'd never noticed before. I tried talking about it with Danee.

She was sympathetic but skeptical. "The suit was filling you up with god knows what drugs. You were probably high as a kite."

"True, but it wasn't like that. I know what those drugs feel like and this was different. This was *more* real than normal."

But nothing I said got through. Same with Douglas. So when I was finally mobile, I decided to visit the only person who might be able to answer the questions I had.

The Swami.

CHAPTER TWENTY-TWO

I hobbled into reception, where a woman took my details. I had the odd feeling I'd seen her before. On Jubilee? I called on the Investigator mind and an image formed. Danee and I had just landed, were on our way to the hotel. A well-dressed lady walking on Concourse with a large cat on a leash. I dropped my gaze to the floor. Curled up asleep at her feet was the very same large cat.

She smiled sweetly. "Swamiji will see you now."

A few weeks earlier I had been talking with Douglas about the surprising number of religions that had outposts on Jubilee – churches and places of worship were dotted everywhere.

"Where better to harvest souls?" he'd answered.

"Aren't people here for a good time?"

"Sure, but then they get depressed and guilty. That's humans, mate, they're weird."

"I'm surprised you let them in."

"Why not? They're not hurting anyone. We've got all two hundred galactic religions plus at last count sixteen cults and one Swami."

"But not the Movement?"

"Not them. The only one that's not here."

"And what," I had to ask, "is a Swami?"

Douglas chuckled. "Far as I can tell, he's the person they all go to when they got *questions*."

I was ushered into a small room. A very old, very skinny man with a shaved head and orange robes was seated on a large, comfortable chair. There were other people in the room. A young woman, tearful with tissues in hand, a couple of guys and an older woman with a powerful presence and intense look. The Swami was playing a harmonica along with recorded music I didn't recognize. Could have been something ancient from Old Earth. Without stopping, he looked up and gestured to an empty chair.

I sat down gingerly, body still sore, and looked around. The walls were almost completely covered with 2D pictures of religious leaders and saints, including mythical figures from Old Earth. Everyone seemed to be having a good time just hanging out with the Swami.

The older woman stood up and said impatiently, "OK, I gotta go!" then strode purposefully out of the room.

The Swami waved goodbye, put down his harmonica and turned off the music. "Nice to see you all, folks, but now I have an appointment."

Everyone stood. The tearful girl touched the Swami's feet and said melodramatically, "Thank you *so, so* much, Swamiji."

He smiled. "You're most welcome, my dear, just keep away from those *bad* boys!"

He met my eye as she left the room. Was that a twinkle of amusement?

"Col? Pleased to meet you!"

"Likewise."

He had a kindly manner and I noticed his eyes had a special shine to them.

"Do you play chess?" he asked out of the blue.

"Ahem, let me think, I've heard of it...."

"It's an ancient game from the prehistory of Old Earth. Not played much these days, but I love it. Care to indulge me while I make a move?"

Set up next to him on a small table was a game board, made with alternating black and white squares. He briefly explained the rules.

"Who's the opponent?"

"Douglas."

A surprise. They had a relationship, obviously.

"That seems like an uneven competition!"

He laughed. "We have a handicapping system. I'm allowed to take as long as I like to make a move and he has five trillionths of a nanosecond. Apparently that's like five seconds for a human."

"Well, you might want to look at that. He's just given himself an upgrade."

He raised his eyebrows. "Oh, is that so? Who's a naughty boy for not telling me?" He spoke into his kom – "Hey, Douglas!"

"Hey, Swamiji," said Douglas immediately. "Finally gonna make a move? I've been lookin' forward to kickin' your arse!"

"What's this I hear about an upgrade?"

Douglas made a snorting sound. "Col – such a goody-goody! Why'd you have to spill the beans?"

"Don't worry about him. How much faster are you running now?"

Douglas sighed. "OK, OK. Let's cut it down to two-point-five. Happy? Don't tell me you're going to make a new move?"

"Stay tuned," said the Swami, chuckling.

He reached over to the board, moved a piece and then hit a small black button. Instantly a hatch opened on the opposite side. A mechanical arm emerged with a faint clanking sound, moved a piece, then withdrew. Next to the hatch was a digital display now showing a number: *2.335*.

The Swami said, "That's reading trillionths of a nanosecond – so Douglas did his calculation in just over two-point-three. Drats, that was a good move. I *hate* him!"

"Have you ever won?"

"We've been playing each other for nearly ten years and I've beaten him twice. Let me tell you, he doesn't like it!"

"How long do the games go for?"

"This one, six months."

The door opened and the receptionist came in with tea and cake.

"Ah, just in time. Every cell in my body is craving tea! Will you join us, Varan?"

She looked us both over, raised an eyebrow. "I think I'll leave you boys to it."

The Swami thanked her, then poured us both a cup. "Now I'm sure you haven't come here to discuss chess. How can I help?"

I paused for a sip of tea and took a bite of cake. Both were delicious, the tea made with some kind of herb I'd not tasted before. "I hear you answer people's questions."

"Who told you that, Douglas?"

I nodded.

The Swami put down his teacup, threw his head back and let out a long belly laugh. "That's his joke about me. Says it's all I ever do!"

I felt a hot flush of embarrassment. I'd taken Douglas literally, what a fool!

The Swami took note and changed tack, becoming serious. "Can I ask *you* a question, though?"

"Sure."

"Do you ever wonder whether Douglas is really *conscious?*"

"You mean like a human?"

"Yes. Do you think he has an inner world in the same way we do?

"What do you mean by *inner world?*"

The Swami pointed to his chest. "When you go *within*, what do you experience?"

"I don't know, never really thought about it."

"OK, let's do it together then, right now. We can see what's going on."

Under his instructions I closed my eyes and took a breath, tried to be present. There was a feeling of warm darkness, a deep feeling. Over the top of it, a stream of chatter from my mind.

I opened my eyes.

The Swami was smiling benevolently. "*Thoughts* and *feelings*, no? That's what's in there, and a sense of *interiority?*"

"Yes...very well put."

"This is what we swamis do – examine the inner world. We're students of consciousness, that's why I'm curious about Douglas."

"Did you ever ask him?"

"Yes. He said he *does* have an inner world and it feels like 'a column of energy and light' – that's how he put it."

"He *seems* conscious. He's got more personality than most people. But is that real, or just good programming?"

"That's the question! Also, you have to say that when it comes to Jubilee, Douglas actually *is* God."

All-seeing, all-knowing, all-powerful.

"He may as well be God here, but that still doesn't answer the question," I said.

"Want to know what I think?"

"Sure."

"Douglas was made by humans, who are conscious. So that same consciousness is imbued in him. It's all the same thing."

This felt a bit like a cop-out, but I couldn't quite put my finger on why. I sat back in the chair with a sigh. Hanging out with the Swami was unusually pleasant. It felt as though he was totally present to me, *understood* me on some deep level – like no person I'd ever met before. His good humor was contagious and I felt calm and energized. Not dissimilar to the experience in space.

"Something happened to me."

The Swami took a sip of tea and looked at me intently. "Tell me about it."

I told him. About going outside in the suit. Being blown into space and the euphoric state. "I knew I was about to die, but there was this feeling. I can't describe it. Connection. Ecstasy. I keep trying to tell people about it, but they're not interested. They just roll their eyes."

The Swami was quiet for a moment. "I believe the experience you had was real. The ancient Greeks had a word for it: *epiphany*."

"Which means?"

"Revelation." He waved at the portraits on the wall. "These great beings have taught me the soul is immortal. You had an experience of that, tapped into meta-consciousness. The rest of us need to meditate for decades to get there, but you took a short cut."

"So, what do I do with it?"

The Swami laughed. "That's up to you! You could come here to my center and do spiritual practice, deepen the experience."

I shook my head, no chance of that – not for the moment, anyway. With every passing day I grew more concerned about Sana. "There's something very big I need to do – which I need to ask you a question about."

"Fire away."

I spoke for a good while. I told him about my history with the Movement and the night I'd seen Gilham speak. Sana's opposition to them, her kidnapping and the mission to save her. "There's something that keeps nagging at me, though."

"Go on."

"I know for certain, from my own experience, that M4M is monstrous. But when I first saw Gilham speak, I was *drawn* to him. I feel ashamed about it now. A lot of Services people are into the Movement and I could've been one of them. Only because my wife" – I stopped for a moment, emotional – "was wise enough to see through them... otherwise, I might have been sucked in myself."

"You're wondering what that means?"

"Yes?"

"Means you're human. Susceptible to delusion, like everyone else."

"Gilham seems to have magnetism, a power to draw people in and influence them. How can that *be* when he's so clearly a bad person?"

The Swami closed his eyes and was quiet for a long time. So long I began to wonder if he'd nodded off. Then he finally spoke. "I don't suppose you've heard of the ancient mystic G.I. Gurdjieff?"

I shook my head, of course not. He pointed to one of the pictures on the wall, a black-and-white image of a man clearly from Old Earth. He had a shaved head like the Swami but not the robes. His eyes were pools of liquid black and he sported an enormous handlebar moustache. His face carried an expression of deep compassion but also sadness.

"Gurdjieff dates from the early twentieth century, Old Earth. A truly great being. He said sometimes it's possible a person might do a lot of hard spiritual work but be lacking proper guidance from a teacher or master. In some cases that person might develop great psychic powers, but there's a danger the ego may not have been sufficiently dealt with. In some circumstances that person can become what he called a *wrong crystallization.*"

"You're saying that's what Gilham is? A wrong crystallization?"

"I think so, yes."

"And what happens to a person like this? Can they be stopped?"

"Gurdjieff said if someone crystallizes in a wrong way, they can't make any more spiritual progress. They can't change or evolve from that state. They have to be painfully broken down."

I looked at the portrait again. This all made sense. It explained why Gilham had such power over people. It also meant Gilham could only be defeated head-on. He would never compromise, could never evolve. I had an intuition: a time would come, not long from now, when this information would be crucial.

I looked at the Swami. He seemed tired, pained. Was there a history between him and Gilham? I would have to ask Douglas.

"Thanks. This has really helped. But can I ask you one more thing?"

He brightened. "Sure! May as well get your money's worth!"

A joke, the woman at reception had refused payment.

"It's personal. A relationship question."

The Swami laughed and put his hands over his ears. "Oh, what these ears have heard!"

I told him about Danee – I guess you had to call her my girlfriend now – and how she was coming with me on what was probably a suicide mission – to rescue my wife. "And while it's true we're estranged, Sana *is* still my wife. But Danee doesn't seem concerned about it."

"So, what's the problem?"

"I feel weird and guilty. And confused. If we *do* succeed in rescuing Sana, then what? I'll probably have to choose…I guess what I'm asking is – can you be in love with two women at the same time?"

The Swami chuckled. "The human heart is infinite, like consciousness. You can love two women, you could love *twenty!* The issue is rather: what is practical? What is going to *work?*"

"So I have to choose then?"

"You said the odds of success are small?"

"Douglas gives it two per cent."

"Then it sounds like you're worrying about the wrong thing. Do you really have to go?"

"Yes, and I think our odds are better than that, though I can't say why. I could be deluded."

The Swami smiled affectionately. "You should focus on the priority. If your mission succeeds, then you can worry about the other matter, and anyway" – he laughed again – "when it comes to relationships, women seem to have a way of knowing what's right." The Swami hugged me goodbye with a final word. "Col, don't forget that state you experienced out in space. It's your birthright. It's where we all come from and go to, and if you get in trouble on this mission – call on it."

CHAPTER TWENTY-THREE

The night before leaving, we gathered in the control room. Danee and me along with Batum and Douglas. Food was laid out, which we humans ate quietly. It felt a bit like the Last Supper.

Danee's hair had grown long and would soon be plaited into the braids of a Grendevan noblewoman. Douglas asked for our mobiles and held them for a few moments.

"I just loaded you up with your 'return' tickets along with the new identities."

We would 'return' to Grendeva from Jubilee as commoners, or at least middle-class people, coming home after a holiday. I would travel alone, Danee with Batum.

"Once you get through customs on Grendeva, all this history will vanish. Then presto, your new identities as Prince Humphrey and Lady Darmley will appear."

Douglas had it all worked out. Our contact, Prince Fenwick – whom I assumed was the holder of the large betting tab – would have a spacer ready with all the requisite paperwork. Batum would be transformed into a royal domestic droid and then we would be on our way.

"Everything is in place for when you get to Rethne – though I wish you two would reconsider," Douglas said. "Nothin' has happened that might make it easier."

I just looked at him. "You know I have to go."

"Yes, I know," he said, then looked at each of us in turn. "All of you please, Batum especially, look out for that LAI. It's there on Rethne somewhere – it could be the key to everythin'."

We said good night to Batum, hugged Douglas goodbye and headed home for a last night of fitful sleep.

CHAPTER TWENTY-FOUR

The problems started almost straight away at boarding when my 'mobile' was scanned by the check-in robot. A red light flashed, a buzzer sounded and my small bag was spat out of the machine.

"No luggage allowed with this fare class," said a tinny mechanical voice.

"OK, I'll pay extra."

"No upgrades allowed with this fare class."

There were rumblings in the queue behind me. Hurry up.

OK, I'll ditch it. Not much of value in there. I retreated to the back of the departure hall, transferred items to my backpack and dumped the balance in the trash.

"No carry-on allowed with this fare class," said the merciless machine.

"No *carry-on?*"

I took the barest essentials from the pack and transferred them around my pockets – toothbrush, change of underwear – and was finally allowed to board the run-down hauler for the first stage of my trip to Grendeva. Where I learned something else about this fare class: no seating either.

Standing room was filling rapidly, mostly with men. This ship must have been a food freighter in an earlier incarnation because there was a faint stink of rotten bananas, mixing now with other smells – of the grubby and unwashed. People who'd blown every last credit on Jubilee. It was Douglas's rule that all visitors had to have a valid return ticket. However, sometimes as money ran dry, people swapped their nice, direct return for a discount ticket so as to liberate a few more funds. So they could stay and gamble (or whatever) that last, tiny little bit longer. That's what my character, 'Donny', had done. I was traveling on the cheapest, shittiest ticket a small amount of money could buy and it was going to take fourteen days of elapsed time and eight separate legs to reach Grendeva. Maybe Douglas had overdone it with the realism?

I reached up to grab one of the handholds, but was bumped aside by a heavyset man who took it for himself. He looked desperate. Sweaty, unshaven, glazed eyes. What sort of hellhole was this, where even a handhold was contested? I thought about pushing back – in Prince Humphrey's body I was at least a foot taller than him, could have taken the guy out in a second – but was it worth arguing? Then again, this leg was eight hours. A long time standing with nothing to hold on to.

"It's all right, buddy, you can share with me." A voice from behind.

I turned. The voice came from a tall, lanky, dark-haired guy, smiling ruefully. Thin. So thin as to be almost two-dimensional. His clothes looked old and worn and hung off him loosely, but seemed clean at least.

"Very kind," I said, grabbing one side of the strap.

"No problem. Zhang's the name. How're you doing?"

"I'm Donny. Guess I've had better days." I had deliberately chosen old, worn clothes and refrained from shaving for several days.

"Busted?"

"Busted flat."

"Sorry 'bout that. Seen it a million times."

Zhang worked on the Jubilee docks and was en route to Parla, my first stop, said to be a beautiful Earthlike planet. "I work six months straight, ten hours a day. Sleep in a company bunk, eat in the company caf, save every credit. Then it's the rest of the year on Parla in my little beach shack."

It was hard not to envy the simplicity of Zhang's life. The lights flickered and we all staggered as the ship's gravity fluctuated, heavy, then light, then back to normal. This old rust bucket was not going to be a smooth ride.

"Looks like we've pushed off from Jubilee. You never did this trip before, right?"

"Nope."

"Bar opens after the second jump. We'll make a run for it, best place to hang out."

There was the sound of heavy machinery running up to speed, subsonic vibrations coming through the floor. Some grating and clunking and flickering of lights, then the unmistakable lurch of a hyperspace jump – a very rough one, causing us all to stagger again. We would now be back in the 'normal' universe, somewhere off MGNA#12. There would be a wait while they recharged and recalibrated for the next jump.

"So, what do you do on Parla?" I asked, making conversation.

"Mostly I'm working on my writing."

Turns out Zhang was a published poet. "I've had three of mine in the *New Farnando Journal of Literature*. I've had letters from readers, even got one from Douglas!"

Douglas? Funny. It was easy to forget how he could be interacting with thousands, millions of people all in the same moment.

"Douglas is the AI computer that runs Jubilee. He's taken an interest in my writing."

I feigned surprise. "Oh, I get it, that's a real credit to you."

Zhang was originally from a planet called Jinxung. "But left young, never went back. Got my lady friend, Mina, waiting when we land." He glanced at his kom. "In seven-point-five hours I'll be wrapped in her arms." His brown eyes glowed with pleasure; it was hard not to like him.

The ship went through another set of warmups, then executed a second shuddering jump. We would now be around 0.25 parsecs off Parla – not that you'd know. This vessel had no portholes anywhere, just a giant tin can. For the rest of this trip we'd be snailing our way toward Parla on the gravity drive.

"Right, let's go," said Zhang, bolting for a nearby door.

The 'bar' turned out to be a small room with tiny bench-height tables and a bank of dispensing machines at the far end. *May as well get a bite,* I thought. Bodies piled into the room behind us and a rowdy queue formed, pushing and shoving. I stood in front of the food dispenser, where a holo display rotated through a range of mouthwatering items. I chose *chicken and vegetable meal* and held up my mobile. The machine gave a short, nasty buzz: *insufficient credit*. I thumbed my mobile to look – *Available credit: C2.4.*

Two and a half credits? *Less* than two and half credits! 'Donny' had literally no money at all. What was I going to do for the next two weeks? What was I going to eat? The queue behind me was growing restless, so I scrolled for the cheapest item and selected *sandwich pack*. The machine groaned and sighed, and a package dropped into the receiving hollow with a chuntering sound. Zhang tapped me on the shoulder and passed over a can of beer, then tilted his head toward the tables. We took one as far away from the machines as possible, cracked open our beers and toasted. This was going to be my last drink for a while.

"So, you really are skint, eh?" said Zhang. Must have seen my interaction with the machine.

I nodded, embarrassed, and opened my food pack. It contained a row of four precut sandwiches. The bread slices were thin and gray, with darker gray paste in between. A far cry from the plump, nutritious-looking sandwiches in the holo. I took a bite, then pushed the packet away. Hideous. If not toxic.

"Helps if you wash 'em down," said Zhang, tapping the can, "and don't think too much about what's in there. Where you headed, anyway?"

"Grendeva."

He whistled. "Long trip, 'specially on a ticket like this!"

Dear reader, if you're not familiar with the galactic star map, please indulge me for a moment while I explain – I promise it won't be too painful!

Imagine you're looking 'down' on the relatively flat disc of our galaxy. Now superimpose a clock face over it. The galaxy's 240 billion stars are spread around the clock in a set of spiral 'arms' emanating from the galactic core. Looks a bit like a choco-vanilla swirl from Douglas's ice-cream shop. MGNA#12 – the starting point of this trip – is at six o'clock, halfway to the rim. Grendeva sits at eleven o'clock at the 'top' of the galaxy, 65,000 light-years away. That's far and Douglas was sending me the *long* way – traveling anticlockwise around the galactic core from six to eleven o'clock. This was all to avoid systems controlled by the Movement. With his newly improved faculties he'd intercepted a secret

M4M command to scan and monitor passenger movement from Jubilee. They were looking for a Caucasian male, 190 centimeters, missing a right eye.

"So you've heard of Grendeva, then?" I asked Zhang. What were the odds, out of two and a half million settled planets?

"Yup, I do a lot of reading, and your system's *quirky*."

"Guess so."

The less we talked about Grendeva the better, so I quickly ran through my backstory. Donny worked in security and was an amateur poker player. Had always wanted to try his luck on Jubilee. Now heading home tail between the legs – like everyone else on this crappy ship. I looked around and felt suddenly tired. These people seemed so depleted and sad. They were the detritus, the waste material ejected from Jubilee's ecosystem. "I guess this is the dark side of Jubilee. All of us fucked up and broke?"

"Not me," chuckled Zhang.

"Never gambled?"

"Once, didn't enjoy it," he sighed. "Look, Jubilee is what you make of it. Best place in the galaxy or the worst. All up to you."

"Built on the backs of these people, you could say."

Zhang swigged his beer, looked around and shrugged. "Everybody made a choice."

We chatted and the hours passed. I had to use the toilet a couple of times – I'll spare you the details, for it was every bit as bad as you might think. Zhang told me the whole ship was hosed out after each sailing. Finally there was a shudder and flickering of lights, then a loud clunk as we docked at the Parla transit hub.

Zhang went to the food machines, hit a bunch of buttons, then came back with an armful of boxes. "Looks like we're parting ways, buddy – these should keep you going for a little while."

I cringed. What a state things were in, for a *poet* to take pity on me for my poverty. Zhang worked so hard, saved every credit. I held up my hands, *You shouldn't have.*

"It's OK, Donny, I'll put this one in the karma bank. Safe travels!"

Zhang would be staying on board for the final leg to Parla's surface. I was getting off to wait in transit for the next ship. We hugged goodbye. He was skin and bone, but strong and rangy from all that work in the docks. A buzzer sounded. The ship's engine noise – an unnoticed constant – died down and there was only the sound of people bustling to exit. I allowed myself to get caught in a wave of humanity washing me out of the bar and off the ship.

*　　*　　*

Then came the interminable wait. For an hour or so it was interesting to wander around, check out the transit station and drink in the amazing view of Parla, resplendent in green and blue below.

But that passed.

How long can you window-shop and sit in cafés where there's nothing you can afford to eat? I clutched the boxes Zhang had given me. There were six different meals and they all tasted exactly the same, but I wasn't arguing. The hours passed. I sat in the transit area playing with my mobile, then stretched out and tried to sleep. No one approached or spoke to me, which was OK. By the time I finished all the food, thirty-six hours had passed.

Finally it was time to board the next ship. Which was something to do, at least, but turned out to be merely swapping one kind of tedium for another. On the trip to Cranache I stood alone and ignored at the bar, watching others eat and drink. I got so hungry even the vending machine sandwiches made me drool.

At Cranache we landed on the planet's surface. When I explained my plight to a security guard, he kindly directed me to a homeless shelter in the town. There was a soup kitchen around the corner with food that was hot, reasonably nutritious and, best of all, a color other than gray.

After Cranache came Mezai, then the Absolom transit station for a nightmare two days, followed by Hetam and Kendal-Povan. Everything blended into one endless day, a netherworld of waiting, standing, queuing and hunger. I lost sense of time and direction – the mobile would bleep with directions when it was time to get on or off the next ship and I followed its commands without thought. My beard grew long, my breath foul – toothbrush long ago lost, dropped somewhere along the way. Clothes filthy, hair disheveled and the smell coming off me? Don't even think about it.

The lowest point: I was standing in front of a café when a young man walked out, passing me directly. I looked up to make eye contact but he moved around me unseeing, face blank. I got no sense of prejudice or disdain; he simply didn't notice me.

Then I realized something with a start: that blank look had become familiar. Everyone else passing bore it too. *I had become invisible.*

One of the wretched, foul-smelling underclass. Unnoticed and unknowable. Then I saw it: Douglas had sent me this way on purpose, probably for safety. So I could travel to Grendeva incognito – why?

Because nothing is more invisible than a poor person.

I went to the transit area and sat, shocked by my realization. In my former life (a million years ago) I'd had the same unconscious attitudes as these people, but now the shoe was on the other foot. I felt resentful of them, these shiny, clean motherfuckers walking past like I didn't exist. The anger passed, dissolving into a wave of depression. Still thousands of light-years to go, the trip stretched out in front of me, endless. I sat slumped on the bench, resigned, hands in pockets. Where I found something at the bottom of my right-hand pocket.

That was odd. Had to have been there for days.

I pulled out whatever it was. A slip of paper tightly folded many times into a hard little lump. I carefully opened it to find a handwritten note:

Intrepid.
More than he seems.
Celestial light guide him
Through the forest of stars.
Z.

A poem. From Zhang. Written on actual paper, which was eccentric of course, but then he *was* a poet. Was it a good poem or a bad one? Hard to know, it was the first I'd read since high school. He must have planted it in my pocket. Must have written it when I went to the toilet, then slipped it in my pocket when we'd hugged goodbye. I read it again. Zhang was perceptive, awake. He saw through me somehow, but meant well. The poem lifted my spirits and I laughed out loud. So what if I was poor and hungry? I was on my way to save Sana – how was *she* feeling at this moment, a prisoner on Rethne?

Then, a crazy idea. It came out of nowhere. I took out my mobile and thumbed through the contacts, stopping at **Rob, brother.** So Donny had a brother? A fake brother for a fake person, why not? I clicked on the contact and the mobile asked: *FTL call* **Rob, brother?** Naturally this would have to be a faster-than-light call so many parsecs from Grendeva. I clicked *Yes.* The mobile bleeped: *insufficient credit.*

Ah well, stupid idea.

Then: *Reverse charge FTL call* **Rob, brother?** In a dream I pressed *Yes.* There was a hiss, some static and after a few moments a voice.

"Donny, is that you?"

I held the mobile away from me and stared at it in wonder. Perhaps someone had given me drugs? "Yes, yes, it is."

"Wow, Donny, where have you been? We've all been worried."

My mind spun in neutral, unable to process what was being said.

"Donny, you still there, you OK?"

"Ah…it's a long story," I said finally, in a daze. "I've been on Jubilee."

"Man, you did it! How'd you do?"

"Not good. In fact…I'm skint."

He laughed. "I guess that explains the collect call."

"Yeah, I've been doing it tough."

"Donny" – Rob sounded concerned, " – do you need me to lend you some credits, help you get home?"

"Actually, that would be great."

"Would four hundred get you out of trouble?"

"That would be a lifesaver."

"No worries." He paused for a moment. "OK, just did the transfer, you can pay me back whenever."

"Thanks so much, Rob...I'd better go, this call will be costing you a fortune."

"OK, I'll see you soon."

"Yeah, see you soon."

Then a final psychedelic sign-off. "Love you, bro."

"Yeah, me too...."

The call went dead. I sat in a daze.

What the fuck?

But I scrolled the mobile and sure enough it was now showing *Available credit: C400.60.* This situation might be surreal, but the money sure wasn't – and I knew just how to spend it. In short order I picked up a set of new clothes from a nearby store, checked into the transit hotel, basked in an endless hot shower and dined on room-service food washed down with ice-cold beer. Then I set the alarm and plunged into a bed softer than fairy floss.

And so it went for the rest of the trip.

I arrived on Grendeva ninety-six hours later, fresh as a daisy.

CHAPTER TWENTY-FIVE

The immigration officer passed Donny through with barely a look. She was wearing a strange ceremonial uniform of coarse brown fabric complete with a belt and scabbard, the white jacket featuring epaulets. I stepped outside to find a beautiful spring morning, the sun bright and warm, the air scented. Finally on Grendeva! It felt like a year since leaving Jubilee.

The mobile bleeped with directions to somewhere in the nearby capital, Strakencz – my next stop on this odyssey. I hailed a ground taxi and, unsure what to do next, waved my mobile in front of the control unit. It gave a soft affirmative beep and a glowing green light came on – a good sign. We drove away along a smooth raised highway leading to the city. Behind us in the precinct around the spaceport was a cluster of modern industrial and high-rise buildings, but below there were old-fashioned wooden houses and narrow dirt roads. High mountains circled in the far distance – meaning Strakencz was situated in the middle of a giant, lush valley.

Then the most bizarre sight: a man sitting in a wooden two-wheeled vehicle piled high with produce being towed by a large quadruped covered in hair. What the hell was that? I scanned it with my mobile and got *horse and cart*. Wasn't that something from Old Earth? From the *prehistory* of Old Earth? How could this archaic technology be sitting side by side with electric ground cars and space travel? We passed over rutted roads and I spied another person, this time riding on one of these same 'horses'. A female figure wearing metallic clothing. No, not clothing, actual pieces of metal bolted onto her person. The mobile gave me a name: *knight in armor*.

We came up on the city suddenly. This was because there were almost no high buildings, everything squat and low. Old-fashioned wood and brick houses mixed with the occasional modern hardiplaz towers, one of which, I spied reassuringly, had a Galactic League flag flying atop. That meant Grendeva, however backward, was still a part of human civilization, followed protocol for jurisprudence and so many other things. We left the highway and traveled slowly on streets that the mobile told me were called *cobblestone*. Then I slapped my forehead, remembering the data dumped into my brain all those weeks ago.

I closed my eyes and directed my consciousness to a certain corner of my mind. It's hard to describe, but imagine a small black box at the bottom of a deep well. I dived down into the well, opened the box and let what was inside pour out. Images and 'memories' from Grendeva washed over me in a confusing rush. But this was better, the sights and sounds now had names. Beside us was a *steam car* and across the road a shop full of *pigeons* in cages. The streets were crowded. Most people wore a bizarre collection of traditional Grendevan clothes, though occasionally I saw someone, usually younger, wearing Galactic Standard. Were they off-worlders? *No*, came the answer from within, *young people these days are giving up the old ways*.

We stopped in front of an impressive storefront signed *Hendrickson's*. My mobile bleeped, the pilot light turned red and the passenger-side door opened. Guess we'd arrived. I got out of the cab and went to pull open the front door, but instead a liveried servant wearing a long coat and top hat pushed it open from inside.

"Welcome to Hendrickson's, sir," he said with a deep bow.

"Ah thanks," I muttered awkwardly. Two days ago I was the scum of the galaxy eating from rubbish bins and now people were bowing to me.

"Ah Prince Humphrey," said an oily, mellifluous voice from the rear of what I now perceived to be a clothing store. "We've been expecting you, good sir!" The voice belonged to a tall, thin and very stooped man dressed in an old-fashioned jacket and breeches with a tape measure around his neck.

My heart sank as I realized what was coming next – a fit-out. For the crazy clothing of a Grendevan aristocrat.

"My name is Otto. Please, this way." He bowed, wringing his hands and gesturing to the rear of the store.

I tried not to sigh as I made my way to the fitting room.

Otto turned from me and barked, "Shimon! Worthless prick, where are you?"

A small, rodent-like man appeared from the back of the store.

Otto scowled. "Tea and cakes for the gentle sir. Move fast or you'll be feeding fishes in Elberthal River!" The small man disappeared and Otto turned back with an unctuous smile. "So, I hear you've been off world studying, sir? Several years, sir? Need a complete new wardrobe? Well, you've come to the right place here at Hendrickson's!"

As he talked, the tape measure slipped expertly around various parts of my body and notes were made in a tiny book made of real paper. Shimon returned with a tray of tea and cakes. I tried one while Otto barked for more things to be fetched – without doubt the best cake I'd ever eaten. Drawers and boxes were opened, scissors snipped and minor adjustments made while Otto produced a stream of annoying, polite comments.

"Very handsome in that, sir, makes you even taller," he clucked. "The good lady will *love* that one. Nice to be home, can't trust those off-worlders, can you, sir?"

Finally I came before the mirror clad in Grendeva's finest: white stockings, a mottled tartan kilt with ceremonial curved dagger or *khanjar*, ruffled shirt, cravat and plumed cap. Then it was off to 'grooming' where my hair was teased, pancake-white makeup slathered on my face and kohl applied to my eyes to 'help them stand out'. The only consolation was that my buddies back on Brouggh would never – *ever* – get to see this. Such hope dashed moments later when Danee, or should I say 'Lady Darmley', arrived and immediately took a photo with her mobile.

Otto bowed so low I thought he'd fall to the ground. "Lady *Darmley!*" he croaked. "What an honor to have you in our pathetically humble establishment." He bowed his way backward to the rear of the store and screamed for Shimon to bring refreshments.

"Thank you, Otto," said Danee imperiously. "That will not be necessary, the prince and I shall be taking our leave at once. Please allow me to settle the account."

"Of course, milady, of course."

Otto bowed his way to the register, where Danee paid in yellow-colored metal discs that my data file told me were *gold coins*. Then as Otto grimaced and waved, Shimon loaded our vehicle – a gilded horse-drawn carriage, naturally – with a huge collection of bags and boxes, and we were gone.

As soon as we pulled away Danee bent over, put her face in her hands and belly-laughed for five minutes. She came up for air, tears streaming, then looked at me and cracked up again.

She was dressed in the simple clothes of a Grendevan noblewoman: coarse woolen pants, a simple androgynous shirt and hair parted in two long braids. Some might consider that unflattering, but to me she looked as gorgeous and tantalizing as ever and I could not help myself. The moment her convulsions ended, we clutched and pawed at each other with gusto.

"I missed you!" she said finally.

It was a shock to realize how glad I was to see her, how drawn to her I felt.

"Me too, hell of a trip."

"Tell me about it! Took *two full days* and *seven* jumps to get here!"

I just looked at her. How could I put into words the nightmare journey from Jubilee?

The public gawped as we passed along the bumpy streets of Strakencz. Older people bowed and parents held up children to catch glimpses of the 'royals' inside. The change in my circumstances was dizzying. Danee had richly enjoyed herself these past two weeks waiting for me to arrive. She'd made good contact with our benefactors and indulged in all kinds of royalish activities: horse riding, archery, boar hunting in the woods and so on.

"This place *suits* me! I don't have to worry about dressing up, the air is clean, the food delicious and all the men are nicely suppressed. It's brilliant!"

I caught a glimpse of myself in the passenger vanity mirror and scowled. "You like it too much."

We turned onto a long, pebbled driveway lined with trees. In the distance was a giant stone building festooned with turrets, royal banners and whatnot – a fairy-tale castle straight out of a holo-drama. Liveried servants in more crazy uniforms waited at the grand entrance, whisking us and our luggage to Danee's suite upstairs, where we would freshen up before the night's feast. I sat on the bed while a serving robot unpacked the shopping, my reflection glowering at me from the mirror opposite.

"Should I get out of all this? Guess I'll only have to put it back on again later."

Danee cackled. "Now you know what it's like to be a woman!" She lay on the bed, bright-eyed and gorgeous.

"I have a deep need to ravage you right now," I said, "but I can't afford to mess up these clothes and hair."

"Oh," she said, with slitted eyes, "there are ways around *that*."

Turns out that wearing a kilt (which, let's be honest, is just a skirt) does allow easy access to certain parts of the anatomy. Just as things got interesting, however, I looked up to see the robot standing next to the bed, stupidly looking at us for instructions.

"Don't worry, Col," Danee said, "these droids are mechanical – no AI. *Robot,* stand in the corner and face the wall."

"Yes, milady," it said in a tinny voice, then plodded to the corner and turned around.

She smiled wickedly. "Now, where were we?"

Grendeva had not been settled till the last days of the Expansion. On the far side of the galaxy from Old Earth and thousands of parsecs from its nearest neighbor, it was thought by the original surveyors too remote for colonization. Word had got out, though. This dazzling, jewellike planet with clean air, a moderate climate, rich soil and abundant natural resources proved irresistible to settlers.

Then came the Collapse. With a small population and thin industrial base, cut off from galactic trade and communication, the economy had failed. Zoo animals such as horses were pressed into service as the machines broke down. Chaos, barbarism and all kind of nastiness reigned and knowledge of the outside galaxy was lost. This Age of Darkness lasted for millennia, ended finally by Queen Amelia the Just – who may or may not have existed.

In other words, the men had cocked things up so badly, the women decided to take over. In practice feudal titles such as 'Lord' and 'Lady' were maintained, only now of course the Ladies were the ones in charge.

When contact had been re-established a mere century ago, the various policy wonks and sociologists from the Galactic League had dithered and debated and taken things slowly. After all, people weren't eating each other as in some places. The elites were carefully reintroduced to the galactic community through off-world education and a small middle class emerged. Outside the cities, though, little had changed. And what to do about the sexist matriarchal order?

Before the feast, we were ushered into a private room to meet with our benefactors. Lady Fenwick greeted Danee with a warm hug, then shook my hand briskly. She stood ramrod straight and had black eyes that scanned me in cool appraisal.

"And this is Col, yes?"

"Pleased to meet you, Lady Fenwick," I said, then butchered some kind of half bow, half curtsey.

She looked amused. "Pleased to meet you too. It's been lovely getting to know Danee. A compensation, I suppose, for the mess my idiot husband, the prince, has gotten us into." Her voice hardened at the mention of the prince.

He stepped forward, nonchalantly shaking my hand, eyes twinkling. "Pleased to meet you, Col." Then in a whisper, "Or should I say, Donny?"

This voice sounded familiar – Donny's mysterious (and generous) 'brother' Rob. I tried to take this in as we were seated in lounge chairs and served aperitifs by a clanking domestic robot. Danee sat opposite with Lady Fenwick and immediately struck up conversation.

I turned to the prince. "So you're Rob?"

He seemed excited. "Did it suffice!? I believe 'twas a fair impression of a modern middle-class Grendevan man, if I do say so myself!"

"Mmm…yes, well done, but I don't understand, how did you come to answer that call?"

The prince pulled a mobile out of his pocket. "This arrived from Douglas. He said if anyone called, 'twould be yourself pretending to be a certain 'Donny'. My role was to be your brother and send a little money. Good show, it was!"

"Douglas?" I muttered faintly.

"Yes! He said you may or may not have the, quote: 'wit to figure it out'. Obviously, you did!"

Not till the end of my trip, till I was falling apart. I would have to take this up with Douglas – if I ever saw him again. Why hadn't he given me a heads-up about the potential lifeline from 'Rob'? Maybe one of his practical jokes?

We chatted and the prince seemed nice enough. A short plump man with a ruddy face. He and Lady Fenwick were the only two people on Grendeva who knew what Danee and I were up to. He'd run up a very large debt on Jubilee and convinced his wife – Chair of the Council of Wise Women – to go along with our little scheme.

"Now, Col," said Lady Fenwick, fixing me with a laser-like stare, "Danee *assures* me there will be no repercussions from your trip to Rethne. Is that so?"

"I've taken her right through it," said Danee.

"Yes, that's right, um, milady," I said, not quite sure how to address a planetary ruler. "We put a lot of thought into it. Nothing will come back on Grendeva, I am certain of it." If I'd been able, I would have been crossing all my fingers at that moment. And touching wood.

"Make sure it is so. We can ill afford a contretemps with the Movement. Just as we could ill afford the bill my husband ran up on Jubilee." She pursed her lips and glared at the prince.

He shrugged and gave a cheeky, unembarrassed smile. This was surely not the first time Lady Fenwick had dug hubby out of the doodah. A chime sounded.

"Dinner. Excellent!" said the prince.

There was a long table seating at least fifty people, men down one side facing the women with Lady Fenwick seated in the center. The head of the table was unoccupied, waiting I assumed for King Leonard's arrival. I was at the farthest end away from him, presumably lowest on the pecking order.

"And who are *you*, then?" said an old gent with bright red face to my left.

"Humphrey, Prince Humphrey," I said, delving into my Grendevan 'memories'.

"Never *heard* of you. Where'd you say you were from?"

"Ah…well, I didn't, but Cantabriach."

"What? *Speak up!*" There was a large old-fashioned hearing aid fixed into his ear. Clearly Grendeva was yet to be given access to the regenerative biotech enjoyed elsewhere in the galaxy.

"*Cantabriach*," I repeated loudly.

People turned to look – the last thing I wanted.

"Oh *Cantabriach!*" said the old man, chuckling. "I know a few people down there – what's your line of peerage then?"

A nightmare question, the answer to which bubbled up from somewhere deep down. "My father is second Earl of Streslau and our manor is in southern Illyria – all a bit obscure, I'm afraid." But if someone did bother to look, they'd find a complete family history of the good Streslaus, freshly implanted into the peerage records.

"Well, you *are* a long way from home, aren't you, lad? No wonder I never heard of you." He held out a tremulous, veined hand. "Count Ludwig." We shook. "I was in Cantabriach for a wedding once…."

The count launched into a long, boring anecdote from his youth – so boring that everyone nearby tuned out. Fine with me, I wanted to make as few ripples as possible. Bugles sounded and everyone stood. A tall, fit-looking man sashayed into the room wearing mirror sunglasses and the most extravagant clothing and headgear I'd seen yet. Instead of pancake-white makeup, he was tanned a deep brown, either from long hours sunbaking or, more likely, heavy use of the tanning bed. He took off the glasses with a flourish, handed them to a waiting servant, and smiled broadly, revealing two rows of perfectly straight, brilliant white teeth. Clearly the king had access to dental procedures not yet widely available on Grendeva.

He held both arms out theatrically. "Friends. *Welcome!* Be seated."

There was a murmuring and scraping of chairs. Waiters ran around topping up wine – which I'd already discovered was delicious.

The king held out a bejeweled hand for his goblet to be filled. "Let us raise our glasses in thanks on this special day. In thanks to Queen Amelia the Just and our magnificent forebears, who were just so…*magnificent*. Who established this commonwealth, this era of plenty, with plentiful food and—"

"Get to the *point*, Leo," snapped Lady Fenwick.

The king jerked visibly. "Yes, yes, well, anyway, let us *toast!*"

We all drank. It was clear from the last interchange where the real power in the room lay. In Grendeva's matriarchal system, the Council of Wise Women elected the king and could depose him at any time. Leonard was popular – though there was much gossip about his marital status (confirmed bachelor). The holo-streams covered his life in forensic detail: his attendance at fashionable events – always with a new lady – and other appearances consisting mainly of cutting ribbons, hosting dinners and waving to the public from his carriage. Everyone seemed happy with the arrangement.

Waiters plied the table with one delectable course after another. This was an annual event to celebrate the founding of Grendeva's 'modern' system of government.

I was halfway through the eighth or ninth course (I lost track eventually) when the count tapped his bowl of lemon sorbet. "You know, when I was a boy, something like this was an *absolute* luxury! The icemen would take big blocks down from the mountains and sell it to the grand houses. Or grind it up on the street – people would line up around the block. Nowadays, the off-worlders and their gadgets...." He trailed off, then found his point again. "I tell you, nothing is *special* anymore!"

Then came the speeches, details of which are impossible to remember due to extreme dullness. Finally, all was done and it was time for the gentlemen and ladies to retire to their separate salons.

As we broke from the table, Danee fixed me with an intense look and crooked a finger for me to come over. She grabbed my shirt and drew me close. "Get with one of those *sexbots*," she whispered fiercely, "and I will have *these* in a jar!" She was pointing at my nether regions.

I shrugged and made a facial expression signifying innocence – easy to do since I had no idea what she was talking about.

But I found out soon enough. Sliding doors to the dining room were flung open and the men filed into a large room decorated with chandeliers and oil paintings depicting various creatures being hunted down by people on horseback. There was a billiards table, soon in use, and lots of stuffed armchairs. Serving robots appeared, but not like the others I'd seen around the castle. These looked like young women with bright red lipstick, short skirts and stockings. A smaller number of male bots appeared too – catering for all tastes, I guess.

"Brandy and cigar, sir?" said one of the bots, proffering a tray. "Or would you prefer *something else?*"

I smiled nervously. She had full lips and long eyelashes and looked and moved like a real woman – though under the influence perhaps of a stupefying drug.

"Ahm...brandy, thank you," I said, helping myself.

"Anything I can *do*, just let me know," she said with a wink. Then she swished around, skirt swirling upward to reveal suspenders and a perfect bare bottom.

I gulped, remembering Danee's bloodcurdling threat, and started counting backward from one hundred.

"Never indulge?" asked Count Ludwig from behind. "Best you'll find," he said, waving a huge cigar at me, "anywhere on Grendeva."

"Maybe later," I muttered.

I tried to get away, but the count attached himself to me like a limpet. Which turned out to be OK because he took me around and introduced me to all and sundry, burnishing my backstory, explaining I was from an obscure but noble family from far-off Cantabriach.

The king sat on a couch at the far end of the room, sexbot on each knee (male and female), lit cigar and brandy in hand. He was grinning broadly, flashing those white teeth, and holding forth to a cluster of men. Talk in the room became earthy, with tales of hunting expeditions and bawdy stories from misspent youth. In the end, not all that different to a guys' night out on Brouggh – except for the sexbots, with whom there was quite a bit of pawing and groping, followed by short liaisons somewhere out the back. Time crawled.

I was saved eventually when a normal household droid appeared holding a silver tray with a single piece of folded paper. "From Lady Darmley, sir."

I flipped open the note to read, *Had enough? Meet me at the postern.*

With great relief I saluted my new acquaintances – "The good lady calls," – then waved as I scurried out of the men's parlor. I found my way to the rear exit after learning what 'postern' meant.

Danee was standing on the grass outside, gazing up at the night sky. She held out a hand and we walked together in silence.

"I want to show you something," she said finally.

The night was pearlescent from one of Grendeva's moons settling toward the horizon. We reached a small stream and sat together on its bank.

"Look."

She pointed to the stream, where faint lights moved. As my eyes adjusted, I made out tiny shapes, hopping and flopping in the water, glowing with a pale green light. Then I noticed the air around buzzing with flying lights the same color.

"They're called *lucciole*," she said. "That light is bioluminescence. There's worms, little frog-like critters and butterflies – they all glow at night."

The creatures jumped and chirped around together in the dark. Geologically speaking, Grendeva is a young planet. When humans arrived, they found forests, meadows and fish in the sea, but no land animals – hence no need for the plants to develop protective thorns – and no biting insects either. These beautiful glowing things were the only wildlife native to Grendeva.

"This whole planet is benign," Danee said, "except for humans, of course."

We lay on the bank gazing at the stars. As well as being located at the extreme 'top' edge of the galaxy, Grendeva sits hundreds of light-years 'below' the flattish plain where most stars lie. This meant that the night sky was spectacular, the galaxy with its spiral arms of stars spread out across the heavens like a giant glowing disc.

"So, what goes on in the ladies' parlor?" I asked, breaking our rapt silence.

Danee snorted. "Pretty boring, matters of state and all that. And your night?"

"Well…after you've been with one sexbot, they're pretty much all the same."

She tickled my ribs. "Watch it, you."

We lay together, snuggling for warmth against the cool spring night, taking in the light show above and around us. One of those special moments you look back on. Something beautiful before the horror show waiting on Rethne.

CHAPTER TWENTY-SIX

Things moved quickly. A ship appeared the next day, our 'royal' spacer, the *Sandhurst*. Batum came back from the shop, rebuilt to look like one of the household droids, and we inspected him in our suite. He was now one meter tall with old-fashioned ball joints at the elbows and knees, and sporting a slip-on suit complete with bow tie that slid over the top of his silvery metallic body. Perfectly functioning, if a thousand years out of date.

"Happy now?" he asked grumpily, spinning around to give us a good look.

I caught sight of myself in the mirror, decked out in Grendevan finery. "How do you think *I* feel, buddy?"

The robot laughed aloud. "I guess we're all making sacrifices."

A bunch of documents arrived from Lady Fenwick. Our *royal commission* declaring us emissaries to Rethne – signed by the king, stamped and embossed with gold leaf all over the place. Anywhere else in the galaxy these would be electronic. Excellent, the weirder the better. As final preparations were made, we took a walk in the woods and tried to enjoy our last hours on Grendeva.

"I'm going to miss this place," sighed Danee.

"In spite of myself," said Batum, "I will too."

I walked in silence, obsessing about the trip. In the afternoon, Lady and Prince Fenwick visited our rooms to say goodbye and within the hour we were gone, the blue-green orb of Grendeva growing small in our monitors. Danee had appointed herself pilot – fine by me. She tweaked our course in the hours it took for us to exit Grendeva's gravity well. Normally you'd do this work on your kom, but being a Grendevan ship....

I explored our luxurious vessel and noticed something interesting about its interior design. There's a general 'look' to spacecraft we've all become familiar with. Minimalist, square edges, lots of white space. It's been this way for thousands of years and must have emerged somehow from male sensibility because the women of Grendeva, creating their ships from first principles, had arrived at something quite different. Everything about the *Sandhurst* was curved, soothing and feminine. Our master bedroom was decked out with a chandelier, the walls lined with soft pink faux fur, and it featured a four-poster bed with lace canopy.

We needed six jumps for this trip – which, trust me, is a lot. Danee charted a course taking us anticlockwise around the galaxy, passing close to the galactic core. Allowing for a reset between each jump, we'd need forty-eight hours of elapsed time. We stored our mobiles in a stasis locker for the duration – didn't want anything recorded on them that might be compromising.

I played a lot of chess with Batum, which was new to him. He always beat me, of course, but I started to get an appreciation for it.

The ship was crawling with royal household robots. One of them seemed to irritate Batum the most.

"Hey, moron," I heard him say to the official 'security droid'.

"Yes, sir."

"Don't call me that, I'm just another robot, like you."

"Yes, sir."

Batum loosed a string of expletives. "Tell me something, what are your official duties on this little jaunt of ours?"

"Sir, I am a class one royal security droid, sir."

"So, tell me, what's your job? Who are you protecting?"

"Sir, my job is to protect alpha, Lady Darmley, on all occasions and if possible Prince Humphrey as well, sir."

"And how are you going to do that, robot? You're just a dumb pile of metal from what I can see."

"Thank you, sir."

"Don't *thank* me! Do a good job, robot, or I'll have you melted down for scrap!"

"Yes, sir, thank you, sir."

Batum cursed again and walked away.

After our third or fourth jump, Danee called us up to the control room. "You really want to see this!"

She pushed a button and metal shutters slid open. Burning impossibly bright before us was the galactic core. Millions of suns dragged together into a colossal ball of incandescent light. Vast, terrifying, majestic. At its center a supermassive black hole, invisible and hungry, pulling everything into itself.

"It's so bright, I've got the window down to five per cent," said Danee. "I'll have to close it soon or we're gonna cook."

We stood silently, in awe. Galactic forces at their most primal. We were privileged to see this sight only because we were in a royal spacer, built with the luxury of a window, and only because Danee had pushed the envelope taking us this close.

She closed the shutters with an apology. "We'll be jumping shortly. Gotta move or this baby will fry!"

★   ★   ★

Before our last jump to Rethne's system, there was a final meeting in the control room.

"So, this is it," I said. "How are we all feeling?"

"It is what it is," said Batum phlegmatically – and a little mysteriously.

"In a weird way, I'm kinda looking forward to it," said Danee. "Finally some action."

"Agreed. One last thing, very important." I looked at them both intensely. I'd been thinking about how to face Gilham ever since meeting the Swami. "No matter *what* happens, we never drop out of character. I have…information about Gilham, about the way he thinks." Danee raised her eyebrows. "He's a…*wrong crystallization*. He cannot be trusted or reasoned with. Will not compromise. He can only be defeated head-on. So, let's agree? We never back down, no matter the circumstances, no matter *what* happens."

"We never back down," echoed Danee.

Batum looked me in the eye. "No matter what happens."

CHAPTER TWENTY-SEVEN

The jump took us to within five million klicks – eight hours on the gravity drive. Danee brought Rethne up on the monitor and a more complete opposite to Grendeva you could not imagine. A sandy giant with an ancient rocky core. Ice caps covering two-thirds of it, a ribbon of human settlement unbroken around the equator. No discernible oceans or rivers and swirling outward from the equator, bands of brown and red – jagged mountains and valleys, empty and desolate-looking even from this distance.

A huge volume of traffic was in orbit off Rethne, creating a fuzzy halo in our monitors, evidence this unlikely planet was at the center of a large and growing galactic movement. Craft of every size and description were waiting to land or exchange goods. Somewhere in that scrum waited a medium-sized freighter surreptitiously taken over by Douglas. We would not wait in orbit. The *Sandhurst* would land at a private spaceport reserved for VIPs. We got changed: Danee into her simple pants and shirt, me into all the fancy crap of a Grendevan gentleman. I studied myself in the mirror. Kilt and plumed hat, teased hair and ever-so-handsome, made-up face. I would have to look this way the whole time on Rethne. A kept man, mild and subservient. I ground my teeth and reminded myself it was all for Sana.

We descended and our perspective changed from planetary to bird's-eye. We made out buildings, suburbs and factories – not dissimilar to any League planet. Except on Rethne they formed a line of settlement fifty kilometers wide stretching as far as the eye could see. In the distance a dust storm blew a mustard-yellow plume of sand across the city. Coming into view, a small spaceport with a flotilla of ground cars waiting on the tarmac.

As the ship settled, we gathered at the airlock with our entourage of droids and luggage. Danee gave me a wink, then strode out along the freshly unrolled red carpet to the sound of a brass band and soft applause. I followed a few steps behind.

The air was cold and dry, the light sharp. A biting wind blew grit into my face. Gravity was heavy at around 1.5 G – and although that fifty per cent extra mightn't sound like much, I could feel it already in the legs. I walked through an honor guard of public officials, all beaming and applauding. They shared a common body type, short and squat, obviously an adaptation to this heavy planet. At the end of the row stood a tall, thin figure dressed entirely in white. He flicked a strand of dark hair out of his face, strode forward to meet Danee and shook her outstretched hand with both of his.

"Lady Darmley. I welcome you to Rethne with all my heart." He put a palm to his chest and smiled.

"Thank you," said Danee. "I'm sorry, is it Gilham or Mr. Gilham? How does one address you?"

He laughed loudly as if this were the funniest joke ever – though with unsmiling eyes. He wore loose pants and a simple top with a shawl wrapped around his bony shoulders for the biting wind. "Please, just call me Gilham."

"Then you shall call me Juliette, and may I introduce Prince Humphrey of Cantabriach?"

I did a little bow and offered a limp hand, which he shook with little interest. Then, turning back to Danee, he said, "I'm sorry but shortly, I will have to leave you with Mehrqu here" – he gestured to a beaming man in a gray uniform, squat-shaped like the others – "but we'll be catching up tonight. I wanted to personally welcome you to Rethne."

"*Very* kind, what an honor!" Danee directed her highest wattage smile at him, a ray beam usually guaranteed to make men weak at the knees.

Gilham seemed impervious. He tilted his head toward the man and spoke coldly. "Come!"

Mehrqu trotted over. "So pleased to meet you! The car is waiting, let's get you out of this wind!"

Danee turned, strode off and snapped her fingers at me to follow like a good Grendevan noblewoman. I caught Gilham staring at this so I smiled, shrugged and rolled my eyes as if to say, *"Women! What can you do?"* He looked at me for a long moment, face impassive. His lip curled into a sneer, then he turned and walked away without a word.

Perfect. Let him think me a powdered fool.

"I will be your guide here on Rethne," said Mehrqu as our convoy left the spaceport. "I do hope you like our beautiful planet."

At that moment a vicious gust of wind rattled the ground car, whipping yellow sand into our window. Nothing about Rethne seemed beautiful to me.

"That's just a dust storm." He waved at the window. "We get 'em all the time, but then it dies down and it's beautiful and still – especially out in the desert!" His eyes gleamed with enthusiasm. Was he always this bright and cheery? "Shortly we will arrive at your accommodation – which I'm pleased to advise will be the Residence!" He clapped his hands with excitement.

I had glimpses of the streetscape through the thickening dust storm. Most buildings were made of laser-cut orange or brown stone combined with bright-colored hardiplaz. There were pictures of Gilham everywhere – in front of large crowds, shaking hands with VIPs. I was dying to ask what his role in the government was, but that wouldn't be in Prince Humphrey's character, would it? So I just gazed out the window.

The storm died down. We traveled along a grand boulevard with a grassy center. On either side, large public buildings sported Rethnean flags and more pictures of Gilham, and in the far distance a tall, needlelike building rose over the city. Unusually, I made out no League flags anywhere. Our convoy turned onto a small laneway leading to a security gate, which opened automatically. We drove into a vast and beautiful park, the first I'd seen. A rolling lawn spread out before us, landscaped with trees, shrubs, flower beds and what from a distance looked like raised gardens for vegetables. We followed a winding road, made a final turn and came upon a looming, unpleasant-looking structure. A giant rectangle made of brown brick. Slit windows at ground level, a smaller square shape seemingly plonked on top.

"This building," said Mehrqu, "used to be a commercial incinerator and before that a power station. Believe it or not!" I believed it. "And the parkland we drove through was a rubbish dump. The Master had it all converted."

"Is that so?" said Danee. "Rather a large to-do for one person?"

Mehrqu laughed nervously. "Oh but the gardens are open to the public every weekend and they host all kinds of people here, politicians, civic leaders, even *celebrities!*"

Armed guards saluted as we pulled up and another red carpet lay waiting. We alighted to applause from the domestic staff clustered around the front door. I tried to look around casually to see if Sana was among them – but no luck.

Mehrqu pumped us both with double handshakes. "I'll be leaving you here, Lady Darmley and Prince Humphrey. It was wonderful to meet you!"

"You won't accompany us inside?" I asked.

Mehrqu looked down, shoulders hunched. "I'm not allowed in there, only people like yourselves." Then he brightened. "But I'll see you tomorrow at oh eight hundred hours. I can't wait to show you our *beautiful* planet!"

Another man escorted us inside. Shaved head, gray uniform, with a bearing that screamed ex-military. He didn't say a word, merely gestured with an open palm. Inside we found a grand entrance with staircases running from our left and right up to the next floor. Above us was a void filled by an immense crystal chandelier and straight ahead an entire wall made of glass with views across an ornamental lake to the city. I spied a lift, but our host pointed to the right-hand staircase. We trooped up and then along a corridor, our footsteps loud on the polished concrete floor. There were automated sliding doors on each side of us. They swished open occasionally whenever someone got close, momentarily revealing rooms and other corridors. This place was a labyrinth.

After some time we stopped eventually in front of a door marked with a number one.

The man leading us finally spoke. "Welcome to the Residence. Lady Darmley, please…." He gestured for Danee to hold up her palm.

She obliged and he did something with his kom that made the door slide open.

"It's now programmed for your palm. Prince Humphrey?"

I held up my hand and we repeated the procedure.

"My name is Duraqu. You will relax in your rooms for a while." This last as much a command as a question. This guy was tightly wound – I imagined if something pricked his skin he'd explode in coils of sinew and tendon.

"This evening you will be dining with the Master," he said. "Someone will come for you at seven. If you require anything, please page me on your koms." He looked at our wrists, then blinked. "Apologies, I forgot. On your *mobiles*."

He put his palms together in front of his chest, snapped his heels with military precision and made a short bow. Then turned and strode off down the corridor.

The robots followed us inside. A sparse two-room apartment equipped with a low, futon-style bed, lounge and bathroom. I was getting the picture – interiors at the Residence were a certain kind of décor: *religious fanatic austere*. Glass doors led to a small balcony. Without speaking we stepped out to find impressive views of the parkland and lake. It was a relief to be outside. Our room occupied the back right-hand corner, with other balconies running along the rear of the building – presumably more VIP suites. The robots busied themselves unpacking, while the Grendevan 'security' droid took up station at the door.

Batum joined us on the balcony and put his hand around each of our wrists. "Can you hear me?" asked a voice inside my head. "Don't say anything, I'm sending a signal directly to your eardrum. Reply subvocally."

I tried it. "Can you hear this?" I made the words in my mind and throat without speaking aloud.

"Roger that," said Batum.

"How's this?" asked Danee.

We both nodded.

"There is a small surveillance gap here on the left side of the balcony," he said. "That's because it's an old building and also because the Grendevan security droid is putting out a semi-effective cloaking field – so we're OK talking like this."

"What did you think of Gilham?" I asked Danee.

"Weirdo."

"You notice they call him the *Master*?"

"Yeah, that's weird too."

"Big news, guys," said Batum. "I've detected a *huge* AI, just like Douglas predicted."

"What sense do you get of it?" I asked.

"How can I put it in human terms? If Douglas were a big friendly whale, then *this thing,* it's like…a giant tarantula. Nasty, scary. It's constantly trying to penetrate me. I don't know how long I can hold it off."

"Give me a time frame?" I asked.

"Maybe a day or two."

Sobering news.

"But even if it gets through," said Batum, "don't worry, my code will auto-scramble. No data will be compromised."

Maybe not, but the end for Batum. For the first time it struck me that I'd also put him in danger, along with Danee. The robots finished unpacking, lined up in the lounge room and went into sleep mode. Batum joined them, while Danee and I took a rest. It was late afternoon and my body felt tired from even this short exposure to Rethne's heavy gravity. We lay on the bed and talked, but in character.

"What do you think of Rethne, Humph'?"

"I miss Grendeva already."

"Don't worry, dear, we'll be back home before you know it."

And so on. A pain in the butt really – but important to keep up appearances. I flicked through some holo-channels. Lots of propaganda featuring Gilham, some historical dramas – total crap. Did we feel like prisoners? Not quite, but there wasn't exactly anywhere else to go either.

After some time, we hauled ourselves out of bed and got ready, Danee in just a few minutes, myself wearily, taking much longer with all the makeup and hair products. At seven there was a polite tap on the door.

"*ATTENTION!*" said the security robot in a shrill, mechanical voice. "Rethne household staffer approaching, *NO THREAT DETECTED!*"

"Thank you, robot," said Danee, then to the door, "We'll be right out."

They took us through a maze of corridors – all with the same white walls and gray floor – down the stairs to ground level. Batum followed behind, brought along as a domestic.

Talking could be heard from deep inside the building, then moments later we emerged into a large dining room with views across to the lake. There were about twenty people, milling and murmuring, becoming silent as they turned to look, then big smiles and applause. The room contained no ornamentation or furniture of any kind except for a low, round table and an easel holding a board that read:

Welcome to Rethne!

Lady Darnley & Prince Humphrey

Duraqu stood 'at ease' in the far corner, legs apart, confirming for me his role: security. Everyone clustered around Danee, wineglasses in hand, making introductions. All men. One guy appeared to be the alpha. Bull-headed and squat like everyone else, he chatted easily like someone used to being in charge. Minutes later a gong sounded and we made our way to the round table. Each of us stood in front of a cushion, Danee to my left, Batum waiting behind her, ready to serve.

The room fell silent. Expectant. A single empty cushion remained – no different or fancier than the others. The silence grew. I saw a flicker of annoyance pass over the face of the bull-headed man. Finally, a door panel slid open and Gilham strode into the room.

"Welcome, friends," he said with hands pressed together. "Please be seated."

There was rustling and a few grunts as we settled down onto our cushions, some more limberly than others. Gilham sat smoothly with practiced ease and made eye contact with one of the waiters. Plates of food and carafes of wine began appearing.

"Does this please you, Juliette?" he asked, eyes glittering. "We thought you'd appreciate something familiar for your first night."

The food being served was Grendevan. Someone, or a team more likely, had put together a 'package' for our stay. These Movement people had studied us. They were organized, dangerous. I silently prayed our Grendevan cover stories would stand up to scrutiny.

"Just like home!" said Danee. "Though I do hope we may also sample Rethnean fare?"

"Naturally," said Gilham.

Everyone started helping themselves, heaping food onto their plates – everyone, that is, except Gilham, because he didn't have one. A minute later our plates were all full, but Gilham's place was still bare. Nobody started eating; they seemed to be waiting for a cue.

A door swished open to my rear. Footsteps as a servant walked behind me and around the table to Gilham, carrying a jug and single plate. As she put his meal down, I caught sight of her face.

Sana!

My stomach lurched.

Sana. Alive. Wearing a white smock and slippers like the other servants. She seemed OK. Maybe some new lines and a tired look about the eyes.

But alive.

I felt impatient. And worried. Our plan suddenly seemed flimsy and mad.

Gilham spoke. "I offer thanks to the *divine power* for this food and for the company of our gracious guests from Grendeva" – he looked around the table – "and for all of you."

Everyone had heads down and hands clasped in prayer – even Sana, I noticed.

"May our work continue to grow. Give us wisdom, give us strength and compassion. *Praise* to the divine power!"

"Praise to the divine power!" we all echoed.

The food on Gilham's plate was different to ours: a medium-sized spoonful of brown rice and a couple of limp, steamed vegetables unadulterated with any dressing. He held out a glass and Sana poured what appeared to be tap water. She caught my stare – of course she wouldn't recognize me – and her eyes narrowed. A classic Sana expression.

Gilham must have picked something up because he tilted his head. "Sana, why don't you be a good girl and give our honored guests one of your nice smiles?"

Sana, her face unmoving, looked coldly at Danee and me, then raised the corners of her mouth very slightly. "Will that be all? *Master.*"

Gilham waved her off. "Till I call you, Sana dear." He picked up his cutlery and started to eat and on that cue so did the rest of the table.

The meal passed in a blur as I tried to calm my whirling mind. I spoke little, which was probably OK since clueless Prince Humphrey would be way out of his depth here. There was toasting and expressions of friendship between Grendeva and Rethne. Dawning of a new day and all that. The bull-headed man turned out to be prime minister and Danee finally asked the question that had been plaguing me.

"So, may I ask, what is the formal relationship between the government of Rethne and the Movement, and Gilham? Is it all one and the same?"

The prime minister went to speak, then looked at Gilham and stopped.

"Go on," said Gilham.

Talk around the table dried up as people tuned in.

"Well, actually, there is no *formal* relationship. Rethne's constitution is of course secular. But when we're making big decisions, naturally the opinions and teachings of" – he stopped himself from saying *the Master* – "of Gilham, they carry a lot of weight."

"He's an adviser?"

"Yes." He looked flustered. "Better to say, *spiritual leader.*"

Gilham nodded in approval. It was clear from this interchange who had the real power. A door slid open and a group of children filed in, eyes down, all dressed in the same brown robes. They looked about six, though they could have been older given how small Rethneans are. Five boys and five girls.

"The choir!" said Gilham brightly. "Excellent, this is something special."

The children all drew a breath as one, then began. They filled the void-like space of the Residence with a celestial beauty, singing in some language I didn't recognize, definitely not Standard. They sang in multipart harmonies that to my ear sounded pitch-perfect. I guess you'd call it folk music and although I didn't understand the words, it seemed to express some ineffable sadness. It was moving, haunting. Gilham wiped a tear. I don't know how long they sang for but the moment seemed suspended in time. When it was over, we all applauded heartily.

As the children bowed and turned to leave, Gilham called out, "Child, your name?" He was talking to one of the boys, the smallest, with dark skin and light blue eyes.

"Haquan, sir." He stood frozen while the rest of the children filed out.

"Come here, let's have a talk."

The boy came closer, shivering with fear.

"Sit for a moment." Gilham gestured and a cushion was brought. "You are at Miqh-ha? In the music program?"

The boy nodded silently, looking down.

"Don't be scared, we're just having a chat. Why are you at Miqh-ha? Did something happen to your parents?"

He nodded again. "Mommy died at the mines and Daddy is off world."

"Doing *seva* for the Movement?"

The boy nodded again.

"Your father is doing something important, something noble. He'll be back soon and then he will take care of you."

The boy gave a small hopeful smile at that, still looking down.

"Tell me, Haquan, do you like it at Miqh-ha?"

The smile vanished and the boy shook his head.

A shadow passed over Gilham's face – not the answer he was looking for in front of VIPs from off world. "No? Aren't you getting musical training? You've become a very good singer."

There was a long pause. "I miss Mommy."

This was getting awkward.

But then – as so often with Gilham – something confounding and extraordinary happened, which I will try to describe exactly as I saw it.

Gilham's attitude softened. He spoke tenderly. "Look at me, child."

The boy looked up and their eyes locked. Gilham held him in his gaze as the room went pin-drop silent. A minute went by and something seemed to pass between them, the tall thin man and the tiny almost-orphan. The boy sighed and his shoulders dropped. He smiled and color returned to his cheeks.

"See? Everything's going to be OK, isn't it?" said Gilham kindly.

Haquan nodded. He looked around the room with bright, curious eyes like a normal boy. What alchemical power lay behind this? A few moments later Sana returned and led Haquan out through the door behind me.

The room came back to life. There were sweets and more toasts. I drank sparingly, mindful of what was to come later this night. Finally, it was over. After much hand-pumping and backslapping, a servant led us away.

"*ATTENTION!* Lady Darmley and Prince Humphrey approaching. *NO THREAT DETECTED!*" announced a muffled robotic voice as we neared the door. I would have to find the mute button to that thing. Inside a note was waiting for us, lying on our bed along with two chocolate mints. Actually it was a card, official-looking and heavily embossed:

Grendeva Delegation to Rethne: Hul-Quha 37,582
Her Royal Highness Lady Darmley & Prince Humphrey

Day 1
AM Monument to the Lost
PM   The Cave
     Satsang

Day 2
AM School visit
Scheduled meeting: Department of Outreach

PM   Farewell banquet (Residence)

Day 3
Official departure, Aum-Al-Quaim Spaceport

These events had all been programmed by M4M, no doubt with psychological purpose to soften us up for the big pitch – the meeting with the Department of Outreach. *Our* big moment was the 'farewell banquet' – when the plan for Sana's escape would finally be executed. Lord help us. I exchanged looks with the others and we stepped outside to the balcony.

"I can see why you married her," said Danee subvocally as soon as Batum touched our wrists.

I pretended to ignore the pointed compliment. "She looked OK to me, what do you think? I've been worrying what Gilham might have—"

"I don't get that vibe from him," cut in Danee. "In fact, I can't ping him at all. Doesn't come across like a straight guy. Or gay, for that matter. Probably likes having Sana wait on him, maybe a power trip?"

"Your bio-neural patterns were being monitored," said Batum. "Col, there was a spike when Sana appeared. I did my best to smooth it out."

"Who was doing the scanning?" asked Danee.

"The security guard, Duraqu. Networked with whatever that thing is out there."

"And how is that going, Batum?" I asked. "Are you still under attack?"

"Yes, it's stressful, but I'm holding my own for the moment."

I prayed Batum could stick it out for another two days.

"Also," said the robot, "don't eat those chocolates on your bed, they're laced with sedative."

"Really? What kind?" I asked.

"Mild. Just enough to make you sleep soundly."

Crikey, these people didn't leave anything to chance. What might be happening here at night that they so didn't want us to know about?

"All right, that's enough for now," I said. "Time to get on with the mission." Then, remembering the Grendevan security droid, I asked, "Batum, can you mute that sentry bot? Can't have it going off all night."

It was dark, but I'm almost certain I caught a glint in the robot's eyes. "With pleasure," he said.

Back in the room, I opened my jewelery box and took out the ring Douglas had given me. It featured a large, sparkling diamond in a fancy gold setting and looked in every way like one of the many extravagant pieces foppish Prince Humphrey wore. But this one was different. This was an amazing piece of newtech from Douglas's R&D labs that projected a broad-spectrum cloaking field. In other words, it made you invisible and not just to the naked eye – also to infrared and any other part of the spectrum. So as not to show up on a scan, it had no internal energy source and was powered in a very crafty way: by *neural field* – drawing power from the wearer's brain, the best way of doing which was to think about it. In practical terms, that meant keeping awareness of the ring constantly in mind. If that awareness lapsed even for a moment, the field collapsed.

I stripped in front of the mirror, earning a wry smile from Danee. Using the device had to be done naked, of course – otherwise you'd see a bunch of clothes walking around with no person inside. Batum waited. He would neutralize the security cameras and maintain the energy profile of the room as if there were still two people inside. I gave a thumbs-up, slipped on the ring – and vanished.

Danee went to our door and listened carefully. This was a delicate moment, as opening the door would be noticed somewhere. She stepped outside, pretending to take a brief stroll down the corridor, *exercising the old legs*. I slipped out in the same moment and was on my way.

The corridor was lit dimly for evening. It was cold and I suppressed a shiver. Now what? We had arrived from the left and turned right to go for dinner. So let's go that way. I padded off, taking care to be quiet. The plan was to look for two things: the AI – or evidence of it as instructed by Douglas – and of course Sana; it was important to know where she slept. I had a third motivation as well: to snoop. My Investigator mind wanted to know what the hell was going on in this place. A dark blot was spreading across the galaxy, emanating from here. I wanted to know how.

My legs were tired, Rethne's gravity taking a toll. It didn't hurt that I had made Prince Humphrey's body so ultra-fit – although he was a big guy, a liability on this planet. I kept an image of the ring in mind using a mnemonic trick that Douglas had suggested and reinforced with a quick hypno-session. I imagined everything before me as a holo-drama with an image of the ring in the bottom right-hand corner of the screen. The ring spun there on a little plinth, like the feature product on a sales channel.

I took a left, then a right. What was there to see? Nothing. Long corridors with closed sliding doors. The moment I activated any of them, it would draw security. This was a problem.

While having this very thought, I stepped too close and a door slid open, revealing an empty meeting room. I stopped in my tracks, became completely still and started counting. How long before there was a response?

Forty-two seconds.

First there were footsteps, two sets. Then came a flickering light from a torch jittering along the floor. One set of footsteps came toward me from the far end of the corridor in the direction I was heading, another set from behind. A pincer. I stood frozen to the ground like a statue while the first guard walked briskly up the corridor and stopped right before me. He wore a gray uniform, was stocky like everyone here. He stood inches away, looking right through me, scowling while I held my breath. I could smell the coffee on his breath, see the pores in his skin. Judging by that stubble, this shift had been a long one already. I stepped ever so quietly out of the way.

Must keep the ring spinning.

He shone his torch around here and there in a desultory fashion, then the second guard arrived and they stood together, glowering at the errant door. I kept my breath even and slow.

"Nothing?" said the second guard.

"What do you think?" said the first.

I had a sudden impulse, a hunch. I stuck a hand out and the door next to me swished open. The guards spun around, instantly alert, then sighed, shoulders slumping as they shone their torches into the empty room.

"Told you," said the first.

"*Fucking* doors," said the other.

This was perfect, those sliding doors were probably the bane of their lives.

"You do a lap then," said the second guard, obviously senior. "I'll see you back at post."

"OK, see you there."

The second guard headed back to base. The first trudged away with a sigh, waving the flashlight. I followed as he opened doors and checked rooms. Even more perfect, a guided tour of the Residence.

The guard traipsed the corridors with me behind, went downstairs and worked his way from one end of the building to the other, looking into storerooms, under benches, behind every object. These people were nothing if not thorough. Unconsciously the guard must have sensed my presence because several times he whirled around and flashed his light exactly where I was standing. Each time I froze and held my breath, awareness locked on the ring.

I built up a mental picture of the Residence. The ground floor was given over to the public. There were meeting rooms and reception areas, an auditorium, several dining halls and a huge commercial kitchen. The second floor was residential. We inspected a bunch of dormitories and bedrooms, many of which were occupied. You'd think a security guard barging into your room in the middle of the night would be a breach of privacy? Not here. Everyone seemed oblivious as we checked out bathrooms, rifled through cupboards and shone lights directly into sleeping faces. How could this be normal? Were they all prisoners, like Sana?

After forty minutes we struck pay dirt.

She was in a corner apartment identical to ours on the opposite side of the building. Even asleep with her back to me, I knew instantly it was Sana. Had they really given her a VIP suite? Why? Maybe part of Gilham's thing: a show of generosity while forcing her to be his servant?

The good news, the *fantastic* news, was that this room – being identical to ours – had a balcony. A lucky break. You would imagine that being security maniacs they might worry about her jumping from it and running away. But where to? She'd be tracked. She'd be picked up in minutes.

They could never imagine the use we would put that balcony to.

We inspected a few more rooms and then tramped back to the atrium. The guard stood at the balustrade and looked down through the void to the ground floor below. The unlit chandelier loomed, a giant dark mass. The guard appeared to be thinking, then apparently decided something, turned and headed off down the stairs. Follow or not? I already had what I needed, at least for tonight. Then again, when your luck is running....

The guard turned left at the base of the stairs toward the elevator, which was inside a small lobby enclosed by glass doors. Another guard was already waiting there; he looked up and waved. My guy used his kom to pass inside, something I'd anticipated, so at the same moment I held up my ring to capture the code. I followed behind, stepping to the side quietly so neither of them might accidentally touch me.

"How's it going?" asked my guard, settling onto a stool.

"Another day in paradise. You pulling another double?"

"Yeah," said my guy, "thanks to that dickhead Shamir and his *fucking* dramas."

I now knew what this was going to be – a bitch session. Entirely familiar. The kind of moaning and groaning that cops and their ilk indulge in throughout the galaxy. I looked around – what was that guy doing here anyway? What was he guarding?

Of course. Idiot.

This had to be Gilham's private elevator. He could descend directly from his quarters to greet people at the front door. Did that mean I could go up there now? Maybe. The code I'd captured on the ring would probably call the lift – but that would generate interest. To the left of the elevator were steps leading upward. Open with *no door in front of them.* The emergency exit. You wouldn't want to have a security door at the bottom of those steps, would you? Because if you ever needed it, the last thing you'd want is a door in the way. And you couldn't call that a security flaw – not really – because of all the cameras and alarms, and a guard always on duty.

Except that tonight, with me wearing my invisibility ring, it *was* a security flaw. Because it meant I could walk straight up those stairs into Gilham's private apartment.

I stepped around the two men now happily swapping hard-luck stories and crept up the stairs – all white like everything else. I turned a corner and their voices became a murmur. Tried to visualize the layout. I'd seen the outside of the Residence that afternoon – a lifetime ago – and noticed a boxlike structure centered on the top of the building – must be Gilham's penthouse. The second floor. I crept higher, hearing nothing from above. I reached a landing and rested, trying to stop myself from panting, legs on fire from the heavy gravity. We would be at first-floor level now. No exit door. What percentage crazy was this? I already had what I needed from the night. Was I pushing my luck or taking advantage of events?

I pushed off the wall and kept going up. The stairs turned again, just one more flight to the top. I could see already – no door at the end. I tiptoed up and couldn't stop myself from hesitantly peering around the corner – as if I were not invisible. A small foyer, dimly lit with a glowing night light on the floor. Two closed doors on the left and a single door on the right. Wide open. I crossed the foyer in a few short steps and looked inside.

An expansive apartment – could only be Gilham's. Just one single room, but huge, with a mezzanine for the bed and windows on three sides. During the day, the view would be majestic. I crept quietly inside. Where was Gilham? Why was he gone in the middle of the night? I padded to the bathroom partitioned off in the right-hand corner. Looked inside – empty.

Better move fast. He could return any moment, close the door and I'd be stuck here.

Next to the bathroom was a dressing area, nothing but all-white clothes. Along the one solid wall backing onto the foyer were shelves running the length of the apartment holding thousands of *books*. The ancient kind. With paper pages that you turn. For a moment I wondered, could these be the real thing, like you see in the museums? This trove would be worth billions. But impossible. Ancient books from Old Earth had to be kept in those special cases filled with inert gas, otherwise they turned to dust. These were reproductions – an impressive collection all the same. They were all seemingly on the topic of spirituality and religion, filed according to subject, Christianity, Sufism and so on.

Apart from the bookshelf and mezzanine, the apartment held only a low table made of white marble with cushions around it to sit on – like at dinner. He probably held meetings here. What else? Nothing. If it were more furnished, you'd say it was a cool apartment. The kind of place you dreamed of when you were in college. But the vibe was creepy, like the Residence itself. I looked up into the mezzanine and saw a low futon bed like the one in my own room. Lying next to it was a serious-looking book, the very title unintelligible: *The Aphorisms of Siva, Dyczkowski*.

Bedtime reading.

Time to move. I stepped back outside into the foyer, then took the stairs down to find the duty guard – now alone – reading on his kom. I waited in the lift lobby for something to happen, wondering whether I should open the glass security door.

Better wait.

I stood still and focused on my breath. In and out. Mindfulness meditation. I ordered the ring to keep spinning, told my body not to be cold and to stay awake. After an hour, something finally did happen, something interesting.

An older man in military uniform entered from the street and stood in the lobby of the Residence just outside our little room. A *big knob* judging by all the silverware on his chest. He motioned to my unwitting companion, who opened the glass doors to join him – allowing me to slip out. I stopped a few paces away. The general – let's say that was his rank – was tall, maybe off-world? He clapped my guard on the shoulder in a friendly way, drew him in close and whispered something in his ear. The guard shook his head and whispered something in return. They parted, the guard to his room, the military man walking across the lobby to a small door I hadn't noticed before, scanning his kom and disappearing down some stairs.

The Residence had a basement. Where generals went in the middle of the night.

This was indeed something. I'd captured the door's security code on my ring, I could go down there if I wanted to – but surely that was suicide?

Unlike every other I'd seen at the Residence, this door opened on a hinge rather than sliding. I stood before it trying to decide whether to try to open it or not, when the decision was made for me.

The door flew open with force and I was face to face with Gilham, evidently mid-argument. I focused madly on the ring, tried to step away from him as quietly as possible and took a couple of paces backward while controlling my breath. But Gilham seemed oblivious. He turned his head and shouted back down the stairs, "*Enough!* No more excuses. I want it resolved *tonight!*" Then he abruptly strode across the lobby to his private lift.

His face was impassive but he was clearly angry and would have bowled me over if I hadn't moved so quickly. But I stepped aside and darted through the open door to the basement.

CHAPTER TWENTY-EIGHT

The door snapped closed behind me. Worn steps disappeared down into the gloom from where I could hear voices. What had I just done? My body had acted purely on instinct – guess I should trust it. *Go with the flow*, Sana's artsy friends used to say – along with other similar platitudes. Easy to say if you're not standing naked in a stairwell in the middle of the night with only a magic ring between yourself and a planet full of homicidal maniacs. For a moment I thought of turning around and bolting back to the room. I let my pounding heart slow. *It's OK, Col*, I told myself, *don't give up, you can handle this* and various other lies. Somewhat restored, I set off down the steps.

Quietly, carefully. The steps were old and well-rounded, curving downward in a spiral. Easy to forget that underneath the ultramodern veneer, this building was ancient. The voices grew louder as I descended. I stopped just short of the landing, listening from around the corner.

"So *that* went well." A deep voice, sarcastic.

"Like I said, was worth a try." A second, also male.

"So you say."

"So let's decide then, do we act or not? It's not like we have other—"

"Gentlemen," cut in a new voice, harsh and metallic, "we have made it perfectly clear, the long-term position is unchanged. Patience will be *rewarded*."

"Always 'patience' with you lot." The first speaker again. "And look where it got you, eh?"

This last must have been incendiary because the room erupted, everyone shouting at once. I used the chance to slip quietly around the corner, super mindful to keep the ring spinning. I found a large room – guess you'd call it a bunker, a huge one – with corridors leading off in three directions. It was filled with machinery, equipment and a large hologram, seated around which were half a dozen men. Though better to say half a dozen *beings*, because one of them was not human.

Not human.

In the middle of the group, seated in a large comfortable chair, was an Aurelian. Staff in hand, his Drax curled up on the floor next to him. I reeled.

The movement was taking support from Aurelia.

Obviously.

And no doubt the large AI that was freaking Douglas and Batum out was being provided by them too. It explained a lot.

The Aurelian rapped his staff on the floor. "Enough!" he said in that metallic voice.

He wore a black cape pinned at the throat and carried the peculiarly grim countenance and bearing of all his race. He had a long, rectangular face with flaky gray skin and a slash of a downturned mouth. His Drax looked old with patchy fur and cloudy eyes. The Aurelians and goatlike Drax had evolved together and shared some kind of ill-understood symbiotic relationship – part emotional, part sexual – that didn't bear thinking about.

"We either trust the calculations provided or not," he said. Then, turning to a large, fat man, chest afire with medals, "and if we're discussing the past, may I remind the good general of where things stood for the Movement before *we* came on board?"

They were squabbling like schoolkids – didn't matter how much tinkling silverware adorned their chests.

I tiptoed around to get a better view of the hologram. A scale model of the galaxy, its spiral arms swirled out into the room. Most of the stars were lit blue, but a large swath toward the 'bottom' – let's say at six o'clock – was colored green. The M4M zone, Rethne at its center, spreading crosswise around the galaxy and inward to the core. There was a small redoubt in the upper reaches of the green section. One blue light surrounded by green bulging all around it.

Brouggh, I realized with a start.

A 3D image of a woman floated in front of the stars. I recognized her – a public official, maybe a judge? The issue being debated involved Brouggh somehow.

The Drax struggled to its feet and made a small whinnying noise. The Aurelian bent over. "What's that, Hrggranthx?" He paused for a moment, in silent communication, then turned to the other men in shock. "She's saying there's someone here. Someone in the room!"

The men all stood up, looking around, looking at their koms. I backed away slowly, barely breathing, desperately keeping the ring spinning in my mind.

"The room's totally clear," said the man I'd seen upstairs. "Nothing scanning at all."

The others murmured in agreement.

"I tell you, she *senses* something," said the Aurelian. "She says it's a human wearing a cloaking device of some kind. Over...*there*!" He pointed directly at me.

"Ridiculous," said the fat general. He strode toward me, waving his hands through the air like a blind man. Missing me, but only by inches.

The Drax took a few shaky steps forward and stopped, clearly terrified. It sniffed. It looked me directly in the eye. Then without warning lunged forward and bit me on the calf with surprisingly sharp teeth.

I shrieked – couldn't help it, shock as much as anything – and swatted the Drax away. I ran off down one of the corridors while commotion erupted behind me, the humans all shouting, the Drax whimpering – I'd given it a good whack, that little motherfucker – the Aurelian banging his staff and proclaiming triumphantly, "I saw him for an instant! Human male, naked."

I must have momentarily lost ring awareness when the Drax bit me. Too quick for the humans, but not for the Aurelian.

An alarm sounded. *Fuck, fuck, fuck.* I sprinted in blind panic. The dark corridor stretched ahead into the distance seemingly without end, chambers and other corridors running off every few steps. I took a left, a right, another left – all at random. Now I was in another long corridor; it was a catacomb down here.

What to do? Stop. Think. Regroup.

But I'm fucked, there's no hope. I'll never get away!

Panic will get you caught.

I leaned against a wall, heart pounding. Forced my mind to slow. OK, I was in a pickle. True. But invisible. Even knowing that I was here, they couldn't see or detect me. So, what would they do?

What would *I* do?

First, seal the area. Make sure I could not escape. Then what?

Call the *canine squad*. Assuming they had one? They would. Go room by room till the dogs sniffed me out. But that would take a while, scrambling a team in the middle of the night. There was still time.

All the lights came on. There was a clanging sound up and down the corridor as the doors to every room slammed shut. I tried the one behind me – locked. I padded along the now brightly lit corridor. Far behind, voices and the tramping of feet. After jogging for ten minutes I came upon a locked bulkhead door blocking the way. I was trapped. I looked up – nothing but bare rock. These corridors were really tunnels carved into the earth.

If I couldn't get out or get up, what about down? I ran back the way I came, scanning the ground.

Don't forget the ring! There didn't seem to be any cameras down here, but you never knew. It seemed crazy, going this way toward the sound of oncoming soldiers, but it was the only direction left. After a few minutes I found something, a concrete circle in the floor about forty centimeters in diameter with an indented groove through the middle. A plug, screwed into the floor. They'd open it with a tool like a giant wrench that fitted into that groove. Pity I didn't have one of those on me.

I looked around. There was a narrow locker built into the wall adjacent. Its door was unlocked, inside a long hardiplaz instrument, a bit like a hockey stick with a rectangular blade at the base. Which clicked perfectly into the indentation. Bless the Movement for being so anally retentive!

I pushed and strained, but the plug didn't budge. Probably no one had opened this thing in years. Maybe decades. Maybe millennia? I pushed harder and the tool popped out of the slot, sending me careening into the wall. From down the corridor came the sound of many feet getting closer. Soon they'd be able to see a hardiplaz tool moving around on its own. Bit of a giveaway, I'd say.

But what else to do? Everything was sealed off now; this plughole was my only shot.

I grabbed the tool, pushing down firmly to keep the blade in its slot, and tried again. Then had a terrible thought, *What if I'm pushing the wrong way?* Throughout the galaxy, you always close things clockwise and open them anticlockwise. But what if that was different on Rethne? I reversed direction just in case and pushed hard. Still no movement. Got down on my hands and knees and looked carefully at the cement disc, the sound of troops getting ever louder.

There was a curved arrow inscribed in it pointing left to right – clockwise. Faint symbols in another language running along the arrow. Very helpful. But did they mean *open* or *close*?

I slumped back against the corridor wall, hands on my head in despair. Let them catch me, it was all too hard. I closed my eyes. Then bounced straight back up again – not the time for self-pity!

Think, Col, use the noggin. What could those symbols mean?

An answer came to me: nobody would write *close this way* on something like that. If the plughole were open, you could see how the thread ran. You could easily figure out how to close it. No, you'd only ever write *open this way* on your plug. Because the thread can't be seen if it's closed. And because, for whatever reason, *the thread is running the opposite way to normal.*

I grabbed the wrench and with a burst of superhuman strength twisted the plug to the right. It moved. A millimeter only. But it moved!

I pushed again even harder and it rotated a few centimeters this time. I could make out soldiers now, rushing figures a few hundred meters down the corridor. I pushed on the plug again. This time it rotated one full turn before the tool popped out. But it was getting easier all the time. I tried to spin it with my hands, but it was still too hard. I fitted the tool, turned it around and around till the plug wobbled loose. I lifted it out of the hole and a warm, rancid draught blew into my face. Foul. Sewage probably. I didn't care. There was shouting, blaster fire, getting close.

I looked down into the hole, only blackness. It was small, not designed for a person to slip through, but this was my only chance. I hopped onto the edge, legs dangling, then lifted my arms and slid off into the blackness.

CHAPTER TWENTY-NINE

Darkness, falling, flailing in space.

Landing hard, face first with a huge splash. Submerged, rebounding off something solid. Thrashing, no way to tell up or down. Lungs bursting, breaking the surface, air on my cheek. Opening my eyes to see a tiny shaft of light – from the plughole I'd dropped through – way above and far behind already.

Fast water washed me along. I bounced into walls from the force of the flow, tumbled along and within minutes the shaft of light was gone, everything pitch-black. I held up my arms to protect my head as I bashed and crashed along in the darkness, grabbing a breath whenever I could, sometimes taking in lungs full of the putrid water. I don't know how long this went on – though it seemed like hours, it was probably only minutes. Eventually I washed up into something that felt like a still point, an eddy. I reached out, finding a small ledge. I felt along this way and that. It was flat and smooth and, most importantly, dry.

I pulled myself out of the water with both hands, inch by inch. Legs thrashing, for there was no purchase – the ledge didn't run down below the water level; it must stick out somehow. A platform. I hauled myself halfway up, but there was something wrong with my left arm. It had no power and pressure sent searing pain up the shoulder; it must have hit something. I dangled from the ledge in the dark, panting.

OK, brute force won't work. So think.

An idea came. Horrible, counterintuitive – but it might work. Holding on with my right hand, I let the left go and turned upside-down, head submerged in the putrid water. I swung the left leg up and over, felt it touch the ledge, then used it to lever myself up, pulling with the right arm. My head came up out of the water, hips in agony as the strain transferred there. Inch by inch I rose, red lightning bolts of pain flashing in the dark. My chest drew level and then I was over.

I rolled onto my back, chest thumping, ears roaring. I lay prone for what seemed like hours – probably passed out as well, because next thing I knew, I was shivering with cold. I felt over my body for injuries – everything still seemed to be there.

Something else though, something wrong. What?

My fingers were bare. Somehow in all that the ring had slipped off. It was not tight-fitting and the stone could easily have caught on something.

Fuck.

No point freaking out. Didn't seem to be cameras down here and right now there were bigger problems.

I felt around the platform. Smooth, maybe a deck – for observation or maintenance? Had to be. That would mean there was access to it from the outside. I slid my hands around the surface of the platform in ever-widening circles till I hit the wall. Rocky and damp. Ran my hands up in a straight line, trying to find a door, an opening, something. Then I brought the hands down slightly farther along, gradually moving forward in the pitch black.

What was that? Something cold and metallic. Spherical, with a hole through the middle. I felt the wall around it – an edge, circular. Could be a hatchway cover with a turning screw. Except there was nothing to turn with. It felt more like a knob, rounded and smooth. Of course! This would open from the other side, the *outside*. What I had found was just the head of the screw with no purchase on it to turn.

I lay back down. Guess I'd have to swim it out. Dangerous, though, the water running so fast, must be a main sewer line. This tunnel would therefore run into a treatment plant.

Where they would be waiting – the open plughole something of a giveaway.

They'd be scrambling to cover all the escape points – except perhaps this one here. They wouldn't expect me to get out through the tunnel wall. If only that fucking door was openable. I tried to relax, take a few breaths – let something come.

I thought about what I'd just seen.

The star map showed how important Brouggh was to them. It was a bulwark of some kind. An influential planet, head of its own mini league that had kept functioning even during the Collapse. If Brouggh fell to the Movement, many systems would follow.

And what about the alien?

Aurelia was working with M4M. This was important and dangerous information....

Once we humans had developed FTL travel, the galaxy dangled before us like a ripe, juicy peach. We streamed out of Old Earth and in the space of a dozen lifetimes had colonized – some would say infested – the galaxy from one end to the other. Atrocities were committed, indigenous life forms exploited and wiped out. The League eventually put a stop to it all, but even to this day you can still find vulnerable worlds with a League sentry drone positioned to ward off adventurers.

The Aurelians were one race that had resisted. Ancient and proud, with very long lifespans – in the thousands of years, apparently – they'd watched at first with amusement, then with disdain and finally with alarm as *Homo sapiens* rampaged across the galaxy. They went to war and with superior technology scored major victories. But always pyrrhic. Because the Aurelians might have been an ancient and proud race, but when it came to warfare they were slow and ponderous – maybe *due* to those long life spans?

In the blink of an eye, humans copied their tactics, stole their technology and for every ship destroyed churned out a hundred more.

Altogether the Aurelians fought four wars and lost them all. The Truce of Hahgdeon guaranteed their home sector would be a no-go zone – so you could argue the lost wars at least secured a measure of autonomy – but due only to human generosity. For this the Aurelians had never forgiven us. And now here they were on Rethne, in bed with the Movement. Merrily – if that's the right word for them – putting gravel in the League's gearbox. Pretty clever, really.

These thoughts lulled me and I started to doze. No time for that! An idea came: maybe there was something washed up, lying around, like a rod I could slip through the hole in that knob and use to turn it? I searched the platform from one end to the other, it was about three or four square meters. I found debris washed into the corners but nothing of use.

Somehow, though, scrambling around, I must have touched something. There was a small but definite click, the sound of a servo motor, and a panel in the rock wall slid open, letting in blinding light.

I turned away, covering my face and waiting for my eyes to adjust – which seemed to take hours. Gradually I made out the surroundings. I was lying on a hardiplaz platform suspended next to fast-running black water. There was a very old hatch I'd been trying to open – probably rusted closed anyway – next to a modern motorized sliding panel. Through the opening, a corridor.

I had to move before the door closed again. I jumped through, noting a control pad glowing green, which I touched, causing the panel to slide shut. I hoped that didn't set off an alarm somewhere.

I was in a featureless corridor running into the far distance in either direction, dead straight and dimly lit with small lamps encased in wire every hundred meters or so. My eyes had grown so used to the darkness this light seemed blinding at first.

Left or right?

Did I want to head back to the Residence or *away* from it?

Heading away might be better, sacrifice myself and let Danee go on?

But Prince Humphrey would be missing, they'd put it together, so there'd be consequences for Danee either way. Better to head back, at least *try* to find a way to our room without being seen – if only I hadn't lost the ring!

So which way?

I retraced my steps: down into the basement, through the corridors, left, right, right, left. Overall heading north. Then the sewer – the water seemed to be flowing right to left. North again.

So, head south. A right turn.

I jogged at medium pace, hearing only the sound of my footsteps and the occasional drip of water while wrestling constantly with my thoughts.

Why does the mind do that? Naked, exhausted and lost, in mortal danger on a foreign planet, it was as though a Greek chorus was traveling along inside my head, commenting on everything, reveling in the opportunity to make things even worse. *What's the use, Col? You'll never get out of here. You've really done it now, Col!* All true no doubt, but of no use whatsoever. I forced myself to call on the psy-training.

Fuck off, mind, I said to myself. *Fuck off and leave me alone!* Must stay positive, must *believe*.

The corridor continued endlessly into the distance, mesmerizing. Now the adrenaline was receding I started to feel groggy – what would it be, four in the morning? Such a long day in this heavy gravity, my body wracked with bruises, a huge purple one on the left arm, which mercifully wasn't bleeding. *So tired*. Maybe I should lie down, curl up for a moment?

And what, just wait for them to catch me?

I gritted my teeth and kept going. Focus. Something would come along.

And there it was, an arrow and a stenciled sign: *NH43*. A ladder bolted to the wall with a hatchway above. *Pleased to meet you, NH43*.

Did I say that aloud? Not sure. Getting delirious now.

I climbed the ladder. Poked the hatchway cover and flipped it up a couple of centimeters – hard to see. What was through there? Could be twenty armed troops, could be anything. Only one way to find out. I pushed the lid up and jumped through to find a massive underground space crisscrossed with pipework, filled with pumping equipment and the sound of gushing water. Above, the high ceiling dropped down in a long curve like an upside-down dome. What could that be? I had an inkling.

"Excuse me?"

I whirled around: a short, plump man. Middle-aged and balding, quaking with fear – he held a clipboard out in front of him like a shield.

"You're the intruder," he croaked. Then, gathering his courage, he pointed to a door beside him. "In here, quickly."

I was too tired to argue and anyway he seemed friendly. I followed him into a small office cluttered with papers and files. Stuffy and hot, a tiny electric heater sputtering in the corner.

"I've been following events on my kom," he said, wide-eyed.

The warmth in the room penetrated my body – which suddenly realized how cold it was. I hunched over the small heater, wracked with uncontrollable shivering.

"Guess I shouldn't ask where you're from or what you're doing?" he asked. I shook my head. "You know, we don't all blindly follow the Movement on Rethne. I'm part of a group—"

"Please" – I held up a hand – "don't tell me anything. Better."

The man opened the office door, looked outside, then closed it again quietly. "What do you need, can I get you something, some clothes?"

I considered a moment. Maybe it was possible this guy could help? "I need to get inside the Residence unobserved. Is there a way?"

The man sighed. "Very difficult. When I saw the pierpoint alarm go off – that's the sewer hatch you came out of – I realized it had to be you, so I disabled the cameras down here."

"Won't that alert them?"

"Nah, happens all the time. You're safe for the moment. But I can't turn them off inside the Residence."

"What about the grounds?"

"That *may* be possible." He rubbed his chin. "But it's risky."

"I just need five minutes."

He thought some more. "But there's a problem getting you into the grounds. The only way to get there from down here is *through* the Residence."

"What about through the lake?"

The man gasped. "Of course! How did you know the ornamental lake is right above? I guess you League spies must do *endless research* about your operations!" His eyes gleamed with admiration. "But it means putting you into an outlet pipe, which might be possible if we…." His voice trailed off as he brought up plans and diagrams on his kom. "Aha! There!" he said, pointing to a meaningless tangle of drawings. "But we'd better move fast, they're scrambling because of the hatch you opened."

He looked at me with concern as I huddled over the heater. "I *could* get you clothes, but there's hardly any point. You're going back in the water again."

"It's OK, thanks."

"You don't even know my name," he said sadly.

"Better I don't. But thank you. You almost certainly saved my life."

He raised his arms theatrically and we hugged it out, right there in his office.

"OK, let's go," I said awkwardly after a full thirty seconds. I peeled him off me, opened the door to find two soldiers standing there, blasters drawn.

For a nanosecond nobody moved. They must have been 'clearing the zone', going room by room – didn't expect to find anyone. You never do in these situations, not really. You have your weapon drawn, you tell yourself to stay on guard, but after the tenth room or the fiftieth – or whatever – your readiness drops. Human nature. You certainly don't expect to come face to face with the target standing buck naked in a doorway.

But *I* was ready.

More than them, anyway, and certainly better trained. I exploded into action, kicking at the gun of the guy on the left, simultaneously rushing the other. We tumbled onto the floor, his blaster firing continuously, hitting the walls and ceiling, sending sparks and smoke into the air. There was a high-pitched scream. Something huge and metallic crashed onto the floor nearby, cut loose from its moorings by the out-of-control laser. We rolled around in the middle of this mayhem, both trying to get control of the weapon. He was short and strong like everyone on Rethne, but out of his depth, especially compared to buff Prince Humphrey. I held his blaster hand away from me, brought my right arm around and delivered a sickening blow to his chin with my elbow. He went slack in my arms and I was back on my feet instantly, looking for the other soldier, wondering why he hadn't shot me in the back.

The answer was obvious. He lay draped across a nearby guardrail, a tennis ball-sized hole through the middle of his head. Totally smooth, neatly cauterized by the laser.

That takes care of him, I thought.

My new buddy stood nearby panting, holding a blaster with both hands and staring at it in horror. "What have I done? *What have I done?*" he whimpered.

"Put the blaster down," I said. "Very dangerous."

He whirled around. "This is *mine!* He was going to shoot you."

It was true, the dead guard had his own blaster in hand. He must have retrieved it, then been shot by my friend.

"I've never used one before," said the man. "*Oh my god!*"

"All right," I said, "let's point that blaster somewhere else, shall we? Very good. *Now listen*, you were kidnapped by me, held at gunpoint. Got that?" He nodded, eyes glazed. "*I* shot this guy, knocked out the other one. Your DNA won't be on anything, understand?"

"No DNA," he mumbled, delirious.

"OK, good, now take me to that place you were talking about. The place I can get into the lake. OK?"

That seemed to rouse him. He shook his head as if waking from a dream. "This way."

He scurried off around the guardrail, hopping nimbly over the fallen soldier to a nearby ladder, which he climbed with surprising agility, blaster still in hand. There were sounds not far away, metal on metal, maybe voices too.

Dear reader, despite having been a copper for over two decades, getting involved in every kind of scrape, I had until that point never actually killed a person. I stood over the unconscious guard arguing with myself. Logically I should kill him, the danger that he could identify me was too great, but truly I didn't fancy it.

But then what about Sana, what about Danee? Could I put their lives at risk with my moral sensitivity? I took the blaster from his hand, pointed and pulled the trigger.

A small click. No flash, no barbecued soldier.

I flipped it over; standby light red. All the juice gone from that continuous firing. I guess I could have taken the dead guard's blaster and used that instead – but no, so be it. I took this as a sign.

I followed the man four levels up the ladder, the curve of the lake floor next to us now. Large pipes crisscrossed the open space while giant pumps throbbed. At the top we dashed along a platform made of steel mesh, the metal cold and sharp on my bare feet.

Those sounds were definitely getting closer now.

"In there," said my friend, pointing absentmindedly to a hatch with his blaster.

"Wish you wouldn't wave that about," I said. "When I'm gone, you have to wipe it and put it back in your desk drawer or wherever it came from. All right?"

"Yes, yes," he said, unconvincingly.

The hatch was bolted onto the side of a large pipe thrumming with water.

"I have to get in there?"

"Yes, but wait."

He darted off along the platform and a moment later one of the nearby machines went quiet, the pipe still. He came back, pulled a small spanner from his pocket and set to work on the bolts. There were eight of them and each took approximately forever to undo. As the hatch came loose, water gushed from around it, spilling through the grate to the floor far below – latent pressure from inside the system. I looked down and saw the area around the two fallen soldiers was partially flooded now. Not a bad development, washing my DNA from the scene. Finally the hatch came away and I could see there was just enough space to slide inside.

"Jump in," said the man. "This is the outlet pipe. When the pump's going again, it'll take you straight into the lake."

The pipe looked small, especially for Prince Humphrey's extra-large frame. If I got stuck in there, *good night Irene*. I jumped up, slid my legs backward into the pipe, then flipped around face down. This was not going to be fun.

"It's tight, but you should be OK," said the man. I didn't like that word *should*. "It'll take a few minutes to close this hatch back up, then I'll turn on the pump."

The pipe was half full of water. Cold but clear and mercifully not rancid like the sewer.

"What about the cameras?" I asked.

"I'm going to reboot this whole sector. It'll look like I've done that to correct the 'camera fault' down here. You'll have five minutes to do whatever it is you need to."

"That should be enough. Thanks again."

"You're welcome, sir." He teared up. "I've spent half a lifetime down here, hiding away like a mole in the dark. You gave me a chance to finally do something."

He fitted the hatch over the opening and everything went black. The space was incredibly tight; I should have positioned my arms forward like a diver. Instead they were at my sides, leaving me face down in the water. Every minute or so I had to arch my back and crane my neck upward for a breath.

The bolts were screwed back in – a loud, scratchy metallic sound in the confined space. Each one seemed to take an hour. Finally, a double tap with the spanner. All done. For a moment I was seized with claustrophobia. What if this guy was a sadist, leaving me in this tiny prison to drown? I fought the urge to scream and thrash, told the mind to calm. My breath slowed. That guy was *not* a monster, he was on my side. Must have some terrible beef with the Movement though, to put himself at so much risk by helping me.

There was a click, a hum through the water, the sound of gushing. The water in the pipe stirred and I lifted my head up and took a few rapid breaths, oxygenating my lungs as much as possible. Then it was upon me.

Tremendous force and pressure, a sliding sensation. Being pushed through the pipe, water behind and all around. Faster and faster. Lungs protesting, how long would this go for? Then openness. No feeling of pressure, the water even colder but still black – must be out of the pipe. I thrashed around. Which way was up?

OK, be still.

I stopped moving, spread my arms and legs, allowed myself to float. Do nothing and I would inevitably rise to the surface – we covered this in training. But how deep was the lake? I couldn't hold out much longer, lungs on fire, screaming for air. I fought down panic, imagined myself buoyant like a cork, tried to distance myself from the desperate need to breathe.

A sound. Tinkling of a fountain. How could that be if I were submerged? Because I wasn't anymore.

I lifted my head and drew a huge, gasping breath. Forced myself to slow down, be quiet. I was floating in the ornamental lake about twenty meters from the central fountain. How long had I been at the surface? Impossible to know; water and air were the same temperature, cold, and the same color, black.

I paddled quietly to the shore. The Residence was half a kilometer away, brightly lit. I could see the balcony to our room from here: bottom left-hand corner. So close!

Would the cameras be off yet? That guy was smart, he would know how long it would take to exit the pipe. Then he'd do the reboot – I had to assume my five minutes had already started.

But how to pass this final obstacle? The cameras might be off, but without the ring I was now visible and the area teemed. Flyers flew, boots marched and from far away somewhere came the sound of dogs barking. The canine squad! They wouldn't need that anymore.

I lay in the water, getting colder every moment, counting the five minutes down. What to do? This was my one shot, but running across that open grass right now would be suicide.

There was a loud explosion, behind, out in the middle of the park. It sounded like two flyers had collided midair – which was impossible.

There was a tremendous ball of flame, debris raining down and crackling sounds. A tree on fire.

Nearby, a corps of troops had been walking in line doing a vector search. They all ran off toward the crash site. Too weird, too convenient you might say, but whatever – this had to be it. Now or never.

I slipped out of the lake and bolted across the manicured grassland. Tried to keep my mind still, imagined being invisible. The Residence grew larger, loomed over me. I headed for the garden bordering the rear wall. I had just made it to the trees when I heard a voice, coarse and triumphant.

"There you are – finally gotcha!"

CHAPTER THIRTY

I froze. A soldier stood in the grass a few meters away, gun pointed. But in the wrong direction.

"Fucking idiot!" Another voice.

The first soldier laughed loudly, too loudly. Maybe drunk, or high. "Found him yet?" he asked in a mocking tone.

"Lower the gun, shithead," said the other voice, coming into view now.

Two soldiers, both stocky like everyone here, uniforms disheveled – probably been up all night like me. They both stared for a moment at the mayhem on the other side of the park while I stood frozen next to the tree, barely breathing, clearly visible if they turned.

"Perfect shit show," said the first guy.

"Yup. Probably another false alarm."

"Just like always."

They stood a minute longer while I waited in agony. One of them removed a small canteen from his pocket and they both took generous slugs, then trudged off toward the accident site.

As soon as they were out of earshot, I scampered through the bushes behind me, found the balcony to our room and hauled myself up and over the railing. I crawled along the floor, found the door – unlocked! thank god – and slipped inside.

Danee was awake, clearly freaked out. She silently put her hands together as if in prayer, went to hug me, then recoiled in horror. She waved her hand in front of her nose and pointed to the bathroom. The dip in the lake had obviously not washed away the dip in the sewer.

★　　★　　★

I took a long, long shower, head down, letting the burning-hot water wash over me in an endless torrent while the night's events played out in a nonstop loop. How the hell did I get out of that? What a fool I was, placing everyone in jeopardy. And so lucky. Either I was the luckiest guy in the world or someone upstairs was looking after me. Probably both. By the time I emerged, the burnt orange disc of Rethne's sun was edging above the horizon and we went immediately outside to the balcony to talk.

"What the fuck!?" asked Danee as soon as Batum touched our wrists.

I told them. About Sana. About the basement with the alien, the AI and the long, desperate flight. For a minute nobody spoke. It was a cold but beautiful morning with a clear sky, the air shimmering and desert-crisp. Soldiers – grim-faced and nervous – were posted about the grounds every hundred meters and a crew worked in the middle of the park clearing debris. The morning after the night before.

Danee shook her head. "I don't know what to say. You were incredibly brave. And incredibly lucky."

"I'm sorry, I should never have gone down into the basement, I was—"

"It's over, Col. You acted on instinct, so there must be a higher purpose to it. Think of it that way, you can't afford to wallow."

Indeed. Best not to think about the woulda couldas. "We have to keep going with the plan then, work on the assumption they haven't identified me."

She sighed. "OK, if we had any doubts about why we're here, they're now officially dispelled."

I looked at Batum. "I'm going to need some special kind of drugs to keep going today."

He gave a thumbs-up. "I have just the ticket."

"And how are you going with that AI?"

"I'm hanging on, but it's highly unpleasant. Imagine being inside a spacesuit with spiders crawling all over you trying to find a way in."

For a robot, Batum used some highly graphic metaphors.

"Are you OK to come with us today?"

"I think so, yes."

"Then let's get on with it."

Mehrqu was waiting outside with the limousine. He smiled and waved, chubby face beaming. We all made cheery conversation as our convoy wended its way through the gardens, past signs of chaos from the night before. The drugs Batum had given me were coursing through my system now, making everything bright – almost fluorescent – and my body felt jittery and high. Every so often an image flashed before me from the night before, causing my belly to lurch before I could force it away. I tried to focus my attention outside of the car, outside of myself. *Stay present, Col.*

In the far distance, piercing the sky, was our first stop, the Monument to the Lost.

Rethne was a cold, inhospitable planet, but had been colonized early in the First Expansion due to its mineral wealth. The original settlers had lived in domed camps but grew tired of it, naturally, and so the fateful decision was made to terraform. The giant ice caps were tapped, the water split to make breathable air and within a generation cities spanned the equator. By the time of the Collapse, Rethne had boasted a population in the hundreds of millions. But with an unsophisticated extractive economy, cut off from trade and supply, things broke down. Slowly at first and then rapidly. The food, water, waste and energy systems all failed – only the air-generating silos, engineered to last millennia, remained in service. In the space of thirty years, 99.999 per cent of the population had perished.

The Lost.

We stopped before a vast open space. In its center stood a tall, needlelike structure, an obelisk, I guess you'd call it.

"Sorry, but we have to walk now, vehicles are forbidden at Almaqud," said Mehrqu. He got out of the car muttering a prayer, using the same language as the choir the previous night.

The giant space was paved with hardiplaz. As we stepped on it, holograms sprang to life displaying names and faces, some talking, others still images. We walked and walked. The tower for some reason grew no closer and then I realized why: it was far away from us but stupendously high. A trick of perspective.

"How tall is the obelisk, Mehrqu?" I asked.

"Ten kilometers, Prince Humphrey."

"*Ten kilometers* high?"

"Yes! Usually this place is teeming with people, but we have come early, before opening. Pretty amazing, isn't it?"

It was. We walked rapidly for half an hour till our cheeks were rosy, my legs burning after the night's exertions in this heavy gravity. Our breath steamed in the cold morning air and we spoke little – the scale and the atmosphere of this place was overwhelming. Finally we reached the base of the monument.

"You can touch it," said Mehrqu.

I reached out. It was made of sandstone and inscribed with tiny letters impossible to make out. Mehrqu opened a magnifying app on his kom and Danee and I peered through to read:

Abdul, Dureen	97
Abdul, Mara	101
Abdul, Marnee	5

"See, they're a family that all died together – five-year-old daughter, very sad. For a thousand years, since the Muhraq, we've been collecting the name of every person who died. They keep finding new ones, even now. Look!"

Mehrqu pointed skyward. A drone hovered near the top of the obelisk emanating laser-bright flashes – more tiny names being inscribed. The morning light shimmered around us, reflecting off the enormous paved space and making dancing patterns on the sides of the obelisk. The monument was simple, but moving. It clearly meant something that they had brought us here first.

Not all places had been hit equally hard by the Collapse. Brouggh, for instance, had managed just fine, but Rethne? The mind boggled. What would it be like for half a billion people to die all at once? A tragedy so immense you need a tower ten kilometers high to record and remember it. A traumatized society, vulnerable to someone like Gilham.

We headed back in silence to find our ground car replaced with a neat little flyer, Batum and the Grendevan security droid already aboard.

Mehrqu gestured to the door. "Lady Darmley and Prince Humphrey, we're heading to the Cave now, with a little stop along the way for something special!"

We took off, the rising sun on our right. So, therefore heading north. The spire was behind us, far taller than our flight altitude. In only a minute or so, the city gave way to desert. Ahead were the foothills to the endless mountain ranges of 'sub-tropical' Rethne.

Mehrqu pointed and muttered something to himself, then said to Danee, "Look! You bring good luck, it's been raining here for two days now. Very unusual!"

It was true, seen from a distance the hills before us were dusted faintly with green.

When surveyors had come to Rethne they'd declared it *terra sterilis* – not so much as a single bacterium to be found. But with terraforming and human settlement, soil, seeds and microbes were blown out into the hills, gradually colonizing the barren ground, and although rainfall was miniscule, life found perches here and there. Enough to sustain a few thousand survivors after the Collapse. In the far distance, the faint green merged into a light purple color. The size of it all, the barren hills and empty space, had a grandeur. It was beautiful.

Mountain ranges passed below, looking like giant mounds of haphazardly piled rubble, cut through with old ravines and gullies. We started to descend and without warning a sliver of green appeared. A tight little valley with buildings lining one side. And trees, shockingly green. Date palms. We landed at the top of the valley. Below us stone houses ran down the steep hill, all conjoined, the deck of each forming the roof of the house below. It was like a scene from Old Earth – from the *prehistory* of Old Earth.

"This was my grandmother's village," said Mehrqu. "She lived here till she was seven, one of the last people to follow the old ways. She taught me Araq – hardly anyone speaks it anymore – and see, there's our family home there."

He pointed to one of the larger houses as we picked our way down a tiny path winding around the cottages. I noticed a few villagers wearing traditional black clothing.

"So who are these people if no one lives here anymore?" asked Danee.

"Oh, they just look after the tourists. Here's my cousin now."

An older man, small and chubby like Mehrqu, bounded up the hill and hugged him. They talked excitedly in what I now knew was Araq.

"Greetings, my name is Hadan," said the cousin. "We never had royalty in Misfat before, but please, join us for a traditional coffee."

"We'd be delighted," said Danee.

They took us to the large house Mehrqu had pointed out, then upstairs through a maze of mud-walled rooms. A museum had been set up with pictures depicting the old days and displays of various implements made with pre-industrial materials. A final narrow staircase took us onto a roof landing and a moment later coffee was served. Spoon-meltingly strong and tooth-meltingly sweet, flavored with an aromatic spice that was new to me. Around and opposite us were terraces – obviously for cultivating the palm trees – and crisscrossing the town was a channel of water, a tiny irrigation canal. Beyond the valley wall lay the desolate mountains and beyond them, unseen, the endless glaciers of the north.

"The water comes from a cave spring about six kilometers away," said Hadan. "It's only a trickle really, but never stops. It's the reason this place exists. For a thousand years after the Muhraq we grew dates here."

The sound of tinkling water rose everywhere from around the village. A series of stone piles were set out at regular intervals on the top of the valley wall opposite.

I had to ask, "And what are those structures?"

"That's *so* interesting!" said Mehrqu, wide-eyed. "Those are marking cairns. They used a sighting platform below to measure the stars so they could time the water flow. Each family had an allotment. Clever, eh?"

"No clocks then?" asked Danee.

"At first, I believe, yes," said Hadan, "but then everything broke down."

"I didn't realize people lived in villages. I thought it was only nomads who survived?"

"You mean the Behdan!" said Mehrqu. "Listen."

I took a sip of coffee and sat back. The sun was warm but negated by the cold breeze blowing over the valley. I could hear gurgling water and far off, some faint animal noises, bleating sounds.

"You hear it! The *maeizali*. Some people still keep them. They are like a cross between a goat and a camel – perfect for the conditions. It is true that most survivors were nomads, but where there was water they settled and grew things, traded with the Behdan. There are many villages like this."

That coffee was really hitting the spot. Stomach-rotting, but exactly what I needed. The psychedelic feeling from Batum's drugs was starting to recede but everything felt brittle, as if just below the surface of my consciousness lay a bottomless well of fatigue threatening to rise up and overwhelm me.

Apparently Rethne's original settlers had all come from one region of Old Earth that was primarily desert but rich in hydrocarbon reserves. After the Collapse they'd regressed to a traditional lifestyle. I tried to imagine living like a nomad back in the day. Roaming free, herding the wild *maeizali* and all that. Didn't sound too bad, really. Unless of course you *had* to.

We took off heading north again, the tiny green valley gone in the blink of an eye. I spotted some white shapes against the brown mountainside – *maeizali*. We flew for another half hour. A straight line appeared below us cutting through the mountains – a railway. Where could that be going? Turned out, the same place we were: the Cave.

We landed at the base of a steep mountain, clumps of snow and ice on the ground – you didn't have to travel far north before it got very cold here on Rethne. Across from us a huge crowd waited in a long queue, crisscrossing up the hill from the nearby railway terminus. Mehrqu led us to the entrance of a large cave. Inside was a ticket booth and beyond that a foyer set up so visitors would flow in one direction around the room. There were life-sized pictures of a young-looking Gilham in various poses, meditating and so on. As we examined them, holo-writing appeared with commentary.

"So this is Gilham as a young man?" asked Danee.

"As he first appeared," said Mehrqu.

"Appeared?"

"Yes, see?" said Mehrqu, pointing toward a painting, a corny 'artist's impression' titled *The Appearance*. Gilham, with a benevolent smile and glowing aura, squatted on the rocky cave floor talking with black-clad tribespeople. "The local Behdan found him here. Come."

We ventured farther into the Cave through a narrow passage to a small room. There was a cushion on the floor, a few basic implements and a tiny electric stove. Around the walls, tattered pictures of spiritual figures reminded me of the Swami's room back on Jubilee. In the corner, something else familiar – a chess set, a small portable one. This was a lot of coincidences – was there somehow a connection between Gilham and the Swami?

"Here they found him. Legend says he was meditating in this place for a thousand years, deep in *samadhi*. Then an earthquake opened the Cave and there he was."

"Do you believe that?" asked Danee.

Mehrqu thought a minute, then started to chuckle, jowls wobbling. He drew us in and whispered conspiratorially, "I'll tell you something funny. I think it's OK...they say 'Gilham' means *holy one* in Araq – but it's not true!" He tried to go on but was giggling too much, finally controlled himself. "Really, it just means 'not from here'. *Gil* – 'not from', *ham* – 'here'. Funny, eh?"

Of course Gilham was not from Rethne. Tall and thin with fair skin and black eyes, he looked about as local as Danee and I did.

"So where is he from then?" asked Danee. "Originally."

Mehrqu shrugged and laughed some more. "Nobody knows. I think he came to *this* place here because there was water. It is said all he had with him were a few clothes and a big bag of rice. The Behdan recognized him as a holy man and then...it spread."

"But wouldn't there be records of him arriving from some other planet?"

"Maybe. People have looked, but they cannot find anything. Rethne was poor and backward in those days when the Master appeared. We didn't have all these tourists and money like now."

So Gilham just turns up on Rethne. They find him living in a remote cave. Nobody knows where he's from, why he's here or what his history is. Nobody even knows his real name – kinda cool, actually.

There were more caves with giant pictures, then we exited through the fully stocked gift shop, finding ourselves back at the cave mouth. The crowd had swelled. Most looked to be from off world as they stood fanning themselves impatiently in the midday sun. It would be hours before they got inside, a testament to their faith. Armed security guards stood spaced at regular intervals along the queue, big guys wearing turbans.

There were gasps and I looked up. A medium-sized flyer was landing. It had no markings and was painted brilliant white. A door opened and Gilham emerged, waving to the crowd, which roared with excitement. People snapped pictures on their koms, parents held up children.

Gilham stood for a moment, hands pressed together, eyes closed, face inscrutable, then strode over to where we waited, giving Danee and then me a hearty double handshake. "Lady Darmley and Prince Humphrey, it's wonderful to see you here. This is where I did my *sadhana*, my deep spiritual practice."

He barely glanced at me, his gaze fixed on Danee – which was good. If he had any suspicions about the commotion from last night, he gave no sign. Indeed, he seemed friendly and relaxed, but my heart raced all the same. Only a few short hours ago I'd felt his hot breath on me as we stood face to face before the open door to the basement. I tried not to shiver at the swirling memories of what had come after.

"So glad you could join us," said Danee, beaming. "You certainly lived a frugal life here!"

"Oh, you've been through already?" Gilham's eyes flicked at Mehrqu. "I was hoping to show you around personally."

Mehrqu stuttered, "A-apologies, sir, I was told you would not be joining us."

As we were talking, the crowd grew steadily more noisy and unruly. Their idol was standing just meters away. Gilham took notice, looked over and waved – a mistake. A section of the crowd in the middle distance suddenly broke through the rope line and sprinted toward us and with that, so did everyone else in the queue.

"*Security alert! Security alert!*" shrieked the Grendevan robot as it took position before us alongside Batum. The guards pulled out their blasters and started firing into the air. There's a crowd-control setting on those things, which I prayed was being used now. There were cries as people were trampled, the guards bellowing and firing, the mob bearing down upon us. They crossed the open space to the cave mouth in a matter of seconds.

And then Gilham did one of those things that gave me pause.

He strode a few paces toward the onrushing crowd and stood still, arms in the air, eyes closed. The mob encircled him like a wave and stopped dead. Confused. The guards ceased firing, blasters still in hand, and suddenly everything was still, only the sound of the wind moving across the mountain and a baby crying somewhere. The people around Gilham went to their knees and bowed, the closer ones touching his feet. The rest of the crowd bowed as well while he stood there, eyes closed, somewhere far away. The guards moved in and stationed themselves around him, though that seemed unnecessary now. Batum and the droid visibly relaxed.

Finally Gilham brought his arms down, opened his eyes and spoke. Very quietly. "Hello, everybody, I welcome you with love."

A murmur passed through the crowd as these words were relayed. People teared up and clasped their hands in prayer. From wild mob to passive devotees in a moment.

Such a pity, the galaxy almost had a real holy man here.

Gilham chuckled. "So that was exciting, wasn't it?"

There was a ripple of laughter.

He patted one of the devotees on the head and then launched into a discourse – something about the practice of discrimination. A gentle admonishment to the crowd.

As he talked, my Investigator over-the-horizon radar was picking up a disturbance. One of the security guards nearby. A huge man with dark skin and eyes, wearing a brightly colored turban like all the others. He was sweaty and trembling, angry and red-faced. Clearly building up to something. I looked around. The other guards seemed oblivious, mesmerized.

Should I intervene?

Nope.

If this guy was about to do what I thought he was, then all power to him.

As if on cue, the guard pulled out his blaster and ran at Gilham, screaming, "*This is for my mother, you fucking bastard!*"

He pointed and fired.

CHAPTER THIRTY-ONE

There was a bright flash and an enormous bang, but the guard's blaster must have still been set to crowd control. For Gilham was still there, component atoms all in the same order, a shocked look on his face. The guard swore and went to adjust his weapon but his time was up and the other guards mowed him down in a blaze of violet light.

"Don't kill him!" screamed Gilham, but way too late.

The man was instantly turned into a pile of smoking meat, the air reeking of burnt flesh.

The crowd screamed and ran in all directions. Some of the men threw themselves in front of Gilham for fear of another attack. Not likely, I thought. That guy seemed to have been working on his own, had a private beef. He'd probably been waiting for this moment a long time, finally got his chance. If only he'd thought to reset that blaster.

Gilham turned to one of the guards, presumably the boss. "How was this allowed to happen?"

The guard stammered a few words.

Gilham cut him off. "Why did you kill him?"

That was a bit rough; those guys had had nanoseconds to save his life. The real question was why they hadn't picked up something brewing.

The head guard tried to speak and Gilham cut him off again. "*Shut up!* I want a full investigation." Then, waving in our direction, "Get them back to the Residence."

He stormed off into the Cave without looking back.

★ ★ ★

First we had to have the pretend conversation for whoever might be listening – tut-tutting about Gilham's near-miss. Then we stepped outside to have the real one.

"Saw it coming!" I said, perhaps a little too gleefully.

"Me too!" said Danee.

"Me too," said Batum.

That was deflating. Seemed like the only people who'd been surprised were Gilham's own security forces.

"Even the Grendevan security droid noticed," said Batum. "I muted it to give that guy a decent chance."

"How can they be so bad when they're so good?" asked Danee in wonderment.

"It's not them that's good, it's their AI," said Batum. "By trying to hack me, it's revealed quite a lot about itself."

"Go on," I said.

"It's creating all the intelligence and strategy the Movement uses."

"That makes sense," I said, "but execution is up to them – which is where they fall down."

"Correct," said Batum. "It's sending a constant stream of intelligence to a command center nearby."

"Well, we know where that is, don't we?" I said. "Anyway, folks, on with the show – it'll be interesting to see how Gilham deals with it all at tonight's shindig."

The limo arrived at 7 p.m. sharp and ferried us to Rethne's central stadium for *satsang* – the big weekly event featuring Gilham. People streamed from all directions and stood in long lines to be scanned by security. We were ushered straight through a VIP entrance. I don't know what had happened to Mehrqu but we now had a female guide, a typically short and squat woman who spoke little and did not introduce herself. She looked more 'security' than 'hospitality' to me – something hard around the eyes. Maybe they were nervous after the events at the Cave.

The huge stadium was filling fast. We sat in the front row where before us the warm-up band had everyone clapping hands and singing along. They were followed by a dance troupe, then acrobats who performed death-defying stunts on a rope swing. Then some kid, a competition winner who came out blinking in the light and read a long, dull poem in praise of Gilham. Pumped up after all the theatrics, the audience squirmed.

Finally, the lights dimmed. An expectant hush swept the stadium. Gilham walked out and stood center stage with eyes closed and hands clasped in prayer. A small figure in the vastness of the stadium — which erupted.

He opened his eyes and smiled. "Thank you, thank you, I welcome all of you with love." He settled onto a large white chair, sitting cross-legged like a yogi. "How are we tonight? Are we good?"

The crowd roared.

"You know, I have to confess something. A sin."

I took a breath. Where was *this* going?

"Who was at the Cave?" he asked.

Hands went up around the stadium.

"Many of you saw those tragic events first-hand, and everyone else must have heard by now surely, yes? But I must tell you, *the reports are not correct*. The person who attacked me was not deranged and he did not deserve to die. In fact, he would have been perfectly justified had he succeeded in killing me."

The crowd murmured, shocked. A man behind me cried out, "Not true!"

Gilham raised a hand. "Hear me out, please. That gentleman was part of my security detail here on Rethne. He and his family have served me faithfully for over twenty years. So why did he do that?"

He let the question hang.

"You have to remember, a person's actions always make sense to *them* no matter how strange they might appear to you. This guard, his name was Charan, came from a planet called Harmandir. His family are spiritual people. They have been part of the Movement since it came to their system. When I found this out, I asked myself, *What happened? Something happened*. The people on Harmandir did not want to tell me, but I found out anyway."

He closed his eyes, emotional.

"Charan's mother was very devotional. When her husband died suddenly, she became a little"...he paused..."*untethered*. And she started giving large sums of money to the local M4M office. Charan was not aware of this because he was working here on Rethne, working for... *me*." He stopped again. "And then she ran out of money. She became destitute. She went back to the office and asked for help, for some of her funds back. And what did they do? Did they help? No! They cast her out! The poor woman lost her home, ended up on the street, alone and ill. Talking to herself. *No one lifted a finger!* And then two weeks ago she went to a bridge and threw herself off and when poor Charan heard of it, he lost his mind too. And that is why he took those actions today."

The crowd listened with rapt attention, but I could not help a flicker of cynicism. Was it possible for Gilham to have uncovered this entire story so rapidly?

He went on: "So why is it my fault? Because the buck stops with me. If people on a far planet act in my name without compassion, without humanity, then it is *my* doing too."

People were shouting, *No, it's not your fault!*

"You know *all this?*" He gestured to the stadium, the crowd. "I never asked for it, never willed it into being. It just sprang up around me somehow. They call it the *Movement*, but I never gave it a name. This is only what others call it."

Gilham's black eyes, always so cold to me, filled with tears. At least some part of what he had just said felt genuine. Maybe it was true he'd never asked for any of this, maybe running the Movement was actually a huge and unwanted burden? He suddenly seemed vulnerable. If I did not know better, I would have been swept up in love for him.

"Sometimes," he said, "on days like these, I have to ask *what's it all for?*"

There was a long pause, finally broken when a tiny voice called out from the back, "We love you, Gilham!" The crowd laughed, a shift in mood.

He looked up and smiled. "OK, OK. Do you think we can do better? Will you help me?"

"Yes!" roared the crowd.

"All right, that makes me feel happier. *You* make me feel happier!"

I shook my head in disbelief. Had this been a moment of genuine reflection or an extraordinary feat of crowd manipulation?

He was on a roll now, segueing into the usual themes, winding up with a call to arms. "...So let us do our best. We are building something together, something that will fill the galaxy with awe. Thank you. God bless you all!"

We made our way out through the excited buzz of the crowd and swapped more phony polite talk during the brief ride home. As we approached our room, we heard the muffled cry of the security droid going through its familiar hysterics.

"*ATTENTION*, Lady Darmley and Prince Humphrey approaching. *NO THREAT DETECTED!*"

Which was odd; Batum said he'd mute that thing. A moment later we discovered why he hadn't: Batum lay collapsed on the floor in front of our bed, a jumble of disordered chrome. We ran to him looking for signs of life – if that's the right word. I twisted his head around to see a red light blinking rapidly. That didn't seem good.

Faint metallic words came from his speaking grille. "...and then someone...because...the peanuts...."

The flashing light turned a steady red color and there was no more sound from him.

CHAPTER THIRTY-TWO

Batum was dead. The Aurelian AI had finally got to him. With no way of running diagnostics or repairs for the rest of the trip, this was serious. Without him, Sana's rescue was impossible.

We sat on the bed in shock. What to do?

I felt a tickling sensation inside my left ear, then heard a voice. "Veranda."

I looked at Danee and then at the balcony door. We slipped outside to find a cold but still night. No moon because Rethne doesn't have one, but a beautiful blaze of stars lighting the parkland in a silvery glow.

I looked at Danee, put a finger to my lips and waited.

The voice spoke again. "Col, can you hear me? Reply subvocally."

"I can hear you. Is this Batum?"

"*Who else* would it be?"

"I don't under—"

"Fucking AI. Finally got me. But don't worry, everything in that former head of mine's been scrambled. All my live files are in this micro-nano."

How on earth was that possible, transferring an AI-level CPU into a *micro*-nano?

"Douglas thought something like this might happen, so he made a backup. I escaped through a one-point-five-micron–sized hatch in the heel of my foot."

"So you're just going to hang out in my ear for the rest of this trip?"

"Got any better ideas?"

"How are we going to tell Sana what to do for the rescue with you stuck in there?"

Batum told me. It made sense. It just might work – if we were lucky.

"You'd better explain all this to Danee too."

"Roger that."

I felt the tickling sensation again for a moment. Then Danee's eyes widened. She concentrated for a few minutes, then nodded at me. I guess we had a plan.

That evening Danee and I lay together quietly on the bed. I should have been exhausted from the long day, not to mention all the exertions of the night before, but instead I was wide awake. Wired. It was awkward not being able to talk, so she curled up in the crook of my arm in silence. After a while she turned and stroked my chin, looking into my eyes – so much to say, but no way of saying it. We lay there like that for what seemed like hours, images from the previous night playing endlessly in my mind, sleep a million miles away. Finally I reached over to the bedside table and grabbed one of the sedative-laced chocolates so conveniently left by our hosts. I turned it over a few times, took a sniff and then ate it in one gulp.

★   ★   ★

Danee shook me awake from a dreamless sleep. Much more would be required before I was fully recovered. I blinked in the light from a bright, crisp Rethne morning. Several strong coffees later it was a pleasure to find Mehrqu waiting outside with the limo.

He greeted us both with hugs. "Good morning! Sorry I couldn't make it last night!"

Mehrqu was a sweet guy, he just didn't know who he was working for. Our convoy swept out of the Residence and into the city, Batum a silent passenger in my ear. We'd agreed there would be no chatter till back in the relative safety of our room. After a short drive we pulled up outside an official-looking building signed: *Rethne City PS 47.*

Around twenty children wearing navy blue uniforms waited to greet us, standing in a neat row, their teacher behind. An older man stood on the steps to the front door, beaming. The headmaster, I presumed. They applauded as we got out of the car, presenting Danee with a huge bouquet of flowers and myself with a box of chocolates. There was a card taped to it with writing in a childish hand:

Prince Humphrey we are so happy you came to our school.

The headmaster gestured for us to enter. He was short with rounded shoulders, sporting a large bald patch and extravagant combover. He talked nonstop as we passed along the main corridor. "Lady Darmley and Prince Humphrey, what an honor. My name is Adhul."

"Thank you for having us, Adhul," said Danee graciously.

"We've never had royalty here before. The children are so excited...."

I tried to think. This was probably my first time inside a school for years. The smells and sights were familiar, probably universal: stale lunchboxes and sweaty boys, artwork and learning aids festooning the walls. It was soon clear this school was meant for advanced students – the kind of place where little Johnny and Jane are building a particle accelerator in the rec room. We were shown rehearsals for an orchestral group, some older students in the gym doing stunts – impressive, given the heavy gravity – and so on and on. The vibe was weird; I couldn't quite put my finger on it.

Tense.

We ended at the science wing in a class of kids that looked nine or ten years old. They sat wide-eyed and ramrod-straight, their teacher standing nervously at the front. I couldn't help but notice, lying on her desk in plain view, was what appeared to be a nerve wand.

A nerve wand? Talk about overkill. On Brouggh we used them in the jails. Even on the lightest setting, getting zapped by one of those things felt like being flayed alive.

"These are the year fives," said the headmaster. "Maliqu, can you step forward please?"

One of the little girls left her desk and stood before us, cute as hell in pigtails.

"Maliqu, would you please explain to our guests about the periodic table?"

"Yes, sir. The periodic table is an array of the chemical elements organized by atomic number from lowest to the highest."

"Very good, and would you care to recite it for us?"

"Yes, sir." She took a breath and at great speed, but with a cute lisp, launched into it, pronouncing every word correctly. "The elements are hydrogen, helium, lithium, beryllium…."

Adhul cut in when she got to 115, moscovium. "Is there anything special you can tell us about this element, Maliqu?"

"Yes, sir."

"Please explain."

"Sir, element one-fifteen is special because it powers the gravity engines and jump drives in our flyers and spaceships."

"Correct. Anything else?"

"Yes, sir, Rethne is one of only a handful of known planets where a naturally occurring, stable isotope of moscovium can be found."

"Thank you, please go on." The headmaster's tone toward Maliqu was sharp, quite different to the fawning deference he'd shown us.

She continued: "Livermorium, tennessine, oganesson – " all the way up to element 145.

When she had finished, Adhul raised an eyebrow. "Is that all, Maliqu? I think you might have missed one?"

The little girl froze. The room went dead silent. She looked up in shock and her eyes flicked to the desk where the nerve wand lay. She started trembling and a tear rolled down her cheek. "I don't think so, sir, sorry, sir. I think I said them all."

Adhul gave a snort. "Just kidding! That was excellent, Maliqu." He tousled her hair and I noticed she visibly restrained herself from flinching.

We rode home in silence. It was obvious now what that weird vibe was – those kids were scared shitless. And what about the casual sadism of the headmaster? He couldn't help himself. In front of *honored guests* too. What must go on there in a normal day?

I felt suddenly tired. What hope did they have here on Rethne? Everyone traumatized and brainwashed from childhood. One more night and then hopefully we'd be gone forever from this hideous place.

We said goodbye to Mehrqu with genuine fondness – this was our last outing with him – then had an interminable meeting with the Department of Outreach. Endless presentations by pushy, gleaming-eyed young people showing how Movement planets had higher economic output, better physical and mental health outcomes, and so on and on, blah, blah. I tuned out. Which was fine because that's exactly what vacant Prince Humphrey would have done. Poor Danee had to take it all seriously.

We staggered back to the apartment. I caught sight of myself in the mirror – even the feathers in my plumed hat were drooping, like the rest of me. One more job to do – the most important – then we could get the hell out of here.

We woke up a domestic droid and had it unpack the gifts we'd brought and lay them all out on the bed. Danee pointed silently at the one intended for Sana. I nodded. We went out to the balcony for a final chat.

"Batum, you still there?" I asked subvocally.

"Where else would I be?" he replied sniffily.

"What did you think of the school?"

"How would I know? My only input is the audio from your earwell. I'm bored shitless in here, if you want to know the truth."

"OK, well, it's showtime in just a few hours. You ready?"

"Of course."

"Can you check in with Danee? Tell her I thought the kids in that school all looked terrified."

"Roger that."

I felt the ear tingle. A cold wind was blowing now, orange sand haze in the air. The ear tingled again. "She's ready. Said she wanted to knock that headmaster's teeth in."

I chuckled and gave her a thumbs-up.

To Batum I said, "OK, let's do this."

CHAPTER THIRTY-THREE

There was a knock on the door at 7 p.m. and we were taken to a dining room – the same one as on the first night. One of our droids followed carrying our gifts. Tonight we would finally hand them out and it was essential Sana got the right one. The plan was to hug each of the servants in turn as we thanked them. Batum, now riding with Danee, would fly into Sana's ear and explain what to do – he would have only seconds.

Some people I recognized, but there was also a new group, all men. They looked different – older and grizzled. Duraqu, the security guy, stood in the corner near the window, inscrutable. We took our places at the round table, this time already piled high with food. Danee sat next to the bull-headed prime minister again and as before, we all waited for Gilham to arrive.

He strode in looking ebullient, not bothering with any solemn prayers. "What do you think, Lady Darmley? This is genuine desert tucker, like I used to have with the tribesmen." Without waiting for a response, he turned and clapped his hands. "Rakia!"

The men around the table cheered.

"Tonight, we farewell our friends from Grendeva," he said, face impassive. "We shall do it Rethnean style."

The table was full of dips and olives and flatbread and dates. Chargrilled kebabs of meat, fried cheeses and roasted peppers. Gilham had confounded me yet again. Where were the organic vegetables and plain water? He tucked in along with everyone else while waiters brought thimble-sized beakers and filled them to the brim with a toxic-looking brown liquid.

He held up a glass and toasted, "Serafi!"

"Serafi!" the table answered. Everyone sculled their glasses and banged them on the table. The liquid burned its way down my throat like sulfuric acid, lighting a fire in my belly. Had to be sixty proof at the very least.

"That'll put hairs on your chest, Prince Humphrey," said Gilham with a thin smile. And also a glint of something in the eyes I didn't like. "Again!"

The glasses were filled and we toasted another time. This was going to get me hammered. I was never a big drinker even at the Academy and my head was spinning already. Did Gilham sense weakness here, an opportunity to torment hapless Prince Humphrey?

He was looking at me quizzically, so I called on my store of Grendevan 'memories' and something useful bubbled up. "It reminds me of what the farmhands used to drink – *grappa* they called it."

"Is that so? Fascinating," said Gilham. "Again!"

I tried to get food into my mouth between rounds. One thought comforted me: Danee was famed for her ability to handle alcohol (though obviously not the narcotic drink *quaava* that had half paralyzed her on Jubilee) and could drink men twice her size under the table. Hopefully she at least would be able to keep a clear head.

The man to my right nudged me in the ribs. "What you think, off-worlder?"

He was small and nuggetty with a perfectly round head and leathery brown skin. His voice sounded like it was bubbling up from the bare earth of Rethne.

"Of the rakia?"

"Everything," he rasped.

It was becoming hard to focus. I tried to find a suitably hearty tone. "The food is good and the drink is strong!"

He laughed. "Tonight you will drink a manful amount of rakia. Then you will *know* us."

At this rate, all I was going to know would be the bottom of a toilet bowl.

"In the old days," the man said, "we only had what we could carry – *no* pack animals. No wine, no beer. *Only rakia!*" He bellowed with laughter, displaying a mouthful of rotten teeth, and slapped me on the back.

"So, you are Behdan?" I asked.

"Yes. My father, chief. He found the Master with the others – these."

He gestured around the table. They all looked like him: small, dark-skinned and tough. Adapted to live on this planet that was never meant to sustain life. Survivors.

Gilham seemed genuinely fond of them, smiling and drinking, sometimes breaking into their tongue. Sana did not appear. Plenty of other servants were coming and going, but not her. One of the Behdan stood up and launched into a long poem in Araq. The tribesmen fell about clutching their bellies.

When I asked my neighbor for the meaning, he waggled a finger. "Not in front of the lady."

There were toasts. To Gilham, to Lady Darmley, to fallen comrades and to beautiful women. On and on. The table was stripped of food, cases of rakia drained, and to be honest if the circumstances had been different, I might have said it was a fun night.

Finally, it was time.

Danee rose, cool and elegant. Seemingly untouched by all the booze. "Thank you so much for your hospitality – Gilham and your entire team. Even though we are many light-years apart, I feel our two planets are moving ever closer together. And of course, it was wonderful to meet your special guests tonight, true salt of the earth Behdan!"

The men cheered – a little raggedly by now – and held up their glasses.

"Now for a small ceremony. It is our custom on Grendeva that when one is a house guest, we honor those who take care of us with a gift. So, with your blessing…."

This event had been prearranged, of course, but Gilham did not look entirely happy. He scowled for a moment, then waved at a servant. "Bring them all in."

The domestics entered the dining room and lined up. Head chef in his whites and hat, followed by the assistants and serving girls. They all looked straight ahead nervously. Then the room maids and other workers arrived, but where was Sana? Notably absent. It became clear no more staff were coming, so I stood up to help hand out the gifts, head reeling from the drink, panic mounting. Where was she? The plan was falling apart before my eyes.

Danee gestured for our domestic droid to come forward. "Now, is that everyone? It's very important to us that we honor every person."

Gilham leaned back. "Yes, yes, that's all of them. Go ahead, do your thing."

"I seem to recall there *was* someone else, a young woman who served you on our first night?"

He looked up, eyes narrowing. "She's not here, she's got the night off. Go on, hand out your gifts."

That was a lie, of course. Did Gilham suspect something? How could he? Maybe he just didn't want her to have a gift? Either way, a disaster. Danee could not realistically push this point any further. We were fucked. The mission a wash.

But regardless, the charade had to go on. We started with the chef at the top of the line-up.

Danee shook his hand, carrying on with amazing poise as though this weren't all for nothing. "Thank you so much for the wonderful meals. Did you cook for us on the first night as well?"

"Yes, er...Your Majesty." He looked dumbstruck with fear.

She laughed. "I'm not the queen, last time I checked anyway. You may call me Lady Darmley."

"Thank you, Lady Darmley."

"We have something special for each of you. Grendevan gold is prized throughout the galaxy."

She shook his hand and moved on, now it was my turn.

"Well done, good show," I said, reaching into the box for a gift.

I pulled out a shiny gold ring and placed it in the palm of his hand. In the bottom of the box was the bangle earmarked for Sana. All for nothing now. I moved down the line making polite thank-yous, handing out gifts, feeling hollow inside. But also drunk. Lurching. Halfway along I stumbled, knocking the box out of the robot's hands.

The gifts went flying in all directions and the Behdan cackled.

"Too much rakia!" someone yelled.

There was a mad scramble to collect the jewelery, which had bounced and rolled in every direction. I chased a bangle along the floor, went down on one knee to grab it, then found myself looking at a pair of feet in sandals. The feet were dark brown with orange nail polish. Familiar. I looked up. It was Sana, carrying a tray of chocolates.

"*There* she is!" said Danee, taking her by the arm. "You've come just in time!"

"What are *you* doing here?" called out Gilham coldly. "You were *told*."

Sana looked puzzled. "Domenic paged and said to bring these?"

"Well, you can go again, right now."

The jewelery was all back in its box and the servants in line.

Danee gave Gilham her most charming smile. "Well, now that she's here, surely it would be discourteous not to give her a gift?"

Gilham stared at her, his face impassive. The moment hung. Then one of the Behdan chipped in with a comment in Araq. I didn't understand the words, but the meaning was clear: *C'mon, let the girl have her gift.*

"All right," he said crossly, then snapped his fingers for more rakia.

Danee turned to face Sana. "Thank you for taking such good care of us."

She gave her a quick hug, bringing her head close so Batum could fly into her ear. I rummaged in the box for the gift. Which one was it? All their positions had changed when the jewelery went flying and my vision was blurry from drink. Panic mounted. I couldn't take more than a moment, but choosing the wrong one would ruin everything. I grabbed a bangle that looked right and went to place it on her arm.

But Danee reached over. "Humphrey dear, I think *this* one would look much nicer on her."

Thank god for Danee. "Yes, of course, dear."

I put the bangle on Sana's wrist. Her eyes were wide, looking right into mine. Yes, I think she got the message.

"Thank you, good show," I said, feigning indifference.

Then I gave my own quick hug and felt the right ear tingle as Batum returned. Had we just pulled this thing off?

We finished the remaining servants in the line-up, then made our good nights to everyone, who rose from the table to see us off. Lots of hearty hugs, earnest handshakes and promises to return soon for excursions into the desert – and so on. My head was reeling from the drink; I had to play it cool. Just this last night to get through.

Gilham waited at the door to say goodbye. "It's been wonderful to have you here on Rethne. I hope you enjoyed the trip?"

He seemed different somehow – pensive now, perhaps – and no longer rolling drunk.

"Yes, very much so," said Danee. "It's been wonderful. Is this goodbye?"

"No, I'm coming to the spaceport tomorrow to see you off, but I just wanted to say…." He paused for a moment. "It's been eventful, hasn't it? The terrible scene at the Cave yesterday. It's not normally like that here, I didn't want you to get the wrong idea."

"No, of course not. Things happen sometimes."

"And tonight, that serving girl." He paused again. "I've been annoyed with her lately. With her…*performance*. I didn't think she deserved a gift. But my response was inappropriate. Ungenerous. It was good you gave her the gift."

Danee smiled warmly. "Think nothing of it. The right thing happened in the end."

Sure did. Were these Gilham's authentic feelings or just more of his act, more damage control?

To Prince Humphrey he gave a short perfunctory handshake and turned away. Wow, not his favorite person.

We were taken back to our room and collapsed on the bed, wrung out. Did all that really happen? I was seriously drunk, the ceiling spinning. Might be a good thing, might help me sleep.

But sleep did not come.

It was 10:45 p.m. Sana had been told to stand on her balcony at midnight wearing the bangle. Above us in geosynchronous orbit lay a freighter commandeered by Douglas a few weeks before. It would send a flyer down to collect Sana, guided in by the bangle. Not guided by conventional means, but something new from Douglas's labs: EMR, or enhanced magnetic resonancing. Two bangles had been made from the same original piece of metal. One was on Sana's wrist, the other aboard the flyer would tune to it. The flyer was to appear at her balcony, then whisk her up to the freighter, already primed for hyperspace (jumping straight from orbit, which of course is not theoretically possible).

It was the best plan we could think of and only made possible thanks to Douglas and his newtech. Sana had been instructed to leave the bangle behind on the bed – a master stroke. EMR works on the principle that every piece of metal has its own unique magnetic signature. Movement techs could poke and prod it till the cows came home and they'd find nothing but an ordinary piece of gold-plated brass.

We counted down the time. Was that a faint swishing sound we heard around midnight, or just my imagination? We dared not stir to check. Danee took my hand and we lay together, awake. Who knew what the morning would bring?

We must have dozed off eventually because the security droid jolted us from sleep. *"ATTENTION! SECURITY ALERT, SECURITY ALERT!"*

I turned on the light; it was 3:00 a.m. "What's going on, robot?"

It looked at me with impassive mechanical eyes, then turned silently back to the door.

"Why did you sound that alert? What's going on?"

The robot remained silent. It was mechanical, unsophisticated. The Grendevans were given transition tech, centuries out of date. In some perverse way, did this make it harder for the Aurelian AI to hack? Was there a war going on inside that dim robotic brain?

I must have slipped back to sleep because next thing there was a loud rap on the door. I looked at the time: 6:45 a.m.

Duraqu stood outside, grim-faced. "Come with me."

It was not a request.

CHAPTER THIRTY-FOUR

We threw on some clothes and followed Duraqu through the gloomy corridors of the Residence. Two armed soldiers fell in behind us – but with blasters holstered, I noted.

It was early morning, but everything was in turmoil. Through a window I saw the sky full of military flyers and the parkland crawling with troops. The air rang with loud commands and tramping boots – the ant nest was well stirred up. What came next was crucial. Danee and I had to act like innocent people: bewildered, trying to be helpful.

We were ushered into a meeting room containing only a large white table and chairs. Gilham sat on the far side, his face impassive as usual. In the center of the table was Sana's bracelet. A cutting had been made into it and a hole drilled; Movement technicians were no doubt roused in the wee hours to do this work. They would have found nothing.

Duraqu pointed at two chairs and motioned for the guards to wait outside.

"Excuse me," said Danee, "has something happened? I was just—"

"Please!" interrupted Duraqu. "We will ask the questions and you will answer them."

Gilham's face did not move, his black eyes boring into Danee.

"Well, if something untoward has happened," she said, "then by all means whatever we can do to—"

"This piece of jewelery," Duraqu interrupted again, "we need to know its significance. Why did you give it to that girl last night?"

"I'm sorry, which girl do you mean?"

Gilham exhaled sharply.

"You know which girl," said Duraqu. "The prince tried to give her a different piece, but you stopped him, made sure she got this one. Why?"

We had to be careful here, they would be scanning our reactions and biodata. We were trained for that, but would have to be on our best game if we wanted to get out of this alive.

"You mean," said Danee, "that pretty serving girl who arrived halfway through the ceremony? She has wrists *this* big" – Danee made a circle with her finger and thumb – "and the prince was under the weather last night. He was about to hand out something completely—"

"Nonsense," said Gilham coldly. "You are lying. Tell us the truth now." He pulled out a blaster and laid it on the table in front of him, spinning it around so the muzzle was facing us.

A raising of the stakes, I would say.

Instead of reacting with alarm, Danee sat down, so I followed suit.

She spoke quietly, in soothing tones like a mother calming a child. "Mr. Duraqu. Gilham. It sounds like something unpleasant has happened and I am sorry for that. Truly. But whatever it is, the prince and I have absolutely nothing to do with it. We have traveled from Grendeva in good faith to—"

"She's good, I'll give her that," said Gilham.

"The young lady you gave that bangle to has disappeared," said Duraqu grimly. "We suspect foul play."

I had allowed my reactions to spike when we first entered the room, then again when Gilham pulled out the blaster. Now, talking about things supposedly nothing to do with me, I let everything calm down, slowing my breathing, relaxing my shoulders.

"I'm very sorry," said Danee imperiously, "about your serving girl going missing, but I fail to see the relevance and I am losing patience. We are here on Rethne as part of an official delegation from a friendly system. Why are you pointing weapons, making accusations?"

That was excellent. I saw Duraqu blanch. This had to be their greatest fear. Surely. Otherwise, we would be in the basement already, facing immobilizers and eye-gouging.

They weren't completely sure.

Or maybe they were fairly sure, but not enough to risk a diplomatic incident. Not yet, anyway.

"There are other things," said Gilham, leaning back in his chair. He seemed amused, like a cat toying with its prey – what else did he know?

"I'm sorry?" asked Danee.

"Lady *Darnley*," he said with a hint of sarcasm, "why do you have an AI-grade robot in your entourage? I thought Grendeva did not possess that level of technology?"

A question we had anticipated and therefore a weak one.

Danee shrugged. "A gift from our neighbors, the Delphiniuns, now broken – was that *your* doing somehow?"

A quick hack of the Grendevan archive would turn up the receipt planted by Douglas listing Batum as an official gift.

Gilham turned his black eyes on me. "Well then, please explain to me, Prince Humphrey, what were you doing on your first night here? Why did you leave your room?"

A trick question and a very dangerous one. They must have suspected me of being the invisible 'intruder' but had no hard evidence. Therefore the cameras had turned up nothing, same for the guard I'd knocked out – otherwise I would have been arrested already. Had to play this very, very cool.

"Ahem, well, sorry, but I have no idea what you're getting at?" I let my reactions spike then settle down, like someone mystified by the question. "We were in the room all night, I think, milady? Not sure I remember exactly…."

Danee patted me on the cheek. "Our prince gets a little confused sometimes, don't you, my love? He is adorable, but not the sharpest tool in the shed."

Gilham smiled nastily. "Really?" He turned to Duraqu. "So many coincidences since they arrived here – *just remarkable*." Then to me, "That little episode at the Cave had nothing to do with you either, I suppose?"

I nearly laughed – so the heartbreaking tale of Charan and his poor mother was fake news? Danee and I turned to each other in shock.

"The Cave?" exclaimed Danee, wide-eyed. "How could we possibly—"

"Enough now," said Duraqu. "It's time to end this." He leaned forward and looked at me calmly. "We have turned up some fascinating vision of *you*, Prince Humphrey, transiting through the Berekay space hub two weeks ago. What would a royal prince be doing in a place like that?"

A holo image rose from his kom. A still shot of 'Donny' walking along a travellator, half turned away from camera.

I remembered the moment. Douglas had sent me to Grendeva on a tortuous route that avoided systems they controlled, but an M4M kiosk had been set up in one of the transit hubs. I'd seen it too late, so had turned my body away in case they were filming – which of course they were.

The Aurelian AI had been beavering away, scouring inconceivable amounts of data, correlating images from across the galaxy. Using that picture, they could track my journey from the moment it was captured: backward in time to Jubilee and forward to Grendeva.

Fatal.

They'd been toying with us all this time. They had hard evidence. A facial match made by a supercomputer and accurate – I knew – to five decimal places. Absolute confirmation that our story was bogus.

Duraqu allowed himself a small smile of triumph. "So you see, we know very well you are not who you say you are. The League itself would never be so" – he searched for a word – "*clumsy*, so we wish to know more. How and why did you come to be officially sanctioned representatives of Grendeva? What is your real reason for being here?"

He looked at Danee, then me. No one spoke.

"If you co-operate," he said slowly, "there may be a way to work things out with the Grendevans so we can let you go. But first you need to come clean."

More silence.

"And if you do not co-operate, there will be…*consequences*."

He smiled again, broadly this time, a horrible sight. Then he brought up an image of a man on his kom. Skinny with red eyes, bad acne and teeth filed to points. The man who'd gouged my eye out in Brimheed's office. Did they suspect 'Prince Humphrey' of being Col from Brouggh

– impossible, surely? – or did they just show this picture of their favorite torturer to scare people? Either way, it was indeed terrifying.

I kept my bio reactions in check with an iron discipline, but deep inside my mind was reeling. They had too much on us. This conversation was clearly just a prelude to the torture session waiting downstairs. They would make me watch as they tore Danee apart, then do the same to me. A tidal wave of despair crashed over me. How could I have allowed this to happen, been so stupid? The only possible way out was to come clean. Maybe Danee at least could be saved? For just a moment I closed my eyes.

And had a vision. The Swami from Jubilee, smiling benevolently. Pity I'd never see him again – or anyone else. A memory bubbled up. The Swami was telling me something: "*Col, don't forget that state you experienced out in space…. If you get in trouble on this mission – call on it.*"

I was in trouble. I called on it.

A warm feeling arose inside. The same feeling that I'd had while spinning in space: amused, detached, free. I asked myself, *What should I do now?* and got an answer immediately. The answer I already knew: Gilham was a wrong crystallization, so no matter how powerful he might appear, on some fundamental level he was actually weak. I had to hang tough and have faith.

In the holo, 'Donny' looked terrible. Unshaven with dirty, bedraggled clothing and hollow eyes – his lowest ebb during that trip. To the human eye, it didn't even look like me.

So don't give up, use that.

I reacted how the real Prince Humphrey would have (if he were real). Soft, entitled. Prince Humphrey dressed like a hobo on some distant space hub? Impossible!

"You're saying that holo picture is of *me?*" I asked.

"We *know* it is," said Duraqu.

"But I don't understand, how could that—"

"You know very well, *Prince* Humphrey, what we have here is a facial match." He brought up another image showing Prince Humphrey's face superimposed over 'Donny's', correlation points marked out.

"Impossible! I have never once been—"

"Of course you have, your journey has been tracked from Jubilee all the way to Grendeva."

Duraqu and Gilham swapped looks of triumph.

Then Gilham smiled and said in a sly voice, "We also talked to your friend *Zhang*."

I stared at him, dread rising. "I beg your pardon?"

"Yes, Zhang," said Duraqu. "Remember him? He remembered you all right. Needed a little persuading at first, but turned out to be quite the fount of information."

Zhang the poet, my friend. Generous and sweet. What had they done to him?

"Look…just look here," I stuttered, "I don't know any person called—"

"Bring him in then!" said Gilham coldly. "Let's see what he remembers."

Zhang had been brought to Rethne?

Mind-boggling.

Duraqu leaned over to Gilham and whispered something. I didn't catch it all but heard a few words. Terrible words…*didn't survive the interrogation*….

Reactions: guilt and anger. Suppress them, deal with them later.

Gilham bit his lip in frustration and leaned forward, his red eyes boring into me. "Time's up, *Prince*. Speak now while you still have the faculty!"

I met his stare for a moment, calling on that feeling of inner peace, staying calm and unshakably in character. A prince from Grendeva, bewildered and upset, way out of his depth. I turned to Danee, my bottom lip trembling. "*Juliette?!*"

Danee glared at them. "See, now you've upset him! This is all completely—"

"*Enough* of this charade!" shouted Gilham, putting his hand on the blaster. "*Time's up!*"

Something had snapped in him. He seemed suddenly agitated, going from ice-cold to boiling rage in an instant, and I noticed a flicker of concern cross Duraqu's face.

Gilham leaped to his feet. "I knew there was something *off* about you two the moment you arrived."

"We are legally sanctioned representatives from Grendeva," shot back Danee, cool and unfazed.

"*Bullshit!*"

"I must remind you that Rethne is legally obliged to guarantee our—"

"We are obliged to do *jack shit!*"

"And this whole conversation has been completely out of—"

"Where is that *fucking girl?*"

"We know nothing about her."

"Tell the truth!"

"There is nothing to tell!"

Gilham picked up the blaster, his hand shaking with rage, and aimed at us. His face was crimson, eyes blazing. "Tell me where Sana is or *god help me*, I will do this!" His finger tightened on the trigger.

Danee and I clutched each other. If he was mad enough to shoot, at least let us die together.

Then everything happened very quickly.

There was a ruckus outside in the corridor. Growing louder. Blaster fire, bodies thumping and screams. The door to our room exploded inward with a massive blast and we all dived for cover.

Entering through a haze of dust and smoke came the security robot from Grendeva. "*SECURITY ALERT! SECURITY ALERT!*" it shrieked, sending blaster fire in all directions, including a well-aimed shot at Duraqu, who was getting up from under the table. He flew across the room and hit the wall behind solidly. But still in one piece – must have been wearing a deflector vest. The robot threw itself in front of Danee, sending blaster fire back through the smoking door to the pursuing military outside.

Danee got to her feet. "*Stand down, robot!*" she commanded. Then, to Gilham and Duraqu, "This is all *quite enough*. We came to this planet in the spirit of friendship and good faith, and *this* is how we are treated? We have learned *all we need to know* about Rethne and the Movement. The prince and I shall be leaving *immediately*."

The robot lowered its blasters and stood silent, unblinking eyes fixed on Danee. A man in military uniform scurried in through the haze, spoke briefly to Duraqu, who was slumped against the wall, and passed him a note. Duraqu read it, then looked up at the ceiling in surprise. He crawled over to Gilham, now emerging from under the table.

I think everyone in the room was a bit deafened from the blasts. But not me, not in the right ear anyway. Batum riding along in there must have protected it somehow, so I heard most of Duraqu's words even though he was trying to speak quietly.

"...*retrieved FTL call...brother for money...tonal stress analysis hundred per cent authentic...revised calculations...diplomatic incident at this time....*"

They were talking about my phone call, the one 'Donny' had made to 'brother Rob' begging for money. Their AI must have retrieved and analyzed the audio. It was scanning as authentic – because it *was* authentic. At the time I'd been desperate, down on my luck. I'd made the call in a fit of madness and despair, and my vocal patterns were showing up that way – implying 'Donny' was a real person from Grendeva who'd needed money, not someone plotting to impersonate a royal prince and infiltrate Rethne. It was a piece of hard evidence contradicting the facial match and therefore changing the odds for M4M's supercomputer.

Douglas must have calculated I would make that call – he couldn't have just told me to do it or it wouldn't have scanned as authentic. Instead he'd sent me to Grendeva in the most tortuous way possible to force me into it. He had foreseen. His algorithm had outsmarted M4M's.

Gilham stood stiffly and walked out of the room without saying a word.

Duraqu turned to Danee, ashen-faced. "We'll make the arrangements."

★   ★   ★

Our exit from Rethne was as low-key as our arrival had been grand. We were bundled into a van along with our robots and hastily packed

226 • STEPHEN K. STANFORD

bags, and dumped at the spaceport, where the *Sandhurst* waited, already in preflight mode. We trooped up the ramp, the lifeless form of Batum carried by a droid, while two guards watched impassively. Moments later we were gone.

During the interminable eight hours we spent getting far enough away to jump, I made only one comment to Danee. In character, for who knew who might be listening: "Juliette, you were *magnificent!*"

She smiled to herself, then gave me a wink.

We jumped as soon as the gravity window opened, dropped into interstellar space and spent forty-eight hours scanning the ship from top to bottom, not daring to speak frankly till the coast was clear. Ours had been a diplomatic mission, the ship sealed the entire time – but that hadn't stopped them. Batum debugged the software, while the security droid scanned every inch of the ship and its outer hull, destroying countless planted devices. I myself put a suit on and joined the hunt. Finally, when everything was clean and every foreign object dumped into space like the loathsome trash it was, we jumped again.

Safe at last.

I slumped at the controls, then did a high five with Danee. "That was tight."

"You know, I had a feeling we'd be OK, just had to hang tough."

"It got close there with Gilham."

"Self-control issues, I'd say. That's his weakness – you said he had one."

"Yes, I think Sana's disappearance tipped him over the edge and as for their threats against us, I reckon their AI would have supplied everything in probabilities. Fifty per cent chance of this, twenty per cent chance of that. They couldn't quite put it together and then they retrieved Donny's call and it tipped the scales...." I noticed the prince's plumed hat sitting next to the controls and was seized by a fit of loathing. I threw it on the ground and stomped on it. "Thank god. I am never wearing that fucking thing *ever* again."

Danee laughed. "You'll need it on Grendeva."

"Fuck it, they'll have to cope."

"Wow, two *fucks* within a minute, sir, that's the most I've ever heard you swear."

"Well, I am a country boy," I said sulkily, "and anyway, it's been very frustrating, the whole *Prince Humphrey* thing."

Danee smirked. "You've done very well. Suppressing your masculine side for a whole four days."

We took another week transiting to Grendeva. I spent the first two days of it asleep – still run-down from that wild night underneath the Residence – and the last several days in the mediclinic trying to wipe some of the trauma. I was desperate for news of Sana, but didn't dare make contact. Back on Grendeva, Lady and Prince Fenwick debriefed us, then in a stroke of good luck the prince, who was himself heading to Jubilee anyway, offered us a ride home aboard his own ship, leaving immediately. We saw off the beautiful blue pearl of Grendeva from the control room, then spent the next few days hopping across the galaxy.

Time crawled. Looking in the mirror I saw the old Col start to re-emerge, the DNAltering wearing off. My body felt like it was shrinking and my hair was growing out brown. Not Danee, though. For whatever reason she still had the dark locks and generous bust of a Grendevan lady.

I tried talking with her. About Sana, about *us*. What were we going to do about...*all that*? But the moment we'd left Grendeva something had changed. She became reserved, took to sleeping in another cabin and refused to discuss anything. Whenever I thought about it all, my head hurt.

Every hour brought us closer to Jubilee. I saw little of the prince as he kept entirely to his own quarters.

We finally arrived at MGNA#12, then jumped again and Jubilee was before us. Crazy. Chaotic. My home – I realized with a start. We waited at the airlock and were joined by the prince and his entourage of robots, all burdened with luggage.

"Pleasant trip?" he asked good-naturedly.

"Yes, thank you," I said. "So, what are your plans?"

"For *moi?*" he asked, then with obvious relish, "Why, I shall be heading directly to the fleshpots of Jubilee. Post haste!"

Really? Hadn't he just got himself out of hock? And only because of a deal that was highly dangerous for Grendeva.

He must have seen something in my face because he scowled and said, "You judge? *Spare* me the middle-class morality!" Then he turned to hug Danee. "Goodbye, my dear, it was wonderful to know you. Come back to Grendeva anytime!"

The airlock opened and he waddled out, followed by the robots. Through the glass doors I saw two figures waiting for us in the arrival hall. Douglas and Sana.

CHAPTER THIRTY-FIVE

Sana ran to me at speed and jumped into my arms, light as a feather. Mind you, everything felt light now since we were off Rethne. It was the old Sana: vivacious and loving. She wrapped her arms and legs around me, put her head on my shoulder. I felt her cheek was wet.

"You saved me," she said very quietly. "You're my hero." Then in a whisper, "And tonight I'm going to *treat* you like one."

My heart raced. This was everything I'd been longing for, the Sana I had lost years before, but Danee was standing right behind. Awkward. I peeled Sana off. "You have to thank Danee. *Literally* the only reason we succeeded is because of her."

Sana took both her hands. "How can I possibly thank you?" She produced her highest wattage, most luminous smile. "You don't even know me. You risked your *life!*"

They hugged, but over Sana's shoulder Danee looked me coldly in the eye.

Meanwhile, Douglas was hopping from foot to foot with excitement. "Fuckin' hell!" he said, pulling me into a bear hug. "Ye bloody well did it!"

We were taken to the control room, where champagne and nibbles awaited. Batum joined us after a short while, freshly installed in a new body – this one shiny silver and robotic-looking, apparently his original security droid shape from before his conscription as a butler. We toasted. To the mission, to success, to ourselves. It was joyous. Or should have been but for the tension I saw around Danee's mouth. I needed to talk to her, but what would I say anyway?

"Now there's business to deal with," said Douglas, "but that can wait. Tonight we *celebrate*, OK?"

"What business?" I asked.

Sana swapped looks with Douglas. "Events on Brouggh. We need to get involved, but let's talk tomorrow, shall we?"

"OK, sure," I said, "but at least tell us about your rescue!"

Between Douglas and Sana, we got the full story. On hearing Batum's voice inside her head, Sana had understood immediately. "I thought there was something funny about you two – and then I got it." As instructed, she'd waited on her balcony at midnight, when out of nowhere a small craft had appeared. She'd thrown her bangle onto the bed and dived in the flyer. Minutes later, they were far above Rethne when the nanides on her back woke up with a vengeance – programmed to activate more than a certain distance from the Residence. Sana went into seizure, foaming at the mouth. The ship was loaded with goods and heavy equipment, but had only one autonomous robot. Very primitive, with giant clumsy 'hands' for moving cargo. Somehow Douglas got it to open a medi-kit and sedate her – all the while taking the ship into deep space. The freighter flashed across the lower galactic quadrant while Sana lay at death's door. By the time they got to Jubilee her vitals were close to zero, but a waiting ICU team had her in a nano-bath immediately and Dr. Lam removed the accursed nanides.

"I woke up delirious, thinking I was in a bubble bath!" said Sana.

Only a few days later, she was good as new. Better than ever in fact, clear-eyed and free from pain for the first time in years.

"But we're keeping her under wraps for a while," said Douglas. "In fact, that goes for all of ye. Stay close to the control room and your apartments down the corridor. We don't know who might be lookin' around."

That sounded like an ongoing issue. How long would we have to stay 'under wraps'? Sooner or later, they were going to find out Sana was here.

Batum chipped in. "Can I ask a question?"

"I know that voice!" said Sana.

"Yes, you do."

"You were in my ear!"

"That's right, I was in nano form after the AI trashed my old body."

"It was the loveliest voice I'd ever heard!"

Sana in charm mode. When she turned on that ray *nothing*, no living creature *or* machine, could resist.

"My question," asked Batum, "is how come you appeared at *that* critical moment so we could give you the bangle?"

"Oh, that was Domenic, my boss – my friend too. He's gay and, you know, you're not meant to *be* that on Rethne – even though it was *completely* obvious." She rolled her eyes. "Anyway, he *came out* to me, we were close. He couldn't stand the way Gilham treated me. So he probably paged me on purpose to take in those chocolates. Must have wanted me to get a present like everyone else."

"He saved the mission," I said gravely.

"Really? *Domenic?*"

"We'd never have gotten that bangle to you."

"Do you think he's OK? Would they blame him?"

I had a bad feeling about Domenic. It would be just like the Movement to take it out on him in the most sadistic way possible – my poet friend Zhang had merely stood next to me at the wrong time and ended up dead. Unfortunately, Domenic's fate was sealed.

"They'll torture him," said Danee, standing up from the table, "probably to death."

Sana gasped, her mouth an O.

"Sorry, folks, but I'm beat. I'll see you all in the morning."

Danee strode out of the control room without looking back, her face set. I tried to make eye contact, but she avoided it. Not happy. The comment about Domenic was clearly meant to wound – and it had worked. Sana was crying, being comforted by Douglas and Batum.

"Don't worry, he'll be all right," lied Douglas. "I'll see what I can do, OK?"

"Can you?"

"O' course. I have me ways. They won't be keepin' a close watch on him like they was with you. I got a few ideas already."

That seemed to settle Sana down. But the mood was broken. May as well deliver the other bad news.

"Douglas, you knew Zhang the poet, right?"

"Whaddaya mean *knew?*"

I told him about the interrogation.

He stood and walked away from the table. "Those *motherfuckers!*" I heard a sob. "What'd he ever do to anyone? He was the sweetest guy, half-decent poet too. I'm gonna figure somethin' out for him, ye ken? We can't let them win."

We toasted Zhang sadly, another casualty of Sana's rescue, and with that the night really was over. We said our goodbyes and Sana and I headed to her apartment just down the corridor.

As soon as the door closed, Sana clutched me tightly, her head against my chest. A tiny bird, so different to Danee.

"You can't imagine what goes on there, in the Residence," she said.

Oh yes, I could.

"They took the trauma away somehow when they were treating me. But I still have the memories." She shivered.

"You can tell me as much or as little as you want."

"Not tonight."

She took my face in her hands and we kissed very slowly. She took off my clothes, piece by piece, touching my body as if for the first time, and then stripped off. She pushed me onto the bed and we had sex. Slowly, and then urgently. Like new lovers – better even. It was paradise – or should have been but for the fact Danee wouldn't leave my mind.

After, we lay together and talked. She told me how they'd come for her in the middle of the night, about twenty servicemen. There was a guy in charge, one of the gray t-shirts. He'd had a dossier and knew everything. They'd made her write the message on the bathroom mirror, then injected her with something. She'd woken up on a ship to Rethne.

"That was quick thinking with the message," I said.

"Writing the number two?"

"Yeah."

"It just came to me, I thought it might give you a clue."

"It did! Of course I rushed back to Jubilee, but when you weren't here, I figured it out. Saved a lot of time."

"Good." She paused. "You know, I don't think I can talk about all this anymore, not right now."

"OK, but just one more thing. Were you physically harmed?"

"No, in fact on that level I was treated well. But what he did to me psychologically – you'd have to call that torture." She shivered again, then had one of her patented 180-degree mood swings. "You look like a cross between Col and Prince Humphrey." She giggled. "It's very strange."

"The DNAltering, it's wearing off."

"Yeah, Douglas told me. What a ditz Prince Humphrey was – I didn't know you were such a good actor!"

"Who says I was acting?"

She laughed. "I know you, Col, that would have been torture for you!"

Moments later, she fell asleep in my arms.

But sleep wouldn't come for me and instead my mind turned down a negative track. I watched her chest rise and fall, marveling at her beauty. She was a goddess all right. Tonight she was mine, like the old days. The *good old days*. But how long would that last? How long could a man like me realistically hold on to a woman like her? Almost as soon as she'd started performing, the love notes had started arriving from entranced men – *and* women. Then came the dazzling political ascent. Official events and invitations to this and that where Sana would be in her element, working the room and charming everyone. And who was this lump of a guy by her side in an ill-fitting suit?

A cop.

A *cop?*

She was still figuring herself out when we met, then she became a public figure. A major one. Being realistic, maybe – or even probably – she needed one of those guys you saw in the holos. Handsome and charismatic, more powerful, and more successful than me – someone who could hold his own in that world.

Maybe the right person for *me* was sleeping in another room just meters away? What *would* Danee be thinking? I had blindly charged forward with the rescue, put everything else out of mind and then before I even knew it, somehow ended up in bed here with Sana. What a fool.

Such were my thoughts and they churned over and over.

The next morning, we all met again in the control room. I felt grumpy and tired, but Danee seemed back to her normal self, friendly and sweet. It was as though a ball of negative feeling had passed from her to me during the night.

Sana was all business. "Everything's coming to a head now on Brouggh. The Supreme Court is set to release its judgment about the constitutionality of what M4M did, taking over Congress."

Sana was worried about the chief justice, a friend of hers. Born male, Justice Eergan had DNAltered to become female. While hardly unknown, this was nevertheless uncommon and certainly unprecedented for a high official – causing a ruckus on social media. Some years later, the now *Chief* Justice Eergan had caused more tongues to wag by bearing a child through IVF – and conceived *parthenogenetically* with no male chromosome. In other words, without a father.

"Of course, the Movement hates all that!" said Sana. "And she's no fan of theirs either. But she's in a vulnerable situation."

Douglas brought up a holographic map on the table. "This is her house here, in the middle of a wood outside Brouggh City."

It was a large and experimental-looking place, all flat lines and large windows. This judge seemed quite the radical. No wonder she'd hit it off with Sana.

"They've got military checkpoints in front of her house, plus here and here."

"What are they guarding exactly?" I asked.

"Well, that's the point, isn't it?" said Sana. "They set up those guard posts after the court retired to make its decision, supposedly for her protection. But I'd say it's an implied threat, don't you think? She's alone in there with her five-year-old kid."

A lightbulb went off. "Hey, I think they were talking about this, the M4M generals and the Aurelian, in the basement of the Residence! It was

Eergan's picture on display." I described the scene and told them about the events of that night.

"Sounds to me," said Douglas, "like their AI is calculating Eergan will vote the right way for them. They just have to sit tight, put a little pressure on and it all works out."

"Exactly, which is why *we* have to move the needle in the right direction – they won't be expecting that," said Sana.

Our actions would become the *X factor*, outside the envelope of possibility calculated by the AI.

"But how exactly can we help?" asked Danee.

"The chief justice and I know each other," said Sana. "If I could talk to her, offer some protection—"

"I've got a wee gadget that could be handy," said Douglas.

"Then she might feel safe enough to come out and rule against the Movement." I finished the chain of logic.

"But how do you know which way she would vote?" asked Batum. "She may not like M4M but still think their maneuvers were constitutional."

That was a point. Justice Eergan was the pre-eminent jurist of her generation, famous for objectivity and fairness. It's why the people of Brouggh didn't care all that much about her unconventional life choices and why a decision she helped craft would probably be accepted.

"I've no idea how she's going to vote," said Sana, "but people I knew, *legal* people, said their case was weak."

"OK!" said Danee emphatically. "Let's get this straight. You want us to help get you past security and into the chief justice's house on Brouggh so you can let her know it's safe to vote against the Movement. *If* she wants to?"

"Yes."

"I'm in," said Danee.

"Me too," I said.

"And me," said Batum.

There were high fives all around.

We pored over the holo map and a plan started to emerge. We would use one of Douglas's souped-up flyers, one that could jump straight onto the surface of Brouggh. Danee would pilot, Batum was reserve. I would escort Sana to the house through the forest, finding a way past the guards. It was coming together.

Danee started interacting with me, finally, as we figured out flight plans and landing locations. This was good. Working together, same as always. I even started to get a little playful with her, a fatal mistake.

"And none of your bodgy landings," I teased.

"*Please!*" she said. "You're the one needed help getting to Jubilee."

"I hadn't piloted in years. It was only coz you were *supposedly* commander—"

As we talked, Sana looked back and forth between us, a puzzled expression on her face. She must have sensed something, an intimacy. She was always so perceptive about these things, psychic even. "Oh my god!" she said, standing up. Walking away from the table, grabbing her head. "Oh my *god*, I just got it!" She turned and faced me. "You're *together* – you and Danee. Right?"

The room went deathly quiet. I wanted to run, wanted to hide. Wanted to be another person on a planet far, far away.

"Speak!"

"Yes," I mumbled eventually, "we've...been together."

"You took your *girlfriend* on the mission? To *rescue* me? When were you planning on *telling* me that?"

The roof and walls were collapsing in. I would rather have been facing off against a battalion of enemy troops with only a pocketknife.

"I can't believe it," Sana raged. "This is so *humiliating!* How could you not say something? And there's me *all over you* last night! What was *she* thinking?" She gestured toward Danee.

I made some strange throaty noises incomprehensible even to myself.

"Am I some kind of *prize?* Is that what you were thinking last night? While you were *fucking me!?*" She stormed to the door, stopping for a moment to deliver a final blow. "One thing I *will* say, she's definitely your *type*, isn't she!"

This a reference to Danee's hair and complexion, still darkened from the DNAltering.

"She doesn't normally look like this," I said weakly as the door slammed, the only thing I could come up with.

The room reverberated with Sana's tirade. I guess you could say the ball of bad feeling had passed to her.

"Ouch," said Batum.

Douglas raised his hands in surrender – even though I had said nothing to him. "Don't look at me, mate. I might be a quantum AI, but this shit's way above my pay grade."

Danee's head was down, her eyes closed. Was that a smirk?

"This is funny to you?" I asked, incredulous.

The smile vanished. She turned to me coldly, "What did you think was going to happen?"

"I don't know. I wasn't thinking."

"Exactly." Danee examined her fingernails. Slowly. Looking at each cuticle one by one. A tic of hers that she did when thinking. "All right, fuck it," she said. "This mission is too important. I'll go talk to her."

She strode purposefully out of the room while I sat rooted to the chair. There was dead silence in the control room. Even Douglas had nothing to say for once as the minutes ticked by. After what seemed hours, there were steps outside and the two women walked in. They looked flushed and, if anything, a little giddy.

Sana spoke to Douglas, not me. "*We've* decided this mission is too important to let...*recent events* get in the way. So we'll proceed as planned." Then to me, "Stuff happened, Col, when we were together, that I know was...not OK. But last night was just *totally unacceptable*. So when this mission is over, we need to talk." Her voice hardened. "Till then, you should make *alternative* sleeping arrangements."

I gulped. "OK."

With relief, Douglas brought the holo back up and the plan was finalized. We departed in four hours, reconvening at the departure dock. The two women left together and I heard them chatting pleasantly as they walked off down the corridor. What sort of monstrous feminine conspiracy was this?

"Wow, mate," said Douglas, shaking his head, "you really are screwed."

I could think of nothing to say.

He clapped me on the shoulder. "But best not dwell on it all. Keep busy! We'll go get your kom reinstalled, then I thought we could pay a special visit to someone."

"Really, who?"

"Someone who might be able to throw a little light upon your adventures on Rethne." He smiled wickedly. "The Aurelian Ambassador."

CHAPTER THIRTY-SIX

"Aurelia has an ambassador to Jubilee? Why do they need that?"

"Well, they *don't*, o' course," said Douglas. "It's kind of a joke, I think. Or a special punishment. Who knows with them? I heard they hate humans so much, ambassador's a job they reserve for wrongdoers."

I rubbed my left wrist as we walked, still a bit sore and itchy from having the kom reinstalled. But what a relief! It had become almost normal to live without it. Almost. I felt plugged back into the stream of my life, the endless flow of communication, part of me since the age of fourteen. Here on Jubilee, I couldn't access live data from across the galaxy because we weren't *in* the galaxy, of course – not the normal one, anyway. But I still had local files and the Jubilee intranet. This kom had been tweaked so it wouldn't ping when we got to Brouggh, otherwise a horde of police would descend the moment we landed. I would be able to access everything I needed but remain invisible to the network.

"So being ambassador to Jubilee, that's—"

"Like a big FU to him," said Douglas. "Or me. Can't work out which."

"How many Aurelians live here?"

"Just the one. We saw him on your first night."

I remembered. Danee and I had been at the hot pot restaurant watching as he'd walked through the crowd, tall and gloomy.

"How do you know he'll tell you the truth? And won't he report back? Could be dangerous."

Douglas stopped. "Listen, him and me, we go way back, ye ken? We got history. Which I won't go into just now, but safe to say he won't be tellin' anyone back on Aurelia about our conversation. Ye can trust me on that."

While we walked, Douglas brought up a holo call. The Aurelian appeared before us floating in space, seated in a large easy chair.

"McRabito!" said Douglas. "How you doin', ye grumpy bastard?"

The Aurelian grimaced. "The day was going fine until just now."

"I'm comin' over, bringin' a friend. You two are gonna hit it off."

"I'm sure we won't."

The image disappeared. Call terminated.

"See what I mean? *Grumpy!*" said Douglas.

As we walked, I tried to recall everything from the few moments I'd been in that basement on Rethne, then had a question. "Hey Douglas, was that you who caused those flyers to crash on Rethne?"

Douglas laughed. "Who else do ye think?"

"But how? I thought—"

"The *ring*, laddie. Sent a distress message in the instant it lost you. I was watchin' out from the freighter and when I saw your energy signature there in the fountain, decided a little distraction was in order...."

Those flyers are idiotproof thanks to all the built-in guidance control. Douglas must have used some serious voodoo to pull that one off.

To avoid prying eyes we traveled via the upper levels of Sector Two, a mainly residential area. Finally, we took a lift down a few floors and stopped in front of an ordinary-looking door to a residential apartment. A small sign read:

His Excellency Krn Ka Krkrabitoh
Consul General, Federated Systems of Aurelia

The door opened before we could knock. The Aurelian sat stiffly on a large chair in the middle of the room, his Drax beside him on the floor. The apartment was extremely plain but a decent size. As always with Aurelians, I couldn't shake the idea a tiny cloud was positioned over his head, raining only on him. He sat grim and expressionless, waiting for us to speak.

"Good to see you, Ambassador. Doin' well?" asked Douglas.

The Aurelian looked around and shrugged. "Living the dream, Douglas." Then to me, "Of course, it's Consul General, not

Ambassador." The voice was metallic and harsh, same as I'd heard on Rethne.

"Hi, I'm Col, pleased to meet you." I hesitated, unsure how to address him. "Your Excellency."

The Aurelian grimaced, but did not offer a hand to shake or any kind of pleasantry. There were no chairs, so we both just stood there facing him.

"How can I help?" he asked finally.

"I guess y've heard of the planet Rethne?" asked Douglas.

"I think I might have, yes."

"Well, this young fella just came back from there with some very interesting information."

"Is that so?" The Aurelian sighed. "I assume this information has something to do with Aurelia?"

"Ye could say that, yes."

"And you therefore wish to discuss it?"

"If ye'd be interested, we was goin' to."

"Douglas, I'm very much *not* interested, but here you are. So, go on...."

"OK, so it seems your people are giving the Movement assistance with highly advanced technology. Gonna cause a lot o' problems." Douglas nudged me. "Tell him." I cocked my head, reluctant, but Douglas said, "Go on."

I talked about the trip to Rethne, leaving out the rescue of Sana, which didn't seem relevant – or wise – to divulge. When I mentioned the basement and what was in there, the consul general appeared to stiffen in his chair.

"Here's a package from the droid Batum," said Douglas.

The Aurelian closed his eyes for a moment, scanning the data. There was a long pause and then finally he looked up. "So?"

"So? Don't ye see?" said Douglas impatiently. "Y're upsetting the balance o' power! I know you don't like humans much – can't blame you, really. Might seem a clever move, stick it up the League and all that, but it's gonna cause a huge blowup."

The Aurelian looked at us impassively, his black eyes impossible to read. Then he did the last thing I could have ever imagined. His mouth began to curl upward at each corner, then curled some more, turning into a hideous rictus of a smile – there should have been the sound of icicles breaking – then he arched his back and *started laughing*. Harsh, joyless laughter seemingly without end. The Drax lying beside him stood up and whinnied, put its two front legs across the Aurelian's lap and looked into his eyes with concern. The consul general petted it gently, muttering soothing words in his own tongue.

"Typical fucking humans," he said finally.

"How can you say that?" I asked, genuinely mystified.

"Because we didn't approach the Movement, *they came to us*! They came to us cap in hand and stupidly we agreed to give them what they wanted. And now, when it all blows up, guess who's going to get the blame?"

"So you know about it?" asked Douglas.

"Of course, been going on for ages."

There it was – acknowledgement. From an impeccable source. Proof that Aurelia really was backing the Movement – and had been for some time. A galaxy-shaking development.

"It can't end well, ye know that," said Douglas.

"*Of course* it won't end well. It's going to be a fucking disaster and it's going to blow right back on Aurelia."

"So why do it?" I asked.

"Because this," said the Aurelian, standing up, "is what you get when you have *youngsters* in charge of things!" The door behind us opened. "Now if you'll do me the pleasure" – he pointed outside – "let's at least *try* not to make this day any worse."

We walked back to the control room in silence, implications of the conversation heavy in the air.

Douglas made tea and filled me in about the consul general. "Seems there was a big political dust-up on Aurelia and our friend was on the losin' end of it."

One faction, calling themselves the realists, were in favor of some limited interaction with humans, while the other faction demanded total isolation. The conflict had played out over hundreds of years, becoming ever nastier, until the realists finally won out. Krkrabitoh, as a prominent isolationist, had been handed the exquisite punishment of being sent to live among humans as the entirely unnecessary Consul to Jubilee. He spent his days writing caustic political diatribes laced with obscure scripture from *The Wisdom of the Ancients*. Greatly amused, Douglas was happy to send these missives on to Aurelia, where they inevitably caused a fuss. Over the past hundred years, Douglas had foiled two assassination attempts and forged a friendship with the Aurelian.

"As much as ye *can* be friends with one o' them," he said. "And somethin' else, when he calls that lot in power youngsters – remember, they're *all* thousands of years old."

My kom bleeped. It was time.

Douglas walked with me to the airlock, where Danee, Sana and Batum were already waiting. We strapped in and minutes later were on our way to Brouggh.

CHAPTER THIRTY-SEVEN

We popped out of hyperspace straight into a clearing surrounded by a dense wood of silver beerah. Danee had calibrated perfectly – though I still couldn't get my head around the idea of jumping to a planet's surface. Danee and I were in SSB uniforms. That might give us a measure of disguise if things came to that. Sana wore a camo' brown and green jumpsuit, her black curly hair tied up in double topknots.

Was it only last night she lay in my arms?

That seemed over now, forever – the vibe from both women was friendly to each other, ice-cold to me. Batum sat in the copilot's chair as reserve. We decided not to deploy him or to bring Douglas. If something went wrong, there could be no fallout landing on Jubilee.

"Here goes," I said, opening the airlock. "I know I'm not your favorite person right now" – Sana rolled her eyes – "but once we leave this ship, please follow my instructions, OK?"

"Yeah, I get it," she said in a monotone.

"Really! This could be dangerous. You don't have my training." I touched her shoulder and she flinched.

"I said, I get it."

Danee nodded; Batum gave a thumbs-up. Sana followed me down the ramp and we were off into the woods. The house lay a kilometer to our north through thick bush. We walked in silence, Sana behind, as we picked our way carefully through the undergrowth. There would be a guard post at the front entrance and, following Services protocol, another one a kilometer or so behind the house. Deep rear. These guys had been sitting around for a month doing nothing. Bored to death, off guard by now. That's what I hoped, anyway.

In planning we'd had to choose between two options: try to sneak in without being noticed or take them out instead. We'd decided on the latter and I was laden with useful goodies to achieve that end.

It was midafternoon, a sunny but cool autumn day. A cold wind picked up, but we were warm from our exertions. Finally, a glimpse of the house through the dense brush. There was a cleared space ten meters wide running around the perimeter, a hardiplaz wall beyond. We stopped at the edge of the clearing and peered out. Over the wall were the roof lines of the multi-level house, large windows gazing out blankly. It felt disturbingly empty and still.

I wouldn't want to live there in that vast house. All on my own with a five-year-old kid, armed guards just outside the door.

I looked back at Sana and silently mouthed, *"OK?"*

She gave a thumbs-up.

I pointed to a log for her to sit on while waiting then headed off through the bush, much faster now on my own. Amazing to be back on Brouggh! Everything so intensely familiar: the look, the smell of the forest. I'd grown up ranging through country like this.

I kept the house on my left, heading east to the front entrance. It felt good to be doing something active. So much easier than trying to figure out what to do about the women in my life. Through the trees I made out the front driveway, the perimeter curving around to the left. A portable building was set up nearby, a flyer parked beside it. Two officers, a male and a female, lounged on chairs doing stuff with their koms. Very young and very bored.

"What's that?" asked the male officer as a grenade rolled in front of him.

It exploded, releasing a fast-acting sleep gas, and moments later the two guards were snoring peacefully. I crept forward, nose filters in place. The building was empty – just these two. Good. Sometimes there was a third on standby. I released the code Douglas had given me, a sophisticated piece of AI that would install itself on the koms of these guards and respond to basic calls and messages. It would also spread through the local network, excise our presence from the security cameras and delete itself within the hour.

Now for the rear. Possibly overcautious, taking them out, but I didn't want anyone paying a visit to their buddies at the front entrance. I jogged across the driveway and into the bush, circled around the far side of the house and headed to the rear base. Didn't hurt to do a 360-degree reconnaissance.

It was exactly where I expected. Due west of the house, a kilometer back and well camouflaged. Straight out of the SSB handbook. If anyone attacked at the front, they would not expect this second team – except if they knew the handbook, of course. Not that anyone *would* be attacking the house. This show of force was meant to intimidate, not protect, the occupants, but being Services and instinctively bureaucratic, they still did it all by the book.

The other two guys went down just as quickly. They had a nice setup with a cozy little room and an open fire with three chairs around it.

Three chairs?

I swiveled around on high alert just as a third young man walked in from the bush, toilet roll in hand. He stared at me in shock. Then understanding, dropping the roll, fumbling for his blaster. But way too slow. He fell instantly, sleep dart in his neck. Fool! I was rushing. Should have taken more time to study the setup.

Why *three* back here anyway?

Of course, one of them was *visiting*. Was probably supposed to be out front, but by now everyone was bored shitless. He'd dropped over to sit around the fire.

I arranged the three men in comfortable positions. All slumbering nicely. The tranquilizer dart would last longer than the gas, so he should wake up last. He'd have a story to tell, but would it get passed on? Not a good look, to get surprised like that – especially if you weren't supposed to be here. Not conducive to career advancement. Hopefully they'd stay quiet.

I moved off through the bush, quickly now. Came to the house, then jogged along the clearing beside the wall. There were cameras everywhere, but I had to trust Douglas's code. If it didn't work, we were screwed anyway, and speed was crucial. We had twenty minutes to get inside, talk to Eergan and be back on the ship. Half an hour tops. We couldn't chance anyone waking up early. I slowed, trying to find the spot where Sana was waiting.

Her head popped out of the bush, a worried expression on her face. Bad! I had told her to stay put. Typical Sana, not following instructions. Should I let it slide? I decided yes, unfortunately.

"All good?" she whispered.

"Yup," I said aloud. No point in being quiet anymore. "We've got twenty minutes. You ready?"

"Let's do it."

We dashed to the security wall, a featureless gray slab. Perfectly smooth, at least two meters high and made from a special kind of slippery hardiplaz meant to be unclimbable. Unless, of course, you have a Services-issue molecular bonding kit. I slipped on the gloves and checked my kneepads. Sana clambered aboard for a piggyback – *so light*. Through my kom I activated the left glove and placed it on the wall above my head. It stuck fast, joined at the molecular level. Then I lifted my right knee as high as possible and stuck that on too. The kit pads allowed me to attach and release, and within minutes we were at the top. My kom flashed, warning of a laser trigger – rapidly deactivated – and then we were sitting on top of the wall, looking down into Justice Eergan's backyard. Below us was a swimming pool with crystal-clear water, a courtyard with ornamental trees and beyond that a lawn to the back wall. A gardening bot clearing leaves paid us no attention.

Now to get down. Would have to repeat the process.

But no! A stroke of luck. To our left was a ladder leaning up against the wall. Had someone been using it to peer over the fence? Possibly. Probably. I made a gesture for Sana to wait and walked along the top of the wall carefully, one foot in front of the other, then slid down the ladder, only my hands making contact – another Services trick. Moments later Sana joined me on the ground.

We jogged around the pool and through the courtyard to the rear of the house. To find a giant sliding door facing a pergola and outdoor

248 • STEPHEN K. STANFORD

dining area. Nifty design, this place. The door was alarmed, of course, but that was no problem and moments later we found ourselves inside a large living area with adjoining kitchen. We moved cautiously through the house, which was completely spotless. Too much so. We passed a domestic robot polishing an already pristine mirror. There were a series of large open-plan rooms, dining, lounge and media – all empty.

"Where is she?" whispered Sana.

I shrugged. We came to some stairs and I tilted my head. Had to be up there somewhere; the ground floor was empty. We tiptoed up. The stairs were made of shiny marble or stone and spiraled in clear space with no visible means of support – no balustrade either. I reached out to the sides. A restraint was there, but made of some material that was virtually invisible. Meant to look like stairs spiraling up into space – all very fancy.

There was a door at the top. Sana went to pass, but I held her back. I took another step onto the landing. Looked left, then right to see a black object whizzing toward me at great speed. Caught it just in time – a piece of black marble – it would have cracked my head open. The attacker turned to run, letting out a piercing scream. Cut off as I grabbed her and covered her mouth. She writhed in my arms in blind panic.

"Lillian!" said Sana, coming to my side. "It's OK, don't freak out, we're here to help!"

The woman thrashed, eyes wild, then went still. I gently released her.

"Sana?" She brought her hands to her face in shock, then sank to the floor. "Sana, what are you doing here, what's going on? I think I'm losing it." She took a breath, looked up at me, some measure of control returning. "Who's this?"

"Lillian, this is Col."

"*The* Col?"

"Yes, he looks a bit…different to normal, but that's a long story." Then to me, "Lillian and I always used to talk about…you know, *stuff*—"

"She was always *very* complimentary. Would you mind?" The chief justice held out a hand.

I pulled her up and she grabbed Sana in a tight hug.

"Come," she said, leading us down the corridor to a living area that looked out over the backyard. She poured a glass of water and drank it down, still trembling. Pulled her hair back and fixed us with clear blue eyes. "I'm trying to process this. What's going on? Why are you here?"

"It's a long story," said Sana, "and we don't have much time."

There was a pocket-sized – but still lethal – blaster lying on the kitchen counter. Eergan saw me looking at it and smiled. "You're lucky I was down the other end of the house, had to attack you with a ten-thousand-credit artwork instead!"

Indeed. The object she'd thrown was still in my hand. I put it on the table and saw it was a piece of polished black marble in the shape of a vulva. Formidable, this woman. Still in shock, but she stood straight-backed and spoke in a commanding tone, honed no doubt from years running a courtroom. One entire wall of the room was taken up with security cameras, the vision flicking between various angles: along the walls, outside the front entrance – where I noted with relief the guards slept soundly – and into the forest on every side. She asked how we got inside and I gave her a quick explanation. Over the last month she'd retreated upstairs, cut off and increasingly paranoid.

"Once this is over," she said, "I'm getting out of this stupid *rich person's house* and moving back to the city."

I checked my kom. Ten minutes left.

Sana brought the conversation around to the point. "We know the court's decision is due tomorrow, right?"

No need to mention which decision.

"Yes, 3 p.m."

"Lillian, I don't know your thinking. But the reason why we're here is because…well, if you *did* plan to rule against the Movement, we can offer support. If you're afraid."

"Who's *we*?"

Tricky question.

"I'm sorry but we can't say, Lillian."

Her eyes narrowed. She thought for a moment, then came up with her own answer. "I suppose we're talking about some kind of secret League agency. Makes sense."

I tried not to smile. Better to leave her with that assumption – more reassuring than the truth.

She sat down on a stool and ran her hands through her hair again. "You know," she said in a tremulous voice, looking first at Sana, then me, "I've always thought of myself as a courageous person."

"That's how I think of you, Lillian," said Sana softly.

"I always made my choices, *boldly*. But having a child. Everyone says it changes you and I didn't doubt that. But it's been...a *shock*. Look at all that –" She pointed to the wall of security vision. Her voice hardened. "Their case is a piece of shit. I know which way to vote, but it *is* terrifying. Not for my sake, but Daniel's. You've no idea the pressure, not just those guards...."

She teared up for a second, then clamped the emotion down. This had clearly been a difficult time for her, stuck in this designer-everything house, going quietly mad.

"We can help," I said.

"How?"

I pulled out the locket Douglas had supplied. "This is going to sound very strange, but you have to believe me."

"He's telling the truth, Lillian," said Sana.

"This piece of jewelery is a communication device. If you get into trouble, hold it in your hand and call us."

"How?"

"You say this sentence: *It's been ages since we had a holiday.*"

Eergan picked up the locket and turned it over. It was heart-shaped, strung on a gold chain. She flicked it open to find a tiny picture of a baby, causing her to tear up again. "This is like something out of a holo-drama," she said.

I laughed. "Kinda, yes. Say those words now so it's got your voice pattern."

"Seriously?"

We both nodded.

She looked at the locket skeptically and said, "*It's been ages since we had a holiday*. Then what happens?"

"An hour later you go somewhere outdoors, anywhere, could even be a balcony. Somewhere with access to the sky. Wear the locket and have Daniel in your arms."

"And then?"

"Help will come."

"What kind of help?"

"I can't tell you, but help."

There was noise in the corridor, a child's cry and running feet. Eergan was instantly alert.

A small boy ran into the room clutching a stuffed rabbit, a domestic droid close behind. "Mummy!" he said happily.

"Sorry, ma'am," said the robot. "There was a noise, Daniel woke early from his nap."

"That's OK, it was my fault," said Eergan, wrapping the boy in a hug.

He surrendered for a moment, then pulled away to look at us. Hadn't been visitors here for a while, I guess. "Hello!" he said brightly, clutching his mother's pants.

With long blond hair and clear intelligent eyes he looked a lot like her, but not identical in the way a clone would. I would have to look into how parthenogenesis worked sometime – if we ever got out of here.

"Look, Mummy, flyer!" said the boy, pointing to the screens.

I wheeled around. A Services flyer was putting down at the front entrance next to the other.

Very bad.

We had about twenty seconds before they found their sleeping mates and all hell broke loose.

I grabbed Sana. "We've gotta run."

"Wait," said Eergan. "There's a back gate, would that help?"

"Absolutely."

We sprinted down the marble steps, almost slipping off, then through the house and outside. My mind raced. Why was that flyer arriving *now?*

Shift change.

Of course. Why hadn't we thought of that? The time was 15:53, seven minutes early. But still, we'd cut it too fine.

We tore through the backyard, past the pool and across the grass. The gardening droid, still pottering away, ignored us as we shot by. Eergan took us to the far wall, the one facing west toward the rear base. The wall looked seamless without any breaks, but she held up her kom and a section slid away revealing the forest outside.

"Good luck," she said, waving goodbye.

We darted straight across the cleared strip of land and into the safety of the forest.

"Follow my lead," I told Sana as we beat our way forward.

An alarm sounded at the front of the house, reverberating through the still wood. There were harsh cries and agitated voices. Much chatter on the local network. This was a bolt from the blue. They'd be freaked out and disorganized – at least for a few minutes. That's all we needed.

A clutch of flyers appeared overhead, landing in a scatter formation and disgorging troops. Thanks to Douglas's code we would be invisible to their scanners – but not to a visual search. Which is what they were now doing. The Aurelian AI kicking in, of course – and it wouldn't be fooled by that code for long either.

We were halfway back to the ship, moving slowly now through dense undergrowth, when I heard soldiers forty meters to our left, having a hard time of it in all their gear. I caught a glimpse of them through the trees and dived for the ground, pulling Sana down with me. We lay there prone while the troops methodically beat their way toward us through the undergrowth. I slowed my breath and reached behind for Sana's hand. She let me take it and gave a squeeze back. Positive sign, I guess. The soldiers passed in front of us by ten meters or so. They were encumbered, breathing hard, looking around for movement. We lay completely still. Through the thick bush I glimpsed boots tramping, heard a radio crackle. And then they were gone, continuing west toward the rear base. I gestured silently to Sana and we were off again.

More flyers arrived. The air was thick with them now, the forest filled with sound and activity. I turned to see Sana grim-faced, but holding it together.

The thick bush petered out. Before us lay ten meters of open ground and beyond that the stand of silver beerah where the ship waited. Almost there. I motioned for Sana to stay, counted to three, took a deep breath and dashed across.

Purple light blazed, striking the earth and making puffs of dust. I rolled and threw myself into the bushes beyond. Damn, a squad of soldiers to our north.

I hurled everything I had at them over the trees. A cluster of smoke bombs and dozens of sleep-gas grenades – they wouldn't be expecting those. There was thudding and flaring, and the air was instantly opaque. Blasters fired in all directions as my bombs popped, seeding chaos. If I could keep them occupied for just a little longer, we'd make it home.

Why did she run?

Who would know with Sana? Maybe she panicked? Or didn't trust I would get her out?

Whatever the reason, she ran.

Across the clearing, where a bright flash of blaster fire pierced the fog and caught her in the chest. It must have been the final conscious act of whoever fired, because I threw myself into the clearing and dragged her back without being fired upon myself.

"*Batum, she's hit, she's hit, she's hit!*" I screeched mindlessly into my kom, then caught myself. "Emergency, Sana's hit!"

Bright redness bloomed on her chest. Blood bubbled from her mouth; she was trying to say something. I brought my ear close.

"Col," she rasped, barely able to speak.

"Yes?" I answered, my heart breaking, my world falling apart.

"I never stopped loving you."

"I know, me too."

Sana took a deep shuddering breath and died in my arms.

CHAPTER THIRTY-EIGHT

There was a flash of silver through the trees.

Batum, moving at unnatural robotic speed. He ripped Sana from my arms and vanished again within a millisecond.

A volley of blaster fire came through the fog. Running on autopilot I returned fire, for good measure throwing extra grenades, which seemed to quieten them down. I took off into the wood, knowing already what I would find – the ship gone. Three deep indentations where the landing pads had rested.

I stood zombielike.

How could this have happened? How could I have saved her, only to lose her?

A tidal wave bore down on me, immense and dark: of guilt, of grief.

I stood rooted to the spot. The voice of the training spoke to me: *process feelings later, survive.*

For what? A life without Sana? Inconceivable.

I stared at the space where the ship had been, unable to move. Let them kill me, I didn't care.

The fog was dissipating. Sharp voices and the crackling of radio static emanated from around the forest. A purple light sizzled across the clearing, sending a tree opposite up in flames, and my body reacted without thinking. I threw myself away from the blast, dived into a roll, then emerged in a crouch and ran, sending more smoke and gas grenades in every direction. There was a frenzy of blaster fire behind – the fools were firing on each other now.

Flyers poured in from all directions, soon there'd be an army here. What the hell, I had nothing to live for. I would lead them on a merry dance before they got me. I moved off, heading away from the house purely by touch. The air cleared a bit and I came across a gully with a small creek running through it, decided to follow the creek downstream. The chaos and blaster fire were if anything intensifying behind me. What a clusterfuck, wait till they reviewed the footage. These were the kind of armed forces you get in a society that hasn't known real conflict in generations. Plus, throw in an idiot like Brimheed to be in charge.

I moved down the gully, the sounds of chaos fading. The air was clear here, but with so many flyers in the air darting in every different direction, only the built-in collision protection would be keeping them apart. The gulley was slow-going, densely wooded. Eventually a small road came into view about a kilometer away, downhill. I consulted my kom and saw it was part of the long driveway leading to Eergan's house, now far behind me. It crossed over the creek, then ran along the wall of the gully for a couple of kilometers before meeting up with the highway to Brouggh City. A semblance of a plan came to me: I would track the road from the safety of the gully, then see if I could flag a vehicle down on the highway. The more obvious strategy would be to disappear into the endless forest around the house and wait for rescue. But they would think of that, set up a cordon and gradually draw it in.

So do the opposite – head into town.

The creek flowed under the road through a large pipe – which would also be my means of crossing. I waited until there were no flyers, then dashed out of the wood and into the tunnel. It was a meter high with only a trickle of water, so no problem crawling through. I could see sky and trees at the far end, getting closer. The land plateaued, then dropped away to a deep gorge overhung with foliage. I emerged from the pipe, dirty and wet, to find a Services flyer parked under the canopy.

The uniformed man leaning casually against the open door, working on his kom, didn't even bother looking up. "Took your time, Perolo," said Henderzon, my old antagonist at SSB.

I was half out of the tunnel in an awkward position, but still able to reach for a blaster.

"Don't be an idiot," he said, still not looking at me and making no attempt to defend himself. "Come on, get in, we've gotta move."

Sometimes there's a moment in your life when nothing at all makes sense. And sometimes in one of those moments you need to make a split-second decision. This was one of them. I threw myself across the back seat of the flyer, which promptly took off.

"Get on the floor," said Henderzon over his shoulder, then into his kom, "*Possible sighting of target heading south, uploading coordinates now.*" He chuckled. "That oughta keep 'em going for a while."

We ascended and sped north, the sun setting to our left. SSB flyers zoomed past, above and below, while I cowered on the floor. After a few minutes, the sky cleared and I joined Henderzon at the front, my head spinning from this sudden change of fortune.

"Henderzon? Where are we going, how—?"

"SSB safe house, not far from here. Best you don't know all the details."

"But how come you were waiting for me?"

"A lot's been happening, Perolo. There's a group of us – more about that later. I was monitoring the scene at Eergan's house and saw a visual of you. Put it all together."

"How did you—?"

"By looking at a map! Just like those idiots could have, if they had any brains. Where else would you go? Into the woods? Sucker move. No, follow the gully down to the main road and disappear into civilization. I figured it was worth a try, anyway, and here you are!"

The flyer made a rapid descent, landing in the yard of a dilapidated farmhouse. Broken equipment lay among overgrown fields and falling-down fences. An abandoned farm. The kind of place you don't even notice driving past because it's vaguely unpleasant. In reality, an SSB safe house.

Henderzon dashed to the front door, which was secured with a military-grade lock, released it with his kom and held it open. "I'll be back in a few hours. Don't do anything stupid."

And then the flyer was gone.

Don't do anything stupid meant stay indoors, which was fine by me. The house was quite different on the inside, with modern furniture, made-up beds and a clean if slightly dusty kitchen unblemished by anything resembling food. But I had no desire to eat. After poking around in a few drawers and cupboards, I finally found what I was looking for: a large bottle of Services-issue whisky. Guaranteed to be some lying around in a place like this. I poured a large glass, set myself down on the couch and flicked through my kom. Nothing about the trouble at Eergan's house. No messages. Time to get drunk. I downed the first two glasses in one gulp and started work on a third. But I've never been much of a drinker and on an empty stomach, with all the day's exertion and shock, the booze sent me rapidly into a welcome oblivion.

★ ★ ★

Sounds at the front door. I sat up from the couch in alarm, ready for war.

"Only me," shouted Henderzon, wise enough to call a warning. He was laden with supplies and boxes of takeaway food. "You look like shit, Perolo," he said, dropping the bags. "Go clean up while I sort out dinner."

I made use of the pristine bathroom and splashed water on my face. I did indeed look terrible, covered in bruises and cuts, with dark rings around my eyes. There was dried blood on my sleeves and chest. Sana's blood.

Grief fell upon me like an avalanche. And bitter recrimination. How had I allowed that to happen? The scene played in my mind, over and over in a horrible loop.

But in the end the body doesn't care about such things. Food smells wafted from the kitchen and despite everything, my stomach growled, reminding me I hadn't eaten all day. Henderzon had pizza and beers ready, and before I knew it I was tucking in despite myself.

"Thanks," I said.

"Don't mention it."

I tried to make conversation. Anything to get that horrifying replay out of my head. "So fill me in, what's been going on?"

"A lot," said Henderzon. "Firstly, you should know that eye-gouging episode in Brimheed's office was a big wake-up call. Everyone realized that story they'd put out was bullshit and if it could happen to you – such a *boy scout* – it could happen to anyone."

"I hoped it would get around."

"There's a group of us, older hands. Very unhappy 'bout how easily the forces were co-opted and politicized. I got myself transferred to BC to work from the inside. We want reforms and if the judgment goes right tomorrow, we're taking back control." He paused, took a long swig of his beer and finally asked the burning question. "So, you were up to something with Eergan today, right?"

How much to tell him? "Let's just say we're on the same side. Didn't you try reaching out to her yourselves?"

"Yeah, but you know, cops and judges …."

Not a good history there. Especially with socially progressive judges like Eergan. The pizza was surprisingly good and the beer washed it down nicely.

I had a burning question of my own. "I thought you hated my guts, Henderzon, why are you helping me now?"

He paused again, took another long pull of beer. He seemed to be loosening up, the alcohol taking effect. "I dunno, Perolo. Look, I owe you an apology, all right? What happened was wrong and afterward I realized I didn't want to be part of it. That's why I joined the Resistance." He looked a little sheepish. "That's what we call it."

"I never had a problem with you, Henderzon, but you always seemed pissed off at me."

"You were always the fucking golden boy, always got the breaks. How it seemed to me."

I shook my head. If he only knew. "Didn't feel like that for me."

"Yeah, I guess, and this is hard to say…." He looked down for a moment. "It was the *ladies*, all right?"

I think I knew what he meant, some inkling anyway. Growing up in Jerbert, I had been like every other adolescent guy: awestruck and tongue-tied around the local girls, who transformed overnight somehow from classmates into goddesses. But for no reason I could tell, something had changed at the Academy. I'd never put any effort into it. Nor was I especially confident or charming, but for some reason there had always been women around. Pretty ones, judging by the jealous comments I'd got from the other guys sometimes. They were *easy come*. But *easy go* as well – once they saw how all-consuming my career was. And I hadn't cared much either way – not until Sana.

"And then," said Henderzon, taking another swig, "you married that gorgeous black chick, the politico."

I closed my eyes, awash with pain. "I think she's gone, Henderzon."

He didn't understand, of course, so I threw caution to the wind. Told him about the mission, told him about everything.

"Are you sure she's dead?"

"She died in my arms. I *felt* it."

He paused again, thinking. "Did they have a porta-ICU in that flyer?"

Good question. Had we discussed it in planning? Couldn't remember. But it's something Douglas probably would do, load one in case things went awry. "I don't know for sure. Probably yes."

"Well then, you never know."

"She was gone, I tell you."

"Maybe, but those things are incredible. I'm just sayin', don't go jumping off a bridge till you know for sure."

It was good advice, but I dared not hope. We ended up talking until late and Henderzon turned out to be surprisingly good company, a country boy like me. It was big of him to apologize like that.

Next thing there were birds chirping and my neck was sore from sleeping on the couch. I ran a long, hot shower and dressed in the fresh clothes Henderzon had left. He was already gone somewhere, so I made breakfast and checked my kom. Still nothing.

In the early afternoon, a bunch of flyers arrived. Henderzon's group, the Resistance. I was introduced rapid-fire to three men and a woman: Burns, Durns, Sturgess and Chang – something like that – come to watch the decision live. They were tense and fidgety. I got the feeling if the case went badly, they were going to be in big trouble.

At 2:30 p.m. a holo-news channel went up on a large screen, sound muted, and we watched together in growing tension. Protesters, for and against the Movement, chanted and waved placards outside the court. The pro-Movement protesters seemed well organized with neatly printed signs, whereas the opposition looked undisciplined and chaotic – at least that's how the news channel showed it.

Henderzon sat down and passed over a beer. I stared at it for a moment, not normally a daytime drinker, then thought *what the hell.*

"So, you wanna know what we discovered about Lachy Nees?" he asked, smirking.

"You solved it?"

"Took all of fifteen minutes."

"Really, how?"

"Talked to their security."

Always start with the security. They know everything about the families they guard.

"Take a guess what we found."

I'd spent a lot of time thinking about Chairman Nees' son. Why would a privileged teenage boy throw his life away like that and in a manner so guaranteed to hurt his father? An answer popped into my mind from out of nowhere. "Sexual abuse?"

"Sustained. Horrific. From the youngest age. How did you know that?"

"Dunno…just a hunch, I guess. Would I be right in thinking the fruits of this investigation might find their way out to the general public at some point in the near future?"

Henderzon smiled coldly. "Yes, I think they might, 'specially if today's ruling breaks for us."

On screen the eleven justices filed into court wearing black robes – no doubt a throwback to some kind of ceremonial dress from Old Earth. They took seats at a long table, Chief Justice Eergan in the center. She looked nervous to me and why not? Billions of people, the eyes of a whole planet, were fixed upon her. They cut to outside the courtroom and to other places of protest around Brouggh. All silent now, transfixed. Eergan outlined the details of the petition in a long preamble. Her voice was clear and forthright, but the legal issues were too complex for me to follow.

Inside the safe house, nobody spoke. I silently prayed Sana's sacrifice had not been in vain. Finally Eergan arrived at a conclusion. She paused, took a sip of water, ran her hands through her hair and spoke directly to camera. "...Consequently, we find the declaration of *state of emergency*, along with the assumption of dictatorial powers under the *potente* clause XXIV.2, to be unconstitutional and therefore rule for the petitioner in this matter."

Congress would be dissolved, new elections called and the previous prime minister reinstalled in a caretaker role.

We all leaped into the air, cheering. Beer went everywhere. Henderzon and I hugged – who would have imagined that six months ago?

"What happens now?" I asked no one in particular.

"That's the big question," said one of the others. Burns, I think. "How will they respond?"

So far in all their galactic conquests the Movement had restricted themselves to legal and constitutional means, at least initially. Would they accept the court's ruling? Eergan appeared in close-up, the heart-shaped locket clearly visible. The justices filed out and the screen filled with jabbering talking heads and a panel discussion. The people of Brouggh waited.

Chairman Nees appeared. He looked stiff and flushed, and read a quick statement straight from his kom. Even though the Movement strongly disagreed with the court's ruling, it abided by the decision and looked forward to fiercely contesting the upcoming election.

We had won.

Our safe house turned into a Resistance hub. Flyers came and went at all hours. There was much huddling and strategizing and earnest conversation late into the night.

In Harrison, my old mate Aballa was installed as acting chief, and Brimheed was frog-marched to the door.

Repeated across Brouggh as Movement stooges were flushed from office. Unsavory details also came to light regarding Chairman Nees and his deceased son, immediately denounced as fake news but having a rapid and negative effect on his poll numbers.

Still nothing on my kom.

For a week, as life on Brouggh upended, I did nothing but obsess about Sana while pacing the house, taking long walks in the countryside and batting away job offers from my newfound chums. Henderzon offered transport to Jubilee – in just a few more days he'd be able to pull it off – but in the end that wasn't necessary.

Late one afternoon a familiar-looking flyer landed in the yard. I ran outside to find Douglas gesturing through the open passenger-side door.

"C'mon, laddie," he said, "time to get you home!"

CHAPTER THIRTY-NINE

I ran to the flyer and stopped dead a meter away, frozen, blood roaring in my ears. "Sana?"

Douglas looked serious for once, his eyebrows beetling with concern. "Col, we're doin' our best, but the injuries…you might have to prepare yourself for the worst." He brought up a holo of Sana in a nano-bath, her face slack, tubes running everywhere. "They're going to try restartin' her heart and lungs in the next day or so."

I ran back to the house and said quick goodbyes to whoever was around. Henderzon was off somewhere, so I sent a thank-you to his kom. We jumped immediately and Douglas filled me in. Of course there had been a porta-ICU loaded on the flyer. After I'd called the code red, it had come to life instantly. Batum took mere seconds to retrieve Sana but in that time her heart had stopped, so the machine had admitted defeat and snapfrozen her to minus ninety degrees. Danee had bounced the flyer straight into interstellar space, carved the fastest possible route to Jubilee, where a team was ready. For the past week, nanos had been rebuilding Sana's heart and lungs.

On Jubilee I was taken to my old apartment in Sector Fourteen. My stuff was there, but Danee's was gone. I tried calling and messaging – no luck. Paged Douglas, who gave me her new address, but at the last moment I chickened out of going around – everything just felt too complicated and weird. Next morning, I was in the room when they restarted Sana's heart. They say those machines do exactly the same job, but I don't buy it. The moment her heart started, the color in her face changed. She looked alive again.

Each day there was improvement, but her injuries were at the extreme outer limit even for modern medicine. I spent hours by her side – to be honest, I had little else to do. One afternoon, I bumped into Danee in the hospital corridor. We both stopped a few steps apart. I couldn't help noticing she looked especially radiant with rosy cheeks and shiny hair. I stood speechless. She smiled, her eyes warm and loving. Stepped forward, took my hand and kissed it. Then patted it and walked on without saying a word.

What the fuck did *that* mean?

Douglas was no help – and if he couldn't understand it, what hope did *I* have?

"But there *is* somethin' I'd like ye to see," he said, eyes twinkling.

We hailed an aircab and floated down Concourse, the throngs below us. My first time in one of these and definitely a superior way to travel. We reached the intersection of Sectors Eleven and Twelve, the edge of the red-light district. A large black box was stationed at the corner emblazoned with shiny silver letters: Zhang the poet.

Standing on top of the box was my friend. "Hey! How're you doing, Donny?" he asked. "Back from Grendeva already?"

"Hi, Zhang," I said cautiously. "Yeah, I'm back. Are you OK? I heard something…*happened* to you on Rethne."

"Yeah, I died," he said in a matter-of-fact tone. "Tortured to death. But they made this copy of me!"

Douglas was beaming. "Obviously this ain't a real stasis file coz he weren't backed up. But it's a pretty fair digital re-creation based on all the vision and data. What do you think? Now he can be here on Jubilee forever – his *favorite* place!"

I wasn't sure. Zhang was a private kinda guy and his favorite place was more likely the beach shack on Parla, not Jubilee. I had a rush of memory. We were standing together in the 'bar' during that interminable first leg to Grendeva. Drinking beer and picking at the horrible vending-machine food.

"So tell me something, do you *like* Jubilee?" he'd asked.

"I guess so," I'd said. "It's a place where people have total freedom." I surveyed the scene around me, everyone desperate, beaten-down. "Freedom to do what they want and also to trash themselves."

Zhang laughed. "True and you know the irony, right? That freedom is only possible because the place is run by an all-seeing, all-knowing dictator."

"Douglas."

"Yep. Though I love Douglas, don't get me wrong, he's a *benevolent* dictator." Zhang had taken a long pull on his beer, lost in thought. "Ever wonder why they called it that?"

"Jubilee?

"Yeah."

"Dunno, never really thought about it."

"Words are my thing. So I looked up the etymology. It's an ancient word, from Old Earth of course. You know the definition?"

"Some kind of anniversary, right?"

"A *special* anniversary, like twenty years. But there's also a more obscure secondary meaning." He'd raised an eyebrow. "A *jubilee* in ancient times was when they let the slaves go free – like an amnesty."

"You think that's got something to do with why they called it that?"

"Dunno. Maybe. I'm just sayin'...."

Back on Concourse I reached out to shake Zhang's hand and it passed through thin air, the hologram so convincing I forgot.

Zhang laughed. "Sorry, Donny, I don't have a physical body these days! But would you like a poem?"

I shrugged, why not? Zhang frowned in concentration, then a card emerged from a slot in the box he was standing on. I pulled it out to read:

Returned
Unquiet
Benevolent light shining.
Don't be sad, loving heart.
Zhang the Poet

I stared in astonishment. Was this machine called Zhang in some way tuned into my thoughts and feelings? Or was it just Douglas, playing games?

Douglas peered over my shoulder at the card. "What do you reckon? Not bad, eh?"

Zhang was now talking to other people nearby. He offered them a poem too and moments later a card slid out of the box. Zhang had become another Jubilee 'attraction'. Was that a good thing – or was it somehow ghastly?

A message flashed on my kom from the ICU – they were ready to bring Sana back to consciousness. We waved goodbye to Zhang and high-tailed it to the hospital, where Danee was already waiting – as before, not communicative but not cold either. I arrived just in time to see those beautiful eyelids flutter for a few seconds then open. This was the moment of truth. The doctors had been able to repair the body, but what about the mind?

Her eyes opened to slits. She made a low, animallike groan. Her mouth moved, trying to form words, my name perhaps – I dared hope – then, more clearly, "Where am I?" She was surrounded by tubes and equipment, only her face visible above the nano-bath.

"Sana, you're here on—"

My answer was cut off by a loud moan. She started squirming in the bath, then thrashing and shrieking in distress. There was a flurry of activity from the medicos.

"Sorry about that," said a woman I recognized as the chief physician. "We had to bring her up without pain suppressant."

Sana quietened again. Her eyes closed, then opened. She stared blankly at the ceiling.

"Show's over for now," said the doctor.

The next day Sana was able to turn her head toward me and smile. Definite progress. On the third day she started to speak – but slowly, with much slurring of words. I asked what she remembered.

She closed her eyes in concentration. "We were at...Lillian's house" [wiwians house], "then after that...." She shook her head.

"You know your heart stopped? They brought you back from the dead."

She nodded. "...remember now...dark tunnel...saw people...my ancestors…calling me." She stopped for breath. "…said…*you have to go back!*"

"Really? That's what, a life-after-death experience? Amazing!"

She choked on a laugh. "Kidding!"

That's when I finally knew she'd be OK.

On the sixth day there was a visitor. Sana's improvement had been astonishing, the nanos working their magic. She spoke almost perfectly now, but in a strange accent like someone from a world I couldn't quite identify. Douglas arrived with a young guy in tow, squat-shaped with dark hair and olive skin. Rethnean from a mile off.

"*Domenic!*" said Sana, her face lit with joy. "I can't believe it!"

"Yes, it's *me*, I can't believe it either!" He stood awkwardly by the bed, luggage at his feet, then took Sana's hand.

"What happened? How did you get here?"

"I won't go into it all now coz *look at you*. But let's just say after your disappearing act things got nasty. Then somehow this human rights group found out about my plight" – Douglas nudged me – "it seems I've become something of a *cause célèbre!*"

And no doubt an unexpected and highly generous donation was made to that very same human rights group. Douglas had pledged to do something for Domenic. I hadn't believed that was possible, but here he was.

"You're going to love it here," said Sana. She introduced him to me and talked about our mission to Brouggh. "It's a major victory, the first time a Movement campaign has been stymied. We've got opposition groups from all over the galaxy contacting us, asking for advice."

Douglas had found employment for Domenic somewhere in the catering department. He was led off to his new lodgings and a new life. A far better one than he'd lived on Rethne, for sure.

Sana's memory came back about events on Brouggh – she'd been startled by a noise from behind. That's why she took off into the clearing and got shot. No mention was made of the words she had said as she lay dying – that she'd always loved me – and I didn't bring it up.

Finally she was well enough to leave hospital – and then that was that.

She seemed to just disappear from my life again. I was too timid to call or follow up as the days turned into weeks, and she it seemed had no desire to contact me. Then one afternoon out of the blue, she called.

"Col, I'm here in my apartment with Danee, can you come over?"

And then words to make any man's blood freeze: "We need to talk."

CHAPTER FORTY

I had been moping, the days passing with no contact from either Danee or Sana, and I hadn't had the courage to call or go find them, so I'd slumped into a depression. I put something decent on – a newish shirt, better shoes. Went to the mirror and splashed water about, moved my hair into a semblance of order. *Dressing for the gallows*, that's how it felt. Whatever this 'talk' was about, nothing good could possibly come of it.

I knocked at Sana's door, the first time I'd been to her place. Both women were inside, sitting together on a couch, straight-backed, holding hands and facing a single chair. For me, obviously.

The chair of death.

The apartment was recognizably Sana's already. In just a few days and even while recuperating, she'd filled it with artworks and curios. Spun carpets on the floor, cushions and wall hangings. A place where people would feel comfortable, would enjoy hanging out – *Sana's pad*. I sat on the chair indicated. A deep and awkward silence permeated the room.

Danee looked at Sana, cleared her throat and spoke. "So, we've been talking."

"A lot," said Sana.

There was another silence. I dared not break it. Wherever this was going, it didn't feel good.

Sana looked flushed, nervously cleared her throat. "Col, I've come to a decision – a couple of decisions actually. A bit surprising maybe, but if you really think, it all kinda makes sense – if you look at my history."

"*OK*," I said cautiously.

"Firstly, I've decided I'm going to stay here on Jubilee, live here."

"Jubilee? But what about your career?"

"I'm giving it up."

"But I thought—"

"Col, I fucking *hated* politics. I know you thought it was my passion and I *was* passionate about it, but all I ever really wanted to do was get rid of the Movement. Every day of it was torture and now...we've beaten them, at least on Brouggh anyway. So I'm done with it."

Another one of Sana's dizzying about-faces, walking away from this thing she'd put every waking moment into for years, enjoyed so much success with.

"And besides," she went on, "I love it here on Jubilee, the art scene is *fantastic!* And Douglas has offered me a great position. I'm really excited, actually."

Fair enough, good for Sana.

The awkward silence closed in again – because of the hanging question of course, the elephant in the room. And anyway, why was Danee here? Shouldn't this be a private conversation between Sana and me? But then again, what *about* Danee? My head spun.

"And us?" I finally asked, almost plaintively.

"Yes." She cleared her throat again, looked down at the floor, up at the ceiling. "Col, first I have to say that you are absolutely the best, the sweetest guy I've ever known—"

"OK *right*," I interrupted, angry now. Because every man, no matter how clueless, knows at least *this* about women: if you're ever referred to you as a 'sweet guy', then it's terminal – there's always a 'but' coming. "But I'm not the right guy for you, I get it. You need someone who's more successful, more powerful, with a glamorous job, who can—"

"Col, for fuck's sake!" Sana's eyes flamed. "You always carried on and on about that – but it's just your bloody paranoia. I *hate* those kind of guys. All my life, as long as I can remember, it's always been *men, men, men* – everywhere I went, always coming at me, always in my face, and worst of all these hyper-confident, self-important douchebags with the big swinging dicks – not that there's anything wrong with you in that department, *I hasten to add*—"

Danee closed her eyes, smirking.

"But you were different, Col."

"Then what are you saying. What—"

"Let's be honest, I was never very good at the whole *wifey* thing, was I?" I went to object and she held up a hand. "And yes, there were the nanides but it wasn't *just* that, was it?" She looked at me with liquid eyes. "Col, I'm just not wife material. I tried my best, I really did, but I'm not cut out for it."

"So then why—"

"What I'm saying is this: I love you. A lot. I never stopped. If I *could* be any man's wife, I would want to be yours."

I thought through the implications of this. "So that's it?"

"We've been moving away from each other for years. You just haven't seen it coz you're so bloody stubborn."

"But we still—"

"Yes, we still love each other, but here's another thing too: love alone is not enough. A relationship has to be *about* something, has to have a common cause, and we never really had one."

More silence.

"And besides, there's Danee. I know you love her."

I looked down, confused again, not daring to meet the gaze of either woman.

"She's perfect for you. I knew it as soon as I realized you'd been together and that's what made it so hard – knowing that. *Especially* knowing that. Part of me can't stand the idea of giving you up. But I *must*, because…it's best for all of us. But I want us to be friends – and yes that's a cliché which no one ever really means. Not normally – but in this case—"

"We've decided," cut in Danee, "if you agree, that is, that you and I will be together – and I mean *together* together. But Sana's going to live right nearby coz she and I have gotten to know each *so well* during this time. I can see why you love her. *I* love her too!"

They had worked it all out. Divvied me up between themselves like some hoard of loot in a shady backroom deal. I probably ought to have been offended, but what I felt was closer to relief – though my head was still spinning.

"It'll be great!" said Danee, smiling sweetly.

"We'll be *friends*," said Sana. "There'll be so many benefits" – she shot a sly sideways look at Danee – "though not *with benefits* of course."

Danee growled theatrically. "Any hint of that and I'll murder you both, then burn your bodies and dance on your graves."

A tiny glint came into her eyes that I'd never seen before. I say tiny, but it was quite scary all the same.

The ladies sat there together wide-eyed and smiling at me expectantly, still holding hands. Unbidden, a strange thought came into my mind, a not altogether unpleasant one. "So, when you two say you *love* each other...?"

Danee must have guessed where my male lizard brain had gone because she squinted her eyes and gave me her best withering look. "Are you kidding! And anyway, that's not my thing. I mean, I tried it in college like you do and it was OK. But Sana and I are more like sisters." She turned to her. "Which is not to say that you aren't a very attractive woman."

Sana rolled her eyes.

There was silence again for a moment.

I broke it with a question. "So whose idea was this?"

Both women tried to speak at once.

It was Danee's.

"Col," she said, "I realized almost straight away that you and I were going to be together – practically from the first night – but then I saw how much you and Sana loved each other, and on this very deep level, and I thought *what the hell?* But I didn't want to say anything till I'd talked it over with her."

I guess that explained the strange vibe lately. She'd been waiting.

"This way I still get to have you in my life," said Sana, "but I don't have the responsibility."

I looked at Danee. "And you? What's actually in this for *you*?"

"Well, like I said, Sana and I have really hit it off – you don't meet many women like her and, you know, it's not like I'm *conventional* – this is Jubilee, for god's sake! And it could make life easier." She shot another sly look at Sana, who grinned mischievously. "Take some of the pressure

274 • STEPHEN K. STANFORD

off. You've got this idea, Col, that you're some kind of *easygoing* guy, but the truth is, you're actually very hard work, mate."

Sana cackled. "You have *no idea* how much hard work you are."

The two women looked at me intently. I tried to imagine it, living with Danee, having Sana nearby as a friend to both of us – a strange little threesome. The thought of letting Sana go felt incredibly painful, almost unimaginable. I'd spent years obsessing about her, trying every strategy to 'get her back' from fawning attentiveness to faux renunciation, and yet she had danced ever further away from me, always just out of reach. If I took all that away – the yearning, the drama – what was left? Love, sure, and attraction. But maybe something else – *bondedness* – the closest word I could think of. We were bonded by all those events, so many of them horrible, but events we'd survived together. Maybe that was a different kind of love? Maybe it really was friendship?

And Danee? Love, yes, and desire, of course, but also something else. I had been plagued with guilt the whole time we were together, tried vainly to pull away from her, and yet even with all that going on, things had still felt super-easy whenever we hung out. Natural. I was drawn to her by a force that seemed *gravitational* – and also mutual. Like binary stars in orbit around each other.

"So?" asked Danee. "Do you accept it, this arrangement?"

They looked at me expectantly.

I laughed. "How could I say no? Seems like you guys have it all figured out."

"So say it!" said Sana.

I teetered on a precipice: jumping off meant giving up Sana forever. She who had filled my consciousness – every waking hour of it – for years. But had that been pleasant. Had it been healthy? And anyway, could I really imagine life without Danee? The chasm yawned in front of me.

I jumped.

"Yes, of course I accept!"

They high-fived, then Sana pulled out a tray with three glasses and a bottle of champagne – it had been there all along. They had never doubted and I suddenly realized how right they were, how this was the only way things ever could have gone.

We poured, we toasted, we drank – though Danee, I noticed, took barely a sip. On the couch before me, the two most remarkable and beautiful women I had ever known. They would *both* be in my life now, one as an ex – which is how it suddenly felt – how quickly our emotions can change! – and the other as a girlfriend. I felt something strange inside, strange only because I had not felt it in such a long time – happiness.

Then Danee looked at Sana with that sly expression again, and they both leaned back, arms crossed. I realized something else had been going the whole time while we'd been talking. A weird feeling in the air I hadn't been able to put my finger on but understood now with a lurch. They had a secret.

"Col," said Danee, "there's one more thing I need to tell you. I think it's a good thing."

They looked at each other and laughed. My head start to spin again – what fresh awfulness was about to be unveiled?

"Yes, what?"

"I'm pregnant."

EPILOGUE

"Wake up, lazy bitch!" cried Sana. "Your babies are drowning in their own poop."

"Where's Col?" grumbled Danee, emerging from our bedroom yawning, bed hair atangle. "Is he ever planning on being something more than a sperm donor dad?"

Grossly unfair. I spent at least as much time taking care of the twins as she did.

"Don't blame Col," shouted Sana. "*You're* the one turning into a *crack mother.*"

This is how the ladies jibed each other. Funny, though it did get a little tiring sometimes.

I emerged from the bathroom. "Sorry, Danee, I'm about to go on duty – want me to call the robo-nanny?"

She yawned again and patted down her hair. Today was a rostered day off from her job at the Intelligence department, but Sana's joke did have a ring of truth. While never much of a 'girly girl' to start with, Danee was putting even less time into her personal appearance these days since the girls were born.

"Nah, just kidding," she said. "Wanna kiss the bubbas goodbye?"

In the nursery, Anjali and Lila were crying lustily. We each picked one up and indeed a wafting smell of something rich and nasty filled the room.

"Goodbye, gorgeous," I cooed, planting a kiss on Lila's cheek.

She stopped crying instantly, her face and eyes still puffy and red. "Dada!" she gurgled with a shy smile, the kind of smile that turns fathers into squishy dough.

I leaned over and kissed Anjali.

"Bye bye, Dada," she said softly, turning the dough into melted ooze.

They say that in ancient times, on Old Earth, humans were divided into separate and distinct races that shared common physical characteristics. Nowadays, of course, we're mixed up and kids pop out with any combination of skin tone and bodily feature.

But even so, the difference between *our* girls was startling. Anjali was exactly like her mother: blond and blue-eyed, strong of frame and a hearty eater. Lila, in some twist of fate or karma – or whatever – was tiny and birdlike, with dark skin and hair, and black eyes. She was lighter than air and ate no more than two spoonsful of food per day. When we were all out together, people naturally assumed Sana to be the mother – then started having strange thoughts when they realized I was father to both girls.

Ah, the complications of domestic life!

I grabbed Danee for a group hug – me and my girls.

"Will you be all right?" I asked, handing Lila to her.

Danee leaned over and kissed me slowly on the mouth – triggering an instant hormonal response. "Hurry home," she said – and after a nice smooch like that, who wouldn't?

"See ya, Sana!" I cried, heading for the door.

Only silence from the adjoining apartment – she'd probably gone back to sleep.

Was it weird, having her live right next door? Yes and no. On the one hand we'd all fallen rapidly into a stable domestic routine, Sana joining us for meals or just as often doing her own thing, pursuing the many and varied projects that seemed to have sprung up around her on Jubilee. She loved the twins and they in turn adored 'Auntie Sana,' spending as much time as they could with her. She and Danee caught up for afternoon teas and went out together even after the girls were born. Amazingly, they had become best friends. And as for me, Sana had morphed back into my life in this new capacity – almost like a whole new person – and after a while it grew hard even to remember she had once been my wife.

Though sometimes, just occasionally, we would share a joke or remember something from the old days and I couldn't help – guiltily – feeling that a spark was still there, still smoldering somewhere deep down, even if carefully suppressed.

Anyway, it all seemed to work somehow. Us one big, strange family – me for my sins surrounded entirely by females, happily drowning in a sea of estrogen.

I took the lift up to Concourse. Douglas had installed us in the depths of Sector Twenty, on Level Seventeen with the other families. Turned out there were plenty of kids on Jubilee after all – Douglas's 'no children' rule applied only to visitors, not staff.

"Can't really stop 'em *breeding*, can I?" he'd explained.

Naturally, a strict quarantine was in place to prevent sensitive young souls being exposed to the red-light zone.

It was early 'morning' and Jubilee was coming to life as I rode the transit car.

Danee had fallen pregnant on Grendeva. Her birth-control nanos had glitched – happens occasionally – which would normally have triggered an alert on her kom. But of course her kom was uninstalled for the trip to Rethne and, like most modern women, Danee wasn't aware of the signs. I'd instantly agreed to co-parent and she'd carried the girls to full term herself – a rare thing these days.

At Sector Fifteen I decided to jump off the transit and take in the 'morning air'. Why not?

At Sector Eleven my old friend Zhang waved from his black box. "How're you doing, Donny?" he asked – he still called me by this name even after three years of being corrected.

"Not bad, Zhang. How were the crowds last night?"

"Oh, you know, the usual. Handed out two thousand five hundred and sixty-three poems. Close to a record."

"Good work, buddy. Let me know if you see anything, eh?"

"No worries, Donny, have a great day!"

I turned to walk on. Just a few blocks more to my office in Sector Nine, where I worked these days as head of security for Jubilee.

But a voice called from behind. Zhang's voice, sounding strange. "Col!" he cried. "*Beware the Ides of March!*"

I turned around. "What's that, buddy? Beware what?"

Zhang was standing frozen, arms at his sides, a faraway look in his eyes. "Beware the Ides of March," he repeated quietly.

I went to speak, the hologram flickered for a moment, then righted itself. "What were you saying just then?" I asked. "*Beware the tides of March?*"

Zhang laughed, he seemed himself again. "Beware the *Ides* of March," he said. "Where did you get that from, Donny? That's Shakespeare. *Julius Caesar* Act 1, Scene 2, the soothsayer's warning. No one knows that stuff anymore – except ancient history buffs, *and* poets of course."

"You said those words to me, just now."

Zhang gave a wry smile. "You're shitting me, right?"

"I swear, just moments ago you said that line to me, twice."

Zhang looked blank for a moment, then laughed. "Donny, I think you might have been smoking a bit too much of the old...." He did an impression of someone toking on a long joint. "Would you like a poem?"

I shook my head. "Not today, thanks." I didn't think I could take any more of Zhang's enigmatic claptrap. "See you soon."

"See you, Donny."

I turned and walked on. No further interruptions. What the hell was that all about? Who would know when it came to Zhang?

Concourse was filling fast, people emerging from every corner of Jubilee. I took it all in, the residents charging along doing their morning power walks, mixing with the desolate and bedraggled who'd been up all night doing god knows what. Glamorous couples sipping coffee, hipsters and hucksters, a teeming, throbbing mess of humanity.

My people.

My flock to care for.

Who would have thought?

ACKNOWLEDGMENTS

Humble thanks go to SSS and DM, without whom there'd be nothing. My first readers: JB, JH, Lil's Anj', Tim, Sam and Para. Nath' for help with the translator's note. My editors: Scott Pack and Mary-Jo O'Rourke, who saved me from myself. Jez, who showed it was possible. Most of all, to my beautiful wife, Vani, who always gave the best advice, and without whom nothing would be worth it anyway.

To Harry Harrison: Slippery Jim saved my life as a spotty teenager – sorry about pinching the exploding robot gag.

FLAME TREE PRESS
FICTION WITHOUT FRONTIERS
Award-Winning Authors & Original Voices

Flame Tree Press is the trade fiction imprint of Flame Tree Publishing, focusing on excellent writing in horror and the supernatural, crime and mystery, science fiction and fantasy. Our aim is to explore beyond the boundaries of the everyday, with tales from both award-winning authors and original voices.

•

•

Join our mailing list for free short stories, new release details, news about our authors and special promotions:

flametreepress.com